The Felmeres

A NOVEL

Sarah Barnwell Elliott

Sarah Barnwell Elliott.

"Behold we know not anything:
I can but trust that good shall fall
At last far off at last to all,
And every winter change to spring."

—"The Larger Hope," Alfred, Lord Tennyson

First Edition by D. Appleton and Company, New York, 1879

Current edition by Low Country Press, Savannah, Georgia, 2012
Preface © 2012 Low Country Press
www.lowcountrypress.net

Praise for the first edition of *The Felmeres*

"In many places it rises to a height of absorbing interest and is every-where interesting from a psychological point of view."

—Boston Gazette

"A very clever psychological novel...The work is cleverly done, and is thoroughly worth reading."

—New York World

"Its whole diction is the instrument of a well-stored, alert and accomplished intellect. The theme, too, is notably suggestive—indeed, the author of *Middlemarch* could hardly find a situation more suggestive or more deserving of elaborate and earnest treatment."

—New York Sun

"The book is a production altogether out of and above the common order; a book in which the author displays a fine ability for treating a lofty subject firmly and adequately, while giving to it a warm human interest, in which is not lacking the element of dramatic force....It is a very remarkable book. Prophecies are never safe where young authors are concerned, but in the case of this particular author it may be said, at least, that she has produced the strongest and most promising book of the season."

— Philadelphia Times

"This is a very solid, serious novel. It is a sincere and pious effort to cast out the goddess of reason, and enthrone in her place the angel of faith."

—Missouri Republican

"We have read *The Felmeres* with uncommon interest, and we call it a more than ordinarily powerful story. So well are its characters drawn, and the circumstances described, that the story is very engrossing."

—Boston Congregationalist

Also by Sarah Barnwell Elliott

Novels

A Simple Heart

Jerry

John Paget

The Durkett Sperret

An Incident and Other Happenings

The Making of Jane

Nonfiction

Sam Houston

Play

His Majesty's Servant

Preface

L IKE THE STRONG FEMALE CHARACTERS IN HER NOVELS, Sarah Elliott's own life cut against the grain of the cultural expectations of the Southern aristocracy into which she was born. She is almost always described as the daughter of The Rt. Rev. Stephen Elliott, Jr. the first Episcopal Bishop of Georgia. Her relationship with her father did significantly shape her thinking as one can read so clearly in this her first novel. Yet Sada, as she preferred to be called, was very much her own person.

Born the fifth of six children to the Bishop, Sarah Bull Barnwell Elliott entered a life of priviledge. She counted four colonial governors among her recent ancestors. While she was the first woman of letters in the family, her father and grandfather were known for their oratory and scientific writing respectively.

Her grandfather Stephen Elliott (1771-1830) was a plantation owner near Beaufort, South Carolina who defined himself more by his avocation as a botanist. While he served in the state legislature and was president of the Bank of the State of South Carolina from its founding in 1812 until his death, he also had a scientific and literary side.

The family patriarch started *The Southern Review* and wrote the land-mark text *A Sketch of the Botany of South-Carolina and Georgia* for which he is best known.

Her father, Stephen Elliott Jr. (1806-1866) was an attorney in Beau-fort until a vivid conversion experience caused him to seek Holy Or-ders in The Episcopal Church in 1833. Elliott was a noted orator in a time and place when speeches were more highly prized than other works of literature. Bishop Elliott's sermons, especially those preached on significant occasions during the Civil War, were published and widely distributed almost before the echoes died in the church.

Bishop Elliott was a champion of education, including the educa-tion of women. He started a Female Institute at Montpelier Springs, Georgia, where Sada was born. This school fit the Bishop's goal of enlightening young women and men alike with a progressive educa-tion to prepare them to lead the South. It was on the grounds of this school that Sada spent her earliest years. The Institute was intended to be a self-sustaining operation through an 800-acre campus with farms tended by enslaved workers to provide income. That income never kept up with the costs and the debts were guaranteed person-ally by Bishop Elliott. The school's failure bankrupted the Elliott fam-ily. By 1852, the once wealthy landowner was scraping by on his sal-ary as Bishop.

A strong proponent of religious education for slaves, Elliott was nevertheless strongly partisan in the Civil War. He preached the right-ness of the South and made battlefield visits to Confederate soldiers when the fighting came to Georgia. It was said that he died of a bro-ken heart for the lost cause, when he collapsed at the dinner table at home following a parish visit in 1866. Sada was 18 years old at the time of his death.

Bishop Elliott's interest in education had also led him to be one of three founding Bishops who created the University of the South at Sewanee, Tennessee, where Sada Elliott would spend most of her life.

With well regarded men in view, it is easy to see how Sada came to be described in relation to the Elliott men. Yet in the shadow of these noted men of their times grew a unique woman who defied so-cial expectations to forge a substantial body of well-reviewed and widely read books together with shorter pieces in national magazines, many literary reviews, a biography, and a play.

She moved to Sewanee with her mother in 1871, the year after classes started at the university. Other than living in New York City from 1896 to 1904, she would live at Sewanee the remainder of her life.

Sarah Bull Barnwell Elliott

It was while living at Sewanee, when Sada was 31 years old, that *The Felmeres* was published by D. Appleton Company of Chicago.

The story of the beautiful Helen Felmere, whose unbending devotion to duty and honor lead to tragic consequences, interested reviewers who did not anticipate serious themes from a Southerner, much less a female writer. The conflict of faith and reason had occupied her father's ministry in the antebellum period. Sada works through Helen's internal struggles with doubt and the cost of going against cultural expectations and offers a window into the pyschological dilemmas faced by women of the time who did not intend to conform to the culture. While Helen Felmere is very different from Sada Elliott, the essential strength of purpose in being true to oneself drew from the author's personal experience.

Following the success of this novel, she began to publish a number of short pieces. She traveled to Texas where her brother Robert had been elected as Missionary Bishop of Western Texas in 1875. There she wrote articles for *Church Record* that showed her writer's eye for details. She had been schooled by private tutors except for the summer of 1886 when she attended classes at Johns Hopkins University. The following year, her Texas trip helped shape *A Simple Heart*, a novel serialized in the *Independent*. This novel, which was a tribute to her brother's work, was her first foray into writing in dialect and presents the introduction of local color in her fiction, for which she is best remembered. Sales of the novel helped fund a trip with Robert to the Holy Land. On that trip she wrote a series of dispatches for the *Louisville Courier-Journal*. Her beloved brother Robert returned home early from the trip. Sada had to cut her trip short as well when she learned of Robert's death on his return to the United States.

She worked hard to chart her own course in crafting novels with strong female characters. She wrote her most successful novel, *Jerry*, in 1891. Then in 1898, her book *The Durket Sperret* stayed close to home, portraying the tensions on the Cumberland Plateau as university and mountain societies came to live side by side at Sewanee. Sada's final novel, written in 1901 was *The Making of Jane*, which made her boldest statement of her ideal of the self-reliant woman.

Then she set her literary career aside to raise her two orphaned nephews. Once the boys were raised to successful men, she turned to the women's suffrage movement, serving as president of the Tennessee Equal Suffrage Association from 1912-1914.

By the time she died in 1928, most of her major works were already out of print, as in 1915, her publisher, Holt, disposed of the plates to most of her works. Readers of fiction had moved on from their interest in the local color of regional writers.

Reading *The Felmeres* more than 130 years after its first publication, one cannot help but be struck at once both by how current her concerns remain as well as how time has drastically changed the social norms which constrained Helen Felmere's actions. Yet time has not dimmed the clarity of the author's voice as a woman of letters in a culture that did not tend to value either the opinions of women or the writings of its own regional authors. She writes with passion and conviction. The author's own struggle to make her voice heard is the heartbeat that drives *The Felmeres* and her other works.

Perhaps, then, this explains why Sarah Bull Barnwell Elliott has come to be described in relation to the men in her life. Not so much because her relevance is only as the daughter and granddaughter of known Southern aristocrats, but because she continues the Elliott legacy far beyond its antebellum trajectory. She was a product of the liberal education and the progressive household in which she was raised. Sada charted an independent course that might have surprised her father and grandfather had they known of her writing the petition calling on the Tennessee legislature to grant women the right to vote. Yet, given the support of her brothers, Robert and Habersham, we can imagine her father and grandfather too might have changed to see the world a little differently if they had viewed it through Sada's eyes as we all can in reading *The Felmeres*.

Part First

"An immense solitary specter waits:
It has no shape, it has no sound; it has
No place, it has no time; it is, and was,
And will be; it is never more nor less,
Nor glad nor sad. Its name is Nothingness.
Power walketh high; and misery doth crawl;
And the clepsydron drips; and the sands
Fall down in the hour-glass; and the shadows sweep
Around the dial; and men wake and sleep,
Live, strive, regret, forget, and love and hate,
And know it. This specter saith, I wait;
And at the last it beckons, and. they pass;
And still the red sands fall within the glass,
And still the shades around the dial sweep;
And still the water-clock doth drip and weep.
And this is all."

—"Siege of Constantinople," Edward Bulwer Lytton

"About a stone-cast from the wall
A sluice with blacken'd waters slept,
And o'er it, many, round, and small,
The cluster'd marish mosses crept.
Hard by a poplar shook alway,
All silver-green with gnarled bark:
For leagues no other tree did mark
The level waste, the rounding gray."

—"Mariana," Alfred, Lord Tennyson

CHAPTER I

A SQUARE CHURCH STANDING AT THE FOOT OF A LOW LINE OF HILLS; far-ther out, beyond the damp, moss-grown churchyard, a lonely stone house built on the end of the long tongue of land that runs far into the marsh. From this as far as the eye can reach, out even to the line of light on the horizon where lies the sea, there stretches a level waste of marsh, an unbroken green monotony, save where in one place the river shows itself moving slow toward the sea. A barren, desolate picture, lying hot and shadowless under the glare of the summer sky. There is no sound save now and then the sharp quarreling of the marsh hens; no motion, save the throbbing of the heated air. There is not wind enough to stir the reed tops, or to lift the leaves of the solitary maple keeping guard among the sleepers in the churchyard.

And the sun glares down upon the still, dead picture, until the day begins to wane; then the martins come in crowds wheeling about the lonely stone hall, cheery little martins, swooping in and out from under the deep eaves, chattering and chirping to each other, and making the air alive with their busy doings.

Down in the hall garden a little child is watching them so intently that she does not heed the falling of her hat, nor the woebegone picture made by her battered doll, which, held by one arm, droops downward in a desolate manner. For a long time the child watches the queer little birds, that look so black against the amber sky, and seem so busy about nothing. She has often watched them, but never yet has found out what they were after: she wished her father would take her up to see; perhaps he would some day. Then she turned away, and, pushing open a dilapidated gate, made her way down to the marsh. She stopped one moment to gather up her doll, then, with an unchildish, over-thoughtful step, followed a narrow cattle path leading out to the river. Slowly she went, and quietly, until she stood far out on the very bank of the stream—a lonely little figure on the wide green waste.

There she stood and listened to the gentle song the river sang so sweetly all the while. "Where did it come from, and how far was it down to the sea? The sea!" Why was that sad sound she heard called the "sea"? Had her father named it? It must be a very big place, this sea; for the sun and the moon, the fish and the birds, the wind and the darkness all lived in it, did they not? And the sound of it fascinated her, awed and almost frightened her; yet she loved it, and often came and stood here upon the bank, mystified and wondering.

There were many things she was afraid of, and but few that she liked, or that were really amusing, and very few of these things could talk. Nevertheless, she often spoke to the gravestones up in the churchyard, although they did not answer. What these gravestones were she hardly knew; and why they should be put up in rows, some straight up, and some half buried in the ground, and should have names cut on them, were so many mysteries to her. They were of no possible use that she could see, and her father said foolish people set them up. An especial one named "Mary Dunn" made her very sorry, it looked so tired: she wished it could lie down. The flowers were much more pleasant than the gravestones, for they could nod their heads to her when she talked; and, better still, the fairies lived in them. The solemn cranes and the marsh hens that rested in the flats were not in the least sociable; and the little martins in the roof heeded only themselves and their own foolish noises. But the bitterns she liked to hear; she was sure they had something to tell, their tones were so sad.

This place her father called "the world" was surely a curious place. She would have liked to ask some questions of Peter or Jane, but her father would not allow her to talk to the servants; and, except them and her father, nothing in all her world could answer questions.

So she stood by the river and listened to the dull, unceasing roar of the sea. She did not know what it was, but there was a thrill at her heart and a chill over her body as she looked on the wide green waste spread all about her. It was so silent and lonely out in the marsh, so far from everywhere. Should she stay and watch the moon come up? It came up very early sometimes, and looked so clear and beautiful fresh out from the sea.

Ah, the sea, the sea. How it called and called to her all the time. If it would only hush, she would stay longer looking at the river. Or if she could only go once and see what it wanted, maybe then it would let her alone. As it was, who knew but that the sea would come for her some day when no one was near? It really might.

She turned, the sun was fast going down behind the far-off hills, and all the flats would soon be gray and the pools black. Oh, she could not stay. One more watchful, frightened look toward the sea, then she turned and began to walk toward home as fast as her little feet could carry her. Closer she hugged her dilapidated doll, faster and faster the little steps fell; for behind her in the gathering gloom an awful something followed her. Fast and faster she fled, running with all her little strength. A giant hand seemed ever about to grasp her, a cry seemed in the passing wind. Would she never reach the gate? At last.

Panting and exhausted, she leaned against the wall: she must wait and rest here before she went into the house, for she would not let her father see her so foolishly terrified.

She knew it was foolish, now that she stood within the gate, and could hear Jane singing in the kitchen; out in the marsh it was different. Once before she had been frightened in the same way; and, running home, she had met her father at this very gate. It was then he had told her how foolish it was to be afraid of her own fancies; that there was nothing in the world but what she saw, or could see; and the darkness had never eaten any one up. Then he had taken her into the churchyard, ah, she shivered now to think of it, and made her stand there while he went off for a little time into the darkness to show her it would not destroy him. How she clung to a gravestone when he left her, and listened in terrified silence and with trembling heart to a cow cropping among the graves! She wanted to scream, but did not wish to be called foolish again. Ah, how terror-stricken she had been until she looked up and saw the stars that seemed to smile down kindly on her—so kindly that she asked them to take care of her; and they heard her, and brought her father back to her in a moment.

Even now, with all this experience to aid her, she did not feel at all safe, and she looked up for her star-friends. There they were, bright, and peaceful, and kind, seemingly quite ready to befriend her again. It was strange her father did not believe in the stars, and should say they had never been kind to him. More than this, that nothing in all the world had ever been kind to him. Poor father! She would be, always and forever, she would stay with him and love him; and she had told him so.

"And I will," she said, holding up her little hand to the star, "watch and see if I do not."

A half-comprehended, childish vow, maybe; but for all that — true.

She was rested now, and cool, and was glad enough to turn her steps toward the house, where one long stream of light, falling across the garden and wandering toward the shadows of the graveyard, showed her that tea was waiting in the library.

This room was the heart of the child's world. It was a high, long room, walled in with somber books and pictures, with here and there a gleaming white statue, which, catching the scanty light from the high, deep windows, seemed to absorb it all. And the child lived here, with always a feeling of uneasiness about her heart as she felt the painted eyes of her dead ancestors following her, watching all her play and study. At times she forgot them; but one upward look, and all the time dimmed faces seemed turned toward her, and all their eyes seemed crowding on her, so that, overcome with fear, she would creep to her father's side and nestle there until she could again forget.

What had become of all these people, she wondered; where had they gone, and why had they left their dreadful shadows behind them to watch and torment her? She liked all the statues, and made them the confidants of her many wonders and puzzles; and questions, too, she often asked them, but got no answers poor little maid, any more than from the graves and gravestones.

But her dearest friend was her doll. Ah, the comfort of that mutilated doll, who can tell? It helped her to learn her letters; it comforted her about the pictures; and the mystery of counting was solved on the fingers of this same valuable companion. Besides this doll, the child had only a few playthings put away on a little shelf near the wide fireplace, with a little pile of lesson books, a larger one of fairy lore, and a box of special treasures. Two arm chairs there were, for the doll and for the child, wherein they would sit when tea was over, and pass the evening in pleasant conversation. It is true, Cinderella could not talk, but she was a good listener, which went very far. But Helen was content, and to her Cinderella could only be described as beautiful and entertaining. Often the father would put down his book to listen to what the child was saying. Sometimes he would enter into the conversation and explain some of the mysteries that worried his little daughter; but more often he left her to her own surmises, waiting until she should be older before he solved her puzzles.

So the little girl lived on in a curious, unknown world, full of wonders, full of fears, full of things ineffable, which gave rise to thoughts and emotions that no words can translate. And the father, watching her, felicitated himself that her friends were what they were; for they could never harm her, never be false to her, never turn her against himself. She was his only hope and love, this child, and her education was his dearest task. He had sometimes wavered in the course he was pursuing, but not often nor for long. She gave fair promise of common sense, and of strength enough to stand upright without support from the much-cultivated superstitions known as "beliefs."

And so the days, and the months, and the years moved round the child, bringing new wonders and new learning, solving old puzzles, and sweeping away the old mysteries into dim remembrances; slowly but surely turning the "fairy gold" of childhood wonderings into the dried and withered leaves of positive knowledge; robbing the sea, and the wind, and the sky, and the earth of all their mystic charm, and stripping from her heart the "trailing clouds of glory."

And as she watched them fade and die, she knew not why nor whence the sadness came that clung about her. She did not know that this change must ever come to us as we travel from the cloudless sunshine of childish faith into the shadow of the "tree of knowledge." She did not know why the nakedness of all things should be so suddenly revealed to her eyes, or why such cold barrenness was creeping over the world and life. She had learned what death meant in the dim half-revealings that had come to her, and why gravestones were used. Concerning the church she had asked little, and had got little in return; but she often listened to the sound of music, which reached her faintly when the wind set toward the house.

Once she had seen a little into the church, but it only seemed to widen the foundation for her wonders, and not satisfy her at all. She was leaning over the gate, when deep-rolling music came floating about her, and with it voices singing. She slipped through the gate and stood listening, while a sense of intense sadness stole over her, a feeling of awe crept into her soul. She looked up; far above her, soft rose-colored clouds were floating across the sky; and she watched them with a childish feeling of soul-hunger, a longing for something to fill this great empty world and her own sad little heart.

What was it she wanted?

She drew nearer the church: perhaps she might find it there among those happy-looking people, this something she so much needed, and she crept up the steps.

Ah! And with clasped hands and bated breath she looked, and listened. Happy? Oh, no. She was not happy standing there, there was a something that seemed to cling about the music, a something that came to her when she looked at the beautiful clouds, or watched the great moon rise out of the sea. A something that seemed to wrench her heart with pain, and bring hot tears to her eyes. The people were all on their knees; perhaps if she knelt this pain in her heart would go.

Alas, a man came out and, motioning her away, closed the wide doors. She stood quite still for a moment in astonished despair and anger. What had she done that he should send her away? She ran off a little distance and, crouching behind a great tombstone, burst into tears. She was bitterly angry with all the world, it all seemed against her. The people she passed in her walks with her father looked the other way when they met her, or else stared curiously. Even Jane, the servant, seemed to regard her with doubt; and now, how had she been treated.

"I shall hate you for ever!" she cried, raising her hands as though invoking a curse on the church. Then she ran away, ran to the house, then up to her own room, there to sob and cry as though her heart would break. In the dusk of the evening she crept down to where her father sat in the library, and, kneeling beside his chair, told him of her adventure.

"What were they doing, father, and why do the people kneel?" she asked, as he clasped her little hand in his. "They were doing what they call 'praying,' my child," he answered.

"Praying? Like subjects to a king?" she went on.

"Yes."

"But, father, I saw no king, nor any one who was listening to them; where was he?"

"He is only an Idea, child."

"An Idea?" she repeated slowly, "what does 'idea' mean?"

"It means a notion."

The child pondered a moment then looked up wistfully.

"Say it, father, so that I shall know. Why do they pray without anything to pray to?"

The father put his hands each side the earnest face, and, looking down into her eyes, he kissed her gently.

"Trust me a few years longer, darling, then I will tell you all."

"Eternity, Eternity!
How long art thou, Eternity?
No spring hast thou, no autumn gold,
No summer's heat nor winter's cold;
No infant cry begins thy day,
Nor age nor anguish brings decay.
Ponder, O man Eternity!"

—"Eternity! Eternity!," John Henry Hopkins

Chapter II

AND SO THE GIRL WAITED AND TRUSTED, asking no more questions. True, the world was becoming more and more empty every day, more and more bare and dreary. All the fables and entertaining wonders of her childhood had been educated away, and nothing put in their place. Her battered Cinderella had long been laid aside, carefully, for she still loved her, but completely. Her damp little garden, where every day she had stuck up rootless, pale, unhappy flowers, culled from among the graves, was now of more lasting growth, but scarcely less dreary than of yore. And now she watched the waterfowl come and go with an undefined longing at her heart for wings and freedom.

Her life seemed very objectless, and had grown more so every day since she could remember. What was the point of all these days and months and years? Where would they end, and how? Were languages and poetry, reading and drawing, the only things to live for? And when one had risen above laboring for one's daily bread, was this all?

She looked with envy on the busy housewives and happy children whose homes she sometimes passed in her walks with her father, looked, and wondered why her childhood had been so mysteriously lonely, and her home so empty. It was strange, this utter separation of her father and herself from the world; and surely she was old
enough now to know their story?

One day, in the closet of an unused room, she found a little baby
dress, worn and yellow with age. Curiously she held it up to the light.
Had it been hers? Was it the work of her unknown mother, who she
somehow knew was still alive? A gentle warmth of love stole about
her heart, and she handled the little garment tenderly.

Love had shaped it, had put all those careful stitches in, had folded
it away, perhaps, and laid it in that very spot where she had found it.
Then two little letters, marking it, met her eyes—P. F. Who was that? It
was neither her nor her father's name, whose was it? Had she ever
had a brother or a sister? Were they dead, shut up in the great Felmere
vault over there in the church, and she had never known it?

She must ask her father. She was almost a woman now. Loving
and trusting, she had waited as he had told her to do. Her faith in him
was boundless, and she had asked no questions. But now? So she went
down to the library with the little dress crumpled close in her hands,
afraid of what she would hear.

"Father," she said, standing by his chair, "I have found this; it is
marked P. F. Whose was it?"

The old man touched the little dress, then looked up slowly as
one in a dream. The day he had so long avoided had come upon him.

"I have waited so long," the clear young voice went on, "so long,
and you have not told me."

And silence fell again between them. Had the fire no warmth in
it? Was there a window open, or a door, that such coldness crept about
him? Were there people in the hall, did he hear footsteps coming and
going, and voices? He shook himself as though from hands that held
him.

Long ago he had ceased to question the wrong or right of the
course he was pursuing. Long ago he had determined that she should
not be a Christian, but that she should believe as he did; she should be
strong enough to stand alone; she should follow him step by step beyond the portal of the grave, wherever that might lead! Such was his
decision, and so he had striven to train her.

And now, suppose she should reproach him, suppose she should
forsake him. The gray head drooped. Had he been wrong?

"I will wait, father," and the girl's hand rested on his shoulder, rousing him.

"No," he said, without a quiver in his voice, either for the ghosts of the past that were crowding about him, or for the fears of the present, "no, I will tell you now. But do not stand near me, go away; for in this hour you are to hear my life and judge me, you are to choose between me and the world." His voice fell, and in its deep intensity almost trembled. "You must listen and decide not by your love, I charge you, but by your reason."

Then he paused, and the girl, watching him with awestricken eyes, moved slowly back. Ah, it was a pitiful picture, that, where in the great dim library the old man, timeworn and world-conquered, rich in knowledge and experience, sat with hand-covered eyes making himself ready for this revelation. And before him was the girl, tall and beautiful, with a strong, sad beauty that haunted you, fair as any lily, as she stood where the sunlight fell, still and waiting. And all the painted Felmeres, with dead, haunting eyes, brooded over the scene.

At last he spoke. "I am old now," he began, "old and white-haired. I have had many sorrows and disappointments, much trouble and responsibility, and much experience of many things. Through all I have tried to find and follow truth; from all I have tried to gather wisdom and patience, under all I have tried to bear myself like a man. How far I have succeeded I can not tell; for your life will be the only commentary upon and the only result of mine."

Then he told the wondering girl his story: how he had loved and reared his only brother, Philip; and how he had gone from his heart and his home into the wide world, and seemingly had forgotten all. Then he told her of his own marriage, and his short-lived happiness, ending in his wife's desertion of him, and in her carrying away with her their other child, his only son.

"She never loved me, never!" he cried. "She married me at the instigation of her priest, for the benefit of their church; she left me at the instigation of her priest, because I was an obstinate heretic, and unexpectedly a poor one. And she took with her my son, my only son! Blasting and desolating my life because she was a Christian. And in this countryside she is almost canonized because she broke her vows to her God, leaving home, and husband, and what she thought was a dying child, in obedience to her priest and conscience. She is sainted: we are condemned, cast out!"

"Father." It came like a sigh from the girl's white lips. He was murdering all the tenderness in her nature, did he not know it? He was trampling down in his bitterness all her youth, tearing away all the tender, clinging, reverential thoughts she had in her loneliness twined about her unknown mother. Could he not see the agony in her white face? But he did not heed the little cry.

"Do not come," he said, "until you have heard all. Listen while I tell you of this Christianity; then choose between it and me."

Then he explained the Christian belief; and even while he spoke the bitterness faded from his voice, and he told in glowing terms the beautiful story of the Christ's life and death; he adored the Man, but denied the Divinity.

Then came the history of the Church, beginning with those few devoted men in far-away Judea, a humble, insignificant band, growing slowly but surely into a great political power, that, leaving far behind it the simplicity, the beauty, the purity of the Master's teachings, developed in its stead the idolatry and practiced the persecutions of the middle ages. He dwelt upon the corruptions of the three great branches of the Church; telling how they were torn by factions; how they crucified and burned; how they tortured more terribly than the most ignorant savages; how they demanded that men should put aside their reason, and, falling down in blind faith, adore.

Then he paused, and the girl drew a long, tremulous breath. Hurried on by the burning words that chained her attention, confused amid all the terrible revelations that had come to her, her agony and despair were intense. What was this dreadful thing she was to decide? Why not tell her, as he always did, what she must do? Her mother had been a Christian, her weak, wicked mother. Wrong? Who could doubt it? She stood looking out of the window, looking at the gilt cross on the church tower, with a pitiful look of pain.

The wonderful life of the great "God-man" still rang in her ears. This Christ was the grandest hero of whom she had ever heard. She had not realized Him in her casual reading; but now all her enthusiastic girl nature went out in mute admiration! How gladly she would worship so beautiful a God; and had she but lived in the days of the Apostles, when the cause of Christ needed champions, how she would have gloried in dying for it! But now? Now the Cross was triumphant, and one old man, defrauded for its sake of all his life held dear, stood out against it, one poor old man, deserted and alone. The tears sprung to her eyes.

Reason? How could she reason about a thing like this? Yet her father said she must. She covered her face with her hands, and strove to regulate her thoughts. Then strangely through the chaos of her confused mind there rose up suddenly the awful memory of the Christian's hell. Did her father not think of that? Quick her young voice rung through the silence. "Father, if these Christians are right, what will come to you after death?" And the beautiful eyes watched him with a strained, anxious pain in them.

No one knew the agony this silence had held for the old man; and now she turned and asked, "What will be your (not our) fate?"

Was she going too? Had he not suffered enough? Could he not keep one treasure, one love from this winning Christ? He trembled. It was hard to answer with this horror in his heart, with those eyes so eagerly watching him; but he did it slowly, steadily: "Eternal damnation."

His voice clove the air like a sword, and the waiting heart before him, quivering with the blow, broke into a little cry, then there was silence.

Oh, this awful Eternity, this awful Hell. And this old man could balance these dreadful chances with a steady mind? She turned and looked at him as though he were some stranger. Already so near the end, he dared this terrible risk, dared to stand and look this fearful alternative in the face, dared to choose. Her brain reeled, and she turned away with a sickening terror clinging about her.

Her mother had not dared. Ah!

And he told her now to put her heart aside and choose, to put her heart aside and leave him. She turned. The gray head was bowed, the dear face was covered from the light. With a swift movement she knelt beside him, and drew his hands down; and the face he looked on was surely glorified. Surely, for all the self-forgetfulness and self-abnegation of her woman's soul was shining there.

"Father, I have chosen." And the young voice rang very true. "I shall never leave you; always and for ever, here and hereafter, I will follow you. I swear it."

Ah, old man, so carefully platting a crown of thorns for that young life, crowning, yea, and crucifying it. Taking so gladly the sacrifice from that young, untried soul grasping so eagerly the life-gift from those weak hands that had groped so blindly for some guiding star, and had only found her heart.

"In the wail of the wind, in the cry of the sea,
    In the far-away wash of the river,
In the starlight of night, in the sunshine of day,
In the wanness of March, in the blooming of May,
There lurketh a tear alway—alway
    A sadness that haunts me for ever!"

—Unknown

CHAPTER III

THE LAST SEPTEMBER DAY HAD ENDED, dying solemnly and redly down
the western sky. The land lay brown and bare, the sedge rustled
crisply in the wind, and the one stunted maple in the churchyard had
put on, as best it was able, its autumn dress, not very gorgeous, but
still making a dash of color in the landscape that helped to light it up.

Walking up from the river, Helen noted it, and paused, as she
had done many times before, to look on the dreary picture. Now the
one bright maple seemed to cast a deeper gloom over the rest of the
scene, making the house look more gaunt and gray, the graveyard
more desolate, and the church more square and cold. She had a pitying love for the old place, for herself, for her father:

"A white-haired shadow, roaming like a dream,"

—who seemed to cling to this quiet corner of the world as though it
was a secure refuge from all rude shocks a place where Time would
forget him, and Death pass by unseeing.

In the two years that had passed since the explanation between father and daughter, they seemed almost to have changed places. There being nothing now to keep from her, or to guard her from, the father had very much relaxed his supervision of her life; and she, with her womanly instincts fully alive, glad to find something that would aid in filling out the aimless desolation of her days, quietly altered the old routine, and became the guardian of her father's wants and comforts. But more than this she had changed. Day by day she had brooded over the weakness of her mother, until the love she had in her ignorance built up about her name was changed to bitterness; while the emptiness of her own life seemed to spread like a desert before her, nothing here, and no hereafter. And she had vowed to stand by it.

She would stand and watch the martins as in her childhood, and long for the glamour that used to cover the world for her; and she would listen to the foolish clack of the marsh hens and to the solemn cry of the bitterns with a weary attention, wondering that so many creatures had been made to live and die for nothing. And so living, she had changed. A deeper thoughtfulness had come into her eyes, a greater strength into the lines of her mouth; and over all there seemed spread an infinite sadness and shadow of longing.

Helen did not stand long at the gate, for, seeing the lonely stream of light that flickered out from the library window, she knew her father waited for her, and hastened in.

Mr. Felmere sat close over the fire, holding in his clasped hands a letter. Helen paused a moment at the door, struck by his position and expression. What had come to him to make him look more sad? She came softly beside his chair.

"What news, father?" He roused himself with a deep sigh. "Your uncle Philip is dead," he answered slowly.

"Dead!"

"Dead, a week since."

Then a silence fell between them; the girl pondering on this awful thing death, so inevitable, so mysterious, so unsparing toward all. And the father was groping in among the dead years for the little boy he had loved and reared, and who now had died an elderly man. How strange.

The servant bringing in the tea roused them, and Mr. Felmere spoke, "The letter is from your cousin Philip. He wants to come and see us."

Helen looked up interestedly. "I shall like to meet him," she said.

"He also sends me a letter from his father, begging me to receive his son as though he were my own."

"Of course; how else could we receive him?"

Mr. Felmere nodded, and continue, "And you are something of an heiress, my child."

"What?"

"Your uncle has left you exactly one third of his property; the rest he has left to his wife and son. It is yours unconditionally."

"Oh, father! What shall I do with it?" The voice was almost distressed.

"When I am dead, child, it will be very welcome, almost necessary; for, with my pen gone, you would have been very poor. It eases my heart of a great burden; for now you will have more than enough, and I the pleasure of feeling grateful to my dear brother. It was a noble thought."

"You did everything for him, father."

"My child, he was all I had to love; it was my chief pleasure to give and do all for him that was in my power."

"And through me he has striven to show his gratitude to you. But a third is very generous."

"Wonderfully generous for one who has made his fortune by hard blows; for this poor old remnant of a place had ceased yielding an income when he left me, so that I had very little to give him. Wonderfully generous; and I thought he had forgotten me."

"How could that be, father? You were the only relative he had left."

"Very true; but his wife has a large family, and a solitary man is apt to become absorbed in a pleasant connection, such as that is."

"You knew them, then?"

"Yes, they were once my friends."

"And why not now?"

"Ah, well, it was through my non-belief. I fell from the esteem of the world, and without the world's approval you must not expect theirs."

"How despicable!"

"All the world is the same."

Then there was a few moments' pause, until Helen asked, "Are you not allowed to think for yourself in the world? Must every one's mind and belief be cut after the same pattern?"

"In my youth it was almost so, and to be known as a skeptic was almost social death; even to be a scientific man was considered dangerous. But now things seem changed. We skeptics are still *dreadful*, but fashionably and interestingly so, allowed in society, and sometimes even lionized. This toleration came too late for me."

"Then I may have friends," Helen said questioningly, "if I should ever go into the world?"

Mr. Felmere shook his head. "I would not count upon it if I were you. They are at best few and uncertain; and now that you have money, you will receive all that the fashionable world can give you, and I would not look for more."

"I hate the world!" the girl exclaimed vehemently.

"Hate is a strong word," her father answered. "You should not hate anything, for there is nothing that has not some good in it; so that you should weigh all things justly, and strive to value them at their due. Strong feelings are apt to lead one astray."

"From what?" she asked quietly.

"From the safe middle path of philosophic calm, that high level so hard to reach, because so above the usual walk of every-day life; so quiet, because so high."

"In what is it above the usual daily life?" she went on.

"Ah, child. You do not know yet what the din and whirl of life are, or its unceasing turmoil and excitement, an excitement that in time becomes necessary, unless one rises above it."

"Do many so rise?"

The old man shook his head.

"Not many. One has to leave one's friends behind, and this is hard to do just at first. They cry out against you as cold-hearted and lacking in sympathy; so you are separated from them, and you find yourself alone, but peacefully quiet."

"Like the worm crawling to the top of the post," the girl said slowly, and looked sadly at her father, "it may be to die of starvation; but it is out of the dust and above its fellow worms. Still, I think I should like to try the turmoil for a little while. Then, perhaps, being tired of the dust, starvation on the post-top is the lesser evil. But, father, is the all of life a choice between evils?"

The question came pathetically, with an undertone of hopelessness in it.

"So I have found it, my child, until I reached the top of the post. There I found the highest good; for from thence I could see the heavens and the earth spread out before me, and could live in the beautiful order of the universe. How could I help looking with pity on the poor worms I had left down in the dust, who so foolishly strove against fate, and seemed not to know the joy of perfect calm, nor to realize their own littleness?"

"Is it a pleasure to realize one's littleness?" she asked slowly.

"Yes, if it comes through the revelation of the grandeur and perfection of nature; it is the rising 'on stepping-stones of our dead selves to higher things.'"

"And that same height is the trouble," she answered sadly, "it is so lonely up there. And yet I may some day long for it, though I doubt if I could ever attain to it, for I think I must be naturally a sociable creature."

The father had been watching her closely, and showed her by his next question whither her thoughts were unconsciously tending.

"Could you be a Christian, Helen, and force yourself to believe all that they do? Could you reason yourself into a faith such as they profess?"

"No, father," she answered, shaking her head, "I do not see how it would be possible. But I do not think reason has much to do with it; it seems a combination of faith and instinct."

"Weakness and folly!" the father interrupted sharply.

The girl looked up quickly, but did not answer, only pondered in her own mind if it were weakness and folly to take hold of a religion that helped and sustained one exactly in the ratio of one's faith. If her father's creed of annihilation were true, it made no difference one way or the other, for after death they were all the same dust; and if it made them more comfortable, why not hold on to this religion, even to the extent of fighting for it? What comfort was it that all she believed could be logically proved to rest on a basis of reason, when her beliefs were all negative, when her creed could be summed up in the formula, "I do not believe"? Alas, in the loneliness and emptiness of her life she had come almost to think she would rather have been overgrown with the briers and tangles of illogical dogmas and baseless superstitions, than stand on this shadowless plain spread smooth with the "how" and the "why." She drew a deep sigh. What was the use in arguing round and round again in this same circle? She had done it so often, and never but with the one result: that the Christians were wise, to say the least, wise in having provided for themselves a future and a hope, even though illogical and vain; but she, having been so educated as to find belief in this delusion impossible, would have to content herself with the present as best she might. Then, breaking from her thoughts, she asked, "When does Philip come?"

"He does not say, probably not until he hears from me. But you will do well to have a room prepared for him; it is always safest to be ready."

"I wonder how he looks," she went on, "and if we shall like each other?"

Her father smiled. It always pleased him to see the girl throw off her serious air and interest herself in passing events, for she had become too grave. "If he is like his father," he answered, "he is handsome. His mother was not so much so, although her face was quite strong enough; that woman had a powerful will."

"What was her name?"

"Jourdan, Amelia Jourdan."

"An ugly name. No wonder she changed it. Felmere is better; Philip Felmere is very soft." She paused, then asked slowly, "What was my brother's name?"

"Percival," Mr. Felmere answered lingeringly, as though he loved to pronounce the name of the boy he had lost.

"Percival," the girl repeated. "Shall I ever know him?"

"You must take Philip in his place."

Helen did not say so, but she felt that there was a special place in her heart kept sacred for this lost brother, a place no one else could possibly claim; a place this rich, handsome Philip had no right to.

The next day she gave orders for the arrangement of her cousin's room, and they were obeyed; but after the servants had left it, she went in to make a few last arrangements which she had purposely reserved for her own hands. It was a positive pleasure to have some real, necessary thing to do for some one else, some little tasteful, feminine work that was not all cold intellect, something which needed but deft fingers and an artistic eye.

It was a strange thing, she thought, that, grown woman as she was, sewing should still be a mystery to her, and "fancy work" of any kind an untried pastime. Once, after watching Jane furtively, she had tried to knit, but her thread became so inextricably tangled that she gave up in utter despair. She regretted very much that she was so ignorant; but she could not help it, for her father had kept her with him all the time, and thought but little of such feminine occupations. But this day she made a holiday, and during her little preparations became almost excited over the approaching visit.

It was almost the first time in her life that any person except her old drawing-master had come to the house. Now and then farmers had come to pay their rent, or to ask for repairs, but not often; for usually the rent came through the lawyer, and repairs were asked for by letter. Thus Philip's coming was a great event to her. She moved about his room with a little subdued feeling of joy in her heart, a feeling that something was really coming into her life after all.

She put the brightest-covered books on the table, the daintiest vases on the mantel, and the most cheerful pictures on the wall. All she could think of to brighten things, she did; then stood in the doorway to enjoy the effect, and, being satisfied, ran down stairs, and brought her father up to pass judgment on her handiwork. It was a dim old room at best; but to them, so used as they were to dimness, it looked quite bright and cheerful. It was brighter than the rest of the old house with its weary look of departed grandeur, brighter than the marsh, than the churchyard, so to them it was bright. Then, at her father's suggestion, she added the brightest of the rusty maple leaves, and thought with him that she had made quite an effect of color.

Now, however, all was done, and there was nothing for it but to finish her holiday with her usual walk in the flats; so, kissing her father for goodbye, she set forth. She walked along quite briskly, feeling more light-hearted than usual, stopping only now and then to pick a stalk of grass or a drooping flag-leaf, and weaving them into a little sheaf to sketch when she got home. There was not much in her surroundings to make pictures of; and she seemed to have sketched everything from every possible standpoint. Already her portfolio was running over with views of the church and churchyard, the river, the maple-tree, the priest's house on the hill, the Hall and the garden, stretches of gray marsh, and sections of the crumbling stone walls. Always dreary, her little pictures seemed to collect all the desolation and sadness of the place, and give it to you with a sigh.

This evening, however, she was in a lighter mood, and twisted and pulled her little bunches of grass and sedge until they began to look almost cheerful. This little success still more raised her spirits, and she quickened her steps to keep time to the ballad she was singing, a ballad she had picked up from the servants. This little song was the only one she knew; and so much did she love it, that she would often draw near to where old Jane sat knitting, droning the while in a cracked voice this favored song, wherein each verse ended with the refrain, "Joy comes to all before the sun goes down"; and often and vaguely she wondered if it was true, this song. She surely loved music, and often she would try to catch the notes that came from the church. To her it seemed to take a tone from the wind and the sea, from the summer clouds and dreary winter rain, from the falling leaves and rustling marsh; and at times she seemed even to hear all the poor human voices that had wailed themselves away, and were for ever hushed in the churchyard mold. All the saddest side of nature dwelt in music; and as she stood on the riverbank, she listened to its murmur and made her little song keep time. There was surely the same soft rhythm running through all nature, all poetry, all music; for her song kept time to the river, and the river to the far-away beat of the sea; and withal, there was an undertone from the autumn wind, and the low gray autumn clouds.

Why was the world ever made, she wondered, then sighed. Why was *she* ever made? Or, if made, why was her life so peculiar? "Natural results from natural laws," "cause and effect," of course she could understand how, but why? Why, indeed, was anything as it was? It all seemed very senseless to her. She hated "immutable laws" driving the universe on forever and forever. An unchangeable iron fate ruling all. What good to fight against it? What good to obey it? "Ever climbing up the climbing wave"—ceaseless, enduring toil and war, and for nothing. Let things go: death ended all.

She shook herself to rouse herself from this untimely mood. Her father did not like to see her sad, and now she was always so. If she could only stop thinking, she felt sure she would be more cheerful. Alas, if she were only not such a weak creature. And, drawing a long sigh, she turned toward the house.

"Yet could not all creation pierce
Beyond the bottom of his eye."

—"A Character," Alfred, Lord Tennyson

Chapter IV

On reaching the house Helen felt almost despondent, and entered the library in a listless way, with the bunches of grass drooping down from her hand as though forgotten. She closed the door after her, and, looking up, saw in the dim firelight a man sitting opposite her father. She paused, and her father, catching sight of her, said, "Your cousin has come, Helen."

The stranger rose and came forward, meeting her halfway, and they shook hands. "I am glad you have come," Helen said; and he, apparently much taken up with her appearance, only said some formal words in return, and sat down again.

There was something wrong in the meeting, but Helen did not know what it was; and she turned away to put down her hat with a feeling of disappointment, and almost blankness. But she felt the duties of hostess weighing upon her: something must be done to make him feel happy and glad to be with them; and as a last resort she strove to make a diversion with her grasses. "See, father, I have material for another sketch," she said, kneeling down on the rug to show her trophies by the firelight.

"They are very graceful," Mr. Felmere answered rather absently, for he was all the while watching Philip, who had not once taken his eyes off his cousin.

The silence was becoming oppressive to Helen, and she was wondering what had come to her father that he would not talk, and at the same time trying herself to think of something to say, when, to her great relief, Philip broke the silence.

"Do you draw, Helen?" he asked.

She almost started, for it sounded queer to hear her name so familiarly spoken by a stranger; then she answered quietly, but without looking up, "Yes, I draw somewhat."

At this moment dinner was announced, and they left the dim library for the more cheerful dining room. During dinner, as Helen became accustomed to her cousin, she had to confess to a feeling of disappointment. He talked fluently, seemed well educated, was versed in all the light literature of the day, and seemed to Helen to know a great deal; yet there was something lacking in him to which she had always been accustomed in her father, the absence of which would not allow her to like him altogether. Suddenly, in the midst of one of his gayest stories, it flashed across her that his father had only been dead a few days. If it had been her father, could she have been so light-hearted in so short a time? True, there was one mitigating circumstance: these Christians all hoped to meet again somewhere; so, perhaps, they did not mind death so much, it being only a temporary separation. She felt guilty after she had reached this conclusion, took herself to task for so judging a guest, and tried to catch the thread of the story Philip was telling. She found it at last, but when she had succeeded did not think it worth the trouble she had taken. But to Mr. Felmere it was interesting, for it brought back to him his youth in the fashionable world. And this little aroma of the world that had come into the old house roused him, touching him like a hand from out the far past, a hand not all forgotten.

It almost startled Helen to see her father so animated, and to hear him laugh so heartily; for in all her life she never remembered seeing him in such a mood. He seemed a different man; a color came into his cheeks, his eyes shone, and his laugh rung clear and musical. It was not natural to see him thus, and it worried her; she liked him best as he was every day, as he had always been to her the bent, the venerable scholar. It better suited his silver hair and the chiseled beauty of his face. At this point in her cogitations her father chanced to raise his head, and, catching her questioning look, blushed like a girl. "Your cousin makes me young again, my daughter," he said apologetically.

Philip glanced from the one to the other in mute surprise. What did they mean? Did they never laugh and talk? Could they possibly think it wrong?

Helen looked down and felt miserable. She ought to be grateful to Philip, and she was not. She had never in all her life been gay, and could almost remember every time she had ever laughed. The conversation had flagged for a little while after her father's apology, but it was not long before she had the relief of hearing it renewed, and go on as before.

When once more she found herself in the library, she felt more at her ease, for here she could withdraw herself without seeming rude. She did not think, however, that it would be polite to read, so she gathered her materials together and began a little pencil sketch of her grasses. So the evening slipped away, and nobody heeded her. Alas, this was not the pleasure she had expected to derive from her cousin's visit; and she wondered if her life would be always becoming more empty, if every change would leave her more alone.

"That is very well done," said a voice close to her ear.

She started, and looking up found Philip bending over her. Involuntarily she drew away from him. Philip watched her closely, but did not move from where he was.

"Where is my father?" she asked, as for the first time she missed him from the room.

"He has gone to get the miniatures of his parents to show me."

Helen drew some crooked lines on her paper; her father had never told her of these pictures.

"You draw extremely well," Philip went on.

"This is wretched," she answered coldly, and tore the paper across the middle.

"It deserved a better fate," he said, and walked to the fire.

At this moment Mr. Felmere returned with two small morocco cases in his hand. "Here they are," he said to Philip; and they came near the light to look at them. "Your grandparents, my daughter. I do not think you have ever seen them," and he handed one of the pictures to Helen.

It was a very joyous, lovely face that met her on opening the case, not very thoughtful, but full of life and beauty. "How lovely," she said half to herself, half to the picture.

"Let me see?" Philip asked, offering to change pictures.

Helen gave hers up reluctantly; she liked to look at the handsome, happy lady who had died so long ago. The picture she now took was still more handsome, and, though in miniature, a grand head. It was somewhat like her father, yet very different; it was more gentle and sympathizing, yet had the same thoughtful strength in the brow and eyes that fascinated her; and over all there lay a shade of sadness that was haunting. There must have been a hope in life that he had lost, a keynote that he had missed. "Was my grandfather a Christian?" she asked suddenly.

Both gentlemen started; her voice had struck so sharply on the silence, and her question was so strange.

"In his early youth he was, but not afterward," Mr. Felmere answered slowly.

Philip looked from one to the other in an observing way. He wondered how they would talk of religion, or if they would talk of it at all; he hoped not, for it was not a favorite topic of his, and belonged by rights, he thought, to clergymen and old women. So he made some remark that led the conversation away, and Helen was left to the company of her grandparents.

She put the two pictures side by side on the table before her, and compared them. How had they ever come together, she wondered; they did not look in the least congenial. Yet he must have loved her, for he did not marry again until she had been dead for more than twenty years. Poor thing. She had only lived one year after her marriage. Young, beautiful, and happy, what an unkind fate that she should die. And he, sad and lonely, had lived on with only his baby son for company.

She studied his face. What had he lost to put that look into his eyes, his belief, or the love of his youth? This religion must be a terrible loss to any one who had ever really held it, like a cripple casting away his crutch, or a blind man departing from his guide. How could one do without it, having once lived by it? No wonder the poor brown eyes looked sad and lost; and yet, if he could not believe it, he was right to give it up. It was fortunate, she thought, that she had not had to choose and decide. Weak and miserable as she was, she would never have had the strength to see the right and follow it; she would have taken the most comfortable course without question.

When they were separating for the night, she asked her father to let her keep the pictures, and he assented.

"And stay'd and cast his eyes on fair Elaine:
Where could be found face daintier? than her shape
From forehead down to foot perfect again
From foot to forehead exquisitely turned:
'Well, if I bide, lo! this wild flower for me!'"

— "Idylls of the King," Alfred, Lord Tennyson

CHAPTER V

DAY AFTER DAY PASSED — THE WEEKS CAME AND WENT, filling out October's term; yet Philip lingered.

For many reasons this visit had been planned. First, it was his father's last wish, and as such had to be obeyed. Second, a third of the property had come to this girl, and it was just as well to look after her; for, besides this property left by her uncle, this only child of the eldest branch would inherit the family place, and all the relics of their ancient wealth and long descent. To Mrs. Felmere, Philip's mother, this meant a great deal; for, her own family being hopelessly new even for America, she was possessed of an honest longing for old things and old names. It would be something to say her son had married his cousin; and a dear privilege it would be for her to be able to add, in a careless, casual way, that this alliance would keep the name and estate together. It did not matter to her that the estate had dwindled down to a neck of marsh land and a few poor farms; the name of the thing was what she wanted: "Felmere Hall" sounded well.

This second set of reasons would have been enough alone to decide Mrs. Felmere that a visit from her son to his uncle was a proper thing; but there was a third set that wrought immediate action. She had during all her son's life feared his marrying; for, being her only child and her idol, she had a morbid dread of losing the preeminent place she now held in his affections, and with it much of her influence over him. This girl was doubtless very innocent and childish, for not only had she been reared in the country, but by a man; thus there was every hope and probability that she would be easily awed by the pomp of wealth she would find in her new home, and easily led to take a second place in the management of things.

It was thus Mrs. Felmere argued, and she sent her son to see his uncle. She had not long to wait to see the successful beginning of her plans; for almost immediately her son wrote of his cousin's beauty, adding that she was educated far beyond most of the women he knew, and was withal gentle and ladylike. All this fully satisfied Mrs. Felmere, and she heartily encouraged him to remain. She wrote a sisterly letter to Mr. Felmere, and a motherly one to Helen, then rested from her labors, feeling she had done her duty by her son, and had partially converted his father's foolish legacy into a good to herself and her child.

And Philip was happy. His mother, who had ever made him feel her power, was pleased that he should love his cousin; and his uncle seemed to quite approve his suit. About his cousin he did not know exactly what to think. She seemed a simple-hearted girl, and one who might be easily won, and yet he could not say he was altogether satisfied with his progress; but still he hoped that time and opportunity were all he needed, and so lingered.

Helen, meantime, went on her way in quiet unconsciousness of all the plans, of all the hopes and fears that revolved about her. That Philip could ever be anything more than a cousin never for one moment crossed her mind, for in all her life she had never had any thought of marrying. She felt herself so different from others that she never questioned but that her life would continue to flow in a different channel, and end with a different result from theirs. Her one thought was of herself and her father living alone and satisfied, cut off from all the outer world. As her father had said, she put Philip in the place of a brother; he was not by any means her ideal brother, but yet, in lack of better, he sufficed. Nor was she altogether happy in his stay; for, although he was kind and attentive and made her father more cheerful, yet she missed the old oneness of their lives, and the unbroken companionship that had existed between her father and herself before his advent; and she went so far as to look back with longing and regret to the old monotony, and to wonder if her cousin would never go.

At last one day, as they stood together on the river bank, Philip talking gaily, and Helen listening quietly, and as usual moralizing on him and his ideas, he suddenly stopped his talk and asked, "Do you care for me in the least, Helen?"

She looked up, surprised, and answered simply, "Yes, Philip, I am quite fond of you."

"How fond?"

"I do not know. I have never weighed it."

"*Will* you 'weigh it,' as you say, and tell me before I go?" He pleaded almost impatiently.

"I will try, but when do you go?"

"In a very few days" he answered. Then they turned their steps homeward. Philip was sorely troubled, for the perfect calmness of his cousin had blotted out all shadow of hope he had had in his own powers, and left him only his uncle to look to for success. So he pondered the situation as he walked toward home, and Helen, equally silent, wondered why he had asked so many curious questions.

That night Mr. Felmere and Philip sat up talking until a late hour, and Helen fell asleep wondering what it all meant. She surmised that it must be about that stupid money. She was very, very sorry that her uncle had left it to her; for, besides the worry of it, she would have much preferred to work for her own living if need be. It would have filled out her life and given her an interest in whatever she undertook.

The next day Philip walked to the village of Felmere, saying he would not be back to lunch. Helen listened gladly, and rejoiced that for one day she would have her father to herself.

Alas, that day. She knelt by her father's chair as of old when Philip was gone, and leaned her head on his shoulder. "My own father once more," she said.

"How, child what do you mean, Helen?" he asked gently.

"Only that I have you all to myself for today," she answered.

"Helen," her father began slowly, "I wish to talk to you very seriously today, and it is for this reason that Philip has left us alone."

Helen lifted her head and looked at him in astonishment. "Has he anything to do with your talk?" She asked.

"Yes, he is the subject of it."

Slowly the beautiful head returned to its resting place, but the girl said nothing. She could say nothing, for an indefinable fear was creeping over her that effectually kept her silent.

"Are you listening?" Her father asked.

"Yes, sir."

Then he began, "Philip is the only son of my only brother, and you and he are the last of the Felmeres."

"*My* brother," Helen interrupted jealously.

"To me he is dead!" Her father answered, more sternly than she had ever heard him speak; then continued, "I love Philip and trust him; and he loves you, my child, not as brother or cousin, but as a man loves the woman he hopes to make his wife."

Could he not feel the wave of blood rush back upon the heart resting so near his own? Could he not feel how heavily and slowly it beat? And did he not know what the white lips would have answered him had they the strength?

But he only made a little pause, then went on, "I cannot hope to live more than a few years longer, and when I am gone you will have no friend on earth. Give me the comfort, my darling, of leaving you to Philip's care, as Philip's wife. I am old now, and dread to leave you alone. You know that life has held little for me; will you not give me this pleasure at the last?"

The young heart seemed to almost stop, the young voice seemed almost smothered. "I do not know him, father. I do not love him."

"How could you be expected to love a man who had not asked it at your hands?" There was no answer, and the pleading went on, "Love will come with time, my child, and Philip is all I could ask or expect for you. He is young and handsome, he has money and position; he has a comfortable home, and a mother anxious to welcome you as a daughter. How better could I provide for you?"

The bowed head was raised, and the beautiful face and eyes had a gleam of desperation in them. "Father, I have my own money, I have this house, and somewhere in this world I have a brother who will come home to me. Let me stay as I am. I do not wish to marry!"

"Your brother is less than nothing to you, Helen; and, if you must hear it, you are too young and too beautiful to be left unprotected. Now listen to what I propose. Philip, when he leaves us, is to travel for some time. Enter into an engagement with him, to be fulfilled when he returns. Do this for me, child, and you will put more rest and happiness into my last days than I have in any wise looked for."

The girl rose; this last appeal for her father's happiness touched the purpose of her life. "Give me today to think, father."

"Very well, my daughter; only remember how much I desire this thing."

"Yes, sir." Then she left the room. She felt bewildered. How had it all happened? And why had she not suspected it before, when she might possibly have put a stop to it? And now! She walked to the back door, where old Jane was feeding the chickens. "Jane!" She called, and the woman came to her side.

"What is it, Miss Helen?"

"Jane, if my father should die, would you not stay here and take care of me?"

"Yes, I would indeed, Miss Helen, for all of my life," and the servant looked at the mistress in much astonishment, and at a loss to account for this breaking through of the barrier that had always separated them. "Is the master sick?" The woman asked after a little pause.

"Oh, no! But, Jane, I thank you very much." And, squeezing the old woman's hard hand in both of hers, she went away hurriedly to her own room.

Jane watched her curiously; what did it mean? In all the long years of her service she had learned to love the beautiful, gentle creature, and had long and earnestly mourned her unbelief. She had often wanted to pet the girl in some humble fashion, and if possible convert her to her own simple creed; but the master's orders had been too strict to be tampered with. "Poor child," she muttered as she watched her go. "With no mother and no God, trouble will come hard."

And poor Helen, locking her door, sat down to think. How was it possible that she should marry Philip? Yet how was it possible that she should deny her father this request? Should refuse this one boon that he asked? His happiness was hers, and with him unhappy, what would her life be? And if he should die before she did, the remorse of having refused him would never leave her. What should she do? Either way she looked at it, it was hopeless; in either case she would be miserable; and why not keep her misery to herself, and so make her father happy? Philip and his mother would be kind to her, so why not accept this as her fate, and be patient? Her little span of unhappiness could be borne if she made up her mind to it, and why should she not? What was there that she expected better than this now offered her? There were no reasons why she should not marry Philip, except that she did not love him; and this love, her father said, would come with time. He was wise. He must know. Life at best was a poor affair. Why not put a little happiness into the last days of one whose life had long been so dreary? She would do it.

She would do it if Philip would accept her conditions: first, that she should never leave her father; second, that she should never become a Christian; third, that Philip should not stay longer at Felmere, but go away at once, and never come back so long as her father lived. Hard conditions, and she sincerely hoped he would not accept them.

She did not again go down to the library, but spent the day in her own room, trying to convince herself that she would be happy in some way, and that in any event it was not probable that she should live long. At last the day was spent, and evening and Philip came together. She saw him coming across the graveyard, walking slowly, with his hands in his pockets, his head down, and a general look of dejection hanging about him; and she went out slowly to meet him. He did not hear her coming, and started visibly when her voice sounded at his side.

"Philip, my father says you wish to marry me."

There was not a tremor in the voice, nor a shadow of hesitation. "Yes, Helen," he answered slowly, too much surprised even to take his hands from his pockets.

"I do not love you," she went on, with painful honesty, "but my father says that will come in time."

"Indeed!" he began eagerly, but she motioned him to silence, and continued in the same even tone.

"All day long I have been thinking of it, and have come to this decision. If you will promise never to take me away from my father and this place until after my father's death, I will marry you." She ceased speaking, and for a moment there was utter silence save for the far-away calling of the sea. Was he going to refuse her terms? And she began to speak again with the desperate hope of making her conditions more difficult to accept. "I will marry you to-morrow if you wish, but you must never consider me as more than your cousin until after my father's death. You must go away from here, and not come back until that awful day when he shall leave me, never mind if it is for twenty years. Do you understand me?"

"Yes," Philip answered slowly, and still stood looking down and thinking. At best, his uncle would not live more than five years; this was a short time to wait. In fact, it would be wiser to wait under any circumstances, for they were both young. At last he looked up. "I agree, Helen." And he held out his hand.

She shivered slightly and drew away from him. "Remember, Philip, I do not love you, and am only doing this because my father desires it."

"I remember," still holding out his hand, "but you will learn to love me in time."

"That is a bare chance. If you, however, are willing to run the risk, I have nothing to say save that I will try honestly to love you. There is now but one more thing to tell you: I shall ever remain an unbeliever."

"Yes, and still I accept your terms; they are hard, but I can wait."

She stood silent a moment, weighing idly in her mind whether she most admired his patience in accepting, or despised his weakness in submitting to her terms. It was only a moment, however; then she roused herself and put her hand in his, saying, "And now it rests with you to say how binding the contract between us shall be. I think it were wiser to have an understanding that will bind me and leave you free; so that if you tire of waiting, you need wait no longer. I am safe; I shall never leave my father while he lives."

Philip shook his head. "No, let it be as binding on both as the law can make it. But when I come again, I hope you will not object to my bringing a clergyman with me: I should like to have the public sanction of the church." He hesitated a minute under her steady look, then went on with almost a shade of apology in his tone, "It is the custom in the world, you know."

"Oh, certainly," she answered carelessly. What difference could it make to her?

Then he stooped and kissed her hand, that was all; and they went into the house.

Alone in the dusky library, Mr. Felmere sat waiting. Helen paused near the door, and let Philip tell the decision; then her father called her. "Helen!" and there was in his voice a gentle ring of happiness she had never heard before. "My darling, I thank you."

That was all he said. Then she knelt by his chair and listened to him as he agreed with Philip in his plan, that the next day a magistrate and a license should be procured and the contract between them be made binding. And all that night Helen lay awake schooling herself to what she thought her duty. Poor child, with no mother and no God, trouble came hard.

"I am digging my warm heart,
Till I find its coldest part:
I am digging wide and low,
Further than a spade will go:
Till that when the pit is deep
And large enough, I there may heap
All my present pain and past
Joy, dead things that look aghast
By the daylight. Now 'tis done!"

—"The Merry Man," Elizabeth Barrett Browning

CHAPTER VI

THE SECOND DAY AFTER HELEN'S DECISION DREW ROUND AT LAST, although to her it seemed to linger unnaturally in its coming, a gray, wan day, with neither sun nor shadow, a gray sky drawn over a gray world. The solitary maple tree in the churchyard stood gaunt and bare against the sky, looking as though it were made from the bones that lay at its roots. The priest's house on the hill looked cold and bleak, and the faraway cry of the sea wandered sad and strange across the flats. Helen leaned idly from her chamber window, not even thinking; and if one had asked her what she was doing, she might have answered, "Trying to see the wind," for her eyes were endeavoring to follow it as it swept from the maple tree to the hollyhocks that stood in the Hall garden, then off across the marsh.

At last she saw the magistrate and the lawyer arrive; and in a little while her father called her down. She was glad, for she longed for the ceremony to be over that Philip might go. First the settlements were read and assented to; then the magistrate began a short, simple ceremony, with the lawyer, Peter, and Jane for witnesses, no one else. "Hold up your hand and swear by Almighty God," the magistrate said.

There was a moment's pause, and the girl said quietly, "But I do not believe in your Almighty God."

Philip paled down to the lips. Old Jane raised her hands in horror. Mr. Felmere frowned. The magistrate paused, shocked, and turned to the lawyer. Helen stood quiet, looking from one to the other with a gleam of hope in her eyes.

"It makes no difference," the lawyer said, "if she does it willingly it is just as binding under the law."

"It is the prescribed formula, my daughter," Mr. Felmere said reprovingly, "and you must say it."

"I will," the girl answered. "I only spoke lest it might make some difference in the legality of the ceremony."

Then the magistrate went on, and Helen swore by a God she did not believe in, and took an oath that meant nothing more to her than the simple promise she had given her father. After that they all signed their names, and it was over. A pitiful, heart-breaking farce it seemed to Helen, and to the lookers-on a mockery. A gloom had settled on Philip; and the shocked look that had come over the magistrate's face at Helen's denial did not wear off during the quiet and decorous serving of the cold lunch that came after the ceremony.

Then the lawyer and the magistrate went away, and Philip lingered only a few moments. Poor fellow. His heart was very heavy; he wrung his uncle's hand as he thanked him for his kindness and his affection, then turned to Helen.

"Goodbye," she said quietly, holding out her hand. He took it in both of his, and stood looking into the great sad eyes that met his so unflinchingly, so unansweringly. Mr. Felmere turned away.

"Helen, you do not love me?"

"No, Philip, but I shall try in time to do it."

"Thank you." Then he kissed her as a brother might have done, and left her.

"Gone. What rest," she whispered to herself, and, with a feeling of infinite relief, went to change her dress, putting on one that was carefully selected as having no associations with Philip, or his visit. Very quietly the household settled again into the usual routine, and Helen more than all tried to step back into the old life as it had been before Philip came.

She took up the old books at the old places; began again her regular walks; read to her father as had been their habit every evening since she had learned to read until Philip interrupted them; and actually longed to go back to the thin dresses she had been wearing in September.

Her old thoughts, that had so much worried her, came back to her easily enough, but in a very different light. How foolishly she had hunted up trouble for herself, as though it would not come in due time and readymade, worrying herself about decaying creeds and an impossible immortality, waking to find herself face to face with heartbreaking truths and a miserable present. Death would be bliss to her now, if it came to her before it took her father, for then she need never be Philip's wife.

And Philip carried in his heart a growing terror. A godless woman. A woman who held no higher law than her own will who could be bound by no fetters but her love. What a strange and awful thing. He loved her wildly, madly, deeply; he loved her beauty, her grace, her intellect. She would shine a brilliant star in the world where he would place her, but, alas, unless she loved him, what hold had he over her? How quietly she had stood up and said, "I do not believe in your God." Not timidly, not defiantly, but calmly, unconcernedly, as though it were some trivial matter that it might be necessary to have known, yet something too settled ever to be questioned. God forgive him!

His mother had welcomed him gaily: he was a good son, and had carried out her wishes far beyond all expectation. But her triumph was a little dampened by Philip's solemn looks. "What is it, my son, that worries you?"

"Mother, she is such a fearful skeptic," he answered, almost under his breath, as though it was wrong to mention it.

"Well, you knew that when you first met her; why is it you are only now affected by it?"

He did not answer for a few moments; then he told her of the scene before the magistrate. "And, mother, she said it as coolly as you would say, 'I do not like that book, or that picture.' It seemed to be of almost too little consequence to her to be mentioned. It shocked me terribly."

"Ah, well, she is young yet," the mother said reassuringly, "and we can easily change and tame her when she comes to us and is from under the influence of her father. He must be a wicked old man."

Philip shook his head. "On the contrary, he is charming; he is the most finished gentleman and scholar I have ever met, thoroughly moral and high-toned, and with exquisitely refined tastes. This unbelief is the honest conviction of his mind; else he could not have deliberately trained his only child to it."

"Put it as you may, Philip," Mrs. Felmere answered severely, "unbelief is wicked. I think, however, that the girl may be easily converted. Is she really so beautiful?"

"Perfectly so," the son answered earnestly, as the memory of his wife came over him, "she is faultless in her appearance, though I think in her ideas she is a little too independent, and a little too much given to reasoning things back to first principles. But these faults are due to her training, for her father argues with her as he would with a son, and gives her a why and a wherefore for everything under the sun. Very often I could not answer her. But about her beauty you need have no fears; it is unquestionable."

Mrs. Felmere listened attentively, and nodded her head complacently when he finished. "All the faults you mention are easily enough corrected," she said. "Much more so than awkwardness or ill-breeding; and I would not let them worry me. All she needs is a woman's influence, and I can give her that." So Mrs. Felmere, in her perfect self-confidence, and without the slightest conception of the character she would have to deal with, planned her daughter-in-law's future training.

But Philip knew better; for, although he was far from a thorough understanding of Helen, and had not by any means touched the depths of her thoughts or her unbelief, yet he felt sure that, strong-willed as his mother was, she would be powerless to change his wife. He did not say this, however, as he did not care to have a fruitless argument; and besides, he thought that it might be wiser to let his mother build her own ideal, and dream her own dreams about the girl, than to give her a bad impression of her. But he realized fully that he had made a mistake, and his remembrances of Felmere depressed him.

It was a new thing to him to have painful thoughts, and he strove to throw them off by change of scene. He had never in his life been able to live under a burden; whatever annoyed him he cast aside without a glance at the consequences; and in time it was so with this.

"Name and fame! to fly sublime
    Through the courts, the camps, the schools,
Is to be the ball of Time,
    Bandied in the hands of fools.

All the windy ways of men
    Are but dust that, rises up
And is lightly laid again."

—"The Vision of Sin," Alfred, Lord Tennyson

CHAPTER VII

THE WINTER SETTLED DOWN GRIMLY OVER FELMERE HALL. The snowdrifts were deepest there, the clouds heaviest, for the wind had a wider sweep in which to gather strength.

To Helen it seemed that through all that long season the sun never shone; there was nothing but snow and ice, sleet and fog, the wild cry of the sea, and the long howl of the wind. She never remembered such a winter. At last the outside world became so dreary, that she was driven into an effort to make the home life more cheerful. Of course, books were the first things she thought of; and the only occasion when she felt in the least obliged to her uncle for his money was when she saw the look of intense satisfaction which came on her father's face as he turned over some long-desired book.

This was a pleasure to her, but her aunt's letters were not. The monthly letters Mrs. Felmere wrote Helen were truly a burden; and through them Helen was learning to dislike Philip's mother. She believed her aunt to be somewhat of a hypocrite, and said so without hesitation. Mr. Felmere, driven to the wall, acknowledged that there was truth in her argument, but warned her against the danger of allowing this feeling to gain strength.

"Accept your aunt's failings as facts, my child, and bear with them as calmly as I hope you will with all the unavoidable ills of life."

"And I do not doubt that they will be many," the girl answered.

"Very probably so, but be careful that you do not make most of them for yourself."

"How, father?"

"By this spirit of intolerance of which you are possessed. You must not despise the stupid nor those who find interest in trifles. I tell you there is much wisdom in being able to lose one's self in small pleasures. True wisdom and happiness lie in adapting yourself to whatever state of life you may be driven to fill; else you will always be tearing yourself against the corners of other people's prejudices, and making your existence a burden. Another good rule is to keep your opinions to yourself until they are asked for, then announce them as mildly as you can. Above all, be polite to fools, for they are the most dangerous enemies."

Helen laughed. "Does the world so abound in fools?" she asked. "It does indeed, and necessarily; for every man, having an ideal of a fool other than himself, creates many. Therefore you should learn to tolerate, and especially those who think you a fool; for of course there will always be some who do."

"I am sorry I shall have to go into the world," she said slowly.

"It is the fate of every one, sooner or later," her father replied, "and the only plan is to enjoy as much as possible its pleasures, to politely ignore its opinions if you know you are right, and to strive to become wiser through witnessing the folly of the many."

"If I could only have you for my guide!" she cried bitterly, laying her head on his knee.

He smoothed her hair gently as he answered, "That can not be, my child, for now I am too old. But I feel that you will be safe, guided by your own good sense, and Philip's love; and this feeling makes me willing to die."

"Oh, father, hush! Without you the world will be empty."

"There will be Philip."

"Don't mention Philip," she cried sharply, "for if Philips grew on every tree, still would the world be empty!"

"Helen, Helen, how silly. Where are all my teachings? Where is the philosophic calm that is to raise you above yourself?"

"Will this philosophic calm fill all my heart and life, quiet all my love, and dry up all my tears?" she asked.

"Even so—it can."

"Ay, and turn me into stone!"

"No. One can be calm without being petrified; can pity the sorrows of others and his own, yet, accepting them as inevitable, see the folly of grieving over them. Child, I tell you there is a height that, once reached, frees you from all trammels. There you can stand, and, looking down, see the world beneath you like anthills, and its troubles like the black insects that crawl in and out."

"Would not such a height cause a woman's brain to turn?" Helen asked. "For I was almost persuaded by Philip that woman is altogether a lower animal."

Mr. Felmere answered slowly, "So some men think, but I cannot see why. Your mind is surely equal to Philip's. But even in this, my daughter, and more, perhaps, in this than in other things you should be quiet, not asserting that your mind is as strong, but show it—prove it by your very quiet."

There was a little pause, then Helen said suddenly, "If I should choose to break my oath to Philip, there is nothing to prevent."

Mr. Felmere looked up quickly, "Nothing, save your word."

"And if I chose to break my word?"

"You would shame me for ever!"

"How?"

"Because you would be breaking faith, and all the world holds this code of truth to your neighbor."

"Why?"

"Why? Why, else how would the world be kept in order? Think of the anarchy that would ensue, the lying, stealing, murder, and all disorders that would be rife among us. How can you ask why?"

"But if I cared more for my own comfort than for this principle, what then?"

"Why, then the law would hold you to it, for you were willingly bound."

"And the law could drag me to Philip's house and make me live there, I know that. But, father, how can an unbeliever be kept up to the spirit of his promise?"

"In no way," Mr. Felmere answered, "save by a love for the truth and for your fellow creatures, a love that should be cultivated, for it is not natural. Cultivated, else we would be lower than the beasts; for look throughout nature, and you will find all things, even the smallest insects, working under laws that are for the good of all living creatures. And shall we be lower than they? Shall we alone look only for our own benefit, and leave our neighbor in the ditch?"

"It would be wiser under some circumstances," Helen answered. "If my neighbor were rich in every sense of the word, mentally, physically, and financially, a man who would advance civilization and science, and so aid all humanity, why, then of course help him out of the ditch. But if he were an indigent cripple, who only consumed, giving no return, must we not leave him there? He could only do harm to his race, and in no way advance civilization."

"He could help civilization by showing himself an example of how it strives to raise all, and to ameliorate the woeful condition of the poor," Mr. Felmere answered promptly.

"And is it not," Helen went on, "by bolstering up the weak and diseased, and by prolonging their lives, that the whole human race is degenerated? For children inherit the weakness of their parents. Therefore the man must be left in the ditch, and civilization is a wrong to the human race."

"Even so," Mr. Felmere answered, "and at the present stage civilization may do somewhat of evil in that way. But in ages to come may it not so advance as to raise the whole to a higher level; when men and women will be educated enough and pure enough to see the virtue and good of 'natural selection;' when the profit of the world will be to a man as his own good? Do you think this an impossible dream?"

"Not impossible, perhaps, but improbable; and I must say that Christianity seems to me a very valuable institution, giving, as it does, to the ignorant masses a system of rewards and punishments which, being to them of divine commandment, they fear to transgress. I think it would be a dangerous thing to free them from this, to them, divine law, until education has reached a for higher level than it now occupies."

"Very well, and let them keep it; but only acknowledge that a noble nature rises above rewards and punishments."

"Perhaps, but only the few are noble, and the laws must be made for the many."

"And in the future may not the few be base and the many noble?"

"It is but a chance."

"Nay, child, it is more than a chance. Judge the future by the past. We are no farther in advance of primeval man than the future man may stand in advance of us; and where would that place him?"

"On the barren height of passionless expediency," she answered.

"On the glorious height of perfect philosophy," Mr. Felmere retorted quickly, then more gently, "My child, you lean to the weaker side."

And she answered, "My father, I am a woman."

"So, plodding on through life's dull mist,
We meet our fate and know it not."

—Unknown

Chapter VIII

A T LAST THE FURY OF THE WINTER WAS SPENT, and the tired earth had rest. Day after day the patient sun came and warmed it, until over all the land a pale-green shadow crept, and a fresh sweet smell came borne on the pure warm air. And down at Felmere the one heart young enough to long for the sweet glad spring watched with hopeless eyes to see it come. A mental and physical languidness came with the warm southern air, and, without energy either to study or paint, Helen spent whole days out in the sunshine. The garden and churchyard were quite alive with the buzzing and humming of many insects, and she liked to stand and listen to them. At other times she would watch the snails and slugs come out on the old wall and wind their slow way so aimlessly to and fro, leaving long shining tracks to show where they had been.

She spent long hours resting under the maple tree, following with dreamy eyes the white clouds drifting across the sky, and hearing with half-heeding ears the faraway song of some ditcher or cowboy. She would half envy the laborer and the living creatures about her their careless content; even the stupid slugs and snails were better off than she, in that they did not realize the uselessness of things. They did not know there was nothing to strive for but the perfection of some far off generation of the human race; and that when, after years and ages of pain and longing, through oceans of blood and tears, and endless streams of broken hearts and bitter strife, this much-desired end should be attained, the end would come, and all would go for nothing. Happy slugs that could not realize the end of all; better, far better to grovel in the lowest depths of ignorance than to rise to this despair of knowledge.

One afternoon at the end of May, she leaned half dreaming from her window, watching a sudden rainstorm driving across the marsh. How swiftly it came, and in what solid sheets the rain seemed to fall, hiding all the land. Presently it reached her window, and, with a little dash into her sweet fair face, drove her away. She shivered as the cool wind struck her, and closing the window went down to the library, where every evening a fire was made for her father. She had scarcely taken her seat when she heard a sharp knocking at the front door, and feeling great pity for the hapless creature waiting there, ran to open it herself.

"Can you give me shelter until the rain is over?" a man's voice asked.

"Certainly," she answered, "come in," and, opening the library door, led the dripping stranger in. "Father, this gentleman has been caught in the rain," she said, "and seeks shelter here."

Mr. Felmere rose and held out his hand. "I am only sorry, sir, that you did not reach us sooner. Helen, call the servant to show the gentleman a room."

"Do not trouble yourself," the young man began, but Helen had already gone, and he could only do as he was bidden, put aside his knapsack, and take a seat.

Helen, meanwhile, being in quite a little excitement, went herself with the servant to make preparation for the stranger's comfort; and it was not very long before she returned to the library followed by Peter.

There was quite a little cloud of steam about the poor wet man when she entered, and he, looking thoroughly uncomfortable, seemed as though he would be glad to follow Peter anywhere.

"I wonder who he is, and where he came from?" Helen said when she heard the receding footsteps fading in the distance.

"He introduced himself as Felix Gordon," her father answered, "and said the rain had caught him while sketching in the marsh near the river. He seems to be a gentleman, and will of course have to remain here tonight, as this rain promises to continue."

"I hope he will be easy to entertain," Helen said, with a remembrance of Philip's first evening.

"He seems well-bred and at his ease," her father went on; "and if he is one of a family of Gordons I once knew, he is a gentleman. But the name is a common one, and I doubt if he even knows them."

"It will be pleasant if he is one of your friends," Helen said almost anxiously, "for then you will have something in common."

"He seems quite intelligent," her father answered. "I do not think conversation will be hard to make."

Then he returned to his book; but Helen in her low armchair found it more entertaining to think. During Philip's visit she had often and bitterly longed for the lost monotony of other days, and was for a time honestly glad to get it back again; but, having once had a taste of a more exciting kind of life, she found the monotony she had so longed for rather irksome. She was consistent in that, if given the choice, she would have instantly chosen the monotony in preference to Philip— inconsistent, because this stranger was welcome to her. She argued all this out as she sat looking into the fire, and drew a little sigh as she recognized the fact that, in spite of all her reasoning, all her training, all her indifference, Philip was still a disagreeable thought to her. A hopeless look came over her face. Was it worthwhile to go on training and schooling herself? Would it ever do any good?

The rain still poured in torrents, the evening darkened rapidly into night, and the only cheerful thing seemed to be the firelight. It burned cheerily enough, making ghostly flickering shadows in the far corners, touching into brightness the dark pictures and pale statues, throwing its fullest glare over the white chiseled beauty of the old man, and falling in vivid lights and shadows about the girl.

The picture satisfied the artistic eye of the stranger standing unperceived within the door. The extraordinary beauty and sadness of the girl's face and the cold calmness of the old man's expression touched him, the one looking as though he had met his fate, and by submission had conquered it; the other, the younger and fairer, as though her fate was even now touching her, and with a heavy hand.

It was only a moment that he stood thus, a moment wherein he saw their true souls gleaming on their faces, unconsciously unveiled.

Then he came forward, and they, rising, greeted him as though he had been some welcome friend. It made him feel almost thankful to the rain for his introduction, and, taking a kindly offered chair, he joined the little circle about the fire.

The souls had gone out of the faces now, and he only saw before him an old student and his beautiful daughter; but in that glimpse he had discovered enough to make him wonder what their lives had been or rather, how life had ever touched them in this quiet, out-of-the way place.

Some talk ensued about the weather and his accident; then Mr. Felmere asked, "What did you find to make a picture of down in the marsh?"

"The desolation is in itself a picture," the young man answered.

Helen looked up. So some one else found poetry in bareness.

"You are an artist?" she said.

"It is my profession," he answered simply.

"Then you know all about it? "

"Not all, but somewhat," smiling at the eager comprehensiveness of the question.

"I mean, of course, in comparison with a beginner."

"Are you a beginner?" He did not particularly desire to see her attempts, but he did wish her not to stop talking, for he liked to see the expression come and go on her face.

"Yes, and there is something very wrong in my attempts."

"I shall take great pleasure in looking over them," he said, with undefined expectations as to perspectives and impossible lights and shadows.

"My daughter is a very ardent artist," Mr. Felmere said, making excuse for the girl's abrupt introduction of her dearest occupation. "Outside of books, she has nothing else to do."

Then dinner was announced, and passed more than pleasantly, as Mr. Felmere really found in the young man, a son of an early friend, one of the veritable Gordons of his youth. This pleased Mr. Felmere, and he insisted that Felmere Hall must be made the young man's headquarters, from which to make his sketching tours, instead of Felmere village, and Felix assented gladly.

Once more settled in the library, Felix asked for Helen's drawings. One after another he looked at them, and laid them down. There was imagination, life, and power in them all, and visible signs of thorough teaching. He scanned them carefully and thoughtfully, forgetting to make any comments in his effort to look into the soul that conceived them. What was it that made them such dreary pictures? The marsh was not strictly the marsh, but seemed rather the allegorical depicting of some desolate life; and the churchyard made death seem a hopeless thing. Then, taking up a pencil, he put in with one or two strokes what Helen felt the picture needed, and yet that which she had not been able to give it—that which her master did not seem to comprehend as a want in the picture.

"How do you know so well what I wanted to express in my picture?" she asked, looking at him with increased respect. "My master did not know."

"Because, perhaps, I think the same thoughts about the scene that you do, and thus know what you mean. Your master does not think with you, but he has taught you well."

Then he went on criticizing all she had done in colors as well as in mere sketches, all the while making in his own mind a picture wherein Helen should stand as "Elaine the Fair." Later on she would make a wonderful Guinevere, for even now her face was far too thoughtful and too strong for the simple maid of Astolat.

So the evening passed swiftly, and Helen was surprised when her father signified that it was time for them to put up their work. "And your luggage shall be brought from the village in the morning," he said to Felix, "and I hope you realize, Mr. Gordon, how much pleasure you are giving us. We lived our lives contented here until my nephew Philip came, but since then we have been lonely, and your coming is a gratification."

And Felix fell asleep that night wondering who Philip was.

"What find I in the highest place
But mine own phantom chanting hymns?
And on the depths of death there swims
The reflex of a human face."

—"In Memoriam," Alfred, Lord Tennyson

Chapter IX

So Felix stayed. He sketched, even as Helen had done, the marsh, the church, the churchyard, the Hall, and the river; then he made a journey inland.

During his absence Helen worked hard at a task he had set her to do, a sketch of her father, which he wanted as a study for a picture of King Arthur as he stands forgiving his fallen queen. She faithfully copied her father's features, but stole the expression from the miniature of her grandfather. She worked honestly at it, striving to finish it before Felix's return, which might take place any day. She was anxious to do it without advice from him, and have it ready for his criticism.

One evening, after she had finished and put her work away, she went to sit under the maple tree, on a broad flat tombstone that made a very comfortable resting place. She half expected Felix this afternoon, but did not chance to see him until he clanged the churchyard gate behind him. How his face lighted up when he saw her; how little he said, how strong the clasp of his hand. Then, unstrapping his knapsack, he threw it and his staff down together and took his seat beside her.

"I feel like a pilgrim," he said, "who after long toil has at last reached his shrine."

"Two weeks are not very long," she answered, smiling. He shook his head. "Time varies," he said, "being sometimes a short long time, and again a long short time; for, although very old, Time seems still in his unequal youth, and is not to be depended on. He is fortunate to keep his youth so long."

"I do not know that I count him so fortunate," Helen answered slowly. "I am not sure I look on youth as very desirable."

"Why?" Felix questioned quickly.

"There are various 'whys.' One has so much to learn from youth to age, so much to bear."

"So much to love, so much to hope, so much happy work to do," he interrupted, shaking his head at her reprovingly.

"Is there?" she asked sadly.

"Is there? Why, of course there is! Have you never felt that life lay all before you, to shape it as you pleased? That there was nothing you could not wrest from Time, from Fortune, from the world? Have you never felt that you loved all your fellows, and that somewhere in the universe there was one love waiting for you—one love that would last through life and far beyond the portals of the grave? Have you never felt this?"

"Never."

He looked at her thoughtfully. "Why is that?" he asked at last. "You are young."

Perhaps he now would touch the secret of her soul.

"I do not know," she answered, shaking her head, "all of life is a hopeless 'why' to me."

"Life cannot be all query," he went on slowly, "for until man defaced it, it was a full, rounded, perfect work from God's own hands; and even now it has been left with us to round yet again to perfectness; and if capable of perfection, it must have answers, must it not?"

"I should think so," then more hesitatingly, "if one can believe the answers."

He turned on her a startled face. She lowered her eyes beneath his gaze, and there was silence between them while he scanned her downcast face, and tried to see how much there was of truth in her words. "What is it you mean?" he asked at length.

"Only what I said," she answered, and gathering again her self-possession, she went on, "only that I do not believe, and therefore life is all a query to me."

"What is it you do not believe in?"

"Ah, that would be a long list. Better let me say what I do believe in."

"Tell me that, then — what you *do* believe in."

"Matter and Force."

"No God!" he said, almost under his breath.

"Only the Unknowable."

Involuntarily he made a gesture to draw away from her. She saw it, and, paling visibly, rose from her seat. He started forward and laid a detaining hand on her dress. "Do not go," he said earnestly, "talk with me a little longer. I am sorry for you."

She paused, looking down on him from her stately height; and he, answering her look from his lowly position, thought he had never seen such a queenly face and bearing.

"Why sorry for me?" she asked.

"Because you have no hope."

"Nor any fear," she answered.

"Why need we fear if we live aright? Our religion is not one of fear, but love."

She sat down again, saying slowly, "It is not so the Church teaches; it is not so the masses are governed. But do not let us discuss it. You believe, and are happy; so would I be if I could, but I cannot, and what matter? Death ends all."

Felix sat silent, looking with wonder into the hopeless abyss of the life before him. Was it strange that her face showed so much sadness? Alas, he did not see how life was at all bearable to her. Force and Matter what an awful void. "How is life bearable to you?" he asked at last.

"Just as it is bearable to you, I suppose," she answered.

"I have the comfort of Religion," he said.

"And I of Reason."

"How can Reason comfort you in sorrow or in death?"

"It tells me they are inevitable. Why be so foolish as to mourn?"

"And when death comes, can you bear to give up those you love, having no hope of a resurrection? Is death to you simply a returning to dust?"

"Yes," she answered, "and a redistribution of force. Perhaps, if the world lasts long enough, the same force and matter may come together again and make another Helen Felmere, poor creature." and she smiled a melancholy little smile over the thought.

Felix looked shocked. "Can you laugh at it?" he asked almost reprovingly.

"Which do you mean," she asked, "the other Helen Felmere, or death? Indeed, I need not ask which, for I smile at both; and neither of them is anything to me. Death is nothing. One pang of dissolution, and I know no more. As has been said, 'Life is like the flame of a candle: what becomes of the flame when blown out? Where was the flame before it was lighted?' Neither the one nor the other concerns me. I have only to do with the light, and why not smile?"

Felix put his face down in his hands. How terrible this was! How could he answer this blank fatalism? Where would the argument begin that would confute it? He raised his head. "How did you become such an utter unbeliever?" he asked.

"I was educated to it. My father is the same."

"And your mother?" thinking of his own mother, who had been all in all to him, and who had trained him so faithfully, so earnestly, that the unconscious carelessness of the girl bewildered him.

"I never knew my mother," she answered bitterly, "and at the best she must have been weak, very weak."

All the blankness of her life seemed due to her mother, and she judged her without mercy. Felix looked at her sadly. "And you think you are strong?"

She shook her head rather hopelessly. "No, I am only trying to be; I am young yet. But do not let us talk of this any longer, tell me of your journey, and show me your pictures."

Felix did not answer; he could not all at once get over the effects of his discovery. He had never until now really conceived what doubt was; for he had unquestioningly accepted his faith at the hands of his mother, never dreaming that such wholesale infidelity existed outside of certain books and a few misguided people who lived in foreign countries. But to meet it in everyday life and, worse than all, in a young woman, was shocking. His life had been spent in the study of his art, and of Nature in her loveliest forms, through whose beauties and perfections he had learned to love God the better. A joyous young life, full of faith and happiness; and to meet another life seemingly as fair and young as his, and to find that it was only a seeming, a bright web spread over a hopeless nothingness, was fearful.

And so he sat silent, gazing out across the wide marsh.

"Have I shocked you so much that you cannot talk?" his companion asked at last.

"Yes," he answered slowly. Then, feeling that this was almost rude, he turned to his knapsack, saying, "I have not accomplished much in my journey, only these few sketches," and he spread them out before her.

But Helen scarcely heeded his last honest "Yes," or the effort it was to him to come back to everyday topics; for she looked on all that had passed as fair expression of opinion, such as she was accustomed to daily, and turned to the criticizing of the sketches without an effort. Presently she said, "I have finished the work you left for me to do, and have put my best efforts on it. Now, if it is bad, it is my misfortune, and not my fault."

"I am sure it is good," he said, and the happy look came partially back to his face," and I am glad you have done your best, so that I can see what your best is."

"And my best by my own acknowledgment," she added.

"Yes, you have condemned yourself."

Then Helen rose and led the way into the house. The sun had gone, and all the red afterglow had faded from the marsh; the evening was darkening fast, and the air felt cool and damp.

"We have stayed out too long," Felix said, shivering slightly.

"No, it is only because we are in the churchyard. It always seems damp and cold the moment the sun leaves it. I have often noticed or imagined it."

"And that amounts to the same thing?" holding the door open for her to pass in.

"Not always," shaking her head. "And now shall I bring the picture?"

"If you will, and I shall wait here, for here the light is best."

It was not very long before she came back and handed him her work. She did not feel nor show any hesitation; for, as she said, she had done her best, and expected justice.

He took it and scanned it closely for a few moments, making no comments. "It is your father," he said at last, "yet not your father. Where did you get the expression from?"

"I took it from a miniature of my grandfather," she answered.

He held it off at arm's length. There was a sad strength in the face, and a tired look in the eyes, that exactly suited his ideal of King Arthur as, disappointed in his life's work, he stands desolate amid the "ruin of his years."

"There are many faults in the picture," he said slowly, "but that expression is worth more than I can tell; indeed, it is wonderfully well done, and if the picture is a success I shall owe it to you." His voice fell a little at the last words, and took a more gentle tone as, turning to her, he went on, "You have far surpassed my expectations, and I shall spare nothing in working it up; indeed, it will be as much your picture as mine."

And Helen, leaning against the door, listened happily to his praise, finding it very pleasant. Perhaps some day she could paint pictures that would be praised by all the world. Ah, how she would enjoy that. Then she spoke slowly, looking gravely up into his face, "Do you think I could ever paint a picture that would be admitted into a gallery?"

"Yes, if you will work; and I shall take great pleasure in giving you all the help I can."

"If you will, I promise to be very obedient, and work very hard." Then in a lower tone, "And you do not know how much you will be doing for my happiness in putting an ambition into my life. Will you surely help me?"

The face lifted to his was so pathetic and humble in its pleading, and withal so beautiful, that Felix would have said yes if she had been entirely devoid of talent; as it was, she had a great deal. "I surely will, and look on it as a pleasure."

"And must we not have a room to work in?" she said almost joyously, her young life springing up happily to meet this first little touch of pleasure, "and will you help me write tonight for fresh materials?"

"Of course, and arrange your studio for you with pleasure."

"Then will you not work at 'our picture,' as you are pleased to call it, while you are here? It will give me so much happiness to see you do it; and father, too, will be interested. Please, will you not?"

There was a moment's pause, then he answered, "Yes, if you wish." He would at that moment have done anything for this fair heathen, so beautiful did she look in her animation, and he wondered if she knew how beautiful she was.

And she, standing in the doorway, did not see the graveyard spread before her, but a long vista of grand possibilities, an ambition that would fill her empty life.

That night the important letter was written, and the miniature from which she had caught the expression for the "King Arthur" was brought down.

"Was his life very sad?"

"I know very little of his life, save that in his early youth he was a Christian, and that afterward he gave up Christianity."

Their eyes met—his questioning, hers observing.

"No wonder," he said in a low tone.

"Christianity must be a terrible thing to lose if you have once depended on it," she answered.

"You acknowledge that?"

"Yes, for, having learned to depend on it, one would be lost without it. But not having been trained to it, I cannot bring myself to believe in it. It would be very comfortable if I could."

"Suppose you try," he said quietly.

She shook her head, half smiling at the strange request, then answered sadly, "No, I would rather be as I am since it is my father's wish; nor can I change the whole habit of my life. But cannot we be friends although we differ?"

"Indeed, yes!" he answered quickly, then, lowering his tone, "I will always be your friend, and will never cease to plead for the peace and safety of your soul."

He was so very good and kind, she thought. Ay, and noble. Who could doubt it, looking in his clear gray eyes? And she answered, "You yourself will give me peace if you teach me how to use my one talent, so giving me an ambition, an aim. May your God bless you for giving me this happy work."

This was surely the most pitiful life he had ever heard of, Felix thought, capable of being so rich, and yet so poverty-stricken. He picked up a sketch of Helen's, and, while he put a few idle strokes in it, said in order to hide his deeper feelings, "Painting to me is not a work, it is a pleasure, and when a thing becomes a pleasure, it ceases to be a work, is it not so?"

"There is energy spent in it," she answered, smiling, "therefore it is work, though it may not be labor."

"Very true. You will teach me meanwhile to weigh my words, and in this age of superlatives it will be a good lesson to learn. It is a fearful age!"

"Fearful?" she asked, half laughing.

"Yes, I think I may say 'fearful' for things seem rushing ahead at dangerous speed. I have too much love and veneration for old things to admire my age and generation."

"I admire it," she said. "To me it is an age of progress of liberal thought and fearless investigation; an age wherein old creeds will die, and the world be liberated from all the old trammels of ignorance and superstition."

"God help us then!" he said quickly, "for it will be an age of fearful sin."

"Of course there will be confusion; then order will come again, scientific, philosophic order. But do not fear, we shall not live to see it."

"Maybe not, but think of those we leave behind us."

"Let the future alone," she said. "Our own trials and sorrows will be enough for us; we will bear them and die, and those who come after must also learn to bear and die."

"That is very selfish," he answered slowly.

"How?" looking up in surprise.

"You think only of yourself."

"If I do, that is not selfish, it is but just and natural. Every one must think more for himself than for others; how else would the world go on?" She paused a moment, then said, "Out in the world are there many women who do not believe?"

"I do not know of one besides yourself," he answered honestly.

Helen sat silent for a moment, then said: "I hear of many men who are unbelievers in the world; why should unbelief be considered more a sin in women?"

"As immortal souls there is no difference," he answered, "but for women it is more dreadful in that they have the training of the children, and owing to this, the evil would spread more rapidly, and soon the whole land would be infected."

Helen looked up. "I go into the world, then, a walking pestilence? An incurable plague-spot?"

The color swept over Felix's face, and he looked at her almost reproachfully. "I meant nothing personal," he said slowly.

Then there was silence between them until Helen, looking up, asked, "How can honest men allow their children to be bound by trammels they have broken for themselves?"

"Because, I suppose, they find that to believe is happier than not, and so leave their children in peace."

"How short-sighted," she said, "for if the many were unbelievers, then the weak would not be frightened by the fear of hell into a false religion. If all were emancipated, and the superstitions dead."

He interrupted her quickly. "Then we should have a hell right here among us!"

To his surprise she answered, "Perhaps it would be so just now, but it is the future I am thinking of; then things will be different, and we shall be prepared to rise a step, and be moral and righteous without rewards and punishments."

"How your argument clings to reward and punishment. Is that all that you find in our religion?" he asked.

"That is all I can find to make it live," she answered, "unless it be blind superstition, and a clinging to old things. But this sort of talk is so unavailing, let us go back to art."

And Felix, sighing sorrowfully, did as she suggested. He was so utterly unlearned in her side of the question, he was so little prepared for the arguments she advanced, that he did not know how they were to be met; and he took himself bitterly to task that he could not fight a better battle for his cause.

"I said, 'I toil beneath the curse;
But knowing not the universe,
I fear to slide from bad to worse;
And that in seeking to undo
One riddle, and to find the true,
I knit a hundred others new.'"

—"The Two Voices," Alfred, Lord Tennyson

CHAPTER X

THE ARRANGING OF THE STUDIO WAS A GREAT PLEASURE TO HELEN, certainly the greatest she had ever enjoyed. A room with a good northern light was selected as the favored apartment, and was quickly divested of all unnecessary and unpicturesque furniture. It was a great regret to Helen that all her new apparatus had not come already; but Felix contrived to make the room have a very littered and artistic appearance by spreading out as far as they would go their joint sketches and his materials.

"Make it look like a real studio," she pleaded.

And Felix, standing with his hands in his pockets, looking at the part of the work already done, answered, "If you will let me put everything crooked, fill all the corners with trash, hang all the windows with cobwebs, and suspend dirty paint rags from every available nail, you will then begin to approach a real studio; but I must confess that I prefer clear decks."

Helen laughed. "I think I agree with you. If the room chances to grow artistically littered, I will not change it, but I prefer things clean and straight. But will it not be delightful when all the things come? I shall so enjoy unpacking and arranging them. Indeed," she went on more thoughtfully, "I have never been so happy in all my life before."

"Have you ever been away from this place?" Felix asked, pausing in his work of tacking a sketch on the wall.

"I have never in all my life been away from it any farther than I could walk, and as a child I used to think the world began out by the sea and ended on the hilltop. I used to long to go away, but now I begin to love the life I have lived, and to dread leaving it for the world. You, I suppose, are quite amused that I should fear what you have always lived in."

"Indeed," he answered, "you are mistaken in thinking I have always lived in the world. My home is almost as secluded as this; it is only a little farmhouse, and very poor compared with your home."

"And have you brothers and sisters?" she asked. She was holding the hammer and tacks for him while he arranged the pictures, and with her question there came a wistful look on her upturned face. She would so like to hear of his home; she felt sure it was a cheerful and happy one.

"No brother, but two sisters and my mother; I wish you knew her." And his face lighted up as he spoke of them.

"Are they beautiful?" Helen went on.

Felix smiled a quiet little smile as he stepped back to look at his work. "Beautiful?" he said thoughtfully. "I do not know. To me they are, especially my mother, who is the wisest and most beautiful person to me in the world. I wish very much that you could know her."

"I wish I could," Helen answered; then went on, "And you are all Christians, and happy in your faith?"

"Yes, thank God!"

Helen turned away sadly. This pure, good man was glad and thankful his sisters were different from her. She was silent for a few moments, looking out of the window, and Felix, not knowing the pain he had caused, went on hammering busily.

At last Helen turned and said, "I have never met a Christian woman except Jane; in fact, she is the only woman I have ever known at all. I should really like to see a Christian home. Will you tell me about yours?"

What a pitiful request it seemed to Felix. "Tell me about your home." How lonely the life must have been that had to beg for even the reflection of cheerfulness. And she had never known a woman, had all her life lived alone with her father in this dim old hall standing so desolate between a churchyard and a marsh! Of course he would tell her. Ah, if he could only take her there and let her have a little taste of gentle, womanly sympathy.

He did not tell her this, but said instead, "Yes, I will gladly tell you of it, all there is to tell. My home is only a little red farmhouse, built on the southern side of a steep hill, fitted into a crevice as it were, and nestling away from the wind and snow. The fields all lie below it in the valley, and steep paths lead up and down. There are an orchard, a great red barn, and a barnyard that was the delight of my boyhood's soul. In the world my sisters would be called 'old maids,' but they call themselves the 'ladies Singleheart,' from some quaint book they have read." He paused, with a smile of pleasant memories about his lips.

"How happy you must be," Helen said musingly.

"We are. One of my sisters is an artist, the other a musician, and they are the happiest, busiest people I know. And my mother, ah, you should know her, she is so wise, and holy, and beautiful! Each winter I look forward to the next, and in the next am never disappointed. I wish you could see my home."

The work of tacking up sketches was finished now, and they stood idle, looking out of the window Helen thinking of all she had heard, Felix thinking of her. At last Helen spoke, "And if I should go there," she said, "I should be to your mother and sisters, as I suppose I must be to you, a lost soul doomed to eternal torments."

Felix started! "How can you talk so?" he said quickly.

"It is the truth," she answered quietly. "How could you have any hope for my soul?"

"As long as you live, there is hope," he said, "and Christ is patient to save."

"Ay, your Christ is very beautiful, if I could believe in Him as you do."

"And you will?" he pleaded. She shook her head. "I cannot, there are too many mysteries, too many superstitions, too many dogmas, too many churches. I cannot take all this for truth; my reason revolts. More than this, if I could believe, where should I go for orthodox views? To the Anglicans? The Church of Rome is 'Antichrist,' and the sects a mere fungus-growth of societies. To the Greek Church, all the rest are at the least schismatics. To the Romanists, all the outside world are heretics. So where should I go?"

"Go to the Christ," Felix answered solemnly. "He is the one great Truth that underlies all the loads of nonessentials that the churches have piled upon it—the one glorious Love that blots out all our sins and all our mistakes. Believe in and follow Him; this is all you have to do!"

Helen looked at him as though surprised, then asked slowly: "How can I? How can you believe in such perfect love, and at the same time in eternal punishment? And what is the use of creating man at all, unless for happiness? Your God is omnipotent; if he made things at all, he could have made them differently. "We are of no use to him; he could have been glorified in much higher ways. And more than this, what need had he for glory? Was not all his? Can you call it mercy to create beings 'who are born to trouble as surely as the sparks fly upward'? What use in such an elaborate scheme of salvation, when he could save with a word? Why all this need of trouble, and sorrow, and death? Tell me."

"How can I tell you? "Felix answered. "If we could know and explain all things, 'then were we as gods.' But do you know of any better belief?"

"Mine is much more simple,"she said. "We are all evolutions of force, at death this force is redistributed. Order and right are one disorder and wrong are one. Whatever can be logically proved is truth; all else is theory, hypothesis. I expect no hereafter. I dread no hereafter. Whatever of good comes to me in this world, I will enjoy; whatever of evil, I will bear. This is my creed, and it seems to me simple enough, and easy to be understood."

She spoke slowly and deliberately, and each word sunk into Felix's heart like lead—cold, heavy, and hopeless. "And this suffices you?" he said.

"Why not?" she answered, brushing back the hair that the wind had blown across her eyes, and turning to look up at him from where she leaned with her arms crossed on the windowsill. "It answers all my questions much more satisfactorily and easily than your belief does, for it is only necessary for a person to accept one sentence of your creed, and he is involved in endless contradictions and hair-splitting doctrines. No, you keep yours, if it pleases you, and let men hold it as a power over the masses until the time is ripe for the throwing off this yoke of religion and church. As I have read, 'Force and Right are the governors of this world—Force until Right be ready.' To me Religion is Force, Science is Right. You shake your head? Even so, if you are happier." And she turned again to her former position.

Felix, leaning against the side of the window, listened and looked down on her sadly. She was so beautiful as she leaned out into the clear morning light, the sea wind blowing the loose waves of golden hair across her face so that it sometimes quite covered the violet eyes, and then only touched an exquisitely tinted cheek beautiful as her namesake, for whom "many drew swords and died," and Felix, like the poet, could have said, "Myself for such a face had boldly died."

"Whenever I listen to the sea, I always wish I knew something of music," she said at last, showing how far her thoughts had wandered from the former topic of conversation.

Felix roused himself from his reverie to answer, "Do you know nothing of music?"

"Nothing in the world except what I hear sometimes from the church over there, and though that seems very beautiful to me, I can imagine music that would far surpass it. Do yon know anything of it?"

"Somewhat. My sister teaches me a little every winter when I am at home. She is organist in the little church we attend, and sometimes when the weather is too severe I go in her place. But I can only play very simple things. Can we get into the church?"

"I do not know," she answered, "I think it is kept locked."

"Would they not lend you the key?" he suggested.

"I do not think so. The priest and people about here look upon me and my father as very wicked. Poor, ignorant souls. They do not know any better. I would not ask for the key." Her tone was more hard and bitter than Felix had ever heard it.

"Have you ever been to church?" he asked.

"Never but once." And then she told him the story of the insults offered her in her childhood. He listened interestedly, with all his sympathies excited for the lonely little child, and when she finished her recital, he found himself really indignant.

"How pitiful," he said, "and how hard to treat a little child in such a way, poor little soul. But were you never lonely as a child?"

"I was sometimes," she answered sadly, "but, childlike, I made friends of all living things and many dead ones. I also made many wonders for myself that kept me very busy and served to entertain many spare moments. Besides this, I had my father, and he was everything to me playmate, friend, mother, nurse; in short, he is my world! Is it any wonder that I adore him?" And her whole face lighted up and softened with the love of which she spoke.

After that she often talked of her childhood, of her brother, and of her mother's flight. But she never spoke of Philip, indeed, she seldom thought of him now except to write her weekly letter, and she found that very irksome. One day, after a long discussion about the Romish Church, Helen finished her criticism by saying her mother had been a Romanist. They were at work in the studio unpacking the new materials that had arrived, and their argument had seriously hindered their work, but it ended just as Helen got through with her story.

Felix shook his head sadly. "It was a cruel influence to use," he said, "and your mother must have suffered bitterly."

"I do not know how much she suffered," Helen answered. "I only know she brought it on herself by running away from her duty, and in thinking of her, I only remember how cruel she was to my father." Her opinion was given slowly, and with the hard, unsympathizing justice of youth.

"You are too hard on her," Felix answered. "Think how desperate she must have been to be able to bear the parting from you, and you so ill."

"Then why did she do it?"

"She thought it was right."

"Then the assurance of having done the right should have comforted her, and I have no doubt that the priest up there on the hill promised her endless rewards. The truth of it was she wished my father to consent that my brother should be trained to the church, and he would not. But with even this for a foundation, I do not see how she could have allowed herself to be persuaded into thinking her action right; for she had sworn at her altar and to her God to live with and love my father through all, and she did not do it; and such an oath should certainly be binding on a Christian." The girl's voice was so unpitying and cold that Felix was more pained by it than he could tell.

"And such an oath *is* binding," Felix answered, "but the Romish Church claims the authority to annul any oath, or loose any tie, however sacred."

"Her claiming it does not give it to her," Helen answered. "And the promise was made to God, and only, as it were, witnessed by the Church. No, I tell you my mother's action showed great weakness."

"Are not the best among us liable to weaknesses and mistakes?" Felix went on. "Does our being Christians make us more than human?"

Helen answered quickly, "If you honestly believe, according to the promises, you ought to be endowed with more than human strength when the day of trial comes."

"And I have no doubt that your mother believed herself endowed with that very strength, but she thought it was given her to fly and leave you. Do you not think she loved you?"

Helen shook her head. "Whether she loved me or not, I do not know, but you are leaving the point. Does it make a thing right for one to think it so? Is there no absolute right or wrong in your creed, that my mother could so grievously err, all the time thinking herself right?"

"We can only act up to the light we have; and though your mother was not right, and her thinking herself right did not make her so, yet she did think so, and acted on her conclusions, and, however weak and wrong, she will, I believe, have much mercy at God's hands. Have you no pity for her?" he pleaded.

"No," she answered quietly.

Felix went on, "Granted that she was weak, is there any greater suffering than weakness, anything to be more pitied?"

"Or despised," she added.

"Do not say that!" Felix cried, horror-stricken, for to despise a mother, however sinful, was too dreadful.

"It is the truth," she answered, looking curiously into his face.

"It is not the truth. All humanity calls for pity and charity for weakness."

He paused, and she turned again to her drawing with almost a look of amusement on her face. How absurd to make such an assertion, when it was a well-known fact that in many tribes and nations the weak, either mentally or physically, were so despised as to be put to death that they might be out of the way. It was not worth an argument. To her, humanity was a mass of lives higher than the brutes, but of no account unless they were able to benefit their kind. To him, humanity was the multitude of throbbing, suffering souls, raised, purified, and made holy by the love of Christ.

Presently Felix went on, "Put yourself in your mother's place: what would not you have done to save your child? Think of what eternal punishment was to her, and of her brooding over that one thought for years think of her terrible sorrow in having to leave you, and can you not pity her?" He stopped his work and came to her side as he went on. "And if you should meet her some day, meet her, old and worn with poverty and trials, you would be sorry for these hard words."

She looked up at him, her eyes brimming with tears. "You pity her, for you judge her by your strong, good, loving mother, and you blame me. Do it, but in doing it, think whose fault it is that I am as I am. Think how different all might have been, my home, my life, myself! I tell you I cannot, I will not forgive her!" She brushed the tears from her eyes, and in a lowered, hardened voice went on, "No, nor pity her; for if she is right, she left me to eternal damnation." Her face was white, and her blazing eyes looked steadily into his.

What could he say? Ah, if his mother were only here to help him, and to comfort and set right this sad young creature, whose life had been so strange and lonely so deliberately misguided. At last he spoke. "If you think this," he said, "is it well to dare a risk so terrible?"

"My father dares it," she answered doggedly. "He is my all, and I will follow him without the shadow of a turning. If there is a hereafter, mine shall be the same as his." She stopped abruptly, turning away to her easel and Felix, watching her silently, felt a horror creeping over him as he thought of her future. Could God let so fair a soul as this be lost through the fault of another? Would that be just? God was strong to save, and she, poor child, had never seen the light. If a just God reigned supreme, how could such a dreadful sacrifice be permitted? He shivered. He was doubting. He was faltering where he had stood firm. He was almost judging God! He covered his face with his hands, and tried to think. What was this that had come to him—this wild love for this lost soul, this love that shook his whole being, his faith, his trust? God help him!

"What then were God to such as I?
'Twere hardly worth my while to choose
Of all things mortal, or to use
A little patience ere I die."

—"In Memoriam," Alfred, Lord Tennyson

CHAPTER XI

THE BLACKEST DAYS OF ALL ONE'S LIFE ARE THE FIRST DAYS OF DOUBT, when all things seem to fall away, and you are left to battle, single-handed, with spirits of darkness, days when all the faith and trust of your life seem based on shifting clouds, that change their shape and color for every breath of argument that touches them. Where is right? What is truth? Is there any right or truth? Who can tell whether or not they are figments of the imagination?

So the bright summer days were shadowed for Felix, shadowed with vague doubts, the first questionings of his faith, the first faltering of his trust. He went about his daily tasks of sketching, teaching Helen, and diligently working at his picture of "King Arthur," but all the while the words rang in his ears and heart, "For all my mind is clouded with a doubt," a doubt that slowly grew into the face of the "great king."

Yet Helen did not know. One afternoon Felix came to her, saying, "I have the key of the church. Will you come over and let me play for you?"

She paused a moment. She wanted to hear the music, but did not like to go into the church, for it seemed to her like enjoying a pleasure at the hands of an enemy.

"If father will let me," she compromised, and went to ask him. "Mr. Gordon has the key of the church, father, and is going to play the organ. May I go with him?"

"Surely, my daughter," he answered, smiling at her eagerness. "I have no objection, only do not stay too long."

So she kissed him for goodbye, and went her way, she and Felix, with the sexton's little son, to blow the organ bellows.

Helen, all eagerness to see the inside of the church, and to revive her childish visions, did not heed the child until, while Felix was unlocking the door, he spoke, pulling at her dress to attract notice. "Lady, are yer so bad?"

Helen turned in astonishment. "I? Am I so bad?"

Felix caught the words and stopped to listen, almost glaring at the boy. The child quailed, "I didn't mean nothin', "he stammered out.

Helen, having by this time recovered from her astonishment, became curious as to what the child meant, and said reassuringly, "Do not be frightened, child; tell me who said I was bad."

He hesitated a minute, then, putting her between Felix and himself, said promptly, "Daddy, but mammy says she don't much believe it."

Felix listened, silent. Helen went on, "What does daddy say about me?"

"He says you don't believe there is nothin'."

Helen laughed. "Is that all?"

"No, he says yer soul will burn in hell fur it, he do."

Her face flushed slightly, and Felix said sharply, "Tell your father to be careful that his own soul does not burn for speaking evil against his neighbors."

Helen looked up surprised. "Do not speak so harshly," she said slowly, "the child means no harm."

"No, marm, I don't, but that's what daddy says, he do."

"Well, hush!" Felix cried. Helen watched him curiously. What did it mean, this sudden anger? It was not his soul that was threatened. There was a frown on his brow, and his eyes looked dark with anger as he answered her look, but he said nothing, and she and the child followed him silently into the church.

The organ was near the chancel, and the child went with Felix, while Helen stopped halfway. There were no white-robed priests nor boys moving about, but the sunlight shone through the window above the door just as she remembered it, and now as then touched all the gilding and coloring about the chancel with an almost supernatural hue glittering on the candles clustered about the high white altar, and making a great cross that surmounted the whole seem a living light. She stood mute, gazing on what to her were the symbols of a dying creed, but a grand one, this Christian creed, even if old and decaying. A creed that had comforted many in this weary world—had lightened life's burdens, and sweetened the bitterness of death; a creed that had been for generations a dominant power, and whose death throes would convulse the world.

Low and tremulous the tones of the organ stole upon her. Soft and deep, they seemed to pervade her whole being, thrilling through every nerve. She leaned against a pillar and listened. High and higher the music rose, a wail, a cry that pierced her soul, slowly sinking down to one low sob lingering softly through the senses. A voice rose with it, a rich mellow voice, almost too piercingly sweet to be a man's, almost too full for a woman's.

She listened mute, bewildered. She could not say what she felt; she did not know that she felt at all. The world had floated away, gone from her like a mist before the sun. The church and its creed vanished from her view; a great and terrible knowledge rose up before her, dark and dreadful. She surely dreamed? It could not be true, this knowledge that had come home to her like the keen thrust of a sword, the knowledge that in all the world this was the only voice to her!

She covered her face with her hands, and still the voice rang on, with the words, "No light, so late, and dark and chill the night." She wrung her hands. All her life had been chill darkness and now? She paused, standing mute under the glare of this terrible light that seemed to have touched the lowest darkness of the abyss that yawned before her, an abyss that must swallow up her life. And she had no God to cry to in her sorrow, no human soul to fly to in her distress; she stood alone in her misery.

She turned away and stole out into the churchyard, crouching down behind a great vault. She closed her eyes, and covered her face with her hands, rocking back and forth. "I love him, I love him," she whispered to herself, "I love him." And Philip? She hushed; the horror of it overwhelmed her! Then, as one in delirious wanderings, she came back to the words, "I love him, I love him." The rocking back and forth ceased, and a flood of tender little thoughts swept across her heart; pure little thoughts like gentle doves came fluttering round his whispered name—*His* name, the sweetest in all the world. And Philip.

Then the swaying recommenced, back and forth, back and forth, as though to rock her heart and soul to sleep. And on the air there floated a little moaning sound as of one enduring more than human agony.

The evening darkened. Felix would soon be coming, and he must not know this grievous wound. She rose and crept back slowly into the church. Ah, it was so cold and damp, as though the death-dews from the churchyard had collected there, and were striking through her. The last lingering light streamed through the western window, and the cross and the altar were all bathed in a tender flood of light. The girl looked at them wistfully. If she were a Christian, praying might bring her comfort. If she could only feel that there was one "Supreme Father" who felt her sorrows, and to whom she might appeal for sympathy. She stole up to the altar steps; she stood there, but could not kneel. What good could a prayer do her? She covered her face with her hands. Those happy women in their faraway home on the hillside—they could pray, and praying think their sorrows were sent them, in mercy; they could rise above this iron fate that crushed her. Ah, if she had but lived in such a home. But now where should she turn? Where could she turn? Alas, she had no refuge; this agony must eat forever into her soul! Would it help her to pray there before that cross, to kneel and rend the air with inarticulate cries? This was all that she could do, for she did not know how to pray. Should she cast herself down like some poor stricken animal and moan out her pain?

She looked up; the shadows were gathering fast and deep, so that the cross alone retained the light, the great altar growing shadowy and dim, and still the music rolled on, and its softness seemed to soothe her. Perhaps it would help her to put her sorrow into words, and make a little prayer. Poor and meager it would be, but if this God was what they said He was, He would surely hear her; and if He heard her, would He not comfort her? Could He not send peace to her soul, driven and tossed?

The light still lingered on the cross. She clasped her hands, and her thoughts rushed swiftly back and forth, bewildering her. How could she pray, and leave her father? Had she not sworn to stand by him, and would she fail him in the first hour of trial? A coldness seemed to gather about her heart, and her hands fell apart. What good could it do her to kneel before a gilt cross. She looked up. The cross was blotted out. The light had gone.

"Like one that on a lonesome road
Doth walk in fear and dread,
And having once turned round walks on,
And turns no more his head;
Because he knows a frightful fiend
Doth close behind him tread."

— "The Rime of the Ancient Mariner,"
Samuel Taylor Coleridge

Chapter XII

THE FIRST RUSH OF SORROW that shows us the underside of life, the first blinding pain, which to inexperienced youth seems unexampled and endless, how can it be endured? How is life possible with this dull emptiness staining all the world, dimming all the sunshine, and lending darkness to the night? Will it not kill us? Alas that it does not. That, recovering from this first blow, we live on and learn the great depths to which suffering can go; learn to know that every pleasure has an underside of pain, and that every hope comes lined with fear of disappointment. Until, at last, we learn to work out our lives with calm patience, untinged with any glow of expectation save of that which cometh after death.

So in the vigor of their youth these two suffered, suffered in proportion to their strength and freshness.

Felix was almost in despair. Whichever way he turned, there was no outlet from this sorrow, or from the gathering doubts that were crowding thick about him. Were these doubts well founded? He could not say. He could not let go the faith and hope of all his life; for what was existence without them? Could he go back and tell his mother that he was tainted with unbelief, that he, her pride, her hope, her darling, had gone from her, leaving her desolate in her old age? He could not answer himself, but he felt and knew there was one practical question which rose up for solution, and which could not long be pushed aside: what should he do with the love in his heart for this fair infidel?

There was not much use in questioning himself as to the right and wrong, as to the happiness or unhappiness consequent on the one course or the other. One thing he knew, that he loved her; and every hour made him feel that he must tell her so, come weal, come woe. This decision ended neither his doubts nor his wretchedness. When he tried to tell Helen, and settle his fate, the words seemed to choke him; he felt that he was about to desert those three loving, lonely women, or at least to sow dissension and misery in their happy home. Then he went over once more the same weary round of thought, and determined to conquer himself one way or the other. He still had some self-possession, and resolved to separate himself from her for a little while, so that he could think more calmly.

Ah, what a relief this solution was, and how gladly he strapped on his knapsack and set off for a few days' ramble. They said goodbye at the churchyard gate, and she watched him go across the churchyard and up the hill, where pausing he waved a last farewell.

She answered it, and turned away hopeless. It would soon be an eternal farewell; and yet, she pondered, why should it be? She drove the thought away, and went indoors to her father. She longed to tell him all her trouble and ask for some sympathy, but she could not, for she was bound, and this would but make him unhappy. It could not now be helped, and she must bear it alone. So she kept her sorrow to herself, and, taking up the book she had been reading, sat down on a low stool close beside her father's chair—her place since childhood; and now, as then, he did not speak, but laid his hand caressingly upon her head.

She sat still a moment, then drew the hand down and rested her cheek against it. It was all she had here or hereafter, this old, tremulous, failing hand. When that was gone! The tears sprang quick to her eyes, and she let the dear hand go for fear they might drop on it and betray her. So her tears fell silently, and the book was not read. And he, so near her, was all unconscious of the wasting desolation which was devouring the young life beside him, and of the young heart turning bitterly from its first "Dead-Sea fruit"—dust and ashes.

So she came and went in her daily occupations, he noting nothing in her that spoke of change, more than that the summer weather made her manner a little more listless, and her step a little slower. The autumn would set all straight again.

But old Jane, with her keener woman's eye, saw deeper. She had watched these two young things coming and going, working, walking, talking together through all the summer days. What could they do but love each other? "Poor lamb, poor lamb, she must be warned."

So one day she went into the studio where Helen was at work, and after a few moments silent watching said, standing humbly back, "Miss Helen, do y' not count it true that y' are married to Master Philip?"

Helen turned quickly, the red blood rushed into her face and throat. "How, Jane?" she asked.

"By the laws of man, Miss Helen, not by the blessing of God, it is true, but still y' are married, are y' not?" The old woman came a step nearer—she so loved this motherless, godless girl.

"Yes, Jane, I know it, I know it!" Ah, what a bitter cry the last words swelled into.

"And yet, Miss Helen," the old woman went on more gently, "y' are walkin' open-eyed into a great sin—not to you, maybe, but to both o' them." Helen turned away silent. "This last one is little more nor a boy, scarcely older nor you, Miss Helen, an' he don't know what he's doin'. Y' should tell him about it, Miss Helen, 'deed y' should."

Still Helen stood silent, and the old woman turned to go. She had done her duty by the girl and her master, and she had no more to say. It was a dreadful sorrow for the poor child, but better that than sin. Ay, far better!

And Helen let her go, the kind old woman who in so many ways had shown a tender sympathy for her in her loneliness. Even now, though hard to bear, her humble reproof was gentle. When she had gone, Helen leaned her head against the side of the window near which she was standing, and tried to think. She did not love Philip. She did not believe in the God by whom she had sworn, and why need she keep her oath? In time to come it would only be an endurance of Philip; why not tell him so honestly, and confess that she loved this other? This course would surely be more true.

Her father only wished her to have a protector, and Felix would do as well as Philip. But would not the oath be sacred in Felix's eyes? And if she broke it, would he still care for her? No, he would not; she felt assured he would not, for he would regard her as married and belonging to another. If she should tell him of it and bid him go, he would still respect and love her; else, she were lowered in his eyes. Ah, she could not bear that! She wished him to look on her as pure and high, although an unbeliever. Then she must let him go! Yet how could she stand and see him turn away, knowing she would never look on his face again, knowing that through all the waste of years that lay before her she must go alone?

Alas, she must bear it. What use in thinking of it? She could not tell him she was sworn to Philip, and yet beg him to take her away, plead that the oath was nothing, tell him that she loved only him. She shivered. She could feel now the look those honest eyes would turn on her. Then, again, even if he consented, could she let him soil his fair name and heart by helping her to break this vow? Could she tempt him to this thing that would be so foul a sin to him? And if he consented, could she love him? She did not answer; she was afraid she could nevertheless love him.

But then her father, how could she so disappoint him? Now, when he was resting after a long, sad life, resting on the thought of her safety, could she wreck his hopes, and put his last days out of tune with her wild love and weakness? No, a thousand times no.

So she answered, and went on with her work. But day after day she would go back and battle over the same ground, wounding and tearing herself with her arguments for and against. Living with Philip was a dreadful thought, and yet at every turn it seemed to force itself upon her. To drag her days out without a sign of love or hope—she could not do it. She would die rather. Self-murder would be no sin to her, and as she did no good in the world, and feared no God beyond, why not die? After her father's death, why need she endure the curse of life? And all the while she struggled with herself, she gave her love vent in painting Felix as "Sir Galahad." It was a dim, dark picture, save the face, and that was idealized and glorified by love, until it looted out of the canvas upon her as though from some "happy place God's glory smote him on the face."

Morn and noon she worked on it, touching and retouching it, until the day fixed for his return; then she put it in her own room with its face turned to the wall. Felix had traveled far, but had not accomplished much in the way of sketching. Upon the great question, he had only decided that if Helen would marry him, he would cast consequences to the winds. Indeed, he had come to two conclusions: first that he only doubted through ignorance; and second, that he could not live without Helen. This was all he had accomplished, and the worth of it remained to be proved.

"Death is the end of life; ah, why
    Should life all labor be?
Let us alone. Time driveth onward fast,
    And in a little while our lips are dumb.
Let us alone. What is it that will last?
    All things are taken from us, and become
Portions and parcels of the dreadful Past."

—"The Lotos-Eaters," Alfred, Lord Tennyson

CHAPTER XIII

DAY AFTER DAY PASSED AFTER FELIX RETURNED, yet not a word was said. They worked on their pictures, chatted about the books that were read aloud in the evenings, and were almost happy.

"Let it last," Felix thought, "to speak might break it."

"Let it last for ever thus," Helen thought, "to speak will break it!"

And so it went on. The summer waned, yet Felix came and went, walking in a dream. He was almost sure that Helen loved him, but why say anything? Why not be quite sure first?

All this time Helen worked diligently under him, and made great progress. Soon he would be gone, and his words and teachings would be all she should have left; so she laid them well to heart, striving meanwhile not to allow herself to think of the time which she felt sure was coming, the time when all would be a blank.

The "King Arthur" was finished at last; even Felix could find nothing more to do to it, and consented to take it down to be criticized by Mr. Felmere.

He was much amused when he found himself put in as the King; and after commending the picture highly, he asked who was the model for Guinevere.

"A creature of straw," Felix answered, laughing, "a lay figure, you know. You see she is crouching at his feet, her face down, and the hair falling so as to hide her almost entirely, and thus there was almost no need of a model. The hair is Miss Felmere's. She let it down for me to paint. Do you think the picture will prove a success?"

"I do. I admire it exceedingly," Mr. Felmere answered, and, Helen echoing all his praise, Felix felt as happy as though his name was already famous.

So they packed it up, as merry as children, and sent it off—bidding it many farewells, and wondering who would buy it, and if they would ever meet it again.

"It would be like meeting a dear old friend and comrade," Helen said.

"More than that," Felix answered, "it would be a breath of sweet air from this summer, the happiest of my life. It would be all our talks over again—all our walks, all our pictures, all our books." Here he paused a moment, and then went on more slowly, "Meeting it again would be either a great pleasure or a bitter pain." His voice sunk.

Helen turned to look out of the window. "I hope I shall never meet it then," she said, "for I am sure it will be a bitter pain. All things end that way in life, at least so far as I have gone." Then she left the room, and Felix, pausing in his work, pondered over her words. She was *sure* and it lay in her hands to make it sure. Was she going to send him away? He must ask her, must at last end this happy uncertainty.

Yet two days passed, and it was not done for somehow he feared to break the silence. At last, becoming ashamed of his weakness, and urged by the feeling that it ought to be done, he determined to put his fate to the hazard. They stood on the riverbank, silent and thoughtful. It was altogether a new process to him, and, while thinking how to begin, he idly shredded a bit of dry sedge, casting the fragments into the stream that eddied by so broad, so blue, so ceaseless in its flowing.

The sun was sinking in a flame of crimson and amber, and the evening light lay long and low across the flats. Above, two little golden clouds were poised motionless against a pale-green sky, and far away one great white bird flew up slowly from the sea. The bit of sedge was all shredded now, and Felix, seeing the bird, thought, "Before that bird reaches us, I shall know all."

But Helen, watching, saw with a woman's instinct what was coming, and struck in suddenly. "I have never told you of my cousin Philip," she said, and fixed her eyes on the heavy bird that seemed to fly so slowly.

Felix did not move nor look up, and his voice was uncertain with a nameless fear as he asked, "What of your cousin Philip?"

Now that she had to speak, Helen felt her oath close about her as an iron band, and wondered vaguely how she had ever thought she could break it. The bird was flying faster now; the summer breeze was howling in her ears, and the river seemed to beat the patient shore. Then, as she spoke, a silence fell on all.

"So far as the law can bind me, I am his." Her voice sounded weak and far away, and she wondered if she had really said those words. The bird flew over them; the color faded from the little clouds; and as one in a dream she turned and walked away.

Felix, stunned and silent, stood and watched her as she went, with the red light the sun had left tinting her white dress and fair hair. Fading away from him, slipping slowly from his grasp, but surely this only love of his life! He could not think; he only knew he must go without delay, for she was bound to another as fast as the law could bind her! The *law*—that was all? She did not love him then, and had she not often said that no oath could bind her unless she willed it so? Great God! How dare he think of such a thing when even she, an unbeliever, had turned away! He must go; he was too weak to stay another day.

Helen passed out of sight into the house. She had never once looked back, had never once faltered in her going. She had set herself a task: it was to reach the house before her strength failed her. If she could only find a place to hide herself in for a little while, she thought she might somewhat ease herself of this terrible blindness and agony. Once in her own room, she stopped and looked about; surely nothing had come to her, nothing was changed. She sat down and tried to think, but she could not; nor could she in any way give up to her pain, it held her fast and kept her quiet. But so far she had been true, and this must do for the present; yet she felt as though all life had gone out of her.

Without any aim in her going, she went to the window, and looked out; she saw Felix coming up from the river, walking slowly and heavily. She knew he would go away, and a vague wonder seized on her as to what excuse he would make to her father for his sudden departure: what could he say? The thought roused her. Her father must never know a word of this; she must manage to warn Felix, and already she was too late to do anything more than reach the library before he did. She slipped down stairs and reached the library door just as Felix was about to enter it.

Felix paused, and, looking at her intently, said slowly, "I must go at once."

"Yes," she answered in a rapid whisper. Then, her voice seeming to fail her, she made a gesture toward the room in which her father sat quietly reading, and clasped her hands imploringly. A dim idea came to Felix of what she wanted, but he was too bewildered to fully understand. One moment she paused to collect herself, then entered the library, with Felix following her. She approached her father at once and spoke clearly and quickly, yet all the while with a feeling of wonder that she could do it! "Father," she said, "Mr. Gordon has heard some bad news, and is going away."

Mr. Felmere laid down his book and looked up. "Bad news?" he repeated.

Helen turned to Felix imploringly. He understood her now, and replied instantly, as though impelled by something stronger than himself, "Yes, sir, very bad news, but not of my own family. It calls me away, however, and I must go over to Felmere tonight in order to take the early train in the morning."

Mr. Felmere rose, holding out his hand. "I am extremely grieved," he said, "that you should have to leave us, and under such circumstances. We have to thank you for a very pleasant summer, and I need not tell you how much we shall miss you, nor how happy we shall be to see you whenever you can come eh, Helen?"

"Indeed, yes," she answered, then turned away toward the door at the lower end of the room.

Felix made his thanks and his farewells to Mr. Felmere very creditably; but before he finished Helen had left the room, saying something about Peter and the wagon for his luggage.

Felix heard the door close; then, with a bitter feeling at his heart, he turned and left Mr. Felmere. Would she let him go without a word? Had he so mistaken her, and did she not care for him in the least? He put his things together, and watched Peter take them down, with a heavy heart; then, once more bidding Mr. Felmere goodbye, and insisting that he should not come out into the night air, Felix passed into the hall. Here he paused a moment, and looked about as though he expected something. It was but for a moment; then he turned and left the house with a bitter sigh.

He heard the wagon rolling away in the gloaming, and almost wished he had gone in it. But only for a moment he thought this, for as he reached the churchyard a white figure rose from among the tombstones, and stood in his path. "Miss Felmere!"

"Mr. Gordon!"

Then her two little hands were hard grasped in his, and her eyes gazed into his as one looking on a dying face that the grave will soon hide. "I did not mean to hurt you," she said. "I would have told you sooner, but when the knowledge came to me that I had done you wrong, it was too late."

Oh, the ringing sadness in that voice! Could he ever forget it? "You could not have helped it," he answered gently. "I loved you from the first."

Then they stood silent, while the summer breeze whispered through the reeds, and the evening shadows blackened round them. "Goodbye," she whispered at last. Her voice seemed gone, and she felt weak and weary. The grasp of his hands grew closer. "You must let me go," she went on hurriedly. "I must not stay. I am Philip's, and that makes it sin to you. Through me you must not sin. Go now!"

Ah, how sharply the words struck home. His grasp loosened, and ere he knew it she had raised his hands to her lips, those slim brown hands that were so dear to her, and was gone. The movement was so sudden and so swift, that when he turned, the shadows had almost hidden her. He clenched his hands as if to hold himself from catching her; one spring would do it. The moment passed, and she was gone, and, turning slowly, he strode away from out the place of death.

"Then as a little helpless, innocent bird,
That has but one plain passage of few notes,
Will sing the simple passage o'er and o'er
For all an April morning, till the ear
Wearies to hear it, so the simple maid
Went half the night repeating 'Must I die?'
And now to right she turn'd, and now to left,
And found no ease in turning or in rest;
And 'Him or death,' she muttered, 'death or him';
Again, and like a burthen, 'Him or death'"

— "Idylls of the King," Alfred, Lord Tennyson

Chapter XIV

D AYS PASSED, and that same clinging strength that had come to her
down by the river stayed with her still and kept her quiet. She
shed no tears, she made no moan that any soul could hear, and, without any seeming loss of interest, went about her daily avocations; but
there was an undertone to all her thoughts, and an under-strength
born of the hope that she would die. What use in living now? What
use in any work? She had "drunk life to the lees," and for her there
was nothing left.

That love of which she had read and dreamed had come to her
and touched her still life, until it danced and sparkled then had faded;
and yet not faded, but rather had been put away and put away through
strength born of that very love.

More than all, she was glad to think that her father knew nothing
of it, and should not know; for why should she tell him that her life
and heart lay wrecked about her? There was no need for more than
one to suffer, and it would be only cruelty to tell him that he had set a

seal of eternal bondage on her, and thus destroy his last gleam of happiness. And if she did not die before he did, why then she would die with him. Death was nothing, less than nothing, a welcome change.

The days crept by, and old Jane, watching the girl grow so wan and heavy-eyed, feared she really would die; so the old woman waited on her tenderly, doing nameless little things for her, laying little traps to provoke her appetite, and making little surprises for her, but to no use, Helen only thanked her, and passed on.

At last the faithful soul thought that to see another in worse plight will sometimes soothe us; so she told Helen of a poor woman beyond the village who sadly needed aid, and begged that she would go with her to see her.

"But all the people think me so wicked," Helen answered, with a bitter recollection of the sexton's little son, "that they will not let me in."

"No, no, Miss Helen, ye must not think that for they all know that in all your life y've never harmed so much as a fly. They all think it wrong that ye do not believe, Miss Helen, and it is very wrong, ye don't know how wrong. But come, won't ye? Maybe the new walk will help ye."

"So it might," Helen answered, "I will go." So she put her hat on, and, taking her purse, set out with the old woman as guide on her first mission of mercy. Jane had put on her black silk, for she knew they would be the village talk for the next week, and for the same reason she walked the narrow streets with her head held high. She rather enjoyed her importance, and felt quite proud of her young mistress, who was so beautiful that the people in the street stopped and turned to look at her. More than this, the Felmeres were the only gentlefolk for miles and miles, and had once owned all the countryside. True, they did seem cursed now and dying out, but even that was a mark of honor. So old Jane stepped proudly and bowed patronizingly to her passing friends.

Finally they came to the bakery, and here Jane stopped. "We had best buy something here, Miss Helen," she said, "to take to the poor soul."

"What shall I buy?" Helen asked, at a loss, and as she spoke the baker's wife bustled in.

"Good evening, Mrs. Judson," Jane said in a stately way. "Mrs. Felmere has come to get some bread for poor neighbor Elmore."

Helen looked up quickly. What did Jane mean by calling her "Mrs."?

Mrs. Judson, being a silent woman, only bowed, and immediately proceeded to put up the bread. But the "Judson girls," as the neighbors called them, who were peeping through the glass door, thought their mother demented not to talk. To think of being face to face with the beautiful Mrs. Felmere, who was surrounded by so much delightful mystery, and not saying a word! A girl who had been married so curiously, and who was so rich and wicked for they had heard the whole story, legacy and all, from the magistrate's daughter, and had quite longed to see the heroine of it; and now she stood in their very shop, and their mother would not talk! Was ever such a grand opportunity lost?

And Helen, quite unconscious of what a source of interest she was to the community, leaned quietly against the counter and looked out into the street. Presently, among a group of little children gathered about the door, she recognized the sexton's son. A little pang shot through her. She wished to speak to him for the sake of associations, so she called him in. "Now," she said, "choose what you most want, little boy, and you shall have it."

The child's eyes opened wide in wonder, and the Judson girls nearly pushed their noses through the door in their eagerness to see.

"Choose, child," said Jane, "don't keep a lady waiting."

So with much hesitation he made his choice of candy and cakes, and Helen, ordering a large bundle of each for him, sent him on his way rejoicing.

It was quite a long walk to neighbor Elmore's house, and Helen was tired enough, but she thought, with a little feeling of rest at her heart, "Perhaps I shall sleep tonight."

When at last they stopped, she was shocked to see what a bitterly poor place it was Jane ushered her into. Low and damp, it seemed to be overrun with dirt and children. It was not until she became accustomed to the dim light that she discovered the bed in one corner on which the poor consumptive was lying, huddled together under some fragments of blankets and old clothes. Helen looked about her in wonder; she had read of such things, but only believed them in a vague way; now she saw for herself.

Jane bustled about and found a chair for Helen, then turned her attention toward making the poor woman more comfortable. She had brought, besides the bread, a basket of stores from home; and as Helen watched her unpack them, and saw the greediness with which the sick woman's eyes followed her every motion, she wondered how such an existence was possible. Presently their conversation caught her ear.

The poor woman was speaking, "Father Paul was here yesterday, and made a promise he would try and put me in a better house; he'd do it, too, if he had the money."

"Yes," Jane answered, "he is a blessed man, is Father Paul, a blessed man and holy."

"True enough," the woman went on, "and he spoke most beautiful about my sickness; it was sent in mercy, he said, and I must bear it. All the same he would try and put me in a better house."

Helen was puzzled. This awful want and sickness sent in mercy? How could that be? Then she broke into their talk, and asked, "How much will it take to put you in a new house?"

The women turned quickly. They had almost forgotten her. Mrs. Elmore answered, "I dunno, Miss . . ."

"Mrs.," said Jane, "the young lady is Mrs. Felmere; she is married to her cousin."

The angry color flashed into Helen's face. What did Jane mean by this behavior? And yet, she spoke the truth. For a moment Helen forgot the sick woman and her house, and was away in the summer just gone. Ay, it had been sweet, very sweet; she sighed, alas, too sweet.

"Father Paul can tell ye, Mrs. Felmere," the sick woman it was who called her back to herself, "he can tell ye how much it is, and where the house is. And oh, lady, if ye wud do it fur me, if ye wud, I'd pray to all the holy saints fur ye, and the Blessed Virgin and Her Son to care fur ye for ever!"

"She will do it, neighbor," Jane answered quickly, "I know she will, and I will stop and ask Father Paul myself about it eh, Miss Helen?"

"Yes, Jane."

Then they rose to go, bidding the woman goodbye amid many blessings called down on them by her poor thin lips.

Once out in the open air, Helen felt much better, and, being more at her ease, spoke freely to Jane. "My father will not like me to have anything to do with Father Paul, and you know it, Jane."

"Sure, Miss Helen, I know that, none better; but if y' cannot do your own way now, when can ye? And I know them aster will be glad for y' to help the poor, an' take some satisfaction in somethin'."

Helen walked on in silence for a few moments. "Suppose Father Paul should insult me?" she said.

"Sakes alive, Miss Helen! An' he a priest! Never in this world!" Jane felt almost insulted. "But here he comes himself," she went on in a little flurry, as she spied Father Paul coming toward them.

Helen looked up. She felt some curiosity to see the man who had driven her mother away, the man who had so materially altered her life. He was tall and slim, with a strong, stern face, clear cut and dark. The rim of hair that showed below his black hat was snowy white, but his dark eyes still had all the power and light of youth. There was something about him that very much attracted her, and she kept her eyes fixed on him until Jane spoke to him, when he ceased his conversation with a group of children gathered on the sidewalk.

"Good evening, Father," she said with a low courtesy.

He looked up first at Jane, then at Helen, and started slightly. "Good evening, Jane," he answered, still looking at Helen.

Jane went on. "This is my young mistress, sir, Mrs. Felmere. She is married to her cousin, ye know, sir." Father Paul bowed, and Helen also; and Jane, looking curiously and anxiously from one to the other, continued, "We have been to see poor neighbor Elmore, and Mrs. Felmere would like to put her into a new house if ye'll tell her how much it would be."

Father Paul's face brightened a little. "Mrs. Felmere is very kind," he said, "and the room I had thought of for Mrs. Elmore is rented at two dollars the month. Moving her will be a few dollars more; but I shall have enough for that."

"I have told her I would do it," Helen answered gravely, "and I would prefer doing all. If you will have her moved, please, and her room decently furnished, I shall be ready at any time to pay for it."

The voice was so clear and true, and the face he looked on so beautiful and sad, that Father Paul felt a kinder feeling creeping over him for the young creature. "I shall do it with much pleasure," he said, and, lifting his hat, passed on.

"I wish you would not call me '*Mrs.*' Jane," Helen said impatiently as they went on.

"Indeed, Miss Helen, begging your pardon, but it's best; and if we had always done it, this last trouble wouldn't 'a' come."

And Helen, feeling the truth of the words, walked on in silence. She was Philip's wife, and that other must always be as a dream, a dream that had passed away, a gleam of sunshine that had stolen through the cloud of her fate, and fading, had left a double darkness behind it. Even so, and she must bear it. "Father," she began, after they had settled down for the evening, "I have been visiting this afternoon with Jane."

"What is this you say, my daughter? Visiting, and with Jane?" he repeated slowly, looking at her questioningly.

"Yes," she answered, "but only to see a poor sick creature who needed help. I did not think you would object. Do you?"

"Let me hear more of it," he said.

"Well, she is a poor consumptive named Elmore; she is poverty-stricken, and has several little children." Then Helen paused, for she wished to bring in Father Paul's name very gently. "She is living in a wretched hovel," she went on after a moment, "windy and leaking. The priest, she said, wished to move her into a better place, but had not the money, so I told her I would do it. Was I wrong?"

"No, if you wished to do it," he answered.

Helen went on, "On our way home, we met Father Paul, and Jane stopped him."

"Did you speak to him?" Mr. Felmere was looking into the fire with a frown on his brow.

"Yes, sir, and he was very polite. I told him what I wished to do for the poor woman, and that if he would have her moved and make her comfortable, I should be ready to pay for it at any time; then he thanked me and went on. Are you angry?"

"No, not angry, nor do I object to your visiting the poor if it amuses you, but I prefer you to see the priest as little as possible." And as he spoke his voice grew harsh.

"Of course, father." Then more slowly, "He has a fine, strong face, and after seeing him I am sure he thought himself right in what he did, and you know, father," looking up persuasively, "we cannot do more nor less than what we think is right." She paused suddenly as she found herself using so glibly Felix's argument.

"Perhaps," Mr. Felmere answered slowly, "but still he wrought the evil, and from what motive I could not know. As it is, an eternal gulf divides us. I hope it is eternal; yet Paul Donaldson was one of my earliest friends." And leaning back in his chair, he gazed into the fire with an unforgiving look on his face.

Helen sat silent and thoughtful. Father Paul had been his friend. How strange. She would have liked to ask something more about him, to solve a little further this new mystery, but she feared too much paining her father. What a hard life her father's had been, harder even than hers, yet she so bemoaned herself, and he stood silent! He had had his wife, whom he so dearly loved, driven away from him by his friend. Was her life as sad as that? His had been one long endurance; so would hers be: his through losing all he loved, hers through this and worse, the endurance of what she now almost abhorred. She covered her face with her hands. Never mind, death should come, and death would end all.

After this she continued visiting the poor and miserable about her, going among them constantly, and giving them comforts that nothing but money could buy and give. Nor was it long before she found herself not only interested, but with an actual affection growing up within her for the children in the village. The mothers, too, soon learned to like her, and to be glad to see her coming, giving her the most comfortable chair, and telling her their little trials and joys as they would to one of themselves. She seemed at once to possess herself of their confidence, for she showed a true sympathy for them in their troubles.

She did not confine herself in her rounds to the extremely poor, but visited also the better class of farmers and their wives. She liked to go among them, and often she envied them, these rich poor people, who so patiently tilled the soil and drew their living from it; who looked no further than the next day, and, thanking God for all they had, asked no questions—a simple faith that to her looked very beautiful and happy.

And if the happiness of the human race was the object held in view by the advanced minds of the age, she thought they made a mistake in not giving to the world this faith as a resting place. It was more easily reached than "philosophic calm." That calm her father thought he had attained to; and yet she felt sure that if he knew of her unhappiness, he would at this moment be equally unhappy. Was this "calm"? Alas, she did not believe such calm could be reached until the death of all human affection had been accomplished.

And was this imperfect result worth the suffering and strife it cost? She hardly thought it was. She stood a better chance of attaining this height than her father had done, in that when he died her last heartstring would be broken!

And in the autumn evenings, as she walked home through the yellowing fields, passing by happy homesteads, she would sigh and turn her head away, with a feeling of hunger at her heart for something she had not, longing for that one heart she could not have, longing for the light and the love those dear eyes would have shed on her, and homesick for the home those dear hands would have led her to; wondering where he was, and if all were well with him, and hoping with a wild strength that somewhere in the world she might meet him again.

So once more she watched the dingy maple drop its leaves, watched the wide green marsh grow brown, and the snow drifts gather between the graves. One year ago. Ah, if she could only claim that year again, and live it over or if she could bury it.

"After this sad farewell
To a world loved too well;
After this silent bed
With the forgotten dead—
What then?"

—"And After," by M. MacGregor Campbell

Chapter XV

THE WINTER SLOWLY GATHERED IN, and Mrs. Elmore lay dying. Her feeble hold on life was lessening each day, yet she did not seem to cling to it, nor to be sorry that her time had come.

Helen watched her almost curiously. It was strange to be able to stand and look on this fellow mortal fading toward the end of her span of certain life, and nearing helplessly that vast and wide mysterious uncertainty of which no man could tell. Would the woman be afraid, she wondered, or would her religious faith, as it professed to do, uphold her at the last?

One afternoon there came a hasty messenger. "Would Miss Helen come? Mrs. Elmore was dying and wanted her."

"She would go!"

There was no refusing such a request, and, calling Peter, she ordered the sleigh, and made her preparations for going.

It was a wild, ghastly evening. The wind was howling, and the snow lay thick and white over all the land. So deep was it that the shapes of the graves had disappeared; the wall looked a blank, and the marsh seemed one frozen sheet.

Helen shivered as she looked abroad. How dreary to die on such a day. How awful to be put away beneath the snow.

Then all was ready, and they set off, but it was a long, slow drive, for Peter at his best was never a reckless driver, and today he seemed to be afraid to let the horse do more than crawl, and with all Helen's patient urging seldom got beyond a fast walk. Finally, finding her words of no use, she let the old man alone, and sat silently thinking of the scene that was to be gone through with. She had never seen so much as a bird die, and she wondered what it would be like; and as she wondered, they reached the long level hilltop, where, the wind having full sweep at them, she felt the cold strike through her like a sword. She shivered. Would death be like that—only slow and creeping, gathering about one with a horrible, irresistible slowness? She wished Jane had come, or that her father had prohibited her going. It was too cold; she would turn back. Turn back? Was she afraid, and of what she had said was nothing? And still Peter drove slowly on, hearing no suggestion of turning back.

If she could help the poor woman to bear it, of course she would. Some day she would herself have to face this mysterious something that sooner or later claimed all—this death she had in her wild agony promised herself, and then she would want some comfort and help. It was strange that she should be so terrified by the thought of even seeing it borne by another, and she had promised it to herself as a boon. She hid her face. She was so pitifully weak. She was weak, and had more than once confessed it to herself; but as she pondered on it, it more and more came home to her how terrible it must be to die alone, to die without a human creature to stand by you, or the warm touch of a living hand about your own, to go out into that dark void without one farewell word.

Ah, the awfulness of this mystery. She dreaded the ordeal very much, but through her dread there stole a gleam of hope that in witnessing it she might catch a glimpse of what it was that made these Christians believe in a beyond. But if she did, what good to her? She had sworn not to go with them. Poor woman. Would she be afraid? Would her God help her?

They reached the house at last, and saw Father Paul's pony looking as though it was leaning against the post it was tied to. Poor little thin pony. Helen doubted much if it were ever thoroughly filled or warmed. Its master did not look over-well-clothed or fed himself; and as the parish was a poor one, she thought it more than probable that her surmises were true. Peter had brought two blankets for his horse that was quite fat enough to do with one; so Helen ordered him to put one on the poor pony. "And, Peter," she said, "you will leave that blanket there when we go." She somehow longed to help all living creatures, for some day she might need help herself. She imagined the poor beast looked at her gratefully, and Peter certainly did. Then she gathered up her dress and went into the house.

The sick woman's room, thanks to Helen, was comfortably furnished and warm; and the bed had thick decent covering on it. The children, too, were well clothed, and looked better cared for than most children of their class.

Mrs. Judson, the baker's wife, sat near the fire with the little things gathered about her; the doctor stood at the foot of the bed; one or two neighbors sat near; and the priest stood by the dying woman talking to her. The services for the dying were all over, the farewells had all been said, and now they only waited to see her die.

All turned at Helen's entrance, and the face of the dying woman seemed to brighten a little as she motioned Helen to her side. A sort of awe came over her. The room was so still, the crisis was so dreadful, and who was right? Father Paul moved to the other side of the narrow bed, and Mrs. Elmore grasped Helen's hands, looking at them a moment as in wonder. "So warm, and strong, and young," she whispered, "and mine, look at them!"

And Helen looked, so pitifully thin they were and cold. Ah, they struck a chill through her, more piercing far than wind or snow. Then her eyes met the poor, patient, dying eyes below them, and filled with tears.

"You are so beautiful," the woman faltered, "so beautiful and good. I know the good God will save your soul. And I have prayed fur ye yes, more times nor I can count, fur I don't know much. I am but a poor creetur, but y'ave been so good to me I wanted to do somethin' fur ye, and it was all I could do, but I did it earnest-like an' true, an' if the dear God answers my prayers y' shall be saved." The poor voice faltered; she seemed almost gone.

Father Paul gave her some stimulant, and with this little foreign strength she motioned him to pray. He knelt, obedient to the signal, and the poor woman, still holding Helen's hands, now almost as cold as her own, tried to push her on her knees; but Helen could not kneel, and all the company, some kneeling, some standing, were watching and waiting.

Helen shook her head. "It would be a mockery," she said hurriedly, and all the bystanders seemed to draw away from her all save the priest and the dying woman.

"Oh, humble yerself, child!" the woman said, "or the Lord will humble ye in some dreadful way."

But again Helen shook her head; she could not leave her father. Then they let her stand, and the prayer went on. It seemed to Helen to be a sort of commendatory prayer for the dying, and as she listened she thought that surely this would comfort the poor creature if she believed it. And she seemed to do so. It was simple, too; any one could understand it.

It ceased, and there was a sudden stillness. "Was the woman dead?

The face on the pillow looked so strange, so gray and pinched! What a horrible thing death was! And the priest, standing there with the crucifix in his hand, held high before the dying woman, seemed cut in stone.

Helen tried to draw away, but the grasp of the cold hands tightened with that terrible death-strength that has so much of pitiful impotence in it, and she was constrained to stay where she was. And she stood as though spellbound, gazing down on the drawn face, watching it with a strange fascination she could not master.

Slowly the eyes opened beneath her look, and fixed themselves on hers—so beseeching, so pitiful, so fearfully bright, lighted with the last rays of the fluttering spirit. A dim glassy look crept over them; there came a convulsive shudder, a rattling in the throat; the jaw dropped, and the hands that held Helen's were dead! The flame had been blown out. Where was it?

A horror seized Helen; she tried to loosen the hold of the dead hands; she must go, she must reach fresh air or die. Those dreadful hands were freezing her very blood.

Father Paul looked with pity on the horror-stricken face, and gently loosened the dead woman's hands. She was not used to death, poor child.

Once outside, Helen stood still to let the wild winter wind sweep over her. Then she rubbed her hands with snow: that coldness was life-like warmth to the clammy ice-chill of those dead hands. Oh, if she could only rub the scene from her memory that shudder, that sound, so terrible, so awfully mysterious, so hideous.

Old Peter seemed to take years to uncover and unfasten the horse: would he never be ready to take her away from that dreadful place? At last he was ready, and they started on their slow, crawling journey over the snow. So slowly they went that they scarcely seemed to move. She was bitterly cold. The wind blew full on her, the snow nearly blinded her; and old Peter, doubled up in front, looked scarcely human. The memory of the death scene clung about her, and she shivered as she looked around her in the falling shadows. If they could only go a little faster!

The night had settled down when they reached the churchyard, and, in the shifting white light that seemed to be shed by the falling snow, the tombstones looked like restless spirits wandering to and fro. Helen closed her eyes: she wished Peter would say something, or was he dead too? She roused herself. She was unnerved and foolish, and ought to be ashamed of herself. So she sat up and fixed her eyes on the light from the library window, determined not to be so foolish; but, foolish or not, she had to confess that in all her life she had never heard so sweet a sound as Jane's cracked voice calling to them as she opened the gate, and in the grasp of her father's hand and his warm kiss there was something very delightfully real. Ah, she was very glad to get home.

When she came down stairs after changing her dress, Mr. Felmere watched her curiously. He knew where she had been, and why she had gone, and had let her go almost as an experiment. Now he was watching for the results. She came in slowly and knelt in front of the fire, holding her hands as close to the blaze as possible. "Are your hands so cold that you need scorch them, daughter?" he said.

"Oh, yes," she answered, "terribly cold."

"Then let me rub them for you," he went on.

She was more than glad to turn and lay them in his soft warm grasp; it would perhaps destroy the death-chill that seemed to cling to them.

"They are very cold," Mr. Felmere continued, as he stroked them gently. "Did you not wear gloves?"

"Yes, father, but you cannot know how that dead woman clung to my hands. Oh, it was so awful!"

"Why did you allow her to hold them?" he asked, almost impatiently; for now that he saw how nervous and overcome she was, he was sorry he had let her go.

"I could not help it," she answered, laying her face down on his knee, "she called me, and I had to go, and then she held them until she died. Father, death is awful."

"Not if you look upon it as a release, my child," he answered slowly, "not if you think of it as a rest from toil and sorrow, as a sleep that has no waking, a night that has no morning. It is not pleasant to look upon, but it should have no terrors for the thoughtful." And he gently kissed the little hands he held. "I know all that," she answered, "but still there is a horror about it I did not expect; such an awful, lifeless stupidity crept over the face, such a resistless convulsion, and such a sound as I hope I shall never hear again. Then she was nothing. That is the worst thought."

"How?" he asked.

"I do not know exactly," she answered, "but, as I watched her dying, life seemed so useless, and death so horrible. One moment she looked at me so beseechingly, a knowing, thinking being; the next, the eyes were dim, the jaw fallen, and she lay there a lump of lifeless matter. She had spent her life in caring for that useless body, in clothing it and feeding it, and what was the result? Nothing? After a long life in which she loved herself, cared for herself, and thought herself something, stood up before the world a creature to be considered among her kind, a loving, hating, sorrowing woman, then the end comes. And *is* she nothing? To me it all seems so unmeaningly dreadful, this long life to no purpose."

"And therefore," Mr. Felmere answered slowly, "we should not spend our lives grieving over small sorrows, over useless desires and longings, and in useless strivings; for death soon comes and destroys all."

Helen was silent. If this were so, why live at all? At last she said, "Father, what was the use or beauty of that poor life, lived at such a cost of suffering, and now swept away?"

"Her life was the result of natural laws," Mr. Felmere answered quietly. "That it was not useful or beautiful we do not know, but if not, it was her own fault. She did not reach up to a higher life, she did not recognize the beauty and order of the universe by which she was surrounded, and so did not put herself and her life in accord with it. She had but one, and that the lowest, end of life in view—her daily bread."

"And she did not make that," Helen answered, "so why look for a higher?"

"Her failure was the result of ignorance," Mr. Felmere returned, "her ignorance, the fault of her progenitors, and their ignorance could possibly be traced back in the same way. So it was her own fault, and the fault of those from whom she came, that her life seemed useless. Our lives are in our own hands, to make or mar as we please, to be made beautiful and useful in accordance with the laws of order, or to be ruined and defaced as we see fit. But in either case we have only ourselves to look to, and ourselves to blame."

"And how, then, can I make my life useful and beautiful?" the girl asked.

"By educating yourself up to the highest of which you are capable, and so reaching happiness for yourself by the full and harmonious development of all your faculties. This will make your life beautiful. Your example, and the assistance your education will enable you to give your fellow creatures, will make your life useful. But surely, my daughter, we have argued all this out before?"

"Yes, father," she answered, "but I seem to lose sight of abstract beauty and order when I come in contact with the hideousness of starvation and death; and I have to argue myself back into the belief that there are such things as order and beauty to live for."

Mr. Felmere answered, half musing, "I can very well understand that also, for I have often been myself almost led to exclaim against the incongruities of life. But we know that these laws do exist, and in order to be happy you must work and live up to them; you have no alternative."

"And this is all," she said, and rose as the servant announced dinner.

"Yes, all," her father answered, following her, "but more than enough to fill a lifetime."

"A lifetime," she thought, "but a *life*—would it fill that?"

"Oh, hush! what more remains to me,
But this dead hand whose clasp is cold in mine,
And all the baffled memory of the past,
Buried with him? What more?"

—"Electra," Edward Bulwer Lytton

CHAPTER XVI

SIX YEARS HAD PASSED SINCE HELEN'S MARRIAGE WITH PHILIP, and five since Felix had faded from her life, and in these years she had done much. Through a rigorous and undeviating self-discipline she had won for herself a certain calmness and strength that showed in every movement and expression, a calmness that might have been called coldness but for the sad soul lurking deep in her eyes, and the gentleness gathered tenderly in the curving of her lips. She had made herself much beloved in the country all about her home, her name being with many almost a household word, and it was this love she gained and gave that kept her heart and soul warm and safe from hopeless torpidity from being frozen over with the coldness of her future and the bitterness of her sorrows. At home she moved about the guiding spirit; she cared for, thought for, and provided for everything; and in a negative fashion she was happy.

In all these six years she had never failed in her weekly letter to Philip but once, and that was the week when Felix went away. Philip's letters were only of interest to her as a study of his character, and it was the only way in which she could know him; for, according to the agreement between them, he could not come back until her father's death. He had looked eagerly, hopefully, but vainly in all her letters for some softening of this clause in the contract, some faint shadow of relenting and invitation to come again, if only for a day. But, alas, he never found it. Her letters came like clockwork—always one length, always one temperature, always beginning "Dear Philip," and always ending "Very sincerely"; never even dropping to the more familiar "My dear Philip," and never by any chance ending with "Helen," but always the full stiff "Helen Felmere."

He was learning gradually what sort of nature he would have to deal with, and he was also learning to doubt his ability either to govern or guide it. But in proportion as he recognized this coldness, and the relentless strength of this beautiful creature, the thought that, with all her pride and strength, with all her beauty and talent, he had succeeded in binding her, made his love take fresh root in his vanity, and so fascinate him afresh. He was sometimes guilty of almost wishing for his uncle's death, that he might claim her. While he was traveling it did not make so much difference, but now for three years he had settled down as head of his father's business, and he wanted her at home. He kept up with society, that he might at once place her in the front rank. He amassed money, that he might enable her to shine the more resplendent. He entertained, that his home might be a place where people would come often, and so spread abroad the fame of his wife's beauty.

On the other hand, if Helen ever allowed herself to think of her marriage at all out of the proper routine where it had its special place and time, it was with utter dread of this day that she knew must come. She watched with intense wretchedness the breaking down of her father's health, the pitiful decaying of a strong man. For a long time she had been doing all his writing and reading for him, and his mind still continuing clear and strong, his inability to do for himself was pathetic. But Helen never let this appear, trying to let their habits change almost without his knowledge; he was her one thought, and she cared for him as a mother for her child, watching closely for every sign of a wish and trying to anticipate it.

"I shall be glad to go," he said one evening as they sat together in the firelight, "I am so fast becoming worthless."

Helen, sitting in her old place on a stool at his side, laid her head down on his knee as he spoke.

"You are my life, father, my world. How are you worthless?" she said. She felt the tremulous touch of his hand on her hair, and a knowledge of desolation swept over her as she thought of the time when the touch of that hand would be gone from her life forever.

He answered slowly, "And this thought of your intense love haunts me, and this certainty of the suffering you will endure gives me the only pain I now feel. Else, my life would pass away calmly and without a regret."

The light in the room was dim, the light of his eyes was dim, but a blind man could almost have seen the glorious beauty of the face that looked up into his, shining with the light of the last sacrificial fires she could build for him. "Father, I promise not to grieve," she said slowly, "that is, not openly, nor yet morbidly. Only tell me how it must be, and I will do it I promise!"

"Are you strong enough?" he asked, straining his eyes to read her face.

"Yes, father!" and the voice rang clear and true as when in her ignorant youth she had sworn to stand by him for ever!

"Then, child, say that your grief shall not overwhelm you; that you will make it your private sorrow, and not allow it to be a bar to any wish of Philip; that you will put on no outward sign of mourning, and never speak of what you suffer. I know all this will be hard, but any of these things might fret him. Men are so impatient of any sorrow that they do not feel. These precautions may seem useless, but I know men of the world better than you do, and I am so afraid of standing in the way of your happiness. Will you promise all this for me?"

"Yes, father, I will. This sorrow shall be mine, and mine alone, as it ought to be; so do not let it trouble you any more." And again she put her head down on his knee. Her happiness, her love, her life had all been put under foot for him: why not her grief? If it pleased him, why not cast this last luxury aside, and tread her path barren even of tears?

Once more she felt his soft old hand wandering about her brow and hair as he went on talking. "You have been a good daughter, and I thank you, darling—you, who have been the one steady brightness of my life, which else had gone out in darkness. You have never thwarted a wish or desire of mine; you have never knowingly given me a pang, and loving me as you do, my child, this knowledge will be your reward."

"Ay, more than a reward," she answered, drawing his hand down to her lips, "for nothing can ever dim the joy of it!"

"I knew it," he answered, smiling tenderly to himself, "and so I told you, and when I am gone, I believe you will carry out whatever you know to be my wishes. Thus I am certain your happiness is secure, for what I wish is entirely for your good. First of all, that you should be a faithful wife to Philip, and never leave him," his voice grew tremulous as he touched on the sorrow of his life, "never leave him for any pique or fear, any anger or ill-treatment, for nothing save his own command."

"Yes, father."

"And, child, you must strive to be reasonable and patient with him and all the world. I tell you this because I know you will find many things in him and in the world that will provoke you, but you must strive to be tolerant and gentle." He paused here, then went on more slowly, "And if in your life you should ever meet your mother or your brother, you must not feel any anger against them for me, but rather pity them for having committed what to them was a sin, and in the eyes of all the world a wrong. Now I charge you to be kind and gentle to them both; for as I near my end, a feeling comes over me that I should at least have made it my care to see that they did not want." His voice sunk, and Helen held his hand more closely as though to comfort him.

"Father, she left you of her own free will," she said, with a strange feeling coming over her as she listened to the first self-accusations she had ever heard from his lips.

"So she did, my darling," he answered slowly, "but she was young and easily swayed, and I should have been more patient and have tried to win her back. In any case, the boy was mine, and I should have provided for him. However, it is too late now, for he must be a grown man if living. Ah, it was a cruel thing." His head drooped as he finished, and a silence fell between them.

Helen had never before heard him speak in this way of her mother; indeed, only once or twice in all her life had she ever heard him so much as allude to her. And now, what did it mean? Were these his last wishes, and was he going from her now? She crushed the thought down in her mind and turned away from it; she would not think it. But still she found herself laying all his words away in her heart, treasuring every tone of his voice, every nervous break that came between the sentences. He should not go.

Presently he spoke again. "My child, I wish you would write to Philip. I do not like leaving you alone."

Had her heart stopped its beating? Had the fire gone out entirely? Was the sea surging in the room all about her, and was that her voice that answered? "Yes, father," then a little pause. "Shall I light the lamp and write now?" Poor voice, it sounded very weak and very far away" and did the words her father uttered strike her? They must, for with every one a sharp pain shot through her.

"Yes, this very night; the letter must go in the morning."

Then she was conscious of going to the table, lighting the lamp, and writing. She knew every word she put down; she remembered for all her life how every line of that note looked, and how a sudden feeling of hatred to Philip seemed to cover it all! Her father was going, she was to be given up to Philip. Ah, if that note could only kill him. And if he dared to come and share the last hours of her father's life with her, she would shut the door upon him. He should not come in. He did not care for her father; for had he not said in one of his letters that he longed to claim her, and did not that mean he would not mourn her father's death? But the note must be written, for her father desired it.

The next evening Philip, sitting in his office, read it with a feeling of exultation. At last his time had come, and his waiting was over.

Dear Philip,

My father requests that you will come to him. Of course you will come immediately.

Very sincerely,

Helen Felmere

This was all, only these few terse words. No sign or shadow of any wish from her for his presence; not one line that wavered not one uncertain word or stroke to betray the strain under which it was written, the strain of bitter sorrow and growing hatred. But he did not look for any of these things; he cared for nothing but that he had been sent for. No thought crossed him of the agony this old man's death would cause, of the fearful doubt that veiled his last hours, of the woman left broken and desolate. He only remembered that now he could claim what he so long had waited for; after these six long years he was to be rewarded.

He could scarcely wait for the next day's express train. Indeed, if he had only had himself to consult, he would not have waited, but would have wasted the next day at way stations on the route just to feel that he was traveling, but his mother showed him the folly of such a proceeding, and persuaded him to wait.

And in the still watches of that very night, while he lay dreaming of the happy morrow, and while she of whom he dreamed paced up and down her room, striving to strangle down her heart and its crying in preparation for that morrow, the old man met death alone.

He had no voice to cry for help; he had no human hand to cling to; he had no hope! Alone the dread hour came to him; alone he struggled with the inevitable, alone, and in the darkness. If at the last he caught a glimpse of what lay beyond the portal of the grave, if at the last he found there was a Hereafter, if at the last he had the awful agony added to his own anguish, the agony of knowing that he had doomed his child's soul to eternal misery. There was no one to hear the warning in his moans, or see the horror in his dying eyes. The secrets of that deathbed no mortal ever knew; for the darkness tells no tales, and the darkness was the only watcher there. And all night long the wild sea moaned and the night winds howled about the hall; then the gentle morning light stole in and looked upon the old man, dead.

And later on, his daughter came and found him with the sunlight making a glory in his silver hair. No wail broke from her, no sob, no tears shone in her eyes; only an irresistible shuddering as one in mortal agony, then a stillness, as of death. Had she not promised? She set the house in order, gave all directions to old Peter, then shut herself and her agony in her far off room until Jane should tell her all was finished.

Then, in the dear old library, where all spoke of him, where from child to woman she had lived and learned with him, where one thing after another she had given up all for him, she stood alone with her dead. One last lesson she would learn from him, looking down on his calm dead face, one last lesson of self-control. And she, learning it, stood mute. Once more she found herself without a God to cry to in her misery, without a comfort in her desolation.

There was no time hereafter when she might hope to be reunited to him. For him there was only the grave, for her, only memory. Wailing and weeping would do no good, and more than this, had she not promised?

Philip, coming in almost joyous, found her thus. She turned away at his first entrance, but only for a moment; then she turned and met him quietly, raised her face for his kiss of greeting, and led the way from the room. She could not allow him to stay there with her. This grief was hers, and sacred; Philip had no share in it.

In the hall she paused and told him of all her arrangements. The next morning her father would be laid in the family vault in Felmere church; this right had been reserved to the family for generations, and no objections could be raised on the score of his being an unbeliever. She wished no services at all; they meant nothing to her nor to him. As to the marriage ceremony, she hoped Philip would allow no interval of time to elapse between that and the funeral, and afterward she wished to go away immediately. Quietly and methodically she said it all, and Philip, much relieved by her calmness, assented gladly, saying he had brought a clergyman with him, and there was no reason why all should not be done as quickly as possible. Then he made a halfway suggestion of mourning.

But Helen answered with proud quiet, "It was my father's wish that I should not show grief for his death in any outward manner, and it was his particular request that neither you nor your mother should alter your daily lives in any way for him. He was nothing to any one but me, and I must ask you never to mention his name to me. I need no sympathy, nor any outlet for my sorrow."

Better silence him at once, she thought; for he had not that in him that could comprehend her sufferings, and his attempts at comfort would only torture her.

And Philip did not object, for he felt no positive sorrow and had no real sympathy to offer.

So the next morning the dead man was carried to his grave, the grave of all the Felmeres. The door of the vault grated harshly, and swung heavily on its hinges; for it had not been opened since he, young Hector Felmere, saw his father laid there. Silently they put him down, and Helen, ere the door was closed, stepped in to lay one flower on his coffin. One moment she paused and looked about her to the right and left where her ancestors lay. Some day they would bring her there. Ah, very soon, she hoped.

She turned to come away to leave her father forever. The rush of this thought almost shook her from her calm. One moment she steadied herself with one hand on his coffin—one moment, that was all; then she rejoined the watchers outside.

The door was closed and locked, and all was done. No prayers for the soul departed, no words of comfort for the soul left desolate; all was cold, dreary, hopeless.

Then came the marriage ceremony. Only some of her village friends were there, who wept, poor simple souls, to see her "go to be wed, with the dust of the grave still unshaken from her white dress!" Alas, what mattered it to her? Was not the dust from that tomb spread henceforth all along her path, deadening all the sounds of life and joy that might happen there? What was a simple smirch or two on her wedding dress? She went through the service mechanically, but did not kneel for either prayers or blessing. She did not believe.

When that was done, the worst was over, for the parting with Peter and Jane, and the last look at her home, weighed as nothing with what had gone before. "Jane," she said as the old woman clung about her, "keep everything just as I leave it. You and Peter will be supported here as usual, but let nothing be changed. I will come again some day, and all things must be as I leave them." Then she kissed the old woman, with a long, loving kiss, her last farewell at Felmere and was gone. Gone out into a life and a world she dreaded gone, guarded only by her own strength and a promise to a dead man.

PART SECOND

"Thousands of human generations, all as noisy as our own, have been swallowed up of Time, and there remains no wreck of them any more; and Arcturus and Orion and Sirius and Pleiades are still shining in their courses, clear and young, as when the Shepherd first noted them in the plain of Shinar. Pshaw! What is this paltry little Dog-cage of an Earth; what art thou that sittest whining there? Thou art still Nothing, Nobody: true; but who then is Something, Somebody? For thee the Family of Man has no use; it rejects thee; thou art wholly as a dissevered limb: so be it; perhaps it is better so!"

—"Sartor resartus: the life and opinions of Herr Teufeldröckh,"
Thomas Carlyle

"And the days darken round me, and the years,
Among new men, strange faces, other minds."

— "Morte D'Arthur," Alfred, Lord Tennyson

CHAPTER I

M RS. FELMERE, PHILIP'S MOTHER, WAS CERTAINLY IN HER ELEMENT; for there was nothing she liked better than the bustle and confusion and excitement consequent on the arrangements for a gay winter, and of all her gay winters this was to be the gayest.

The Jourdans were all curiosity to see Philip's wife, and had been much disappointed that he had not brought her home immediately after her father's death, instead of taking her to travel. But Mrs. Felmere nodded wisely; said it was her arrangement that they should spend the months of mourning in travel as she preferred that Helen should make her appearance all at once, and not creep into society as she would have to do if she came to town while in mourning. Then she would go off into descriptions of Helen's extraordinary beauty and talents, and into discussions of large plans for the winter's campaign, and for the reception of the young people. Evidently she expected much increase in importance from the possession of this beautiful daughter-in-law, and the Jourdans waited with doubtful pleasure and questionable curiosity to see this wonder.

"If she was such a marvel, how had Philip managed to catch her?" So they whispered to each other, but only whispered, for the Jourdan family stood rather in awe of their strong-minded sister Mrs. Felmere.

And all the while she wrote her son the most minute descriptions and directions on the subject of Helen's trousseau, which he was to buy in Paris, and begged Helen to be careful in suiting her style of beauty. Helen would read the letters in the most dutiful manner, but could not remember them; so she let Philip do as he pleased, and buy whatsoever seemed good in his sight. She only hoped she would be able to keep her temper and be patient under the host of trifling annoyances she saw ahead of her. She was a little curious as to society, yet feared much that she would not like it; in which case she would still be obliged to go out into it. She carefully pondered all the advice her father had given her; tried to look hopefully out to her future; then tried to be philosophical over the failure and fruitlessness of her efforts, and bent her will to crush out the undercurrent of thought that made her wonder if in her husband's circle of friends she would meet Felix Gordon.

So all the long bright summer was spent in going from place to place, places she had longed all her life to see, places that she now looked on and walked through with quiet apathy. More than this, she seemed unconscious of the devotion Philip lavished on her. Philip was good to her, and she thanked him, but did not in any way seem to realize his admiration.

And Philip, watching her, began to wonder when this cold calm would wear off. At first, after her father's death, when he met her down at Felmere, it had been a pleasant surprise to him; for he had expected and feared tears and wailings, and, not finding them, was agreeably disappointed, and was thankful that his wife knew what self control meant. But now he thought it time for her to have overcome her grief enough to look at him, and treat him in some other way than she had done heretofore.

Her scrupulous politeness was wearying to him, and although as Mrs. Philip Felmere her every action was worthy of all admiration, yet he also was worthy of some consideration. But she did not seem to agree with him, and, although he left no means untried, he had to give up at last, and only hope that the settling in her new home and among new people might rouse her.

When the winter found them with their faces turned homeward, he was hoping much from the change, she dreading it, and more than all the long after life with her aunt. In all her life she never felt more desperate than when she stood in the doorway of her future home, with her future full before her.

The meeting between mother and son was ecstatic but short; then Philip turned, "Mother, here is Helen," and Mrs. Felmere came with open arms to the stately young woman who had kept herself rather in the background. As it was, her arms closed round a mass of silk and furs, and she had to wait until the owner of them chose to bend her head and receive the proffered kiss.

But Mrs. Felmere was not to be daunted, and as she led them to their apartments, she gushed on irrepressibly. "Some of her family were to dine with them that day," she explained, "to meet dear Helen, so that dear Helen must have as much time as possible in which to rest and dress before the appointed hour."

"Dear Helen" looked and listened, and the mother-in-law grew restless under the grave quiet of the daughter, and left the room a little anxious. What it was Mrs. Felmere could not say, but there was something very trying in this young person's manners; it was worse than trying, it was actually exasperating.

Philip followed his mother downstairs; and Helen, glad to be alone, yet with nothing to do, stood near the window and looked down thoughtfully on the people and vehicles that passed so ceaselessly to and fro.

Her musings were interrupted by the entrance of the men bring-ing in the luggage. "How stupid," she thought, "to have such a quan-tity, and at the best, what extremely frivolous things fine clothes are." And she was almost impatient with the maid who came to ask what she would wear for dinner. "Anything you please," she answered. "I do not in the least care." So the woman with ready tact chose a dress she had heard Mr. Felmere praise as it was wise to please someone.

The party assembled in Mrs. Felmere's drawing room was made up entirely of the immediate Jourdan family. There were Mr. John Jourdan, banker, and Margaret, his wife; his son, young John Jourdan, commonly known as Jack; and his daughter Amelia. Besides these, who were known as the "John Jourdans," there was the old maid aunt of the family, Miss Esther Jourdan, who was also the terror, keeping her connection well in hand with the lash of an unmade will. The only member of the whole family who did not bow to her rule was her young brother, Arthur Jourdan, who now leaned on the mantel watching with skeptical eyes for the advent of Philip's wife.

They were all rich and moderately well educated, these Jourdans, with good complexions, sound teeth, and strong digestions—a fair-haired, sturdy race, with neither souls nor livers. Helen was introduced by Mrs. Felmere to each one separately, "This is your uncle John, my dear, and your aunt Margaret. This is Aunt Esther, and this Uncle Arthur; but he is so little older than Philip that you may call him Arthur. This is Jack, and, last but not least, Amelia, my namesake and goddaughter, of whom I hope you will make a friend."

Philip watched a little anxiously as the ceremony proceeded, he was so much afraid that Helen might in some way offend them; for she was so very different, and at times so strangely abrupt and peculiar, not to say eccentric. But he need not have feared. It all went off quietly enough. She distinctly repeated all their names and prefixes after Mrs. Felmere, and kissed them all most dutifully.

There was only one little pause. When Mrs. Felmere explained about Arthur's age, Helen asked him gravely which he preferred, "Arthur "or "Uncle Arthur," and he answered, "It is as you please, Helen."

She said quietly, "I have no pleasure in the matter," and turned to Jack. Miss Esther smiled to see Arthur snubbed, for it was such a rare occurrence, but Mrs. Felmere looked grave and frowned very slightly. The dinner passed off very successfully; for Helen, seated between old and young John, was much amused by young John's hearty boyishness and old John's honest admiration. There was something contagious in the merry flow of Jack's spirits, and she found herself chatting and laughing in a way that was quite unusual for her. Philip bloomed out under this, and Mrs. Felmere was in her glory.

Arthur watched Helen with growing admiration. She was surely the most beautiful creature he had ever seen. He must certainly make his peace with her. "Have you ever been to a ball?" Jack was asking.

"Never in all my life," she answered.

"Then tomorrow night will be your first. How queer!" he went on.

"Am I to go to one tomorrow night?" she asked.

"Why, have you not heard? Aunt Amelia has not told you?"

"No," Mrs. Felmere answered from the end of the table, "I thought tomorrow would do as well."

Jack nodded. "Then I will tell her now," and he went off into a description of a grand party to be given at his father's house in honor of Philip and Helen.

"You are very kind," Helen answered, "and I hope I shall like it; but I do not know how to dance."

The whole company looked aghast—not know how to dance!

"What have you been thinking of, Philip?" Jack asked, reproachfully.

"We have not been going out, you know," Philip answered with mysterious solemnity.

Then a little pause fell on the company, and the hot blood rushed angrily to Helen's cheeks. How dared Philip allude to her father in this strange company, or allude to him at all. She paused a moment to steady her voice, then said coldly, "We might have gone, Philip, if you had said so, for there was nothing to hinder us."

This was a little more shocking than her not knowing how to dance. Such plain speaking was not usual in the world. Philip's excuse was very proper. Why not let it alone? And it remained for Arthur to break the silence that ensued. "It will give me great pleasure to teach you how to dance," he said quietly.

Helen looked up quickly and gratefully for this interruption to her angry thoughts. "Indeed, you are very kind," she answered, "and I shall do my best to learn."

"It is a very easy matter," Arthur went on, "if one has any ear for music, which you no doubt have."

"I cannot say," Helen answered, shaking her head, "I have never taken a music lesson in my life."

"She was educated entirely by her father," Mrs. Felmere put in quickly, seeing a little sneer on Miss Esther's lips.

Helen looked around from one to the other with a shade of wonder in her eyes, then said a little proudly, "I have no accomplishments at all, save perhaps painting; I can do something at that."

"And one accomplishment is quite enough if you do that one well," Arthur said quietly.

"Yes," Helen answered slowly, as though considering and concluding on her deliberations, "yes, I do paint well."

"That is honest at least," Miss Esther remarked, with a trifle of sarcasm in her tone. She had been panting for an opportunity to snub this newcomer into a proper appreciation of her special merits. Helen looked up surprised.

"And is not honesty a desirable quality?" she asked.

"Very desirable," Miss Esther answered, with a little toss of her head, "if there is a trifle of modesty mixed with it."

"There are such things as false modesty and affectation," Helen went on quietly, to the great amusement of the family, who never by any chance answered Miss Esther, "and I despise both. If I think I paint well, why not say so?"

"Would it not be just as well to wait and let others say so?" Miss Esther's ire was rising.

"Others might not think so," Helen replied, and a general laugh followed her speech.

"You do not mind over-estimating yourself then?" Miss Esther asked.

"If it is my honest opinion of myself, then to myself I am not over-estimated, and if I am satisfied with myself, what are the opinions of others to me? Indeed, they do not disturb me for one instant." She was looking at the old lady gravely, and listened most attentively to her answer.

"There are some people who are humble enough to think that there are others a little wiser than themselves, and with sometimes a little better taste and judgment."

"If one is confessedly inferior," Helen answered, "it would be wiser, perhaps, to ask the opinion of all before deciding for one's self, but I think it is much happier to be honestly aware of your own powers, and honestly self confident."

To Helen the conversation had now become an abstract argument, and as such she pursued it. Miss Esther, however, not having been trained to this sort of exercise, after the manner of most women, continued personal, and answered bitingly, "In short, be conceited."

"No," Helen said gravely, "that is one step too far; that amounts to self-admiration, while what I mean is simply self-approval. The one is putting yourself above and beyond your fellow creatures; the other is only putting yourself on a level with them."

"And you consider yourself on a level with the highest?" queried Miss Esther.

Helen laughed as she answered, "I could not answer that question, Aunt Esther, until I had met and estimated all the people in the world."

"Of course you know I mean the highest you have met," Miss Esther snapped.

Helen smiled. "With one or two exceptions known long ago, yes."

"Bravo!" cried old Mr. Jourdan, and the young men were quite delighted to find some one who dared to contend with Miss Esther.

Mrs. Felmere and Mrs. Jourdan, however, felt anxious as they looked at Miss Esther's angry face and remembered her fortune and unmade will; so they strove to mend matters by making a movement to leave the table.

That night, after all were gone, Mrs. Felmere called her son aside and told him he must speak to Helen, and warn her of the danger of making Miss Esther angry.

Philip looked doubtful, and after pondering for a few moments said with a deep sigh, "We had better say nothing about it, mother. Helen is very peculiar about some things, and I know that about this she will think differently and will probably say so. More than this, I am quite sure she will not heed me."

Mrs. Felmere looked amazed, then angrily scornful as she said sharply, "I would be ashamed to acknowledge that, Philip, and since you are afraid, I will speak to her myself."

"As you please," Philip answered, shrugging his shoulders and driving his hands deeper into his pockets, "but you will find I am right."

And Mrs. Felmere without answering left the room.

"Ah, me! the clinging touch of those days—
    those days so utterly dead!
The ringing sadness of last farewells—
    farewells so quietly said;
The falling shadows of lonelier times, dark
    days in the midst of strife;
The longing for peace, and faith, and love that
    were ours in that old life."

—Unknown

CHAPTER II

FOR THE FIRST TIME SINCE THEIR MARRIAGE, Helen missed Philip when on the morning after their arrival he went to his office; indeed, she more than missed him, she felt deserted and almost in danger, being left alone with Mrs. Felmere. That a collision between them was inevitable, and that her hours of peace were numbered, were two facts of which she was sure. She could only hope that the shock would be a slight one, enough to show each of them the position the other intended to occupy, yet not enough to make a decided break. It was a disagreeable thought and expectation, but there was no use in trying to escape from it, for it must finally be faced. She had feared many years ago that this would be so, but now that she had seen Mrs. Felmere, her surmises had ripened into knowledge.

So she pondered as she stood in the front drawing room, looking over a photographic album filled with meaningless faces which, fortunately or unfortunately for herself, she did not see. She was very homesick for old Felmere, for Peter and Jane, for anything simple and natural. She had been so shut up in cities and hotels, had so stupidly followed the beaten fashionable track in traveling, had been so tied down to conventionalities and nonessentials, that she longed for the broad clear flats, and the wild fresh wind that dashed about the hall down at Felmere. And now that she was at home, she looked about her and wondered if in all the world there was anything more dreary and un-homelike than these grand parlors teeming with silk and velvet and gold, yet with the rug in front of the sham fireplace turned wrong side up. It was a little thing, yet to her it spoke volumes. Then, in irresistible contrast to this brand new affair, too handsome to be used, there came to her memory the old worn rug in the library at Felmere, worn almost white at the corner where her father used to sit; burnt in innumerable little black spots where the sparks from the open fire would fall; and persistently rolling itself up at the four corners. Ah, how pathetic was the picture of that old Felmere rug, and to her how beautiful.

But this was dangerous ground, and she hastily turned her eyes and mind to other things. She looked curiously at the miserable little gas fire, entirely for show, and at the awful holes in the walls, so black and unlovely, where the real heat came in, could anything be more dismal, except perhaps the album before her? And, turning over the leaves, she wondered vaguely what could have been in the minds of the originals of the pictures when they allowed themselves to be so represented. Did they for one moment imagine that people seeing these would consider them correct likenesses; that any one would be deceived into thinking they always had their hair arranged so wonderfully, or their heads in these painfully graceful positions, or these sweet smiles always on their lips? But they, perhaps, had been brought up in just such a home as this, where on all sides they were trained to and surrounded by shams; and how could anything different be expected from such an education? Alas, how utterly small it all was.

As she reached this point in her reflections the door was opened, and Mrs. Felmere joined her. Helen looked up as her aunt advanced, and wondered a little at her grave looks; but, not liking to ask the cause, she went on turning over the leaves of the album after an idle uninterested fashion.

Mrs. Felmere watched her a moment in silence, then said slowly, "Helen, I have come to have a few moments' talk with you. I wish to take a mother's privilege and give you a little advice. May I?"

Helen looked up gravely, and for a moment scanned Mrs. Felmere's face; then she looked down again, answering quietly, "Certainly, aunt, if you wish."

The permission was not very encouraging; nevertheless, Mrs. Felmere went on. "I only wish to say, my dear," she began, "that it is utterly useless ever to argue with my sister Esther, and it is much wiser not to anger her, wiser for many reasons. She is getting old, and perhaps a little peevish, but through all she is very fond of Philip, and I should like her to be fond of you as his wife."

Helen assented, and Mrs. Felmere, seeing her so quiet under her little lecture, put Philip down as a goose for his fears, and warmed to her subject. "Her health is not good," she continued, and at her words Helen felt a little contrition for having provoked an old sick person, "and as she is very wealthy, we, Margaret and myself, and Philip," Helen looked up with a gleam of surprise in her eyes, "feel a little anxiety about her will; for she is entirely untrammeled, and can leave her money where she pleases."

"And Philip wants her money?" Helen asked slowly, as Mrs. Felmere paused.

"Yes, of course!" she answered quickly and sharply, being made impatient by the tinge of scorn in the girl's voice and the contempt she saw gathering about her lips, "of course he wishes it. Money is not to be picked up in the streets, and every sensible man will and ought to take all he can honestly get. Philip has a right to hope for a more prominent place in Esther's will than any of the family, unless, indeed, you spoil all by angering her."

Helen did not look up. She felt ashamed to face any one who could acknowledge such motives, ashamed for them; and she answered almost sadly, "I had better avoid her then."

"Oh, no!" cried Mrs. Felmere, "that would be worse still; that would be neglect, and it would never do!"

"Then will you tell me what I must do? For I must confess to being almost at a loss to understand you." Helen began to be restive, and her voice had an impatient ring in it as she strove to control her desire to vent her honest scorn of this groveling after money.

"You must be kind and attentive to her, as you should be to all old people," Mrs. Felmere answered instructively, "be patient with all her little tempers, and seem pleased with her little jokes. To an amiable person it is a very simple process; Amelia does it admirably."

"I have never tried to act anything in all my life, Helen answered slowly, as her aunt ceased speaking, "and I am afraid I am not an amiable person. I beg you will let me avoid her." There was a moment's pause; then she added sharply and quickly, "As for her money, I abhor it!"

Mrs. Felmere raised her head in angry astonishment, and the color in her cheeks deepened swiftly. "That is foolish," she said in a stinging voice, "and if you do not wish the money, you can at least be unselfish enough not to ruin Philip's prospects."

Helen shook her head. "I cannot think Philip wishes for Aunt Esther's money to this extent. If he does," she paused, and in the pause Mrs. Felmere watched her closely, "if he does, I cannot stoop to any such means to aid him in getting it."

Mrs. Felmere grew angrily white as she listened to this quiet opposition, and her voice shook audibly as she answered, "And Philip shall get it without your help, and if you prefer making enemies for yourself in place of friends, I cannot help you. But, thank God, I am still here to see to the interests of my son!"

Helen turned away, sorry that the breach made was of such width; she had tried through it all to be tolerant, but she had not succeeded in even keeping the peace. She must now make an effort to mend things, and turning at the door she said apologetically, "I will ask Philip, aunt, and what he wishes I will try to do. I am sorry I have displeased you."

But Mrs. Felmere answered coldly, "It is of no consequence; whatever is necessary I can do myself as heretofore. I am sorry I troubled you at all. Philip advised that nothing be said to you about it; I now see he was right."

Helen closed the door slowly, and turned away pondering deeply. So Philip did want this money to this sordid extent, and was ashamed that she should know it. She had readied her room, and stood looking out of the window into the street. She did not wish to think any further on the subject of the morning's discussion. It was a pity it had ever come up, and to change the current of her mind she began in childish fashion to count the different kinds of carriages that passed. Suddenly she stopped. This was very weak. It was silly and cowardly to turn away from realizing facts. Why not at once look them in the face, and weigh them for what they were worth? This morning she had found out that Philip loved money more than she had supposed; that he would stoop to what she considered deceit to get it; that he laid his plans with his mother without consulting her—she was of no consequence! This last thought she put on one side: it was not because she was of no consequence that she was not consulted, but because

Philip knew she would not aid in any such scheme. She was glad of this, glad that he knew her opinions on such matters well enough not to put her in the disagreeable position of giving them. Then a sort of despair crept over her as she brought home to herself the facts that these were the people she had to live with, and that this man was her husband.

She walked from one window to the other under the "pressure of this thought, and stood looking down into the side street. What a close horrid place a city was, and what had become of her "philosophic calm"?

Her father was right: to be at peace one must rise above the littlenesses of everyday life; for they seemed to be more trying to one's philosophy than the greater trials of life or rather, those things that were deemed the greater trials. If the happiness of Philip and his mother lay in the attainment of this money, she had no right to put difficulties in the way; the more so as she believed that happiness was the one end in life.

And it was in this frame of mind that she went down to lunch. Mrs. Felmere was a little stiff in her greeting, but as the time went on she talked politely of the round of entertainments prepared for Helen, of the habits and hours of the household, and ended by asking if the last quite suited her.

"Philip," she said, "never comes home until dinner. He might perhaps alter this habit if you wished it, but I have never urged it, as it seemed to suit both his father and himself to take their lunch down town. The office is such a journey from this place."

"I hope neither you nor Philip will change anything on my account," Helen answered. "It is entirely immaterial to me how the day is divided. My only tastes are painting and reading, and they can fit in anywhere."

Mrs. Felmere bowed, then looked up; for the door had opened, giving entrance to Arthur Jourdan. The interruption was a pleasant one to both the ladies, and in consequence his welcome was warm. He joined them in a glass of wine, and while drinking it told them he had come to try and teach Helen something about dancing before the ball that evening.

"I thank you very much," Helen answered, feeling really grateful to him, "and you are very kind to have thought of it."

"It is a pleasure to me," Arthur answered kindly, "and now if Amelia will play for us, will you?" turning to Mrs. Felmere.

"Yes, whenever you are ready."

It was certainly very amiable in Arthur, Helen thought, to take so much trouble for her pleasure; and she wondered if she would be able to learn, she feared not.

Arthur, however, was determined that she should, and quite wearied his sister's politeness and fingers before the long afternoon was half spent. But she said nothing; for Philip, coming in earlier than usual, seemed so pleased with the state of things, that she was content to go on and make no sign of weariness; for was not Philip's pleasure hers? So she thrummed away monotonously the same waltz over and over again, until Helen laughingly declared that if she did not know the steps she certainly did the tune, and that she was too tired to dance any more just then.

Mrs. Felmere was glad to be relieved, and joined Helen and Arthur, who were following Philip into the library to see a picture, "a favorite of his," he said, "which he had been keeping for years as a gift to Helen."

The library was a long room, not very well lighted, but richly furnished with all the appliances for a literary life, as the libraries of most wealthy un-literary men are—furnished thoroughly at first, and remaining so because unused.

Helen looked about her, wondering what use Philip found for a library, and secretly planning to spend most of her spare time here until she arranged a studio for herself.

"Here it is," Philip said, as he drew away the curtain hanging in front of an arched bay window, revealing a gilt easel on which rested a painting. Helen paused a moment, then, paling painfully, came forward slowly as a somnambulist might, slowly as though uncertain of her steps. It was Felix Gordon's "King Arthur."

Philip stepped hastily between her and the picture. "Do not look at it, Helen. The likeness is very strong, but I did not think it would affect you so much."

She looked at him as though not quite understanding him, but, obeying his gesture, turned and left the room. Upstairs, in her own room, she paused and tried to collect her thoughts. "What a strange fate!" she whispered to herself, and covered her face with her hands. And so she sat, feeling weak and powerless before the throng of old memories that came about her, until Philip, rapping at the door, said his mother was ready for a drive; would Helen go with her? But Helen felt much too tired, she said, and begged him to make her excuses for her.

She stood near the window after that, and watched them until they drove away; then she went down swiftly to the library so glad to be alone with her picture. She knelt down in front of it, and gazed on it with all the love and sorrow of her short life glowing vividly in her face. "My own, my darling picture," she murmured, laying her cheek against it, putting her arms about it, and kissing it as passionately as though it lived. "I am so glad, so glad to see you!" Then she drew away and looked at it.

Alas, it was no longer a joy! The fair, sweet past that rose before her seemed almost to numb her heart. She could see her father as he sat reading, all unconscious that she was stealing his lineaments from him; she could see Felix as he stood in the hall door scanning and praising her work; she could hear him talk as later on he worked the head into his picture; could see the slim brown hands, so skillful and graceful as they plied their task those dear brown hands she kissed so sadly for goodbye. She could almost smell the fresh salt wind; could almost hear the wild, sad cries of the seabirds flying to and fro, and the peevish chatter of the marsh hens in the flats!

Ah, so vivid, so vivid it all swept over her as she gazed on the sad grace of the picture; and again the words came back to her, "It will be a sweet breath of air from this summer, the happiest of my life; it will be all our talks over again, all our walks, all our pictures, all our books; meeting it again will be either a great pleasure or a most bitter pain!"

Alas, a most bitter pain.

Sweeping into the ballroom that night, her shimmering satin and sparkling jewels seeming to radiate light, people called her "wonderfully beautiful" and looking again, "strangely sad." For the thoughtful eyes seemed to look into every soul they met, and, drawing thence the drop of bitter sadness always hidden there, revealed it to you in their violet depths. A strange and strong fascination seemed to attract attention to her. People saw her beauty, but wondered at something in her they could not understand.

"Surely," the gossips began, "there is some mystery or misfortune hidden somewhere in her life, there must be."

And Helen, looking vainly among the shifting crowd for that one bright boyish face, always bright and boyish to her, felt a new excitement creeping through her veins, an excitement deep and powerful. Always expecting, always hoping, always listening for some echo of his name and fame, she talked and listened eagerly to every stranger.

Arthur, always close beside her, always ready to help or entertain her, watched the flickering color come and go, watched the flash-
ing of her eyes and the sorrow in the depths of them, and wondered
why she had married his commonplace nephew.

But in the dim day-dawn, when all the house was still, the sad-
eyed, envied, beautiful Mrs. Philip Felmere crept down to where the
picture was slowly growing into color under the morning light, and
knelt before it as before a shrine. And there, forgetting her "lord and
master," forgetting her host of admirers, forgetting her enviable beauty
and riches, she went back to the faraway summer down in the old
house among the flats once so dreary, now so glorified.

So the sad, troubled face of the "Great King" grew slowly into
light, sad and troubled as the face of him who had lost his God, sad
and troubled and strangely like the face of the woman who knelt desolate in the gray dawn, the woman without religion, without love, without hope.

"And, indeed, her chief fault was
this unconscious scorn
Of the world, to whose usages woman is born."

— "Lucile," Edward Bulwer Lytton

Chapter III

THE WINTER OPENED WITH A FASHIONABLE RUSH: balls, germans, din-
ners, theatres, operas—everything in fact that could be done to
absolutely annihilate time. And Helen, in the thickest of the fray, half
way scorned and half way enjoyed it all. To Mrs. Felmere, however,
the winter was somewhat shadowed, as she found that the possession
of her beautiful daughter-in-law was not unmixed delight and triumph;
for Helen had, among other peculiarities, a quiet way of putting all
the conventionalities which were the creed of Mrs. Felmere's week-
day life to the crucial test of reason, and as often as not putting them
aside. Mrs. Felmere could not deny that Helen was very polite in her
manner of doing this often, indeed, seeming to do it with a calm unconsciousness that the feelings of any person would or could be hurt
by a difference of opinion on such subjects, but this fact did not make
her course any the less disagreeable. On the other hand, if there was
anything Helen desired to do, and in which she saw no harm, she
would unhesitatingly do it in spite of, or rather in disregard of, the
world's opinion.

Another thing that Mrs. Felmere could not recover from was Helen's perfect candor whenever her opinion was asked. She never for one moment considered expediency. Nothing was ever shaded off or added to what came from her lips, and Mrs. Felmere was becoming afraid even of telling so much as a polite fib where Helen could hear her. It was surely very trying to have such a disagreeably exact person always about you. But the open and quiet expression of Helen's unbelief was one of the hardest trials Mrs. Felmere had to bear, for she was superstitiously religious, and on this score poor Philip also suffered, for, lectured by his mother into lecturing his wife on this point, he was always met by a silence half contemptuous, half amused, and wholly pitying. It surely did not promise to be a happy household.

On the second Sunday after their arrival, Mrs. Felmere insisted that Philip should make a point of Helen's going to church, and afterward dining at Miss Esther Jourdan's house. Under great stress of harassment, Philip made his point, and, much to his happiness, was met by a quiet acquiescence, on the ground that, as she looked on churchgoing as one of the family habits, it would be impolite not to conform. Mrs. Felmere also was surprised at this, and, looking back, was compelled to put a retrospective faith in the headache Helen had given as an excuse the Sunday before.

A handsomely respectable, well-lighted, well-heated, comfortable church; a richly rustling congregation; a grand organ, a brilliant choir, and an oratorical rector: such was the "holy temple" where the Felmeres worshiped. Not ritualistic? Oh, no. Not Methodistical? Oh, never. What then? Why, respectable "middle church." Yes, deadly respectable, excessively "middle church," cold unto death.

Mrs. Felmere took one comfortable corner of the pew, and Philip the other, and Helen sitting very straight in the middle mused on unselfishness!

The service opened with airs from "Traviata," which to Helen, with the opera and its story fresh in her mind, seemed a trifle incongruous. She listened and admired until the service began; then with much curiosity, but without pretending to follow, she studied her prayer book and watched everything with much interest.

The sermon did not in the least attract her, nor did the singing, notwithstanding her love for music; for to her it all seemed ill-matched and caused a sort of sorrow to come over her that this should be so. She remembered her girlish ideal of Christianity, an ideal built on her father's description of its rise and spread and could not but feel a little sad at having to give it up. She had pictured something so grand and solemn, so far-reaching in its services and prayers; and it was not there at least not in this church. She had so often imagined the Christians' reverence for their God, and their love of their prayers to Him, and how deep and thankful their trust would be. Alas, in this light, un-mysterious church, she heard the priest saying these very prayers off in oily, familiar tones, and with a self-appreciative, patronizing man-ner, as though he were conferring a favor on the Lord by his service. Among the people she saw that few knelt, leaning forward in prefer-ence, and that all of them, kneeling or sitting, rattled off the responses as though speed were at a premium. She looked, and listened, and wondered. This sort of religion could not surely benefit any one, and was she not as well off as they were? But she kept her thoughts to herself, not even remarking on the hurry to get away that seemed to possess every one as soon as the service was over, rushing out into the aisles with the greatest air of relief, and chattering to each other in the most frivolous manner and about the most incongruous things; yet this to them was a holy place.

They drove from church to Miss Esther's house, where the whole family made a point of assembling every Sunday, making it, as Helen thought to herself, strictly a duty day. She watched them all with keen, unloving eyes, and drew many conclusions that it never entered into their wildest dreams to conceive as possible regarding themselves. Jack and Arthur she really liked, for they were strictly honest and kind to her. Philip, too, would have been so, if his mother had not con-stantly forced upon him a course of advice and lecturings.

During dinner, the talk turned on the services, and Mr. Jourdan, addressing Helen, asked her what she thought of them. Mrs. Felmere and Philip looked up anxiously as they heard the question; for, al-though they had tried to impress on Helen that it was considered al-most a disgrace for a woman to be an unbeliever, and especially so in their circle, yet they knew that she had not heeded them, and would not now, if she so minded, hesitate to confess herself before the as-sembled family, and so cover her husband and mother-in-law with mortification, and reveal to all the "skeleton in the closet."

But Helen answered without the shadow of a scoff, "It was not what I expected, Uncle John."

"And what did you expect? "Miss Esther asked sharply.

"I do not know exactly," Helen answered quietly, "but something more quiet, more solemn, I might say more deep and reverential."

Mrs. Felmere and Philip were surprised at these simple answers, and felt much relieved that danger had been avoided, not knowing that Helen had made up her mind to avoid as far as possible all discussions and contentions with Miss Esther. But the fates were not so propitious as Mrs. Felmere had imagined; for Amelia Jourdan, having heard vague hints of Helen's unbelief, and being curious to hear more, entered into the conversation. "You are a Ritualist, then?" she asserted interrogatively.

Helen looked up quickly. "I do not quite understand you."

"I mean you are fond of forms and ceremonies, and hang your faith on non-essentials," Amelia explained, letting her voice linger fondly on these "war cries" of her party.

"No," Helen answered, shaking her head, "you do not now quite understand me. You are perhaps not aware that this is my first experience of church services."

The family looked interested and curious, and Mrs. Felmere and Philip utterly miserable, as Amelia pursued her inquiries. "Why, are you a sectarian?"

"No, not at all."

"A Romanist?"

"No, nor that either." Then Helen paused and felt a little pity for Philip and his mother, both looking so nervous and restless just opposite her.

"What are you, then?" Amelia said quickly, afraid someone would stop her.

"Your cousin was not trained in any special church," Mrs. Felmere answered reprovingly.

Helen smiled and looked up at Arthur, who sat beside her and knew pretty well what the truth of the matter was. He returned her smile and shook his head warningly, for he was anxious for her sake to keep the peace, but he saw plainly that his sister had made a false move.

Amelia was silenced, but Miss Esther, who had taken a strong dislike to her new relative and longed to see her humbled, and, moreover, had an amiable desire to clip Mrs. Felmere's too triumphant wings, here asked of Helen, "And which church or denomination do you intend joining, Mrs. Helen?"

There was a moment's pause until the harsh voice died away; then Helen answered quietly and frankly, "None. I was not brought up a Christian."

Amelia's curiosity was satisfied, as was Miss Esther's spite, and an ominous silence fell on the shocked company. It did not last long, however; for poor Mrs. Felmere, whose mortification was only exceeded by her anger, broke the silence in a smooth cold voice, which Helen had learned to know meant warning of silence to her. "My brother-in-law was very peculiar in his views," she said slowly, "and made the mistake of bringing Helen up in accordance with them, but she will join us before long, I hope."

It was a frightful blunder, this speech, and Helen would in pity have let it pass but for the slur on her father; that made her blood tingle, and must be answered. "Perhaps he thought your views, if not peculiar, at least very wonderful," she said quietly, but with a light in her eyes that Philip did not like, "and perhaps he thought, and with as much reason, that you were mistaken."

Mrs. Felmere turned very white, and leaned back in her chair quite silenced; for further argument would only insure further disclosures. So she put away as gracefully as she might her wounded pride and wrath until some future time, when her family would not be there to triumph sympathetically over her discomfiture with her beautiful and much-vaunted daughter-in-law.

The women rather veered away from Helen after dinner, but Arthur, seeing it, and feeling angry with them for their treatment, came and sat by her. She made no remarks about the conversation at dinner, nor yet about the present loneliness of her position; but taking up a book of etchings, she began idly to turn over its pages, allowing him to choose his own subjects and talk as he pleased. Slowly she turned over the leaves of the book, uninterestedly listening to Arthur's talk, all the while commenting in her own mind on the people she found herself among. They seemed so narrow, so small-minded, so low in their views of life, and yet what higher views had she?

Suddenly she stopped with a page held tight in her hand. She rose abruptly, leaving Arthur in the middle of a sentence, and stepped nearer the light to examine one of the pictures; only a moment she looked at it, then closed the book slowly without a word, and came back to the sofa weak and pale. It was only a sketch of Felmere church and churchyard, with the initials F. G. in one corner. Why was it that he met her at every turn? Why was it that those old days should so haunt her present misery?

"You are ill," Arthur said quickly, as he saw how pale she looked, and he brought her a glass of water. He was so kind, and seemed so true, that Helen determined to ask him a few questions; for even if he did surmise anything, she did not think he would talk of it.

So when he again took his seat she began, "Are there many rising artists that you know anything of, Arthur?"

"Yes," he answered, "there are several, but I only know them very casually. I have a friend, however, who has just returned to town and, by the way, is very anxious to meet you who knows all that sort of people, and can tell you all about everybody."

"Who is it?"

"Mrs. Vanzandt."

"Vanzandt," she repeated, "is she a friend of my aunt?"

Arthur laughed. "Not altogether loving friends, but they keep up what you might call a guarded and armed fondness. To tell you the truth, she has once or twice taken the social lead out of Amelia's hands, and among women of the world this does not induce affection."

"Yes," Helen said, nodding her head, "I remember now what it was Aunt Amelia said, and that I drew the conclusion at the time that I should be apt to like Mrs. Vanzandt."

"It is more than probable," Arthur answered, "for she can make herself and her house very charming if she chooses. I am really very fond of her."

"Where is her husband? "

Arthur shook his head. "I do not know; they were divorced many years ago, rather a dark story, I believe. But people do not heed or remember that now, for she is rich and in a certain way charming."

"Money seems to be a great power," Helen said musingly, "and I have never realized it until now."

"And you will be made to realize it more and more the longer you live," Arthur answered.

"I think I would prefer being poor, really poor," Helen went on, "so that I should have to work for my living. I am very tired of this easy, useless life, and I feel penned up, inane, and altogether a burden on my own hands."

"What would you like to do? "Arthur asked.

"I should like to be an artist," she answered. "I am very fond of painting, and I think I could succeed, but I have not touched a brush since I have been here." And she sighed.

"You need not sigh so pitifully," Arthur said, feeling a great sympathy for his lovely companion creeping over him; for a beautiful woman looks so sad when she is sad, and an ugly woman so ugly!

"I did not mean to sigh," Helen answered, and felt impatient with herself for giving way to even that much feeling, but she found she was being sadly shaken out of her self control by these prying people.

"I should think you could easily arrange a studio for yourself," Arthur suggested, "your house is full large enough."

"I intend to either that, or hire one," she answered, "and then you may introduce me to your friend Mrs. Vanzandt, who you say deals in my sort of people, I mean artistic people."

Arthur laughed. "Not only artistic," he said, "but literary, scientific, musical, and commonplace people of all grades and employments. A strange conglomeration sometimes, but always entertaining."

"I should think much more so than the conventional stereotyped people we meet at balls and parties. They seem to have lost all command of ideas." And Helen yawned slightly, as though even the remembrance of them wearied her.

"Even the recollection of them makes you sleepy," Arthur said, laughing, "but you should not allow yourself to get really sleepy, nor indulge yourself in any hopes of getting home for an hour or two yet, as the Reverend Mr. Tolman always comes in for a sociable cup of tea on Sunday evenings."

"Who is he? "Helen asked "the man who preached this morning?"

"The very same, and as you are a fresh importation, you will have to bear the brunt of his conversation."

"I shall not object," Helen answered, "indeed, I shall like to meet him and hear what he talks about. I was out when he called. But is he married, and will Mrs. Tolman come with him?"

"No, he is not just now married, but I do not doubt but that he will replace his wife before long, for the women all 'adore' him, Amelia Jourdan among the rest."

Helen looked up quickly. "Do you mean, Arthur, that Amelia would like to marry him?"

"To all appearances, yes." And Helen, listening much interested, detected the trifle of scorn that came into his voice as he went on. "Amelia is not a beauty, you know, nor so rich as to be an heiress; so she will be quite willing to compromise on the church and a certain salary. The family actually seem anxious for it."

"Is she in love with him?" Helen asked gravely.

"In love?" Arthur repeated, looking at her curiously, "do you think that a necessary part of the contract?"

"Yes," she answered, then, after a moment's pause, she added more slowly, "that is, if you desire or expect the faintest shadow of happiness."

"So she lives without the 'shadow of happiness,'" Arthur thought, and feeling more than ever sorry for her, he answered slowly, "I do not know about Amelia, but girls as a rule do not count love in after they have passed their earlier youth; but from that time they act on what they are pleased to term a 'common-sense basis,' choosing a man according to his money, his position, his morals."

"Do they put morals last?" Helen went on gravely.

Arthur shook his head. "There is somewhat of mystery surrounding that point," he said, "but it seems to depend on how much a man is worth. If he is very rich, and is not pulled out of the gutter during the day, they will marry him on the plea of reforming him: it is quite a missionary spirit they show." And he pulled his mustache meditatively.

"Is this so everywhere, or only in this city?" Helen went on.

"Everywhere that I have been," he answered. "The love of money seems to be in a state of development; we shall soon be able to rank it as a feminine instinct."

Helen laughed. "You make me think that you have been at some time a sufferer from these or like causes."

Arthur shook his head. "Not one only has treated me ill on this account, but whole dozens of them. Of course there can be no other reason for their not being charmed."

"Of course, but, Arthur, what is it that so influences them to the love of money?"

"They are brought up to it," he answered slowly. "As soon as a girl has teethed, money and matrimony are the two aims and ends of life that are set before her, and as after a while existence would be a blank without these two things, they are naturally the main objects of pursuit."

"It is pitiful," Helen said, "and I had formed such different ideas of the lives and education of Christians."

Arthur looked at her in surprise. "Where did you get your idea of Christians from?" he asked.

"From my father's descriptions, and from the Bible," she answered.

Arthur felt nonplused. He was too honest to pretend that the Christians he moved among guided their lives by the Bible. In fact, he had more than once, in observing them, thought that they could only be called Christians in contradistinction to "Jews, Turks, infidels, and heretics," and not because they had any of the real life of Christianity in them; and yet to this unbeliever he could not bring himself to acknowledge this. Finally he said rather deprecatingly, "I am afraid that the religious training of the present day is rather ecclesiastical than biblical; at least I should be led to this conclusion from my observations of the results."

"It seems to me the blindest folly," Helen answered, "not to hold to such a beautiful religion when you have the choice of doing so."

Arthur looked up surprised, but his reply was cut short by the entrance of Mr. Tolman.

Helen watched Amelia curiously as she greeted him, wishing to judge for herself of Arthur's conclusions. Amelia was reverentially gushing, and Mr. Tolman held her hand in both of his while he told her in a fatherly way how glad he was to see her, and how well she looked. Arthur saw that she was watching, and smiled significantly as she looked up to him for confirmation of the scene.

Then Mr. Tolman was brought toward where they sat. Helen scanned his face curiously during his introduction, and all the while he shook her hand and made his speeches about "dear Phil's wife," and "dear Mrs. Felmere's happiness in such a daughter," she was reading him. He did not leave her a moment in which to say a word until they had been seated for some little time; then he asked her "how she liked city life?"

"Very well," Helen answered gravely.

"Only 'very well'! Why, how is this, Phil?"

"It is not Philip's fault," Helen answered in her literal way, "it arises from my being country-bred. I like the quiet best."

Philip looked a little anxious, and Arthur smiled as he watched the growing perplexity on Helen's countenance as Mr. Tolman rattled on. "Prefer the quiet? Why, how is that? Miss Amy here does not, I warrant."

Amelia looked a little sad, and Mrs. Jourdan said she thought "Amelia had quite tired of society lately."

Helen looked around quickly; she had not at all observed this weariness in Amelia; and Mrs. Felmere, seeing the look and fearing a speech from her, hastily filled the little pause with words to the effect that "the dear child longed for a higher life."

"A sisterhood," Arthur suggested from not an altogether amiable motive, and Miss Esther, scenting a discussion, smiled grimly.

Mr. Tolman shook his head. "Home is a higher sphere for a woman than any other," he said reprovingly.

Helen was listening attentively. "I thought only Roman Catholics had sisterhoods," she said, while Mrs. Felmere looked reprovingly at Arthur.

"So it has been until of late," Mr. Tolman answered instructively, "but now there is a branch of our church which seems to think religion lies in copying Rome; in sinking back into mediaeval darkness and superstitions; returning to images and pictures, to bowings and scrapings, and playing at 'What o'clock, old witch?' all round the church. To me all this is abhorrent and foolish."

"I agree with you entirely," Miss Esther said severely, "it is actual mummery and idolatry."

"Miss De Sayle has entered the sisterhood," Amelia said with a tinge of pious pity in her voice.

"She was never afflicted with much sense," Mrs. Felmere rejoined contemptuously.

"To me it seems less of a sin to be a regular Romanist at once than a bad imitation," said Mrs. Jourdan.

"What is it they do in the sisterhood that is so wicked?" Helen asked, looking from one to the other.

"They take an oath of celibacy," Arthur answered gravely from where he leaned on the high back of her chair. Helen turned to see if he were in earnest, and Jack laughed merrily at the look of surprised consternation that came over the faces of the company.

"No, Arthur, but I really wish to find out about them," Helen went on, turning to Mr. Tolman.

"They profess to devote themselves to charitable works," Mr. Tolman answered.

"Profess? "Helen repeated. "Do they not perform them? Are they not true in what they say?"

"I, for one, do not believe they are," sneered Miss Esther.

"All affectation!" said Mrs. Jourdan.

"The dress is becoming and romantic," added Mrs. Felmere.

"But tell me really," Helen asked of Mr. Tolman, "do you not believe in them?"

"Yes," he answered slowly, as though, he were weighing the matter, "yes, I believe they mean to be true."

"Then what is wrong in them?" Helen asked gravely. "If they are striving to do right, and give up their lives to charitable works, why so abuse them?"

"Softly, softly, my dear young lady." Mr. Tolman interrupted. "I do not for one moment abuse them!"

"Indeed, but you forget," Helen rejoined quickly, "you intimated that doing good and being true was a 'profession' on their part, and not a practice."

Mr. Tolman colored up. "I was, perhaps, a trifle hasty in my choice of words, madam," he said. "I do not mean to cast any slur on their works or their sincerity, but I do think the system a mistaken one."

"Why? "Helen went on, wishing to make him express himself firmly on the question.

"Because it leads to superstition and empty forms; because it is copying Rome; because I do not think God meant women to cut themselves off from their duties in any such way." And he looked around complacently on his audience.

"But if they think this mode of life their duty?" Helen urged.

"Then they think wrong," Mr. Tolman answered promptly.

"Why?"

"Because, I say, God never meant them for any such purpose." His tone was becoming a little impatient; he was not accustomed to such contumacy.

"How do you know that so certainly?" Helen went on quietly.

"How do I know anything?" Mr. Tolman retorted. "In no way, I think, except by experience."

Helen answered, "and I cannot see how you can know God's purposes in that way, since I suppose you will admit that you cannot even so prove that there is any God."

Mr. Tolman looked aghast. Philip walked to the other end of the room. Mrs. Felmere was pitiably mortified and the rest of the ladies looked in a sort of pious "I told you so" state. Mr. Tolman's metaphysics were rusty; he could dogmatize on ritualism, but he had not attempted to philosophize on the "Absolute" and the "Infinite" since he had come to be a popular orator in a rich city church: in fact, shortly after his call to this highly respectable salary, he began to have queer feelings in his head that prevented much study on his part. So now, with a retrospective sigh for the disadvantages under which he had labored, he shook his head slowly and sadly, and, falling back on faith, answered solemnly, "We need no such proof."

"I know you do not," Helen answered. "I only wished to find out how you can know so positively what God means, unless you can with equal certainty know God. You may say you do not approve of sisterhoods, but I cannot understand how you can so dogmatically assert that God does not approve of them. If I remember rightly, St. Paul advises women to remain unmarried and to do the works of the Lord, does he not?"

Here Mr. Tolman was on firm ground again, and rejoined quickly, "St. Paul may have advised it, but you may also remember that he tells us he spoke there without inspiration!"

As he finished his voice sounded almost triumphant, and as it ceased Helen's answer came in quietly, "Very true, but may not these 'Sisters' think the uninspired advice of St. Paul is better to be followed than your uninspired opinion?"

The point was made so simply that Mr. Tolman scarcely realized it, and when even Miss Esther joined the young men and Mr. Jourdan in a little half-smothered laugh at his expense, his state of mind could not have been described as tranquil. He looked at his adversary a moment in silence, then asked, "Are you a Romanist or an Anglican ritualist?"

Helen did not wish that her unbelief should again come under discussion, for there was no use in making her husband and mother miserable before strangers, however silly such misery appeared in her eyes; so she simply answered, "I am not either."

"What are you then?"

There was a painful silence in the room as she answered: "In your vocabulary there are many names for me: Utilitarian, Materialist, Skeptic, Positivist, Atheist. I call myself a Rationalist. I think that more nearly expresses my position."

Miss Esther nodded her head once or twice, then leaned back in her chair in a state of happy resignation; Mrs. Felmere muttered "Horrible!" while Mrs. Jourdan and Amelia looked exceedingly sorrowful.

Mr. Tolman turned away from Helen as she ceased speaking, and walked the length of the room once or twice in silence. At last he stopped near Philip, who, overwhelmed with these exposures and the weight of the family displeasure, leaned against the mantel with his head bowed on his hand.

"How has this happened?" Mr. Tolman asked slowly.

Helen heard the question, as did the rest of the company, and listened intently for Philip's answer.

"How was it done?" Mr. Tolman repeated in a more authoritative tone. "She was educated to it," Philip answered sullenly.

"And you knew it?" Mr. Tolman went on.

"Yes."

There came a quick, sharp sigh from Arthur, and Helen's chair shook under his grasp. He made a quick movement forward as he said, "And wherein do you presume to blame him?" The question cut sharply through the silence. Jack twisted round and round on the piano stool; Mr. Jourdan looked exceedingly annoyed and the women utterly demoralized at this new development. Mr. Tolman, turning, answered slowly, "'Be ye not unequally yoked together with unbelievers,' have you never heard that, Mr. Jourdan, 'for what part hath he that believeth with an infidel?'"

"And why did not you impress all this more deeply on Philip in his early youth?" Helen asked quietly, but with a shade of scorn creeping into her voice. "You were his spiritual director. Why did you not make him appreciate more fully the vileness and blackness of unbelief and reason? With all due deference, I think you and my aunt are more to blame in this matter than Philip; for six years ago, when he came first to look after his father's legacy, he did not seem to think there was any sin in what he was doing, neither did my aunt!"

There was a bitter, bitter ring in her voice as for the first time she put in words the knowledge she had felt creeping over her of her husband's utter weakness, and the knowledge of why she had been dragged from her peaceful seclusion. Ah, if her father could only have foreseen the results of his plans for her happiness and comfort; have seen her standing up to defend her husband's weakness, and to excuse his sin in marrying her.

It was a bitter moment to her, no one knew how bitter; for, womanlike, she had striven to build a pedestal on which to set her "lord and master;" had searched diligently in him for the wherewithal from which to weave a mantle or a veil of ideals to cover his smaller faults and shade his failings; had striven to raise him high enough for her to look up to! And now, now, when one manly word or look would have for ever put him on a higher level in her heart and mind, when one brave, authoritative gesture, even, would have ended all this impertinent prying and reproof, he stood silent, and his wife defended and despised him.

Helen had been trained to no charity, and so could only despise weakness; she had been taught no forgiveness of injuries, and so only felt a contempt for the meanness which prompted them; she had been educated to no paltering between right and wrong, only to a straightforward code of reason and self-control. She could not now pity Philip, nor excuse his mother, and she no longer cared who knew the true state of things. They had torn down the flimsy screen that hid their motives: why need she hide that she despised both them and their actions? They were cruel to her; she was careless of their standing before the world. Ay, anyone and everyone might think what they pleased; it was no longer any concern of hers.

All this she thought as she stood looking round on the silent company, and her last scornful words seemed still to reverberate through the room. Mrs. Felmere sat rigid with anger; Philip did not move; and Mr. Tolman felt a sharp pricking in his conscience that betokened the truth in her words.

"You may be right," he said slowly, "perhaps I am to blame. I can only pray God's forgiveness for my fault, and that you may be brought to a better mind."

Then he said "Good evening," and walked away through the darkness to his home, with a dim sense of the folly in the weak wranglings and jealousies of theologians over non-essential ecclesiastical differences, when there was opening in the midst of them a black abyss of utter destruction for many wavering souls. Alas for the blindness of theologians. Rationalism derides them; Judaism mocks them; Science pities them, watching them as they march to their downfall splitting hairs over "real" or "objective presence," over green or red altar cloths, over broken bread or wafers!

Whatever Christ meant in leaving His memorial among them, He did not mean them to battle over it; He did not mean to raise strife and contention among them; He did not mean for them to let go of peace, charity, love, patience, gentleness, meekness, long-suffering, tenderness, and to take instead malice, envy, hatred, "and all uncharitableness." Christ taught no such religion as this!

"But standing apart as she ever had done,
And her genius, which needed a vent, finding none
In the broad fields of action thrown wide to man's power,
She unconsciously made it her bulwark and tower,
And built in it her refuge, whence lightly she hurled
Her contempt at the fashions and forms of the world."

—"Lucile," Edward Bulwer Lytton

CHAPTER IV

THE FORMAL, IRREPARABLE BREACH HAD BEEN MADE; all had chosen sides, all had shown their colors, and all thought of repairing the mischief was given up. Hereafter there could only be an armed peace, to preserve which would require the most watchful care. There was no forgiving to be done, for the deepest wound had been dealt to Mrs. Felmere's pride, and that is a wound that seldom heals; almost anything else a woman can forgive, but this seems always to rankle.

For Philip, Helen could now only feel pity, could only bring herself to a state of endurance; what little influence he had possessed was entirely gone, and his words were as an idle wind in his wife's ears. For, in the war of words that had swept over the family on Sunday night, he had not only failed to defend his wife, but had suffered *himself* to be reprimanded; had allowed himself to be put down in the presence of all; had lowered himself irretrievably. He was now spoken of in the family as "poor Philip," and in his wife's eyes he was so "poor" that, ignoring and unheeding him, she went on her own way, seemingly in a state of quiet indifference. All advice or reproof from her mother-in-law or husband was listened to in respectful silence, but quietly unheeded when it did not suit her. She would not consent to quarrel, nor in any way allow herself to be ruffled, and this to Mrs. Felmere was exasperating, and her self-control was not always so perfect as to hide this fact. And so between them, as might have been expected, "poor Philip's" life was a burden; for where can any more pitiful position be found than a weak man between two willful women?

For Helen, however, the tiresome round of everyday fashionable life was pleasantly broken by Mrs. Vanzandt, Arthur's friend, who since her return had opened her house to the gay world with much noise and bustle. She and Helen had immediately exchanged calls, and were mutually pleased, for each found in the other something different from the common run, something fresh and interesting. Mrs. Felmere saw, and was displeased; she had no love for Mrs. Vanzandt, who, though a much younger woman than herself, had of late years been her rival in social matters; her rival to the extent of outshining her on one or two occasions, and thus giving sufficient ground for maledictions and many innuendoes from Mrs. Felmere. But Mrs. Vanzandt gained for herself the consideration and afterward the honest liking of Helen. Above all, Helen found in Mrs. Vanzandt a true love for art, with knowledge enough to really appreciate talent in others, and the necessary kindliness to admire it.

"Why do you not fit up a studio?" she asked of Helen one day as they were out together for a drive.

"My aunt dislikes the smell of paint," Helen answered.

Mrs. Vanzandt's eyebrows arched themselves in a significant manner. "She used to come often to my studio and sit for hours," she said.

Helen shrugged her shoulders. "In such cases one can only acquiesce," she answered.

"Very true," her companion rejoined, then continued rapidly, "But you must have some place to work in. If you will, you may have the room next to my studio. The light is good, and as the room stands it is quite useless to me. Will you come?"

Helen was touched by this unexpected piece of kindly interest. "You are very kind," she answered, "and if you are sincere in your offer, I will accept it with gratitude."

"Gratitude, indeed, when it is an absolute favor to me! You will make my house a new place, and soon fill it with pleasant people for me; I am getting too old and stupid to do this for myself." And she drew her pretty little dark face out as long as possible.

Helen smiled as she caught the queer little expression, and, thinking how pretty her companion was, wondered what the story of her past life had been.

"Indeed, I am getting old," Mrs. Vanzandt went on, shaking her head slowly, "and if it were not for my hot suppers and a clattering tongue, my former friends and admirers would be as cold as charity, and poor Valeria Vanzandt would be 'shelved.' But so long as I can acceptably feed the men and flatter the women, I can count on something this side of neglect."

Helen looked amused and puzzled. "Why do you worry yourself to keep up friendships that are based on such low motives?" she asked.

Mrs. Vanzandt looked at her a moment in silence, then said with mock gravity, "It is really astonishing to hear a person talk in so wild a way in this advanced age of the world and society! My dear, how old are you, that you can still foster such delusions? 'Friendship,' 'low motives,' it is wonderful! Indeed, I do not know when I have been more shocked."

"Then why do you value this society and life?" Helen went on.

"What else is there to value?"

"Honest friendship and honest love."

Mrs. Vanzandt shrugged her shoulders. "My dear child," she said, "I was born many years before you were; I have seen many more phases of life than you will ever see; I have moved in much more and more various society than you have; and my testimony is, that unless you can enjoy the society of selfish, low-toned people, who are for ever watching for their own interests, you had better leave the world. And unless I can keep a chattering, flattering tongue in my head, and give handsome entertainments, I shall be, as I before remarked, simply shelved."

"And would you not be willing to be shelved from among such people? "

"No."

"Why not?"

Mrs. Vanzandt paused a moment, and a sadder look came over her face as she answered, "What else have I?"

"Can you not make some higher aim for yourself?"

"Can you make rope out of sand, or 'bricks without straw'? It is my life, child, this same mean, self-seeking world and I cannot do without it."

"Have you not your religion?" Helen went on in a lower tone.

Mrs. Vanzandt turned quite round to look at her. "My dear, you continually shock me from my self-control. What do you mean by such an attack? Has 'Chadband' Tolman converted you? I hope not sincerely, for you are a better Christian than any of us. But since you ask me, I make you the same answer I made the Reverend T. I am not rich enough to wear my Sunday clothes all the week. I should die of melancholy if I were to indulge in religion all the time."

Helen sighed. This beautiful religion she had almost longed for, how different its effects were from what she had imagined. "My experience has been small," she said after a little pause, "but it has been enough to make me long for the seclusion of my early youth."

"I can readily believe you,"Mrs. Vanzandt answered, "and pity you too, at least your awakening."

"I fortunately did not expect much," Helen said. Then she quite changed the subject by asking who was the most rising artist.

"There are several of them who stand nearly abreast," Mrs. Vanzandt answered, "but there is one young man who bids fair to distance them all, and now that I reckon up, he is no longer such a youth. Gordon. Felix Gordon."

At last she had heard of him. At last the hunger of her ears was satisfied with the echo of his fame that reached her! But it was harder to listen to than she imagined it would be, and she had to turn and look out of the carriage window.

"He is almost a genius," Mrs. Vanzandt went on, "and such a nice dear fellow. At least he was when I knew him several years ago. I hear he has changed a great deal of late."

"How long have you known him?" Helen asked, "and how long is it since he became known to the public?"

"Let me see," and Mrs. Yanzandt paused reflectively, "I have known him off and on for seven years, but he has only been known to the public in the last five. His first real success was a picture called 'King Arthur.' I think your husband bought it, did he not?"

"Yes," Helen answered, "he did, but where is Mr. Gordon now?" She found it more difficult than she had expected to speak of him quietly.

"I do not know exactly. He is a wandering, uncertain sort of creature; you can never be sure of him for a day, but he usually puts up one fine picture for sale each winter, and they always sell. But is it not time to turn toward home? Remember Mrs. Tilmont's tonight."

So the horses were stopped in their stately pacings around the park, and turned homeward; and Helen, pondering on what she had heard, sat silent and let her companion talk.

So at any time and in any place she might meet Felix Gordon; people knew him, and he was sought after and admired. Indeed, she might meet Felix that very night; for were not the Tilmonts, strictly speaking, blind followers of Mrs. Vanzandt, always trying to have at their entertainments the same sort of people that Mrs. Vanzandt had?

With these and such-like thoughts haunting her, Helen went through the ordeal of dinner almost in silence; usually so impatient of the state and stupidity of this meal, she today scarcely noticed them. At last Philip, becoming annoyed at her silence, spoke to her directly on the subject. "Are you ill," he asked, "that you are so silent?"

"Am I unusually so?" Helen answered, with the tone and manner of one stepping out of absorbing dreams. "I was not aware of it." Then, after vainly searching among her thoughts for something to say, she ventured upon the remark, "I suppose we go to the Tilmonts' at ten."

"I am not going," Philip answered rather shortly, "I have a headache."

"Indeed? I am very sorry." Then Helen turned to Mrs. Felmere, "You will go, of course."

"And leave Philip sick?" Mrs. Felmere asked severely.

"I supposed that with a headache he would prefer being left alone," Helen answered quietly; then turning to the servant said, "Tell Andrew to have the carriage by nine, and you come to me for a note."

"Are you going?" Philip asked as the servant left the room.

"Yes. I will send for Arthur. He never has any engagements, and will be glad to escort me." And she rose to leave the room.

"Can you not stay at home one evening?" Philip went on almost fretfully.

"I suppose I could if I liked," she answered, "but why should I?"

"Because I am not well," he continued, as he swallowed a glass of wine.

Helen waited until he had finished, then said provokingly, "If that is true, so much wine is not good for you." And, not waiting for further discussion, she left the room. Since her afternoon's conversation with Mrs. Vanzandt, she felt as though she would not for any consideration miss an entertainment where there was the remotest chance of meeting Felix Gordon; she had been watching and waiting for all these days and weeks for even a mention of his name, and now that she had heard it, the longing to see him redoubled itself. She took great pleasure in dressing for Mrs. Tilmont's, and bestowed more than usual care on her adornment; and when she had finished, she surely had reason to be satisfied with her success. Before the last touches had been given, Philip came in fully dressed and equipped for the ball. Helen looked up quickly from what she was doing. "Have you recovered?" she asked.

"No," he answered severely, "but I prefer taking you myself, sick as I am, to allowing you to go with any chance person."

His wife smiled. "Your own uncle?" she said.

"So he may be," and as he spoke, Philip's manner became majestic, "but that does not exempt him from observations in the town."

"Is your mother going?" Helen went on, stepping carelessly over the subject of Arthur.

"No."

She sighed as though relieved, and, giving Philip her fan and flowers, led the way down to the parlor, where Arthur sat waiting.

"She is *too* beautiful!" said one of a group of gentlemen, as Helen passed into the ballroom, "and to be tied to Phil Felmere must be awful to her."

The man he was speaking to was Felix Gordon, who, turning quickly, saw Helen, magnificent in jewels and satin, sweep by him. Her dress touched him, the perfume of her flowers floated about him, and the music of her voice as she spoke to some one near at hand drowned all the voices and laughter. He had in a moment gone back far, so far into that fair dead summer. If she had been beautiful to him then in her simple white dresses and plainly braided hair, what was she now? She carried her jewels and her laces with regal stateliness, and yet as if unconscious of their splendor. In the years that had passed since Felix last saw her, her beauty had become thoughtful and more soulful, and to Felix the proud coldness which hung about her added a strong charm.

He watched her as she made her slow progress to the upper end of the room; he watched her make her salutations to her hostess; and then she turned so that her beauty shone full upon him. He drew nearer, stationing himself just outside the circle of which she was the center; unseen by her, he stood close to her, watching the play of her features, the changing expressions that flitted across her face, the expressive gestures that almost told him what she was saying.

It was a happy moment, a moment that made his heart leap; but he could not stand it long. Should he go and speak to her? Should he not rather go away and leave her undisturbed in the careless enjoyment she seemed to find in her present life?

"Felmere watches her like a cat," said a voice near him. Felix started.

"Where is Mr. Felmere?" he asked.

"That short, light-haired man just behind Mrs. Felmere."

And Felix, looking, found "the light-haired man" with his eyes fixed on him. Look for look they gave each other; then Philip spoke to Helen, and she, raising her eyes, met the one face in the world she cared for. After so long a time, after such hungry longings, after such vain struggles, they met at last.

And Philip, watching, saw in that instant a look come over his wife's face he had never seen before; so gentle, so longing, so bitterly sad. What did it mean? Never had that beautiful face so softened, never had those shining, liquid eyes so yearned for him.

But he need not have feared. That one look was all; then Felix turned away and went out into the cold darkness of the street, and into his narrow life that seemed so empty turned away, for he felt he was not strong enough to stand and fight.

And as Helen saw him turn away and knew that he had gone, a desert emptiness and silence seemed to reign throughout the rooms—an emptiness and blackness of darkness.

"Who was it?" Philip asked in her ear.

She started from her thoughts. "Felix Gordon," she answered, with an unconscious lingering on the syllables of his name.

"Do you know him?" Philip went on.

"I did know him."

"When?"

"Five years ago."

"Where?"

"At Felmere; he spent the summer there."

"After I was there?"

"Yes."

Then Philip stopped. She had answered his questions so quietly, so un-evasively, that he was afraid to go on, afraid to go deeper and find out that something more which he felt sure was under all this, and which he could not reach without a point-blank revelation of his suspicions. And should he question further, would she scorch him with one of those surprised, pitying glances she sometimes gave him; or would she answer with her cool, literal honesty, and confirm his fears? Alas, he feared the latter; feared a quiet "Yes" that would make him more than miserable; feared the indifferent "of course" sort of look that would come with it, killing more utterly, if that were possible, all hope of her ever caring for him, this woman who owed him her love!

He watched her as she moved amid the dance, always a prominent figure, always the leader of any company she entered—the admired, the brilliant, the fascinating woman whom he owned, but that was all! As he watched her, he almost felt willing that she should have been the wife of any other man if she would look at him as she had done at Gordon. Ah, he *hated* Gordon!

He leaned against the doorpost revolving many things in his mind, while he followed his wife's every movement. He always did that now, some said from jealousy, some said from love, but no one rightly knew. If Helen would dance with him, he would dance, but not else: he made no engagements save with her, and these he made as diligently as any stranger would have done; and she treated him very much as she did her common acquaintances.

"A queer couple," the world said, and the men called her the "coolest hand on record."

So Philip stood and tortured himself until his turn came to dance with her; then, after no little elbowing, he managed to make his way through the circle of which she was the center, and to catch her attention. "Is not this my dance?" he said, in the same conventional tone that every one else used to her.

And she, looking up with the careless look that is common on such occasions, answered, "Yes, I think it is," and went away with him.

"I would like to know the mystery of that match," said one of the circle she had left as he watched her go off.

"There is no mystery in it," was the reply, "she married him for his money."

"I do not believe that," said a third, "for she had money of her own. More than that, she is too proud and too honest to so deceive any one. I would take that woman's word against all odds."

"Then why did she marry him?" asked the second speaker. "I cannot tell, I am sure, but certainly from some higher motive than money."

And the first speaker, agreeing, said, "I prefer mystery to such a solution; for I have never met a woman who answered so perfectly my ideal as this one. Only one thing she lacks, softness, and if she loved her husband, she would have that."

"You are quite eloquent," said a bystander who had hitherto been a silent listener.

"It is but natural I should be, with such a text." The speaker was a middle-aged man with an honest, earnest face, and evidently meant all he said, and he now stood watching Helen with a sad, kindly, almost fatherly look in his eyes.

"She is magnificent!" said the second speaker, "but I would prefer a little religion in my wife. Women ought to be religious. I cannot trust one who is not, and this woman deals in the most bold unbelief."

"I noticed that she flung you in that last argument," his middle-aged companion observed a little maliciously.

"So she did, and cleverly too, but I would not like a wife who could do that sort of thing." His answer was honest, and a little laugh from the listeners followed it.

"Well," said the middle-aged gentleman, "if she loved me, I would marry her, metaphysics, skepticism, and all, though I have never yearned for a metaphysical wife; for if that woman loved you, she would do it without stint and with the blindest faith."

"I wonder," said the second speaker, "if she has ever had a love-scrape? She does not look it."

"I venture to say she has," answered Helen's middle-aged champion, "for she has the saddest eyes I ever looked into. They go all through me."

And Helen, waltzing with Philip, did at that moment look at him with those same sad eyes, and say, "Yes, Philip, I loved him, but I could not help it."

"And now?" Philip went on, with a white shadow creeping over his face.

"Yes."

That was all honest, quiet, irrevocable, utterly damning to all his hopes, perfect death to all his happiness, small as it had been. He escorted her to a seat, then left her, and she, watching him go, felt in her heart a deep pity for him, and for the mistake he had made—made in spite of her warnings and his own common sense.

"So I have said, and I say it over,
  And can prove it over and over again,
That the four-footed beasts on the red-crowned clover,
  The pied and horned beasts on the plain,
  That lie down, rise up, and repose again,
And do never take care or toil or spin,
  Nor buy, nor build, nor gather in gold,
Though the days go out and the tides come in,
  Are better than we by a thousand fold;
For what is it all, in the words of fire,
But a vexing of soul and a vain desire?'

—Cincinnatus Hiner Miller

CHAPTER V

So Philip, bitterly unhappy, went about his daily tasks. He did not have even the excitement of watching her, for Helen was very honest, almost too honest, he thought; she told her secret too readily, too much as though it were a matter of course that she should not love Philip. No, there was no use in watching her, for whatever she did she would do openly. The misery was that he did not know what she would do; for, since she did not love him, he had no hold over her. He did not know the promise she had made her father; he did not know that she had been trained never to diverge from her word once given; he had not learned that her whole nature tended upward; and he could not comprehend in its fullness the truth of the character he had to deal with. He only knew that, unless she so willed it, there were no laws on earth that could bind her.

Helen, meanwhile, entered into every species of gaiety, longing and hoping to see Felix again, yet all the while dreading to meet him, and glad that he did not come. She had accepted Mrs. Vanzandt's offer, and had furnished for herself a studio in her house, spending there much of her time. It was not long before she became known among a certain artist circle, which found her studio a pleasant resort, a place where they could meet informally and talk on the subject that most pleased them.

Mrs. Felmere watched this growing intimacy with much wrath. Wrath that was not silent. Helen listened politely to all she had to say on the subject, all the while surmising that Mrs. Felmere's chief cause of disapproval lay in the fact that Philip's wife, who had been for many years held back as the best card in her hand, should go to complete Mrs. Vanzandt's victory in making her house and entertainments more than ever popular. It was doubtless very aggravating, but it was, Helen thought, Mrs. Felmere's own fault. The conversations on these matters were frequent and long, and Helen, when escape was out of the question, listened with patient but heedless ears. Finally things came to a crisis, and Mrs. Felmere turned the force of her attack on Philip: it was his duty, she said, to change the state of things, to break up this intimacy with Mrs. Vanzandt; indeed, if necessary, to compel her to a different course. Philip, as his wife had done, listened quietly until she finished; then, with more wisdom than courage, declined to say or do anything in the matter, and strongly advised his mother to let things alone.

Mrs. Felmere shook her head: that was not the way to manage so contumacious a person; strong measures must be taken. Determined not to be baffled, she made her plans to attack them at dinner, where they could neither avoid each other nor escape her. She patiently awaited her opportunity; then, deliberately dismissing the servant, began her lecture.

"Philip, I have for some time watched and warned Helen about her intimacy with Mrs. Vanzandt, but as she pays no heed to my advice, I think it will be better, perhaps, if you will speak to her."

Helen sipped her wine gravely, and Philip, looking diligently into the bottom of his empty glass, said slowly, "What shall I say, mother?"

"Say that you do not approve," she answered sharply.

"Helen already knows that," he went on as he filled his glass.

"If either of you will show me any reason in your objections," Helen said quietly, "I will heed them."

"Any reason!" Mrs. Felmere exclaimed. "Do you forget how often I have told you that Mrs. Vanzandt has been talked about, and that she is not a proper person?"

"And yet," Helen rejoined, "I found her a leader in your circle, a visitor in all the best houses in town, a high member of your own especial church, and, more than all, much admired by Mr. Tolman. How is she improper?"

"She makes herself conspicuous on all occasions," Mrs. Felmere answered angrily, "fills her house with all sorts of unknown people, and is continually doing queer things."

"And still I see no wrong," Helen said.

Mrs Felmere looked indignantly at her silent son. "Will you say nothing?" she asked.

Philip shook his head. "It is useless for me to speak," he said.

"I should be ashamed to acknowledge it," Mrs. Felmere retorted; then turning to Helen, she went on, "For you, Helen, I have no more words. Your sense of propriety seems never to have been cultivated, and if Philip will not use his lawful authority in this matter, why then the world will have to talk. I cannot help it."

"Why should people talk?" Helen asked quietly.

"Because it has not been the custom for women to have studios, and art receptions, and . . ."

"And does custom make right and wrong?" Helen interrupted gravely. "Must I bind my life between two dead unwavering lines in order that I may suit the customs inaugurated by people who are possibly, if not probably, idiots? Why can I not make customs for myself? Why can I not make these little art gatherings a custom? They are sensible and pleasant, and can have no possible harm in them. They clash with no known code of morals; are better than this 'going from house to house to hear and tell some new thing' that is called among us 'visiting'; and are, besides all this, instructive. Indeed, aunt, I can see no reason in your objections."

"Of course," Mrs. Felmere said in an injured tone, "when people utterly disregard everything but their own will and pleasure, they had best be let alone, but I thank God, there are some who sometimes consider the happiness of others!"

"And allow them to enjoy themselves in their own way," Helen rejoined quietly. "And I cannot see, aunt," she continued, "why I need cut my life down to suit the ideas of everybody, making it a long battle and burden in order to conform to opinions for which I do not care. You know, as does all the world as far as the world knows me, that for me there is no afterlife, no reward nor any punishment. The grave ends all. Why, then, fret out my only life against all the little stones of custom and prejudice? "Why not let it flow on as quietly as it may, so that when death comes I shall be as well off as most? You may never have looked at my life and at me from this standpoint; you may never before have taken these things into consideration when you strove to coerce me into your forms and fashions, but now I beg you to think of them, and in judging me remember that, believing in no hereafter, I do not see the profit in wearing out this little span of which I am possessed in practicing self-sacrifice. I ask nothing either of the world or fate, and I fear neither."

Mrs. Felmere listened with widening eyes as the quiet voice went on, so grave, so cold. She had never before realized the girl's position. She had never imagined the depth and scope of her unbelief. She had never known the width of the gulf that separated them. She covered her face with her hands, and, as the soft voice ceased, burst into tears and left the room. Philip sprang up and followed her, and Helen, touched and surprised by these signs of feeling from her aunt, went after them into the parlor, where Philip was striving to comfort her.

"Aunt," Helen said gently, bending over Mrs. Felmere, "if I have said anything to wound you, I am sorry."

Mrs. Felmere started away from her. "Leave me!" she cried, "leave me! You are enough to bring God's curse down on this house. What have I done, what have I done, to be so punished? God forgive me for harboring such a creature!"

Helen stepped back, and, looking at Philip's white face, she said no word, she was too sorry for him.

In her own room, while her maid laid out her jewels and dress for a reception at Mrs. Vanzandt's, she pondered over what had occurred. How strange a God was this, who would curse one for the sin of another. Poor, weak-minded, superstitious people. She felt very pitiful for them. Then a wild glad hope sprang up within her heart that Philip would send her away. Ah, she would ask nothing more than to quietly go back to Felmere and live at peace; she was weary of this eternal contention and enmity, weary of her whole life.

She was at length dressed, and, Philip declining to go, drove off alone. The rooms were crowded with a brilliant assemblage of the very best people; music, flowers, lights, all beautiful. Every one seemed to be enjoying thoroughly all that had been arranged for their pleasure, and Mrs. Vanzandt seemed everywhere at once.

"Ah, my dear," was her greeting to Helen, "you do not know what has been done for you; you do not know that you have been immortalized; and yet the town, which means 'our set,' is ringing with it."

"I do not understand, "Helen said in much bewilderment.

"Of course you do not, but follow me and you will understand." And she led the way into a small side room, where a crowd was collected round a picture artistically lighted up and draped with red velvet curtains. "I found it yesterday at Pittelli's," Mrs. Vanzandt continued, "it had just been unpacked when I entered and saw it; a most mysterious affair. The artist desires his name to be concealed. Of course I ordered it home immediately. Is it not beautiful?"

Helen paused, astonished, for she stood facing herself as "Guinevere."

Guinevere was taunting Lancelot and casting his diamonds into the river. On the beautiful, stately face there was a world of mingled love and pride, woe and passion, and Helen, gazing in silence, knew the hand from which it came, and listened half consciously to the wild surmises spoken round her.

Slowly she turned away, with a dull pain gathering about her heart that Felix could have conceived her such as this willful, weak woman.

"Do you not like it?" Mrs. Vanzandt asked, watching her closely.

"No," Helen answered gravely, and people listening, especially the women, thought her foolish not to enjoy the distinction. But among the crowd there was one man, the middle-aged man who so admired her, who was pleased with her action and words. He surmised a portion of her feelings, but only that portion he expected from her as a high-toned, pure-minded woman. She did not like the character. She did not like the notoriety. He could not guess that the chief bitterness lay in the thought that the only man, the only soul, in fact, for whose respect and love she cared, could have so painted her.

Alas, "and also this fell into dust."

But the world only saw enough of her sadness to put it down to displeasure that she should have been made so conspicuous: her friends were pleased that this should be so; her detractors put it down to affectation.

A thoroughly wicked woman, according to his code, she thought, and if *he* ranged her so low, what need to care for the rest of the world. 'Eat, drink, and be merry, for tomorrow ye die.' Even so. Her life, as far as happiness went, was a failure; why not substitute excitement, and so dull the pain? And she did it.

She quietly put her husband and mother-in-law aside, and took the lead: she threw open the house, and began a series, seemingly

endless, of the most brilliant entertainments. Her toilets were magnificent, and the bills ruinous. A reckless, brilliant, beautiful woman—
where would it end?

The family, meanwhile, stood looking on in amazement. Mrs.
Felmere would have liked nothing better than all this parade and show,
if she had been given the lead; but, that being taken and held by the
daughter, Mrs. Felmere became virtuously indignant, and with the
rest of the feminine Jourdans set up a piteous wail over "poor Philip"
and his "heathen wife."

But the "heathen wife" did not heed them, and "poor Philip,"
miserable and morbid, raised not so much as a finger to stop or rectify
things. So time slipped by, and the days, and the weeks, and the months
swept on to make the unhappy years.

"Nay, but Nature brings thee solace;
for a tender voice will cry.
'Tis a purer life than thine;
a life to drain thy trouble dry."

—"Locksley Hall," Aldred, Lord Tennyson

CHAPTER VI

A ND SO, AMID ALL THE SORROW AND TROUBLE OF THEIR LIVES, a son was born to them—a fair-haired, blue-eyed child, strong and straight of limb, and lusty as a country child might be. And through the fresh May-time, when Helen lay quiet and thoughtful, so happy in this fresh happiness that had come to her with the child that lay on her arm, life seemed to have a new meaning, and for Philip there grew up within her a gentler feeling. Poor Philip, his life had told on him.

But with Mrs. Felmere the horror of Helen's unbelief, and the almost hatred she felt against her for her beauty and success, and rebellion against control, grew daily. It was a bitterness to her that her son seemed to be again learning to care for his wife, and in a more hopeful way; it must not be. It was a sin to live with this woman and allow her to rear his children, a deadly sin, and one that she could not stand by and see committed. She kept herself aloof from Helen and the child, ever brooding over the failure of her schemes and hopes, and making new plans for the future. She determined, for one thing, that Helen and the child should go away for the summer, and that she should stay in town with Philip. This would give her full opportunity to strengthen and regain her old influence over her son; afterward she could mold things to her will.

So, as she had determined, Helen spent that summer on the seashore, in a quiet cottage far out from the gayer portion of the watering place, and down near the beach. She was glad to go; glad to leave behind her the fret and turmoil of her city life; glad to be where she could sit and watch the great waves rolling in and dashing high against the cliffs to fall back in snowy foam. She was glad once more to greet the deep sad voice that had sounded round old Felmere through all the lonely sunny days and long still nights of her young life. The deep sad voice that, singing to her through all her childhood, had made life seem a rhythmical mystery.

Sitting near the window in the dusky summer evenings, listening to the sweet old song of her early days, and feeling the soft breath of her little one come and go as he slept in her arms, she thought often and regretfully of her own mother. Now that she realized what a mother's love was, there came a softer feeling in her heart for her. Suppose some harm or danger should threaten this child, imaginary or not, would she not fly to the other end of the world to save it? What were Philip, or laws, or oaths of any kind to her in such a case? And she acknowledged the truth of Felix's words when he represented to her the misery of having to leave one child to save the other. Yes, she felt the most intense pity for her mother, often wondering where she was, and if her son for whom she had endured so much had proved a comfort and a joy to her. Poor, sad, superstitious lady, suffering intensely, and for what?

Helen did not go out much, although Arthur, who was staying in the town, came out every morning to put himself at her disposal. Sometimes she went to a reception or a lunch, but without much zest; for she always had her mind divided between the light nothings of small-talk and the secret fear that during her absence the nurse would give the baby cold tea, or commit some other heinous crime. Nevertheless she was much sought out, and her little lawn was made the scene of many a charming reunion, such as luncheon or high tea, croquet, or perhaps a regular game of romps; for her cottage could be considered in the country, and there was surely no harm in a country frolic.

But, outside of all this, this long bright summer was very delightful to Helen. For here her little child was so entirely her own, growing and thriving under her care and love in a way that was astonishing, learning to know her and to stretch its little arms to reach her, and sleeping close to her heart. This child and life had become synonymous terms to her, and in the flush and delight of her joy, she wrote old Jane a letter, in which she opened her heart and revealed herself as she had never done before in all her life, pouring out her feelings to old, ignorant Jane, knowing that she would be understood without being doubted or scoffed at.

"Dear Jane," she began, "I write this to tell you that I have a little baby. Think of that, Jane, my own little baby, to love and to keep all my life! It is a little boy, strong and healthy and beautiful, and I shall name him 'Hector' from my dear father. I have not written to you before, dear Jane, because I have not been very happy, and did not see the use in worrying you with troubles you could not help. I do not like the world nearly so well as old Felmere, and I should be very glad if they would let me come home to you, and show you my child. These people do not understand me, nor love me as my father did, and you. They scorn me because I do not believe as they do, and I scorn them in return. Oh, dear Jane, I would give anything to come home again! I could be very happy with you and Peter to take care of me, and my child to love and live for. But I am better off than I have been; for with this child my life, even here, is bearable. Indeed, I do not see how I managed to live so long without anything of my *very own* to love, and now my life would not be endurable without it. His little hands are so soft, and his little feet are like rose leaves—rose leaves with little toes and toe nails, so tiny and so perfect. I love them so, I cannot bear to think of them growing into great mannish feet, and having, perhaps, to walk through many sorrows and trials before they reach their rest.

"Ah, Jane, I do not see how you can believe as you do, and be thankful, as you say you are, for this life! I think it is a dreadful, hard thing, and I could not love a God who let me suffer so much. You have never tried the world, and so you do not know, but I tell you it is a dreadful thing! These people who call themselves Christians are such shameless hypocrites, and so hard hearted, you would not, I am sure, understand or like them. My father was the best man I have ever known; he never lowered himself by abusing and backbiting even his worst enemy, and these people do it to their dearest friends. More than this, my father was kind and charitable to all, and made me think more of Christianity by his account of it than these people will ever do by their example. Oh, I do despise them!

"But I am away from them all now, down by the beautiful sea, the same sea that comes to you down at Felmere, that I used to listen to, and be afraid of, and love, and it is very beautiful. It seems a piece of home, and I sometimes fancy I hear voices in it when it cries at night, voices that used to talk to me at home. Ah, Jane, I did not know how happy I was until my happiness was gone! I am afraid it is always so. But I have written you a very mournful letter, and I intended it to be very joyful, but my life has been out of tune for so long, that you must excuse me and not grow sad over it. I will try and come back to you some day; then I can rest. Take care of my garden.

"Goodbye. My love to all the people, and to you, and Peter, and the place.

"Helen Felmere"

A childish letter, maybe, and foolish, but it was true, and came from the depths of the heart, wherein, if we are fortunate, there always lies one little drop of that innocent truth and love with which we begin our lives. We may bury it, deny it, hide it, but, unless we willfully murder all our better selves, that little drop is always there, still, clear and sweet. Some there are who have kept their simple childish hearts through all their lives, seeming to draw all love, and trust, and sorrow toward them; seeming to spread a new and wondrous beauty over all the path of life; seeming to see in all about them goodness and worth. Such things are, and we may be thankful for the knowledge!

So Helen's letter went, and old Jane, reading it to Peter as they sat by the kitchen fire, stopped many times to wipe her glasses, while Peter had frequent need to mend the fire. Then they talked it over in their homely fashion, and Jane decided that Father Paul must read it, and help them pray for their dear young mistress who seemed so very sad. And Jane's old heart warmed over the little baby; she longed to see it and to hold it; for once, long ago, she had held children, children of her own, who for years and years had rested in the churchyard; and she and Peter were left without a child to close their eyes.

Her little babies! How long ago it seemed. She was a strong young woman then, and now she was very old. Very old, but she could remember the look and the voice of every one, their little ways, and the touch of their little hands. For, young or old, rich or poor, good or evil, high or low, bond or free, a mother never forgets her children, never forgets their voices or their kisses, and through all her life the clinging touch of their little hands reaches forth to her, the patter of their little feet echoes in her soul, and the lengthening shadows of their little graves fall upon her heart. The mother whose arms have once held a child can always feel its shadow resting there, can always feel the void it left within her life.

"O ye years!
That intervene betwixt that day and this;
Yon all received your hue from that
keen pain and bliss."

—Jean Ingelow

CHAPTER VII

ONE GLORIOUS DAY IN EARLY AUGUST, when the sky was cloudless, and the sea lay darkly blue and softly swelling in the morning sun, Helen, with her child in her arms, stood on the beach watching the lazy waves roll up the shore, leaving little lines of foam and sedge grass, with here and there a tiny glistening shell; watching the complacent sand crabs ambling back and forth with no visible object in their journeyings; watching the gleaming white sails that shone far out on the wide horizon. She was happier than she had been for years, and happier in that she realized it and enjoyed it consciously.

Humming softly to herself the little country song she had learned from Jane, and pausing now and then to look down upon the child, she walked to where the rocks jutted out into a little promontory. The sun was warm, and behind those rocks she would find shade. So, still singing the little ballad, she rounded them.

Alas, facing her stood Felix Gordon. Not three feet of the shining sand lay between them, and her shadow, reaching out beyond her for a little space, was lost in his!

"Mr. Gordon!" The tone was low and almost frightened, and he, paling painfully, held out his hand in greeting. She looked at him a moment, then gathered her little one close in one arm and laid her other hand in his. After so many years, after so many changes, they once more stood face-to-face, hand clasped in hand.

So long he had not seen her save on his canvas and in his memory, that his eyes seemed hungry in their gazing. And her look, so full of the sorrows of her life, wandered sadly from the gray hairs tinging the brown, from the lines across his brow, from his full, dark beard, down to the hand that held hers, then up again to the eyes. She would surely find her young tutor there; she would surely see again that happy, careless look she so well remembered; surely it had not deserted those honest, kindly eyes.

Alas, only a bitter despair shone there; and withdrawing her hand, she turned away. Felix stopped her. This meeting had been decreed by Fate; he had not sought it, and it should not be shunned.

"Will you not," he said slowly, "spare me a few moments out of all your life?"

She turned quickly, looking at him honestly and truthfully as a child might. "It is you," she answered, "who have shunned me; I have wanted to meet you."

"True?" he asked, looking into her eyes as though to read the depths of her heart.

"Yes, it is true; I have wanted to see you." Again she turned away.

Felix stepped in front of her. "You have wished to see me, but now?"

Her eyes met his unflinchingly as she answered, "Now I am not so lonely, for I have in my child a friend," wrapping the child closer in her arms as she spoke, "my little child, who will always love me, and never doubt me."

"Doubt you?" Felix repeated questioningly. "Who has doubted you?"

The blood leaped into her cheeks, and her eyes flashed as she answered, "You painted me as Guinevere!"

Felix looked at her steadfastly as though expecting some further communication; then, slowly, and as from far off, a shadow of surprise gathered on his face, deepening into a look of absolute pain. "If I understand you rightly," he said deliberately, "you sadly misjudge me." Then he went on, with his voice a little shaken by his eagerness of self-defense, "I painted you as Guinevere because you only were beautiful enough and queenly enough to represent her."

"Then I have wronged you," Helen answered, the quick tears springing to her eyes, "wronged both you and myself; for after I saw that picture I thought you had lost all respect for me and faith in me; and if you, knowing me, could so think of me, what right had I to expect any more from the rest of the world? So I let all go. But now I am thankful this is not so, and I beg your pardon." Her eyes and voice were full of tears.

So beautiful she looked, with a faint flush on her face, her crimson lips half parted, and her hair all ruffled by the wind.

Felix stood as if lost to all about him; then his eyes fell on the sleeping child, and he turned away. "It has all been very bitter," he said at last, "and I have been very weak and very wicked, but now the worst is over, and I think I can venture to be your friend. I have loved you, I do love you, and I will always love you," he stopped suddenly, and Helen, waiting, wondered at his strange abruptness. "No," he began slowly, not able to deceive himself, "I cannot altogether say what I hoped to be able to say whenever I should meet you again, but putting this aside, will you be my friend? Will you let me come to see you?"

"Yes," she answered sadly, "if you wish to come, I shall be glad."

In her mind there was no anxiety, no misgiving.

Then he walked home with her through the summer sunshine, talking little, feeling he knew not how, held quiet under the excitement of the hour. At the garden gate he left her, and she for the moment, forgetting where or who she was, stood and watched him as he walked away.

Felix never once looked back, nor allowed himself to think of or to weigh the consequences of the course he had entered on. He stood on the shore and looked out across the shining sea. The summer wind whispered about him, the waves left their lines of creamy foam at his feet, and the sea birds flew lazily back and forth. He noted it all in an idle, dreamy way that seemed to make no impression on him; yet in the after time he could recall it all, and his every thought as he stood wrapped in a dizzy maze of past and present.

He had not arranged the meeting. He had not sought Helen. He did not even know she was on the island; all was accidental, and he would not turn away. All these long years he had hungered for the sound of her voice and the touch of her hand; all these years other women had been as nothing in his eyes; all these years he had pondered over her sweeping skepticism and the causes of it, had studied her side of the question and his own, and wavered. The strain upon his soul no man could know; it had whitened his hair, and taken the strength and purpose out of his life. And with this wavering, the knowledge of himself came to him with overwhelming suddenness, causing him to distrust and to despise himself. So the youth in him died, and in its place stood a gloomy, embittered man.

And at his home those three devoted women watched the change with sorrowful wonder. What had come to their boy, their Felix, the life, the joy, the one bright thing in their world? And he could not explain; he could not tell them of his misgivings that to them would be too dreadful. So he became more and more silent and sad, and they learned to love their changed idol with a new and different love, a love with more of care and pity in it, with more of unobtrusive action and less of words.

Now, after all these years and changes, he stood in the yellow August sunshine, deciding without judging, determining without weighing, without argument, on what might prove the most important step in his life. Yes, he would stay. He must see and know Helen in her full womanhood. Her happiness was dear to him, ay, dearer than his own; he would only stay and enjoy for a little while the sunshine of her glorious beauty. His life had been too barren, and now that he had once more touched her hand and heard her voice, he could not leave her. He could die for her, but he could not go.

"O for comfort, the waste of a long doubt and trouble!
On that sultry August eve trouble had made me meek;
I was tired of my sorrow; O so faint, for it was double
In the weight of its oppression, that I could not speak!"

— "Requiescat in Pace!" Jean Ingelow

CHAPTER VIII

THE NEXT DAY FELIX CALLED AT THE COTTAGE, and found a croquet party assembled on the lawn. He was kindly received, introduced to those he did not know, given a mallet, and set to work. He played in an unenthusiastic, commonplace way, and talked to the young ladies, who were thrown into quite a flutter by his attentions, in the same way. The game seemed longer to him than it really was, and it seemed strange for him to be idling in this careless manner through all the turmoil and excitement that surged like a strong wild undercurrent through his heart and brain. He found himself watching Helen furtively and earnestly, constantly striving to catch the tones of her voice, all the time longing for the people to be gone.

After a while the game was over; then came the lunch, and after that the beginnings of farewells. He watched the company lingering over the last moments with ill-concealed impatience. He drew a deep sigh of relief as he helped the last party into their carriage, and, lifting his hat to their last bow, turned and followed Helen into the house.

She made her way among the flowerbeds to a low French window that, being open, gave a full view of the dainty drawing room. She took her seat inside, but Felix, with her permission, preferred to sit on the windowsill with his feet down among the flowers.

Over the lawn and flowerbeds, over the hedges and clover fields, down to the sea, a fair sunshiny view stretched before them shadowless save for the passing summer clouds. When the sun got lower, the stiffly trimmed cedars and poplars would cast long still shadows across the velvety grass, and so lie there until the darkness destroyed them.

"A fair sweet picture," Helen mused, "with a coloring and an atmospheric softness about it that could never be put on canvas, and a peacefulness that should fall like a healing balm on the most troubled heart." So she thought, while her quiet heart beat calmly; and Felix, at her feet, almost touching her, was fighting manfully with himself, striving to begin temperately his conversation. What should he say to her? Why had he sought this interview? How could he talk of commonplace things?

The wind, brushing a portion of Helen's dress against him, startled him; he looked up quickly, and found his companion regarding him with a steadfast sadness. Then, without a tremor in her voice or a sign of excitement, she said meditatively, "This reminds me, Mr. Gordon, of the evening we sat in the old churchyard at Felmere, when I told you I was as an unbeliever. Do you remember?"

Felix looked up in surprise. How quietly she went back into the very heart of the old days, bringing up the associations he had of all others expected her to avoid. Was it intentional, he wondered? Well, it did not much matter; since she had led up to them, he could but follow. And, he not answering her question, Helen went on in the same musing tone, "I cannot think why it should remind me of Felmere, but it does. It must be the fresh wind, or the white clouds, for there is nothing else here that could bring it up, not even you."

Then she bent her look out toward the sea, and Felix, looking questioningly at the averted face, answered slowly, "In some things I know I am changed, and woefully so. How is it with you?"

There was much in his voice, but she did not seem to hear it, or if she heard she did not heed it, but answered without so much as turning her eyes from the sea, "Yes, I am also changed, but whether for better or worse I have not of late stopped to ask, and when I look back at that poor, high-strung, unhappy girl that you knew, I could almost cry for her. She thought she had lived her life, and her life had not begun; she thought she had conquered herself, and she did not yet know herself. Alas, it was down among the blackest of all black days that she learned all this, and without a human soul to tell it to."

There was a little pause while Felix was trying to see if there was any deeper meaning hidden in her answer. At last, not able to decide, he said slowly, "If I had known that you had no friends," then he paused, forced to do so by the look almost of curiosity that Helen bent on him, a look as though she was trying to fathom his deepest thoughts, and to find if there was a special motive for his words.

She looked at him steadily for a moment, and, he not continuing his speech, she again turned her eyes to the view spread before her, and answered, "No one could have helped me. There are depths in every heart and life that must sooner or later be sounded; depths to which you must descend alone, and from which no love or sympathy that I have found can help you. You Christians cry to your God. I have no God!"

All the sorrow he had felt for her in her early youth came back to him now, as once again the loneliness of her life was spread before him—this soul-desolation that, absorbing the bitterest drop from every sorrow, stands alone and quiet, held still in a cold despair. Her words had quieted him, and he said, "And you are still an unbeliever?"

"Yes."

"And your unbelief has satisfied you?"

"As well, I think, as your Christianity has satisfied you," she answered, looking sadly down on his face, that had gathered in these years an expression of settled weariness.

He looked up quickly and met her look full of sympathy bent on him; but it was only sympathy, and he turned away. "I have studied both sides," he said at last.

"But you still believe?" Helen asked almost anxiously.

He stooped down among the flowers, and picked a fresh, fair daisy. He laid the flower on his palm. It was so frail and tiny, and yet its life and being was as deep a mystery as those greater questions he could not solve. He put the flower on Helen's knee. "It is all a mystery," he said, "as great a mystery as the life of that little flower."

"And you have learned to doubt? "Helen asked sadly, and in her turn laid the flower on her hand.

"No," he said. "I have never been a skeptic; I only wavered somewhat at times."

"And now?" Helen was watching him very closely.

"I strive to believe without questioning, and I will, until such time as God in his mercy shall make it clear to me."

A pain shot through Helen's heart. Had she done this? Had she clouded the beautiful faith her girlhood had known and loved in this man? Then she asked, "Was it my fault?"

Felix looked up quickly. "Your fault! What?"

"Your unbelief."

He looked at her a moment in surprise, then said, "It seems so strange to me that you do not know how weak I am; that you do not know where the temptation to doubt came into my life, the temptation to strive to stand where you stood. To look on the oath you had taken as an empty form to put away all law of obligation, and, casting consequences to the winds, go back and plead with you. But I could not," he went on more slowly, laying his hand on hers and crushing the little daisy under his hot palm, "I could not when I remembered how you had turned away, when I remembered how high and pure you seemed to me I could not even try to drag you down! No, it was not your fault you saved me. And now . . ."

Helen clasped her other hand over his. "Go back to your faith and your God," she almost whispered. "I have no peace to give you. I would do anything to help you to take the doubt and longing out of your life, or in any way to make you happier."

"You can." Then he paused and looked away across the peaceful land and sea. He almost crushed the hand he held. Was she not as high and pure as in the past? He rose abruptly. "Goodbye." He wrung her hand. "I will come again," he said, and turned away with the bitter knowledge surging in his heart that, even after all he had suffered through his doubts, and through the bitter discovery of his own weakness, he would now be willing to live in doubt for ever, and irrevocably confirm his weakness, if in payment he could claim this woman. It was a sickening revelation of himself, and he bowed his head in hopeless humility!

"Let us alone. What pleasure can we have
To war with evil? Is there any peace
In ever climbing up the climbing wave?
All things have rest, and ripen toward the grave
In silence; ripen, fall and cease:
Give us long rest or death, dark death, or dreamful ease."

— "The Lotos-Eaters," Alfred, Lord Tennyson

CHAPTER IX

THERE WAS A BALL IN TOWN THE NEXT NIGHT, and as the hostess was a special friend of Mrs. Felmere's, and had already complained that young Mrs. Felmere kept up none of the family friendships, Arthur had insisted on Helen's going, and Helen, seeing the kind motive that underlay his persuasion, consented that he should come for her. She was ready when he arrived, and called him in to see the baby.

"He is so beautiful, Arthur, you must come and take one look at him." So Arthur, obeying her as men usually did, stood looking at her as she leaned over the sleeping child.

How much more beautiful love and happiness make her, he thought, and if she had only married the man she loved, for he had long ago decided in his own mind that she had loved some one once whom, or when, or where, or what the circumstances were, he could not surmise; but of the one fact he was quite certain, she had loved someone once.

"Is he not lovely?" Helen said, looking up at him.

Arthur immediately bent on the child that dispassionate gaze that men are in the habit of bestowing on the young of their land. "I do not like him," he answered gravely.

"Arthur!"

Arthur shook his head. "He always recalls to me the fact, the miserable fact, that I am a great-uncle; he makes me feel too old."

Helen laughed; she was really relieved that he did not dislike her child. "You are too ridiculous," she said, and drawing her cloak up over her shoulders, she led the way to the carriage.

"You are looking happier and handsomer tonight than I have ever seen you," Arthur said as they entered the ballroom. "What has happened?"

"I do not know, unless it is that yesterday I met my old friend Mr. Gordon," she answered frankly.

"Gordon the artist?" In much surprise.

"Yes."

"Why, where on earth did you meet him?"

Here, they were interrupted by their hostess, who came up leaning on Mr. Gordon's arm. "Mrs. Felmere, I brought Mr. Gordon to be introduced," she said, "but he tells me he has had that pleasure."

Helen, shaking hands with Felix, answered, "Yes, we met each other a great many years ago. Before you were famous," she went on.

"Before I had ever sold a picture," he answered.

"Then, of course, you have much to talk over," Mrs. Beaumont said, smiling and arching her eyebrows in knowing surprise, "and I can leave you feeling sure that at least three of my guests are enjoying themselves."

And, with an especial smile and bow to Arthur, she joined another group.

"Will you let me look at your card?" Felix asked, after greeting Arthur.

She gave it to him, and while he was busy writing down his name, she turned to Arthur. "I never answered your last question," she said, "what was it?"

Arthur looked up, smiling pleasantly. "You answered it to Mrs. Beaumont. I only asked where you had known Mr. Gordon."

"Ah, I did not understand. Why, I knew him long ago at Felmere," she answered, "he taught me all I know of drawing or painting."

"Not quite all," Felix amended, "you had advanced exceedingly well, and you had been grounded thoroughly."

Then others joining the group, Gordon moved away, and Arthur, following him with his eyes, thought, "Gordon is the man!"

And all the evening he watched them as they danced together, and pitied them from the depths of his heart.

"I did not know you danced and went to parties," Helen said.

"I am very fond of dancing," Felix answered. "Did you not see me at Mrs. Tilmont's ball?"

Helen looked away. "Yes, I saw you." Then, after a little pause, "Why did you not speak to me?"

They had stopped dancing now, and stood out on a terrace looking over the moonlit sea. Felix looked down into the honest, questioning eyes, and manfully told the truth, "I was afraid."

"Afraid?"

"Yes, of myself."

Helen stood silent, then the thought that had come to her the evening before, and that she had put away as unworthy of her old ideal, was true? Was he meeting her now against his better judgment? She looked at him gravely. "And now?" she asked.

"Now?" Felix turned away as he repeated the word, for what could he answer? "Now—now I have given up. I cannot go away and leave the only friend I care for in all the world I am too weak."

"Hush!" Helen almost whispered. "I do not want to think you weak. I do not want to lose faith in you. I should have to despise you."

"I despise myself more than you can ever do," Felix answered, "and yet I have given up. Hereafter, I must float wherever the tides drift me. I am too tired to struggle any more."

"And you will do wrong, and say you drifted into it?" she asked, with a tone of scorn creeping into her voice. "Would it not be braver to say, 'It is wrong, but I will do it'?" She paused a moment, then added, "Whatever you are going to do, for the sake of my old trust in you, do it honestly and bravely!"

Ah, how her words and tone stung. This woman who could not pity, but only despise weakness. And Felix answered with deliberate quiet, "Suppose I am neither honest nor brave."

"Then I am sorry," she said bitterly, "and my last delusion as to humanity is swept away." And she turned toward the house.

Felix stepped in front of her. "Wait!" he said quickly. "I cannot lose your friendship in this way, just as I have laid hold on it again."

She paused, and they stood looking at each other in silence—he angry, she bitterly disappointed.

At last, she spoke, "Yesterday afternoon you said you were prevented from pleading with me because in your eyes I was high and pure, because I turned away. Did you ever, on the other hand, go over in your own mind the probable course; of reasoning, and the probable motives, that guided me through that great temptation of my life?"

Felix looked surprised. "Your devotion and promise to your father," he answered readily.

"Yes, that, but did you surmise nothing else?"

He shook his head.

She waited a moment, then went on in a lower tone. "The strongest weapon against my love for you," she said, "was my love for you. I could not bear to let you see me break my word and be untrue; I could not bear to see my ideal step down and succumb to a weakness. I preferred giving you up and emptying my life, to keeping you with the faintest taint on your strength and honor. And now?"

"And now you have lived to find out what you did not want to see," he answered, looking straight into her true, pure eyes, "have lived to know that I was saved through your strength; have lived to see your 'last delusion as to humanity' swept away by me!"

"Have I?" she asked, laying her hand on his arm, "have I lived to see this? Will you let this thing be?"

He trembled under her touch, and his voice sank low as he asked, "Must I go away again?"

"You know the right here better than I can tell you," she answered sadly, "and you must do it."

"I cannot."

"You can, and you must; for the sake of my old faith in you, you must!" Her voice was low and tense, and there was a ring of despair in it that was pitiful. She clung so desperately to the love and belief of her life; she so longed to prove him what she had thought he was, and if he failed her now? Ah, she would rather a thousand times see him dead.

Felix did not answer, and she went on, "You will do right?" She hesitated a moment, then added a saving clause, "But whatever you do, I will trust, and not judge you," and, passing him swiftly, entered the ballroom.

Ah, what a bond her last words had laid on him. And he wondered if she had realized it. "Whatever he did, she would trust, and not judge him," and he knew her well enough to know that whatever she said, she would do.

He paced up and down, thinking. She had left him a loophole; he might stay, and she would trust, and not judge him. He paused. She had also left herself a way of escape; he might stay, and she could not to herself blame him. In short, she would accept his staying as a pledge that he was acting according to his better judgment, and in his own eyes doing no wrong.

Up and down he walked thinking, arguing, fighting, and with no result. He would far rather have had her do as most women would have done, and denounced, commanded, or pleaded with him. Anything would have been better than this calm binding him, this quiet compelling him to do right, or to deceive her.

Was there ever another woman so wise, he wondered? Suppose he should go to her and say he knew he was wrong, but had decided to stay; what would she say? Alas, he knew the answer too well—a look of pitying contempt and a quiet turning away as from a worthless thing. No, if he stayed, it must be done quietly as though he thought he was right; that was the only way.

Should he stay?

And Helen, in the silence of her cool, dim-lighted chamber, did that night ponder many things. The world was such a pitiful jumble, and no one was strong or weak in the right place. The strength she had so much admired in her father, the strength that had kept him still when her mother fled, was afterward regretted. And herself, if she had only been strong enough to resist her father's wishes in regard to Philip, or weak enough now to respect Philip.

It was all very strange, she thought, and, looking out over the shining sea, she longed so bitterly for her father and Felmere, longed for the love and the home she would never have again. She had suffered so much that the years that had passed since her father's death stretched almost into a lifetime; and it seemed her sufferings were not over. For this child, who was almost her life, was but another hostage to sorrow, an entering wedge that would separate her forever from any chance of happiness; for how could she rear him acceptably to Philip and his family? How could she give him up to be a Christian? It was not often she let herself dwell on, or even contemplate, this subject, but sometimes it would come up, and so darken all her present joy. And she was powerless save to wait and watch.

"'We meet at one gate
When all's over. The ways they are many and wide,
And seldom are two ways the same. Side by side
May we stand at the same little door when all's done!
The ways they are many, the end it is one.'"

—"Lucile," Meredith Owen

Chapter X

IT HAD BEEN A LOWERING DAY, with a fitful wind blowing that put a cap on every tossing wave. Just now the sun was setting, and a long stream of glory, breaking from between the clouds, shot across the hills and fields down to the sullen waves. What a glow of color came over land and sea, rounding the ragged outlines of the crags and cliffs, and transmuting as it were the long curve of the beach into a band of gold. Far out on the gray waste of waters a solitary boat-sail caught the wandering beam, and the sea birds, flying landward, were turned to silver as they came.

"A wild, beautiful picture," Helen thought as she sat in the low window, with her feet down among the flowers; so beautiful, it made her sad. Ah, this sadness. Did it live in her, or in all things beautiful?

A step on the gravel disturbed her musings, and looking up she saw Felix Gordon approaching. He took off his hat as he neared her, but did not offer to shake hands, nor would he take the seat she offered him beside her, but leaned instead against the window frame just opposite her. It was a strange meeting and greeting, she thought; but the silence that followed was stranger still. At last he raised his eyes from the tender little daisies among which he stood, and, looking at her, said, "I have come to say goodbye, Mrs. Felmere."

There was a little pause before the last two words, as though he found them difficult to say, and to Helen the name sounded strangely from his lips. "When do you go?" she asked slowly.

"Tonight."

She looked up with a glad light shining in her eyes, and an expression of positive happiness sending a glow over her face.

"Are you so glad then?" Felix asked a little bitterly.

"I am," and the eyes that met his seemed cleared of some trouble. "I am glad because you prove yourself true and strong," she said, and again there was a silence between them, she looking out across the sunset-tinted sea, he looking down on her and drinking in the exceeding beauty of the sad face.

Would he ever see it again? Could he ever see enough of it? "Goodbye," he said abruptly, and his voice struck hard and sharp on the air.

Helen started, then rose and gave him her hand, saying nothing.

"I am going," he said hurriedly. "I could stay longer, but to what purpose? What would these few moments of nearness be to the eternity of separation that lies before me? Goodbye. God bless you!"

He wrung her hand, and, turning away, ground the frail, pink-lipped flowers under his heel. He heard a sigh as sharp and tense as though some heartstring strained too tightly had given way. He turned, and saw the face that to him was all the world look white and suffering, with all the glow of joy and thankfulness faded away.

One swift step brought him back to her side. He laid his hand on her shoulder, and his voice trembled as he spoke. "God will bless you," he said, "you will be happy somewhere. Twice you have saved me in my hour of weakness; twice you have turned me back into the right way, and God will reward you. Remember, I have you, and you only, to thank that I am not a miserable and utter wreck." He paused, his voice lowered and his grasp on her shoulder grew heavier. "If by God's mercy I am saved, may I not hope to meet you in eternity?"

She trembled under his hand, and his words seemed to ring about her like a thousand bells. He was miserable, but he had a hope. She alone stood desolate. How the weight of her misery seemed to crush her down, how it seemed to double itself when she realized how utterly alone she stood. Solitary, outside the pale of all the Christian world. But one had stood there, an old, deserted, white-haired man had stood there, and dared all risks. Her place was at his side.

She stepped from under the hand that lay on her shoulder, and, looking up with a light of devotion shining in her eyes, and a pale, brave face, she answered, "If I deserted my father, remorse would torment me even in the Christian's paradise. This life is all I have or hope for; with it I must be content."

One moment they stood facing each other, realizing intensely the awful distance that possibly lay between them. And while they looked, the crimson glory of the sunset faded, and the world was left to the gray dusk and sobbing wind.

"I will pray for you day and night," he said at last, "that God will save you."

Then, without another word or touch, he left her and strode away through the gloaming.

Gone!

She stood among the gathering shadows and listened until the last echo of his footsteps died away: firm, steady, unfaltering, it faded from her hearing and from her life. It was right, and she had wished it so; but now the loneliness of it came home to her so heavily, and she only now realized how much she would miss him, how much of a link he had been between her and her old home. He had known her father, and had lived with them in their daily life; he was something to make her conscious that those former days were not a dream, and when he was near her she had missed the empty longing and homesickness of her life. But it was well: he had shown his strength and gone away, and she could still remember him with pleasure and trust. This was a happiness to her, and she was glad for it.

After this she drew within herself more than before; lived within her little circle of home, her child, and her art; painted, as in her youth, sad little pictures of the scenes about her stretches of gray sea under a somber sky, ragged headlands with the wild waves surging about them, desolate marshes with solitary birds hovering over them, and dreary fragments of wrecks with dead bodies lashed to them. Here and there among them would nestle a little rosy sketch of her child, or some view of Felmere glorified with a beauty born of love and memory.

So the summer faded into autumn, and the sharp September winds dispersed the gay crowds that filled the hotels and cottages, and left the little seaport town at rest in its own quiet, old-fashioned beauty. And for this Helen was glad. She preferred seeing the long rows of villas on the avenue shut up and desolate; she liked its old-time crooked streets best when they were empty of gay carriages and finely dressed visitors; for in her mind the frivolous crowds that gathered there did not suit the sadness of the winds and the waves.

The place to her was sad with an infinite grandeur that seemed to raise her above and beyond the littlenesses of life; that seemed to still the ever-reaching longing within her that, in her searchings for a name, she called her soul.

Was that her soul? This thing that seemed ever striving to express itself; wailing and sobbing for lack of better speech, tingeing all the beautiful with a shade of misery, and all the high and good with a mist of tears! Was that her soul? That "something" these Christians believed would be saved or damned; that "something," now trammeled with "fleshy bonds," that in its freedom would soar to the Infinite, to enjoy or suffer infinitely!

Was this "divine despair" within her a portion of the all-pervading unknowable? This was something she could neither understand nor quiet; that made the rising storms, the watching the waves lash themselves into a fury, howling and crying as though they were human the hearing the winds wail, and seeing the low clouds hurrying by torn and rifted, the standing alone, far out, and feeling the wild spray about her a fascination to her. And so living, she gathered to herself a patience born of beauty and the nothingness of all; a patience born of pity for her own misshapen lot; a patience and a sadness that pervaded all her afterlife.

At last the day came when Philip wrote requesting her return, the seaside being now, he thought, much too bleak for the child. No hint of wishing to see her, no anxiety on her account, only the tersely given opinion as to the place being no longer beneficial to the child, and the cold request that for this reason she would bring him home.

What did it mean, she wondered? Was his mother influencing him to this extent, and why? She could not answer the question, but the letter made her more than ever realize how sorry she was to leave her little home, where she had found somewhat of happiness, and go back to the false conventionalities of the world, and the hypocrisies of her husband's family, but of course she must go, and the orders for the move were given.

In the next two days she wandered slowly and regretfully from one to the other of her favorite haunts to say a last goodbye. She hoped she would see them again some day, for among them she had been almost happy.

Happy! Alas, had she ever been happy? Was there such a thing as happiness for her? Felix had said she would be happy somewhere. Poor fellow, how he had loved her, and how pitiful his blessing had sounded in her ears; and his faith that she would be rewarded for her course and be happy "somewhere" was so simple and so beautiful. He could not let himself believe that all her life would be of one somber hue; some joy must touch her sooner or later. Ah, he had loved her truly; and for his sake, as well as her own, she hoped it might be, though she could not think it would.

So she reflected, standing alone and far out on a jutting crag, looking a last farewell on her favorite view. The day had darkened before a coming storm; the clouds scudded low in hurrying crowds; the fitful wind, moaning now as sadly as a broken heart, now rising with a sudden dash into a high wild shriek, lashed the sullen waves to a fury, boiling and hurling them to and fro until they howled like human souls in hell's deep agony until it seemed as if, in impotent despair, they strove with thin foam-hands to clutch and hold the mighty cliffs. Already the storm wailed sad among the scanty seaside trees, and far and near the screaming birds flew inland from the rising wind.

With tight-clasped hands, and set white face, and eyes brimful of all heart-breaking sorrow, Helen stood a picture of despair, framed in the wan storm light. The wildness of the storm entered into her; the waves in their anguish seemed to call to her; the sorrows of her life seemed too much for her. Why not end it there? Why drag on a weary existence that she loathed? Why go back to the torments and the trials of her life? Why not now solve the mystery of death, the truth or falsehood of eternity? A swift plunge, a little struggle with the mighty waters, a last sharp breath, a quiet floating on the wandering waves, a resting on some sea-beaten shore.

Why not?

A hand closed on her arm, and a voice said in her ear. "Come away."

She started, and turning quickly saw beside her a small, ill-dressed man, almost a hunchback. She made as though she would have drawn away, but a strange power in the great brown eyes held her, and looking deep in them she wondered what it was.

"Yesterday I saw you with your child," he said, "you must go back to it now."

A rush of love and memory for her little one throbbed through her: how could she have forgotten him!

"Thank you," she said, as though in a dream, and turning left the sad-faced man alone.

PART THIRD

"Full desertness
In souls as countries, lieth silent-bare
Under the blanching, vertical eyeglare
Of the absolute heavens."

— "The Patience of Hope," Dora Greenwell

> "'But woe is me! I think there is no sun;
> My sun is sunken, and the night grows dark:
> None care for me.'"
>
> —"Sunday Reads," Jean Ingelow

CHAPTER I

MRS. FELMERE HAD PROPHESIED A TWO WEEKS' DELAY before Helen would so much as answer Philip's letter, so that Helen's appearance in the sitting room the fifth evening after the letter had been sent gave them quite a shock. She had opened the door quietly, and stood watching for a moment the two silent occupants of the room: Philip in a low-hung reading chair, his book turned down on his knee, his arms crossed, and his head bent until his chin rested on his breast; Mrs. Felmere under the full glare of the lamp, knitting, and casting from time to time furtive glances at her son. The fire in the grate looked dull and red, the place and people somber, and as she came forward, Helen could not help sighing deeply.

Mrs. Felmere dropped her knitting, and Philip, starting up with a hurried exclamation, let his book fall to the floor. "What is the matter? How have you come so soon?"

"You wrote for me," Helen answered, pausing in her approach with a look of surprise on her face, "and I came; did you not expect me to do so?"

"Oh yes; yes, of course," Philip said quickly; then, recollecting that he had not in any way greeted his wife, he stepped forward, seeming much embarrassed, and kissed her.

Then Mrs. Felmere also came and kissed her, and Helen sat down. Then the child received more attention, but being asleep was sent to bed, and the three were left together. "We did not expect you so soon," Mrs. Felmere began, "or Philip would certainly have met you."

"Of course he would," Helen answered, and wondered why Philip could not say that for himself.

"You should have telegraphed," Philip said.

"I never thought of it," Helen answered. "In your letter you said, 'Come as soon as possible,' and did you not know that would be to-day?"

Her voice was very quiet, but all the while the thought coming up to her that this was *home* gave her a feeling almost of desperation. Her temporary servants whom she had just left had always given her a warmer welcome after a day's absence, and she wondered what had come over Philip, at the same time casting about for some polite excuse that would allow her to retire to her own room.

Mrs. Felmere scanned her closely. "You are not looking very well," she said at last.

"I am only a little tired," Helen answered. Then Philip looked at her more narrowly, but he said nothing.

"The family, are they all well?" Helen asked after a few moments.

"Yes," Mrs. Felmere answered, "all except my sister Esther; she is far from well. Amelia is engaged to Mr. Tolman."

Helen looked up quickly. "Indeed! I had not heard that." Then more slowly, "I hope they will be very happy," and she wondered if Amelia loved him.

"She ought to be," Mrs. Felmere answered, "he is everything that any woman could desire or deserve, and even if Amelia does not all at once love him, she is such a good Christian that love will soon come through her submission and desire to please him. But I believe she loves him now."

Philip crossed and uncrossed his legs nervously. Were they going to quarrel already?

And Helen, looking into the fire, answered simply, "I sincerely hope she does, else she will be very unhappy."

"But I say if she does not," Mrs. Felmere persisted, "she will make it her pleasure to learn to do it."

"Perhaps," Helen answered, "but it is a desperate risk." Then she changed the subject by asking if Miss Esther was really very sick.

"Very," Mrs. Felmere answered emphatically, then closed her lips as though that subject were a dead letter between Helen and herself.

But Philip, who felt really very grateful to Helen for not quarreling over Amelia when she had been offered such a good opportunity, and being anxious to help in the diversion from that subject, said boldly, "She does not look very ill."

"I do not know what you can be thinking of," his mother said quickly and sharply, "I have never seen any one break as she has done. It is true she has brightened up a little since Amelia's engagement, for she says it is such a happiness to her to see those she loves uniting themselves with pure good Christians, and so insuring both their temporal and eternal happiness." Then Mrs. Felmere sighed deeply, and a look of resignation came over her face.

If Helen had not felt the truth that was in these words, the truth she felt too deeply every moment as exemplified in her own ill-assorted marriage, she might have smiled at the spite in them. As it was, she answered quietly, without even the desire to retort, "Aunt Esther has always admired Mr. Tolman."

Her listeners were surprised, and Mrs. Felmere, being made rather impatient by the peacefulness of her words, said quickly, "Of course she has, and every one who has any appreciation of goodness and worth admires Mr. Tolman; indeed, he is universally esteemed."

Helen halfway smiled as she answered, "He seems to be very popular."

Philip was much relieved, and Mrs. Felmere was really provoked that Helen should so baffle her. What did this extraordinary patience on her part mean? Was it a plan to win Philip back to herself? A little pang of jealousy shot through Mrs. Felmere's heart, for she had come to feel that she ought to stand first with him; and now she felt it more than ever before in her life. With the growth of this feeling her antipathy to Philip's wife had rapidly increased. It was the force of this feeling which made her forget, in her search of motives for her daughter-in-law's behavior, that Helen had not yet been made aware of the breach which she had been preparing between her husband and herself.

"Had you a pleasant journey?" Philip asked, feeling awkward in the pause that followed Helen's last remark.

"Not very," was the answer, and there was a hopeless sound in the voice, as though the speaker was asking herself would anything ever be pleasant again?

Mrs. Felmere caught something of the tone, and looked up quickly. "Perhaps you were not anxious to make the journey," she said deliberately.

"You cannot be surprised that I was not anxious to come back," Helen answered candidly, wondering the while if her aunt wished to quarrel. "The quiet was delightful to me, I like the country so much better than town."

Philip straightened up in his chair. "It was only on the child's account that I suggested your return," he said stiffly. "I did not at all mean to coerce your movements."

Helen sat quite still while he spoke, and listened with a surprise that was almost painful. It was true she had never loved her husband, and did not now care for him to any great degree, but since the birth of her child she had come to have a more gentle feeling toward him, more as though peace between them would be a pleasant thing, and coming home after her long absence, she had determined for their son's sake to do all in her power to put things on a happier footing in the family. Mingled with this feeling and the good motive inducing it, there arose from the same source, from the love for her child, another feeling and another motive. The knowledge that her husband had more power over the child than she had, power enough to separate her from it, filled her with an intense fear and longing to do all to make her stay under his roof sure. All this came up in her mind and heart as Philip spoke, and, without looking at him, she answered slowly, "I know that, and think it better for the child myself."

Philip rattled the leaves of his book, with a fresh amount of wonder at Helen's extraordinary patience. Mrs. Felmere, knitting diligently, could not make it out, and Helen, weary of it all, excused herself and went to her own room.

Slowly she traversed the long halls and mounted the broad stairway. Slowly her thoughts revolved around the questions, "How could she bear this life?" and "What did this treatment presage?" Their letters had been short and cool during her absence, but not to an extent that would have led her to expect this state of things, and the fact that this was "home" grew blacker as she contemplated it. Home! And no hope for a happier one. Ah, it was desperate.

On reaching her room she found that the servant, out of his own thoughtfulness, had put refreshments there for her. She paused a moment, touched by the little attention, then turned to him as he stood waiting for further orders, and held out her hand in greeting.

"Thank you, James," she said, "this was very thoughtful of you. I shall not need anything more."

James bowed low. He felt honored by her gracious thanks, and asked respectfully after her health and after the conduct of his daughter, who filled the important post of nurse to the child.

"Annie has been very good," the mistress answered. "I am perfectly satisfied with her, and so should you be, James."

"Thank you, madam, and I am," James answered, then left the room. Down in the servants' hall talk was plenty that night. Young Mrs. Felmere's arrival, her cool reception, her beauty and gentleness, Master Philip's weakness in being managed by his mother, and "old Mrs. Felmere's" general disagreeableness, were some of the themes. Then there was a whisper that "Miss Helen" would not be allowed to stay long as Mrs. Felmere was working too hard against her. The coachman had heard scraps of many conversations to this effect between her and her son as he drove them out in the summer afternoons. James had picked up a great deal around the table, and the housemaid had heard long discussions between the ladies of the Jourdan family. It was a "sin and a shame," they all declared; for, although "Miss Helen" might not be a Christian, she was more of a "real lady" than any among them, and the current of feeling set strong toward her.

Before Helen had quite finished her tea, Philip knocked at the door. Annie opened, it, and stood back, holding it wide. He hesitated a moment, then came in and went to the crib where the child slept. Helen did not move, but, thinking that perhaps Philip had come to make peace and explain her reception, she motioned Annie to leave the room. For a few moments he stood looking down on the child, then turned toward the door, and said slowly, "I only came to tell you that I am going with my mother to see Aunt Esther, and that when I come back I shall not disturb you, as I am at present in my bachelor quarters on the other side of the house."

"Very well," Helen answered quietly; then added, "Good night."

"Good night," he repeated, and held out his hand. There was an almost imperceptible hesitation before Helen laid hers in it; then he left the room and went slowly down stairs.

Very slowly he went, each step seeming as though it would be the last in that direction, and as if he would come back. Helen listened intensely. At last he paused. "He will come," she thought.

Alas, his mother was listening. "Philip, I am waiting," she called, and he went on.

Helen covered her face with her hands. She did not love him. Why should she be pained? Even so, but in all the world he was the only creature she had any right to call on in time of need, and above all, he had the power to take her child from her. She raised her head. Was this to be a separation, and why? What had she done to make him take this course now? She had been away all summer, but he had sent her. She did not love him, but she never had, and he had always known it. She was not a Christian, but in spite of that he had insisted on marrying her. Could it be because she had acknowledged to him her love for Felix Gordon? If so, even that was his fault, for he had asked her the direct question, and she could do nothing but tell the truth.

Then, with the memory of Felix, her thoughts seemed to slip away from the turbid current of her present life into a stiller stream, between green banks, by nodding flowers, back to the old days. She had seen him again, and, though changed, yet he was true, and she could feel that there was one thing left living in her life that was not a delusion. And he had said she would be happy "somewhere." It would never be here, and was there a hereafter? She drove the thought away; she would not go back to the old neverending round of questions; it could make no difference to her, for she had made her choice, and would abide by it.

"Somewhere!" How the sound of his voice came back to her with that piteous ring of despair in it, and she could see his white face as it had looked down on her through the gloaming; she could smell the sea wind and the poor little flowers whose lives he had crushed out under his heel as he turned away, and the cry of the waves came to her as she sat alone in the heart of a great city.

The little child sighed in its sleep, and the sound brought all the knowledge of her present life to her again, and again she questioned herself. Would this lead to a separation, and what had caused the breach? She thought over everything she had done or said, and could not solve the mystery.

Suddenly she paused. The solution of it lay plain before her, distinct as the pictures on the wall or the fire that burned in the grate. The love had been all on one side, a hopeless love that had died, had worn itself out, had recoiled upon itself and choked out its own life. She had not cared for it, yet now that it was gone she missed it; she felt lonely and cut off from all save her child.

She went near the crib and looked down on the little sleeper, so peaceful and innocent, and wished from the depths of her heart that she could have blinded herself to the faults of her husband. She had honestly tried to do it, but found that her education had been peculiarly fitted for the discovery of those very weaknesses and shortcomings he had fallen heir to. "Poor Philip," she whispered as she recommenced her walking to and fro; "he has suffered much, and a separation would be much happier for him." She paused in front of the fire. Once she had longed for a separation, and even now would agree to it if she could have the child.

A chill crept over her, and walking to the crib she took her baby in her arms; she would serve as a menial in Philip's house rather than leave her child. Yet, if he commanded her? She paused. Could he command her to leave him without just cause? Surely not! Could she humble herself to the extent of staying in his house against his wishes? Never! And she crushed the child to her bosom with such force that he waked with a piteous cry, and with the sound of that little startled voice all her self control came back to her. Gently she hushed him to sleep, and when again he was quiet, a calmer train of thought had come to her.

Of course she could not expect Philip to give up the child, for he was the last of the name, and a son, and realizing this, she must make up her mind what she would do in case Philip proposed her leaving him. She could not argue these questions calmly with the child in her arms; so, stopping in her walk, she laid him in the crib, then took her seat near the fire. If it came at all, she thought it would only be a private separation, with no law and no publicity about it, so that there could only be a private arrangement as to the child, and how would this be managed? Turn the question as she would, she could see but one solution: six months with her, six months with its father. Would this do? Would it not be the surest way to ruin the child and to make them all bitterly unhappy? She paused. This was too true, and they must agree to live together, or one or the other must give up entirely.

She buried her face in her hands. A thousand times better for her that she should have ended her miserable life than that it should come to this, and if that wretched man had not stopped her, she would have been at peace now. Dead.

She rose, and again began her walking to and fro, for she could not sit still and think calmly on such a subject. Once more she paused beside the child, and, looking on him and beyond him to the future, her lips turned white and her hands clenched themselves convulsively together. She could not bear it. She would appeal to the law before she would give up her child; if the law decided in Philip's favor, then Philip would have to bring the law to bear to force her child away. Slowly her hands unclasped themselves, and a coldness of horror crept over her white face and half-parted lips. Would the law protect an unbeliever? She grasped the back of a chair to support herself. Where had the thought come from? Would Philip think of it? Was there any truth in it?

A feeling of hatred and defiance against Philip and his mother was growing up within her. They should not take her child. She would run away with it, would hide it. How her head ached, and how her brain seemed to throb and swell.

"O father," she whispered, "if you were only here to help me and tell me what to do."

Suddenly a remembrance came to her, and taking a light she went down to the library where the picture of "King Arthur" stood. She put the light on a stand nearby, and knelt before the picture as before a shrine. She had not seen it for so long that now it burst on her with redoubled force.

"Father, father," she whispered, and her sobs swelled into a storm of grief. All the past came back; all the sorrow she had through all her life controlled, all the tears she had smothered, found vent with redoubled force, while the hours swept on and the night waned.

And she did not know that Philip and his mother, passing by on the thickly carpeted floors, had paused and looked on her crouching in the dim light; had listened to her wild sobs; had gone away without speaking or looking at each other gone away and left her to the blank bitterness of her own heart. She was all unconscious that she had been watched, and when she had worn out the violence of her suffering, and her sobs had ceased, she looked up into the face of the "Great King" that seemed to sympathize with her despair; she gazed on it as though she would put life into the eyes and speech upon the lips.

At last she rose. "He would have been calm and strong," she said, "and waited quietly until the trouble came; he would have stooped to no deceit, nor will I. He would have asked for no mercy, and I will not. If any trouble comes, I will bear it, and through all I will study only the good of my child as he did for me."

She paused a little before her last words; for when she thought of it all, she felt that his actions had not at all worked for her good; but he had meant all for her good, and so had acted to the best of his judgment. So she said the words, and then, as one taking an oath, she laid her lips on the unanswering canvas, and left it.

The next morning, before the house was astir, Philip stood on the spot where he had seen his wife the night before stood there scanning the picture closely. "Aha!" The exclamation was made below his breath; then, he straightened himself, and his face darkened strangely. In one corner of the picture he had found the letters "F. G.," and the date "18__," the very year after he had left Felmere. Ah, what a blind fool he had been, never to put things together. Gordon had painted this picture, Felix Gordon, and had probably done it while at Felmere. All those wild sobs, that long midnight vigil, meant Felix Gordon. And Mrs. Beaumont had seen them together at the seaside.

He glared at the picture; he longed to cut it to pieces, to burn it, to dash it from the window, anything that would destroy it and forever remove it from his sight, now that he hated it so much. For a long time he stood there battling with himself, debating, reasoning, planning, but coming to no conclusion save that he was learning to hate his wife.

"Change, reverting to the years,
   When thy nerves could understand
What there is in loving tears,
   And the warmth of hand in hand."

—"The Vision of Sin," Alfred, Lord Tennyson

CHAPTER II

THE NEXT MORNING AFTER HELEN'S ARRIVAL brought a note from Mrs. Vanzandt.

"If dear Helen will come to me this morning, I shall eternally thank her! As refreshing showers after summer heat, so will dear Helen's presence be to me.
   Devotedly,
   Valeria Vanzandt"

These few words, written in a strictly fashionable hand, on strictly fashionable paper, covered a whole sheet, and took at least twenty minutes to decipher, but Helen read to the end with admirable patience, and answered in her honest round hand, on plain square paper, that she would surely come. She said nothing to any one of her intended visit; for on the preceding evening it had been made painfully clear to her that her presence in the house was of no consequence. She therefore quietly ordered her private carriage, and, sending the nurse and child downstairs ahead of her, was about to follow them when Mrs. Felmere, meeting her on the landing, stopped her.

"I think it is too cold for the child," she said.

I do not agree with you," Helen answered, "it is quite pleasant, and a drive will do him good. Besides, I wish Valeria to see him while he is looking so well."

"Of course," Mrs. Felmere rejoined, "it is as you please. I can only warn and advise; I cannot prevent. You know, also, our feeling about Mrs. Vanzandt?"

Mrs. Felmere's tones were those of an injured and much aggrieved person, and Helen, listening, paused a moment before she spoke, then said gently, "I know, aunt, that you do not now like my friend, but you once liked her and made her known to me. Now I cannot give her up, for I believe she is true to me, and I am fond of her."

Mrs. Felmere bowed, and in the action there was a world of unspoken sarcasm. "Yes," she said, "and you intend, I suppose, to continue fond of her in spite of everything?"

Helen did not answer immediately, but wisely paused a moment to think whether she should do so or not. Deciding quickly that it was not worth her while, she turned to descend, when a sudden thought, came to her that made her change her mind. "Aunt," she said, "please tell me the worst thing against Valeria."

And the voice was so quiet and conciliating, so much the voice of a person asking for advice, that Mrs. Felmere was surprised. She had never in all her experience of her known Helen to feign anything, and yet what other explanation was there for this patience and gentleness? After a moment of wondering, she answered, "She is a divorced woman, and we ought not to hold such people in much respect. Besides, the world says she was to blame."

"Do you think a divorce a disgrace?" Helen stood looking straight down into her aunt's eyes in a searching manner that was not very agreeable.

Mrs. Felmere shifted her position uneasily once or twice; then, suddenly standing quite still, she answered in a decided tone, "Yes, I do."

"And Philip also?"

Mrs. Felmere stood still now and scanned the face before her curiously as she replied, "Yes, my son also. All Christians ought to think so."

Helen stood silent and thoughtful for a moment, then went on,

"On whom do you think the disgrace falls more heavily in general, the man or the woman?"

"On the woman," was answered unhesitatingly.

Helen looked at her a moment, as though she had not heard her words and was thinking of something very far away from the subject under discussion. At last she spoke, spoke slowly and musingly as though to herself. "But the children," she said, "suffer the most; for they have the disgrace without being sustained by the strength of the motive that drove their parents to take the step." Then for a moment she stood silent, and Mrs. Felmere watching her was puzzled. "Poor Valeria!" Helen went on after a little while, "I will not believe she was in fault." And, without a word of explanation or a word of farewell, she turned away in a slow, preoccupied manner and went down to the carriage, where the nurse and child already awaited her.

And Mrs. Felmere, watching her from the landing, seemed to catch the look from her face, and in the problem that opened before her forgot the dispute over the child. "Was Helen going to sue for a divorce?" she pondered, "and in such case what should be done?"

"Philip will not go to law," Helen thought, "he thinks it a disgrace. What then?"

Mrs. Vanzandt said all in praise of the child that could be expected or desired, so much that both mother and nurse agreed in pronouncing her a woman of much judgment. Then the child was sent for a drive around the park, and Mrs. Vanzandt made known to her friend the urgent need there was for her presence. "An art reception, dear, tomorrow, and behold, with all my invitations out, three of the best pictures have failed me. Is it not awful? Utterly dreadful, and you can appreciate my despair. And now, I want to beg you to fill their places. Can you, and will you? Your pictures are all lovely, and peculiar also, they will, I know, be admired, for your style is not at all commonplace. Will you?"

Helen looked doubtful. Her pictures were almost sacred to her, and she did not like or wish to put them on exhibition for the public; yet it would seem very unkind, not to help her friend out of her dilemma. "We can send for them," she said slowly, "and determine if any of them will do. Most of them, however, are upstairs in this very house. I have made only a very few this summer, but you can send for them if you like. I will write a note."

Mrs. Vanzandt's thanks were profuse, and the pictures were sent for.

"And now, dear, while we are waiting I will order in a little lunch, and we can exchange a few remarks."

Helen smiled as though she were tired. "You begin then, Valeria," she said, "for I have neither the ideas nor spirits necessary for even a 'few remarks.'"

Mrs. Vanzandt poured out some wine for her friend, then for herself, saying soberly the while, "You should remember, my dear child, the remark that 'to those who think, life is a farce; to those who feel, a tragedy,' and surely you are among the thoughtful?"

"Yes," Helen answered, "I ought to be. I was regularly trained to think. But I doubt, Valeria, if life ever becomes a farce even to the most thoughtful until their feelings are worn out."

Mrs. Vanzandt arched her black eyebrows, and shrugged her shoulders. "I would not wait to wear my feelings out," she said, rather bitterly, "I would, without further demur, annihilate them that is, if I were as you are."

Her companion shook her head sadly. "So you think," she said in a voice full of despair, "but you have never had a child."

The pretty dark face of the woman opposite worked strangely for a moment, and her answer came slowly and with difficulty, "Yes I have."

For a moment there was a dead silence, for Helen was more than pained to have so wounded her friend, and was besides astonished out of all words. At last she broke the silence. "I beg your pardon, Valeria," she said slowly. "I did not know. I did not mean to hurt you."

Mrs. Vanzandt recovered herself. "Of course you did not. I understand. I do not mind it very much now. It has been long enough for me to get over it somewhat, for my child died many years ago, and when it was only a few months old." There was a little pause; then she went on in the same quiet, musing voice, "And I was glad it died, for I could not have kept it; the law would have given it to its father, and this would have made both it and me utterly miserable."

A chill crept over Helen as she listened. The law would in any case go against her, and appealing to it would only insure the loss of her child.

"My dear, you are spilling your wine all over your dress," and Mrs. Vanzandt made a sudden dash with her napkin into Helen's lap.

Helen started, and the glass fell to the floor with a little crash. "I am so sorry," she said, looking helplessly into the astonished face of her friend. "I could not help it. And, Valeria, are you sure about that?"

"About what?" Mrs. Vanzandt's voice sounded almost frightened, and the look of bewilderment increased on her face: was Helen losing her wits?

Helen rose, and walking to a window answered slowly, "Nothing. I have changed my mind, dear, and you must excuse me without an explanation."

Here they were interrupted by the arrival of the pictures; and to Helen, at least, the interruption was more than welcome. Mrs. Vanzandt soon selected what was needful to fill the places left vacant, and, the child coming in as she finished, Helen rose to go glad to be free to think, glad to be once more alone; promising faithfully, however, to come the next day. "And the law will not give me the child," she pondered. "Oh, what shall I do?"

Once more she stole down into the library to ask counsel of the picture, and to seek comfort in the strong face of her father. "He would have been strong," she thought, "he would not have cringed or deceived; he would have been calm and patient. Oh, my father my father."

And Philip, coming in, found her standing there. She saw him coming, but she did not move. "You love that picture," he said, pausing near her.

"Yes."

Philip went on more slowly, "Gordon must have painted that about the time you first knew him."

"Yes, he painted it at Felmere." The voice was very quiet, and the face as unconcerned as though they were discussing the weather, and to her it did seem but little more now, for that time was so faraway, and it appeared such a gentle grief in comparison with the sorrow that now overshadowed her.

But her unconcern made Philip angry. "That accounts, then, for the likeness to your father," he said quickly.

"Yes, my father was our model."

"Ah, you helped in it?"

"Yes."

"You never told me all this before," Philip went on coldly.

"You never asked me before," she answered with studied slowness. She was trying not to be scornful nor cross. It would not be wise to anger him unnecessarily, and yet she did not wish to be too polite or gentle, lest she should be tempted to go further and cringe a little in order to be allowed to remain with her child. And now, since Philip, as it were, put her at the bar to be questioned and judged, she felt as though she would rather die or go away than humble herself to him.

Meanwhile, Philip stood looking out of the window as though arranging his next words, finally breaking on her thoughts with, "There is a new piece by Gordon. It is down at Pittelli's, called 'By the Sea.' Have you seen it?"

"No."

"It was painted last summer while he was at the seaside."

"Doubtless." Why did he not ask her the honest, direct question? He knew she would answer truly.

But patience was wisest just now, and, although she longed to express her contempt for his little hints, she stood quite still and silent, and Philip went on, "Mrs. Beaumont said you seemed to be old friends."

He was watching her closely, and she looked at him steadily. "And was it necessary for Mrs. Beaumont to corroborate the statement I made to you years ago?" she asked.

"You did not meet as old friends at Mrs. Tilmont's ball," he answered slowly.

This was hard to be borne, but, putting a still stronger curb on herself, she kept silent until the first hot rush of her indignation passed, then said with deliberate coldness, "I do not like your tone, Philip; there is something behind which you do not seem willing to speak out honestly. If you and your mother suspect me, there is nothing easier than to watch me, and I am willing that you should do so." She stopped suddenly, for she felt her anger again getting the better of her. She turned and left the room.

That it was natural for Philip to suspect her, was a fact she had often looked at squarely and imagined that she realized, but, coming home to her as it had done in the last few days, reason as she would, she could not reconcile herself to the justice of it. It was true that Philip, knowing that she had little regard for the bonds forged for humanity by either custom or religion, knowing that she was neither guided nor swayed by any of the hopes and fears engendered by a belief in future rewards and punishments had almost aright to be uneasy. Furthermore, he knew she did not love him, and this, to a man of his narrow views and education, was enough to condemn her at once. He could not comprehend a person being true for truth's sake; for all his life he had been furnished with motives other than this.

Helen saw and knew all these things, and, trying honestly to make excuses for him, succeeded until the reflection assailed her that in all their intercourse she had never told him anything but the most unshadowed truth, and that in remembrance of this he ought to spare her these insults. More than this, it was his own fault that he stood where he was; and although she pitied him, yet he only was to blame, and had no right to visit his mistake on her. He had been weak enough to be managed by his mother, and must now abide by the consequences. So she argued as she walked up and down her room trying to calm her temper.

What her father had said was true—peace was better than all, and peace lived on the heights. She must rise above the tangle and torment in which she stood, for she could never step out of them. Then there came to her mind the conversation they had had so long ago about the worm crawling to the top of the post, out of the dust and above its fellows. Her father had been right; she had come fully to agree with him that starvation on the post was better than the turmoil and the dust; and while she thought, the words of the great poet came to her, "On every height there lies repose." Could she not gain some height? Was she incapable of rising? Surely not! She would rise; she would recover her self-control. Philip should not know that she minded his coldness and anger, or in any way resented them.

Philip angry! She covered her face with her hands as the thought of the dreadful power he held came to her. Had she made him angry enough to send her away? If she had, who was there to counsel her? And if he should take her child from her, who to protect or comfort her?

She walked the room in a terror of agitation. She tried vainly to recall her resolutions to do as she thought her father would have done in her place, to wait calmly until the trial came, then to study only the good of the child. Of course she must train herself to face this sorrow and self-abnegation, and she would be wiser to begin at once.

She took one or two more turns up and down the room; then, sitting down and crossing her arms on a table, put her face down on them, and tried to think. Would the child do better without her? As a flash of light the answer darted across the chaotic gloom of her misery: Yes! She crushed her face more closely down, and drove herself to follow out this thought. She would be only a weight about his happiness; a weight to drag him down to where she stood in cold, hopeless misery; a bar that would separate him from his kind; a shadow that, blotting out all hope, would darken all his life. How had her life and happiness fared under her training? Alas, a blankness of despair and misery seemed to sweep over her as she looked back over her empty, aimless days as she looked forward to her hopeless future. Should she doom her child to that?

Once, in the years that were gone, she had heard a poor woman cry out in her despair, "Oh, my God, help me, help me!" and the cry seemed to help her. "And I have no God to cry to," she murmured, "nor any human creature." She was tempted to blot out the almost conviction that had come to her, lighting up like a storm gleam the horrid possibilities that lay before her, making the wild whirl of doubt and despair in which she stood seem wilder. Her father had not thought Christianity best for her; he had not deemed it best to send her to her mother. Why act differently? Why! Ah, who better than she knew why? Who better than she could tell how bitterly the plan had failed? Who better than she could weigh and balance the chances of her child's happiness if he should be trained as she had been, and find them wanting?

She rose hurriedly from her chair; she dashed her hands in front of her as though to fling away her thoughts. "I will not, will not let him go!" she cried. "Let the consequences be on my head; I cannot give him up." She paused a moment and listened as her words seemed to come back to her from all parts of the great room where the evening shadows were gathering. "I cannot, I will not," she murmured; and, kneeling on the hearthrug with the red gleams of the firelight dancing about her, she made a bright spot in the twilight room. A picture that would have made a study for an artist, a sorrow that would have made an angel weep. A hopeless human soul.

"No one can be more wise than destiny."

—"A Dream of Fair Women,"
Alfred, Lord Tennyson

Chapter III

Mrs. Vanzandt's art reception promised to be a grand success. It was an entirely new sensation, and its novelty was in itself almost enough to insure a good result. All the pictures were to be by native artists, and, after a committee selected for the purpose had passed judgment, a handsome prize was to be awarded for the best.

"Artists were always poor," Mrs. Vanzandt said, "and her reception, besides bringing the pictures into notice, would probably sell a few. More than this, the prize, besides being handsome, should be suited to the circumstances and station of the successful artist."

There were, of course, many comments passed on what was called "Mrs. Vanzandt's new freak."

"She does not know what to do with her money," said amiable friends, "and it is just as well for her to waste it in this way as any other."

"She likes to be notorious and conspicuous," said pious enemies, "and we ought to be thankful that she has taken a decent way." (Whether they were or not, has never been proved.)

And Valeria Vanzandt, looking only to the novelty of the thing, with the hope of helping some poor artist as the excuse for her lavish expenditure, enjoyed without heeding the criticisms.

Philip and his mother had both decided to go, making Helen suspect that they went for the purpose of watching her; then, thinking the term watching too strong, she softened it into curiosity to see her pictures. But whatever the real motive was, they announced their intention and carried it out.

When they arrived, the house was crowded, and a long line of carriages stretching down the street told of the wealth, at least, of the company assembled.

The rooms were exquisitely arranged, and the hanging of the pictures and the falling of the light were artistic in the extreme. Added to this, a band of music, hidden amid wonderful flowers in a distant conservatory, made the scene still more charming. The whole was so charming, indeed, that all the fashionable world pronounced it a "wonderful success."

"How lovely!" Helen said to Arthur, with whom she was walking, "what a success Valeria makes of everything!"

"Everything except her own life," Arthur answered, as he watched their brilliant hostess moving back and forth from picture to picture and group to group, criticizing, chatting, laughing, and making all seem brighter for her presence. Arthur watched her until she had passed out of sight into another room, then turned and led his companion up to a gilt easel on which a watercolor sketch was most conspicuously placed.

"Mrs. Philip Felmere," he read slowly as he turned over the card attached. "Did you really do this, Helen?" he went on.

"Yes, I did it years ago, and dressed it up last summer; it is 'Felmere.'"

Arthur scanned the picture closely, and the thought of how dreary it was saddened his kind face; that, lonely and dreary as it was, it was the only home this young creature at his side had ever known; that there she had grown up, a solitary young heart without a gleam of joy or hope to lighten her life, and with only an old man for her companion. "How sad it looks!" he said at last.

"It is glorified to me now," she answered slowly. "Time was when I thought it dreary enough, and longed to get away, but *now*. . ." she ceased suddenly, and Arthur, looking up, saw Philip and his mother approaching them. They also paused before the picture, and Mrs. Felmere, as Arthur had done, read the card.

"It is Felmere Hall," Helen explained.

Then Mrs. Felmere looked more closely. "How dreadfully lonely," was her first comment, "and so near the graveyard. I wonder, Helen, that you did not die of the blues long ago, and I cannot see what charm held your father there."

It was almost too much for Helen's patience to hear Mrs. Felmere speaking in her false, oily tones, and so disparagingly, of this, to her, sacred place, but she did not fail herself, and only answered long-ingly, "It was home, and we had each other. More than this, neither of us was without happiness. Ah, I would give a great deal to go back all, and ten times more than I possess, or ever shall." Her tone had be-come very bitter toward the end of her speech. Not that she had in-tended it so to be, but her life was so fast becoming desperate, that she could not always keep down her despair.

Fortunately, no one was near enough to hear either her speech or Philip's sullen answer, "You can go, and could have gone long ago had you expressed your wish on the subject."

Her face grew crimson for an instant; then the pallor almost of death crept over it down even to the parted lips. What had she done? Would he send her away without her child? These thoughts swept over her, and she spoke slowly, as though with much difficulty, "Thank you, Philip, I should like very much to go in the spring."

Philip stared at her a moment almost rudely, and, turning away without waiting for Helen to finish her speech, walked off with his mother, leaving Arthur pale with rage. Under his stare Helen's ex-pression changed from almost pleading to a look of utter contempt. She could not help it, and the little pity that she felt for him only crept into her face when he turned away.

After this, she and Arthur walked about examining pictures, but without much spirit in their talk or comments, and were much re-lieved when Mrs. Vanzandt came up to them followed by the commit-tee of selection. "We have come, Helen, to take you in to see the pic-ture that has gained the prize."

And Helen, wondering, followed her down the long hall to a small room at the end the same room where on a former occasion the picture of "Guinevere" had hung. The daylight had been excluded, and an artificial light so arranged as to throw into wonderful relief the picture of the hour. As the party approached, the crowd made way for them, and Helen found herself face to face with her picture of "Sir Galahad." Under it were these words printed:

"And there was one among us, ever moved
Among us in white armor, Galahad."

She stood quite still and looked up at the idealized face. It was so long since she had seen it that she had forgotten how beautiful it had been to her, but now it came to her like a new wonder, it shone down on her like a star from out the crimson draperies. Ah, what a glad, pure look there was on the lifted, half-turned face, and the light that touched it was glorious no doubt of that. Her "bright boy knight," how glad she was to greet him once more.

She forgot the crowd, forgot her present life and misery, and stood thinking over the same thoughts that had been in her mind when she painted the picture.

She almost felt that if she turned her head she would be looking through the old studio window across the Felmere churchyard, and would see Felix coming with his knapsack on his shoulders.

"Do you know, madam, that your 'Sir Galahad' has won the prize? It was the chief of the committee of judges who spoke, and his voice sounded clear above the hum of talk about her.

Helen started, and looked up at him, wondering that he did not see the likeness and call it by its rightful name. Then a little shiver ran over her. Suppose he had done so, how dreadful it would have been. It was fortunate she had scribbled that quotation on the back of it; and how in the world had Valeria found it?

"You look so dazed," Mrs. Vanzandt broke in, "and you do not say anything. Are you not pleased to have your genius found out? For every one says there is decided genius in that piece."

"How did you get it?" Helen asked irrelevantly.

"Get it?" Mrs. Vanzandt answered. "You may well ask. Why, I found it in a dark corner of your studio, with its face to the wall, absolutely hidden in the most careful manner."

Helen looked up at the picture sadly. Yes, she had hidden it even from herself since her marriage, and now that she met it in the full glare of all the world, it seemed like laying her heart bare to be criticized by any passerby.

"I did hide it," she answered absently. "And that is what I cannot understand," Mrs. Vanzandt went on, "that you should hide the very best thing you ever did. Why, my dear, it has taken the prize over one of Gordon's pictures; think of that."

The hot blood dashed into Helen's cheeks, and Arthur felt the hand on his arm give a little nervous twitch.

"And by the way," Mrs. Vanzandt went on, "if you had ever known Felix Gordon, I should say you had put somewhat of him in your picture."

Arthur felt the hold on his arm tighten. He saw his companion raise her eyes, and watched while the color faded from the calm face, but she did not turn her eyes from the point where she had first fastened them as she answered Mrs. Vanzandt, "Yes, I feel it a great honor to be thought to have excelled Mr. Gordon, and shall value my prize very highly." Then she looked away, and Arthur, turning his eyes to where she had been looking, found Philip's eager, pale face watching her intensely.

Afterward, one or two persons standing near took up the freshly dropped idea, and said the picture was somewhat like Mr. Gordon; in fact, he must have looked much like it in his youth.

Then Helen turned and drew Arthur with her from the room. "It is very close," she said faintly, "and I should like a glass of wine."

Arthur instantly obeyed her move, and, taking her into the refreshment room, suggested calling the carriage. She paused thoughtfully for a moment before she answered, as though considering the proposal; then refused, on the plea that she was quite well again. But the time after that dragged heavily to her, and Arthur, watching her, saw the effort she made, and felt a sincere pity for her.

Fortunately, it was not long before the company was collected together for the presentation of the prize, which was to be the conclusion of the entertainment. The spokesman of the committee made a little speech, full of well-worn compliments, and, ending abruptly and unexpectedly at the apex of his eloquence, left his audience in a state of stupid surprise.

There was a painful pause of a few moments' duration, while the company looked expectantly at Philip, who, standing stolidly angry, made no movement to reply. It was only for an instant; then Arthur stepped quickly from Helen's side, and, receiving the prize for her, said such pleasant words of thanks that people almost forgot their surprise at Philip's silence.

"It must have been arranged between them," the world said, "yet it was strange Mr. Felmere had not taken Arthur's place, unaccountably strange!"

Helen was quiet under it all. No one could see the slightest change of expression when Arthur took Philip's place and did Philip's duty; no one could discover so much as a quiver of her eyelids when Mrs. Beaumont told Mrs. Vanzandt, in her hearing, that Mrs. Philip Felmere and Mr. Gordon were old and intimate friends, and that there might be some look of him in the picture; nor was there any more show of expression when Mrs. Vanzandt, with a flash of her black eyes, answered glibly and without a moment's hesitation, "Oh, yes, I have just heard all about it. They were brought up together. He was an adopted brother, or uncle, or something very near. Mr. Jourdan has just told me."

And Arthur bowed very low to hide the smile he could not repress; it was such a quick, clever little story, and the motive behind it was so generous, he would have liked to thank her. Then she swept Mrs. Beaumont off into a crowd where this last item could be repeated to advantage.

But no one could have told that Helen heard it, and her only feeling about it was that Valeria was telling a story to shield a person who was fated. Everything militated against her; there was no use in struggling, nothing was left for her but endurance. So she chatted and smiled with those about her, receiving their congratulations and thanking them for their kind compliments, and all the while wondering what would come of this day's work.

Arthur, meanwhile, waited deliberately, and without invitation, for the Felmere carriage, in order that he might ride home with Helen, and, if possible, prevent any discussion of the events of the morning until he had had some private conversation with his sister and Philip. But he need not have feared; for Philip kept utterly silent, spending his time looking out of the carriage window; while Mrs. Felmere made only a few general remarks about the entertainment they had just left. On their arrival at home the party separated, and Arthur, seeing the time was not propitious for his talk, did not stay.

The whole evening Philip spent alone in the library, sitting for hours in one position, brooding over and nursing his resentment. Helen loved Felix Gordon; for him her face would soften and her beautiful eyes grow glad; he had seen it. He clenched his hands. For him she watched and waited with ever a longing in her heart; for his praise she cultivated her talents and worked so diligently at her art; and in her dreams it was his face she idealized, putting a glory and a beauty about it that only the light of heaven could cast. Could he be expected to love and protect and cherish her, knowing all this? Who could measure the wrath and agony he had suffered that day, as he watched her receive the prize for that glorified face, glorified as only love could have conceived it?

"Great God," he muttered, almost wringing his hands, "and if I ask her she will say, 'Yes, it is Mr. Gordon's face. I did it years ago, but its exhibition was a mistake. I am sorry.' Of course she is sorry." Then he put his face in his hands. He could almost hear her voice saying the words he had muttered: a sweet clear voice it was, but always cold to him. Ah, he had made a bitter mistake in marrying her, but then he had hoped for so much.

So he sat until the night closed about him, then he rang for a servant, and without any message or note sent the gilt easel and the picture of "King Arthur" up to his wife. And Helen, discussing with her maid what she should wear at the ball that night, laid down the spray of jewels she held, and quietly superintended the placing of the picture. She knew it meant a great deal, but she had reached that point where hopelessness merges into calm. Nothing but the actual mandate to go could touch her now.

At the ball that night, no one, not even Arthur with whom she went, could have told but that her life was one even flow of prosperity. Yes, she was very calm: no one but the little nurse, watching for her returns from balls and parties, listening through the dusks and dawns of many days, knew of the despair that held her, of the hopelessness that possessed her! And often the little maid would tell her mistress of a kind gentleman, a clergyman, who lived among the poor and helped them: would not her mistress ask his advice?

But Helen only turned away, saying, "Child, this is a trouble that only death can comfort."

And so the days sped by, and Philip told her nothing except that in the latter part of spring he was going abroad, and that if she wished she might go back to Felmere. He did not mention the child, and she would not ask any questions.

"O for comfort, O the waste
of a long doubt and trouble!"

—"Requiescat in Pace!," Jean Ingelow

CHAPTER IV

THE HOUSE WAS STILL, THE FIRES BURNED DULL, the sky was gray, and the wind howled dismally up and down the streets. Helen sat alone, for, being Sunday, all the family, including baby and nurse, had gone to Miss Esther Jourdan's house to dinner. Helen, however, finding she was not welcome, had not been present at these reunions for some time. Now she sat by herself, listening to the wind, and thinking how many days she could remember at Felmere when the wind sung the same song about the dreary marsh that now sounded in the busy city streets, and how in its tones the cry of the weary sea would mingle.

Ah, she did not like to look back, she did not like to think, and she could no longer stay in that lonely house. She rose with nervous haste, and, putting on cloak and furs, and muffling her face in a heavy veil, she went out. The wind was desperately high, and battled with her at every corner in a way that seemed almost malignant. But she would not turn back, she rather enjoyed the struggle; it made her forget her misery for a little while, and almost cured her homesickness and restlessness. She turned from the usual course of her walks and drives, and in a very short time found herself among unknown scenes. The houses were poor and shabby, and the few people she met looked common and tawdry, but this pleased her, for she wished to be where there was no danger of meeting any one she knew.

At last she reached a dreary little park, grown over with grass that looked gray from age, with here and there a few stunted trees and impotent-looking benches, dingy with over-much rain and sun, and scarred by many idle knives. The safest looking of these benches stood under, or rather leaned against, a tree so black and bare as to make one almost doubt the resurrecting power of spring; that tree could surely never again bring forth summer foliage. Helen gave the bench a precautionary shake, and, finding it tolerably firm, sat down, thinking to rest for a little while, but the wind seemed to be of a different mind, and attacked her on every side. It would not let her alone, and finally there came with it a fine, penetrating rain, that made her scan the buildings about her for some sheltering doorstep or porch, where she could stand for a while before turning her steps homeward. After some moments scrutiny, she descried a narrow, dingy church, standing rather back among the high rusty rows of houses. She went nearer, and, hearing a strain of music floating out on the wild winds, determined to seek shelter there. "It is such a poor and mean looking church, I dare say it is free," she said to herself, as, fighting hard against the wind and rain, she crossed the dingy square and muddy street.

Reaching the church, she paused to look for some retired side door that would let her in without attracting notice, or that would perhaps protect her sufficiently without the necessity of an actual entrance. It took her some moments, but at last she discovered the desired place, a side porch built in a little crevice between the church and one of the crowding houses that seemed to lean in on every side. She was not long in making her way to this newly discovered haven, flattering herself that she had found sufficient protection, But only for a moment was she unmolested; then the wind and rain, driving round the corner, crowded her back against the wall, and dashed the cold drops in her face. She could not stand this, and, waiting a second until she heard the music recommence, she opened the door and stepped in. In a moment she was at rest, finding herself in a dim dark corner, quiet and calm, where she could hear the tempest but not feel it. She could see all the tired human faces congregated there, but could not well be seen.

The church was long and dim, with a dark arched roof and high narrow windows. The floor was paved, and the benches, crowded close together, were of common deal. There were no soft hassocks, no cushions, no carpets nothing that could at all remind her of the light, fashionable temple where her family worshiped. All save the altar looked common and unlovely, but there soft lights were burning, and fair fresh flowers gave forth their fragrance.

Once catching sight of the altar, her looks were fastened, for a strange feeling began to steal over her, taking her back to the days when as a child at Felmere she had crept inside the church door and a mysterious reverence and awe, that did not at all seem the outcome of reason, made her, now as then, wish to kneel. Alas, she was no longer the ignorant child of those days, and bitterly she felt the change. She could now realize and see the awful gulf of doubt and risk that yawned between her and that altar; she knew it would be but a mockery in her, and a desertion of her father.

She closed her eyes, and the sounds of prayers and chants passed, leaving her without any distinct consciousness of their meaning, and with only a feeling that they were one long sigh and longing going up from all those weary souls. Suddenly, distinct words fell on her ears:

"Art thou weary, art thou languid,
Art thou sore distressed?"

She raised her head. She was all that; could these people give her any comfort?

Softly the answer fell:

"'Come to me,' saith one, 'and, coming,
Be at rest.'"

She listened eagerly, greedily, longingly, and the sound seemed to float away from her utterly and entirely. She was cut off, she had no part in that rest, that call had no meaning for her. All those hard-worked servant girls and day laborers could listen and find comfort, could sing with all their heart and strength, could believe, and in believing *rest*. *She* could not.

She covered her face again. She envied the lowest there, and would have given all she possessed for the simple faith and ignorance of any one of them.

"'Come unto me, all ye that labor and are heavy laden, and I will give you rest!'"

The voice rang out above her bent head, clear, musical, soft sounding down the dim length of the church that was fast fading into obscurity, losing itself deep in many human hearts.

"O ye who are weary with the burden and heat of the day, laden with sin and sorrow; weary with toil and care, laden with regrets and remorse; blinded with the dust of many troubles, thirsty with the drought of many wants, who, reaching groping hands from out the clouds of doubt, fall prone without a voice to cry, 'Come to me, saith one, and, coming, Be at rest!'

"Are there any here among you who can say, 'I have none of these,' any who can say, 'I have no need of rest,' any save, perhaps, some little child still standing poised on the brink of life, watching with wonder the toilers after this world's rewards, the mourners over this world's disappointments, some fair, pure soul that still looks beyond the dust and pain of mortal warfare, that still can fix its eyes on yon far Paradise, forgetting its roots are in clay? To such I do not speak. I only ask them to come and stand beside me, that, looking down into the depths of their far-reaching faith, my own faint spark may be fresh kindled. It is not to the pure and stainless I come, but to those who like myself are 'weary and heavy laden,' those who search longingly after some shadow wherein to rest. My beloved, for all who believe and trust, there is such rest. Sometimes it touches us even here among the drifting sand heaps of this present life; and I know it waits for us yonder, beyond the grave, beyond the mystery of death and the dread of hell! 'Only believe!' Believe that Christ died for you, that his blood can save you, that he stands waiting lovingly for your halting steps, ready to forgive and blot out the broken promises that mark your days, and listen patiently for the few scattered wandering cries for help that flicker up through all this waste of years! Believe that he still waits and says unto you, 'Come, and I will give you rest! Only believe!'"

Helen did not move, and her eyes seemed to have grown to the pure, pale face in the pulpit above her, almost a boy's face, with luminous dark eyes and a grand broad brow; the face of the man who had saved her life on the cliff.

She listened and looked until the dusk hid all save that white face, shining through the gathering shadows like the face of one who has seen God. And the clear sweet tones rang on and on, commanding, comforting, pleading with them for their own souls requiring of them to believe in Christ. How the words rang about her; how they sounded back and forth through the empty past and future of her life!

"Only believe!"

Desert the old man who had trusted her, the one human heart that in the past had been her own!

"Only believe!"

And for ever keep her child beside her, the one human heart in all the world that would in the future be her own. She covered her face with her hands. To do it would be breaking her oath to the dead, and bring remorse upon her. Not to do it, ah, who could measure what her life would be without her child? She wrung her hands.

"And when life's short day is past,
Rest with thee in heaven at last!"

Slowly the words faded from about her as the choir filed out, and the soft "Amen" sounded miles away.

Once more from under shelter, battling against the wind and rain, but now heedless of them. Nor did she again pity the dwellers in those common houses, the frequenters of the dingy square; for down this narrow back street she had found the Christians her father had described to her. Among the common work people, in a dark, unlovely, free church, she had found herself face to face with the foes she had longed yet dreaded to meet, the foes, the beauty of whose lives and religion had so strong a fascination for her.

This priest was different from the Christians she had lived among. He really and realizingly believed, and there was that in his face that made her know he lived up to his faith. Had he found peace and rest? she wondered. Had that almost boyish face grown pale and harassed, and those shining eyes grown troubled, through his anxiety for the souls of others, or for his own? She wondered still further whether he had ever doubted, and thought she would like to know him and talk to him should like to plead for counsel in her dire distress.

She did not heed the wind and rain nor the lateness of the hour. She plodded on through mud and slop, across crowded streets, around slippery corners, scarcely knowing when she reached her own door, or realizing that she was weary, wet, and cold. She did not even note James's astonishment, nor his gratuitous information, as he took her wet wraps, that "Master Philip and the baby had come, but that the carriage was to be sent back for Mrs. Felmere." She did not see Philip, who had stopped in his walk up and down the long parlors to observe her late arrival and wet condition. She only thanked James for his services, and went hastily up stairs. She wanted her child, she wanted to lay fresh hold on her promise to her father, she wanted to turn away from this temptation to forsake her father and leave the ways of her youth. She did not heed or stay her quick steps until she knelt on the hearthrug where the child was playing, and felt his touch upon her face; then she paused and thought.

"Believe in Christ," and she would forever have him for her own. Ah, the depth and far-reaching strength of those words — "her own," "for ever." And the little arms about her neck were dreadful powers dragging her from the old paths.

"O father, father," she almost sobbed, as she crushed the child nearer to her, "I will be true." Then the clasp relaxed, and the little maid, watching, felt the tears rise to her eyes. She did not understand it all, but this much she knew: her mistress was in some deep distress, and her mistress had no religion. And all the tenderness of her kind, young nature went out in sympathy for the misfortunes of her fellow woman, who was also young, and oh, how beautiful.

"What is it?" the mistress asked at last, "what is it that troubles you, Annie?"

"Only you look so sorrowful, ma'am."

"I feel sorrowful, child."

"I know it, ma'am, and oh, Mrs. Felmere, if you would only go just once to my church."

"Would I come away happy, do you think, Annie?"

"P'r'aps not altogether happy, ma'am, but more peaceful like," the girl answered thoughtfully.

"I did go to church this afternoon," the mistress answered slowly, as she rocked the child back and forth in her arms, "a free church on a back street, where the singing was beautiful, and a good man preached; I know he was good."

"Were he a small man, ma'am, and did his eyes shine?" the girl asked eagerly.

"Yes." Then Helen gave the street and square, and it proved to be Annie's "own" church.

"And didn't he give you peace, ma'am?" the girl went on gravely.

The mistress shook her head. "No, he did not give me peace, for no one can give me that, nothing can rest me but the grave. But he showed me he was a good, true man, one to whom I can go and tell my troubles, and I shall go."

"Now I know you will be happier, ma'am; for Mr. Heath will do all he can to help you; he will show you the right way if anyone can."

"Our ways are very far apart, child," the mistress said, "but I shall go to him and hear what he says."

Then a silence fell between them, and the red firelight danced merrily on their sad faces, and on the peaceful sleeping of the child lying still in its mother's arms; while, in the long dim rooms below, the master and father paced nervously to and fro, angry, wondering, and suspicious. Why had Helen stayed at home from dinner? Where had she been? Had she come home alone at that late hour? And what had troubled her so much as to prevent her from even looking in his direction when she passed? None of these questions could be answered except by asking, and he could not ask. Up and down, up and down he walked, cursing his fate, cursing himself for being so miserable and jealous, and tormenting himself with plans he could not possibly carry out.

In the midst of his self-torture his mother came in.

"What has happened?" she asked hurriedly.

Then Philip, as though it were a relief to talk to some one, told her all: that Helen was out when he arrived, and had not come in until after lamp-light; that she had appeared wet and draggled, and had gone immediately upstairs without saying a word to any one.

"Did she see you when she came in?" Mrs. Felmere asked gravely.

"I do not think she did," Philip answered, "she seemed very much preoccupied and hurried, and did not so much as look in this direction."

"She did not wish to," Mrs. Felmere said musingly, "and her behavior of late has been most peculiar. I have been observing her closely."

Philip turned away impatiently. "You need not watch her," he answered gloomily, "you have only to ask her point-blank questions, and she will answer you without hesitation."

Mrs. Felmere shook her head. "You are deluded, my son."

"I tell you it is so!" Philip answered sharply, as he turned to face her. "In all my intercourse with Helen, I have never known her to deviate one hair's breadth from the truth. The difficulty does not lie there," he went on more quietly, "but in the miserable fact that she does not admit that there is any law that can be binding on her, unless she chooses to be bound."

A keener look came on Mrs. Felmere's face as he finished speaking. "Will she always keep a promise?" she asked.

"I do not know how she looks on that," he answered, "whether she would consider a promise to mean forever, or only until she gave you warning of her intention to break it."

"Why do you not solve the question, then, and ask her first where she has been, and second how she regards a promise?"

They looked at each other a moment in silence, then Philip turned away. "I would rather remain in doubt for all my life," he answered sullenly, "than ask her those questions. No, I will solve the difficulty by going away in April."

"And your child, my son?" Mrs. Felmere's face was really sad as she looked up, and as she went on there was real solemnity in her tone, "Do you think you should go and leave your only son, and the last of your name, to grow up as he may? Do you think you will be doing your duty in leaving him to be reared in utter atheism, so risking his eternal welfare?"

Philip stood silent a moment. "Then, mother, what shall I do?"

Mrs. Felmere did not answer immediately. The plan she had for proposal was one that had long since matured in her own mind, and one she really thought was right; but she hesitated as to the first mention of it. "Helen wishes to go back to Felmere in the spring," she said inquiringly.

"Yes."

"You have told her she could go?"

"Yes."

"The place is low and marshy?"

"Yes."

"And therefore not healthy for the child?"

Philip looked up quickly, as though intending to speak, but Mrs. Felmere raised her hand for silence. "I will take the child and go with you to Europe!"

Her words fell quick and sharp, and she watched closely for their effect. Philip stood still for one moment, looking at her in mute surprise, then turned and walked away thoughtfully. "It would be too cruel," he said at last, standing before his mother.

"Cruel to save your child's soul?" she asked.

"We could educate him as a Christian without taking him away from her," he argued.

Mrs. Felmere shook her head. "Is it more cruel to separate them now," she asked, "or to let them live together and learn to love each other more and more, and then, teaching him the fearful error of his mother, sow grief and dissension between them? For, even if you leave them, they will be separated if he is trained a Christian. Her own unbelief sets a gulf between them, and the day he is baptized they will be as far apart as heaven and hell."

Philip shuddered and turned away, and his mother went on in the same low voice, "Better never let your son know his mother, than know her as she is; better for him not to learn to love one he must lose eternally, better have no faith in Jesus Christ and his power to save than to have faith undermined and shaded by the knowledge that the one he loves best in the world, and who seems to embody all goodness and purity, looks on such faith as weak and foolish!"

"You should have thought of all this before, mother," Philip began, standing before her and speaking slowly, "long before you sent me to Felmere."

"And God forgive me that I did not," his mother answered earnestly. "But this excuse I have, my son, I did not realize what her unbelief was; I could not realize it."

Philip turned away wearily. "She will never consent to give the child up," he said.

"I think I can manage that," his mother answered more confidently, "provided you are enough convinced of the truth in my words to give me the authority to act."

"The truth of what you say cannot be denied," he said, "but it seems too hard and cruel to leave her all alone."

Mrs. Felmere covered her face with her hands for a moment, then said slowly, "I have, my son, told you all I think about this matter, and have only this to add: that to stand and see your child grow up an atheist, to feel that if he should die he would be inevitably lost, to know that when at the last I stand before the judgment I can be held accountable in part for the loss of that little soul, to feel all this is breaking my heart and making my life utterly miserable, utterly miserable!"

Philip paused. He would have liked to wring his hands like a woman. As it was, he thrust them deeper into his pockets while his mother spoke, and when she ceased he said, "I put it all into your hands, mother. It has been a miserable mistake; right it if you can. I cannot." Then he went from the room; and Mrs. Felmere, left alone, burst into tears.

At last she was free to act, free to rid her conscience of this weight that had been resting there. She had been terror-stricken when she discovered the depth and reality of Helen's infidelity, and her family and clergyman had not made light of it. "Little worldly sins could be forgiven at the last," they agreed, "but never before had anything like this come under their ken, and it was too awful to be contemplated." Thus poor Mrs. Felmere had been living in what was very nearly a purgatory of mental suffering, and to gain her point was almost too great a relief. Now the child could be rescued, and the contumacious mother quietly sent home. "Thank God! "she whispered.

And up stairs the mother, alone in her dim fire-lighted room, rocked her child slowly to and fro in her arms, for ever repeating the same question, "What shall I do? What shall I do?"

"If this were thus — if this, indeed, were all —
Better the narrow brain, the stony heart,
The staring eye glazed o'er with sapless days,
The long mechanic pacings to and fro,
The set gray life, and apathetic end."

— "Love and Duty," Alfred, Lord Tennyson

CHAPTER V

IT WAS A POOR LOOKING ROOM ON THE GROUND FLOOR of a third-rate board-ing house, a very third-rate house, and you might, notwithstanding the landlady's assertion to the contrary, put it one grade lower. It was a pitifully bare and common room, with an uneven brick floor; with the two windows either side, the entrance door barred as much with dirt as with iron; with a poor gaunt stove, that for many years had suffered from a chronic case of rust; and with walls that were dingy beyond compare. The entrance door and the two windows furnished one side of the room, the blankness of the opposite wall was broken by a door leading into an inner chamber, while the two side walls could only boast, the one of the stove and a small bookcase, the other of a solitary chair. Between the stove and one of the cobwebbed win-dows, and within reaching distance of the bookcase, stood a deal table littered with books, papers, and writing materials. More than this there only remains to be mentioned a dilapidated writing chair, and two rags of carpet that lay, the one under the table, the other in front of the stove.

"A pitiful, poverty-stricken place," Helen thought, as, entering, she paused to look about her.

Presently the inner door opened, and a man came in. He was miserably attenuated and small, with a stoop in his shoulders that amounted almost to a deformity. But his head was grand past question, and his face and eyes were such as to make one overlook his unfortunate body.

Helen turned as he approached her, and they stood for a moment scanning each other closely and curiously. To Helen there was something in the man's face and eyes that seemed strangely mixed up with her past life, and he recognized in her the beautiful woman whose life he had saved on the cliff, the woman on whose face he had then seen hopelessness written, and in whose eyes he now saw nothing but despair.

"Are you Mr. Heath?" she asked at last.

"I am," he answered, then, bringing the one extra chair from the opposite wall, he placed it for her, and waited for her to speak.

"I have come to you, Mr. Heath," she began after a little pause, "because I heard you would help people who were in trouble, and you should know better than any one how deep my trouble must be."

"I do know how deep your trouble must be," he answered solemnly, for he remembered the day on the cliff, "and I will help you if I can. But what is your trouble?"

"I am an unbeliever, and my husband is a believer. We have one child, a son, and I do not know what to do. I cannot give him up, yet how can I keep him?"

The story told in so few words and in so straightforward a manner puzzled her listener; it was certainly a very strange recital, and at first hearing Mr. Heath was somewhat provoked at the nature of it. A person who was so deliberate and cool, an infidel as this woman seemed, deserved to suffer. What did she come to him for? What did she expect him to say? These were his thoughts until he looked in the pleading face opposite him and recalled the real sorrow in her voice, then he concluded there was something behind that would explain the mystery. So, after a moment's pause in which to change his temper, he asked kindly, "And what can I do for you? And how is it you come to me for advice?"

"I heard that you were kind," she answered sadly, "and I have not a creature in the world to ask counsel of. So, after I heard you preach, and recognized you as the person who had seen me when overcome by my sorrow, I thought you more than any other would realize the depth of it, and help me if you could."

The story looked more pitiful now than provoking, and Mr. Heath's voice was more gentle as he said, "Tell me first how you became an unbeliever, and why you continue so."

"My father educated me in unbelief," she answered, "and I continue so because I cannot believe, and because I promised him I would never desert him."

"Is your father living?"

She shook her head. "If he were, I should need no other counsel nor strength. He would tell me what was proper, and help me to do it."

The story was becoming more puzzling, and Mr. Heath could only strive through questions to find the right clue, but he hesitated before he asked the next question: he did not know how much his visitor wished to tell him. "Did your husband," he began slowly, "know when he married you that you were an unbeliever?"

"Yes," was answered unfalteringly. "He was my cousin, and knew all about me: knew I had been trained an unbeliever, and had sworn to continue so; knew it was only to please my father that I accepted him. Yet, through all, he married me. Now he does not care for me anymore, and I think he will take my child from me, and what *shall* I do?"

Mr. Heath hid his eyes with his hand; it was too wretched a story as it slowly dawned on him nor did he know what to say, for all his sympathies were going with the infidel. Then he asked slowly, "Do you mean that your husband is going to separate you from your child entirely, or that he intends educating him as a Christian, and so only alienating him?"

His companion looked up at him quickly. "One is as bad as the other," she said.

"So I think," Mr. Heath answered, "but surely you cannot expect me to advise against educating your child as a Christian, or to condemn your husband for doing it."

"I do not ask you to condemn my husband at all," Helen said, "nor do I blame him for such a wish, for it is but natural in him. The only question I have to decide is, what is best for the child. When that is settled to my satisfaction, I shall bend all my energies and strength to accomplish it. I have thought about it so much that I am distracted, and so have come to you for help. You looked true, as though you could put aside any prejudice against me, or bias for my husband, and act solely for the good of the child."

Her face seemed to grow stronger as she spoke, but a look of latent agony in her eyes and about her lips touched the man in front of her as no pleading would have done. "I cannot advise anything but that your child be brought up a Christian," he answered sadly, "you could not expect anything else from me?"

"No, certainly not." Then her voice faltered and she had to pause a moment. "And I confess I came here more to be confirmed in that opinion than anything else."

"If you wish him to be a Christian," Mr. Heath said eagerly, "you will be one yourself, and your troubles are at an end!"

"You misunderstand me," Helen answered, drawing back. "I do not wish him to be a Christian because I am convinced, but only because I think it more expedient."

There came a trifle of scorn and some pity into the expression of her listener's face as he asked, "Why is it not just as expedient for him to be an unbeliever as for you?"

"Because my life has been an utter failure! I have been bitterly unhappy, and I want his life to be different."

"And why has your life been a failure?" Mr. Heath went on. "There are numbers of unbelievers to give you countenance; unbelief is actually becoming fashionable. Why is it you have no friends and companions?"

Helen shook her head. "That is not what I meant; you misunderstand me again. I meant expedient in the sense of happy. My nonbelief is so empty, I think Christianity is more comfortable."

"If that is all," Mr. Heath answered, "I do not see the need you feel to sacrifice yourself in giving up your child. If there is to you no principle involved, he should give up his comfort for yours."

Helen looked puzzled: what a peculiar man this was. "Then you think I need not let him go?" she asked doubtfully.

"Certainly you need not, if it is only his comfort in this life that is endangered," Mr. Heath answered. "If you are sure there is no life to come, that death is the final end, that there is no heaven and no hell, that there is no danger of his being eternally damned; if you are sure of this, I would not for one moment think of sacrificing my own comfort for his in such a little matter as this world's happiness. Life is at best a short affair soon over."

Helen sat silent. How strange that this man should give her the very reasons with regard to her son's life that she had urged with regard to herself years ago. "I gave myself all those reasons years ago when I promised my father not to forsake him," she answered almost absently, her mind going back the while; then added more slowly, "but they did not satisfy me."

Mr. Heath looked at her doubtfully. "I do not quite comprehend you," he said. "You tell me first that you have been educated an unbeliever, and have promised to remain so; still, you are not sufficiently satisfied to train your child as you were trained. Did you, believing there was a risk, or a shadow of truth in Christianity, *dare* to make such a promise, *dare* to throw away your immortal soul?"

How his eyes gleamed and shone as he questioned her, and what awful depths there seemed in them as he fixed them on her as though striving to read her inmost thoughts.

She met the look, and her answer came sad and quiet, "Yes, I did dare it. My father dared it, and he, loving me as never parent loved a child before, asked me to dare to stand by him, and I promised, and shall fulfill my promise. I acknowledge I think my life is a failure, but I believe it is owing more to my weakness than my training. I cannot prove this, because I cannot go back and educate myself afresh, but, recognizing the fact that my life is a failure, and not being able to prove wherefore, I must take the most probable causes, and strive to leave them out of my son's education."

"And why," Mr. Heath asked, "do you put down your unbelief as one of these causes?"

"Because it made me different from my kind," she answered readily, "because, seeing every one around me with near motives, my life seemed empty with only far-off ones. I was not content to sacrifice my happiness for an abstract principle of truth that was being preserved for future generations. This life, as you say, is but a short affair, but it was all I had, and I naturally wanted it to be happy. But it has not been, for I was not generous enough to be happy in feeling that I was living for the good of my kind, nor was I strong enough to refuse to give up my wishes when my father's happiness was in the balance. Thus I was obliged to be satisfied with emptiness. It is not because your belief is reasonable, or because my unbelief is unreasonable, that I am unhappy, but because I am not strong enough to stand alone, because I am not noble enough to live a life guided by abstract principles, and barren of all reward or punishment."

Mr. Heath listened patiently until she finished, then asked, "And now that you have reached these conclusions, why do you not for expediency's sake become a Christian, and put some hope, never mind how silly, and some motives, never mind how low, into your life? Why keep to your level, barren nothingness?"

She looked at him questioningly as she answered, "Because I promised my father."

"And you kept your promise as long as he lived but why keep it any longer? If he is dead as you believe in death, it can make no difference to him now."

Mr. Heath was almost sorry he had said it when he saw the paleness that crept over his listener's face. She raised her hand as though to ward off a blow. "But if he should not be!" she cried, and her voice was low and tense, "if you should be right, and I wrong, I could not even then desert him. I would rather bear all the consequences than be in peace and see him suffer! Oh, heaven itself would be hell under those circumstances!"

"And you admit the possibility of a future state?"

"A possibility yes, but not probability."

Mr. Heath paused a moment after her answer, then said, "Admitting then this possibility, I, a Christian, am convinced by you, an unbeliever, that your child should be trained a Christian."

"And must I," she asked, as though not quite understanding the position she had been brought to occupy, "must I let him go?" A moment's pause, then a quick, sharp sigh. "I cannot, I cannot!" she cried. "I tell you, in all the world I have no other soul to cling to; there is no other creature that is all my own! The last words came like a wail, as though the heart had crowded the reason down and now stood clamoring for itself, crying out against being desolated, "I cannot, I will not let him go!"

Her listener waited quietly. He had expected some such outburst; for no woman, no mother, could argue for long in that quiet strain about giving up her only child. And the last cry of agony had been watched for, and patiently he began the same arguments over again. "Can you reconcile yourself," he asked, "to making him run the same fearful risks you are running at this moment?"

"My father, I tell you, let me run them."

"And if we are right," Mr. Heath began.

"I know all you can say," she interrupted, sharply striking her hand on the table, "I know all you can urge, and more. I can see him cut off from all his kind, as I have been; I can see his life stretch blank and hopeless before him; I can see the spring taken out of every action, and the light out of all his days by this nothingness I cling to; but I cannot let him go!" The words seemed to rush from her lips, so fast and passionate were they, ending with the pitiful iteration, "I cannot let him go!"

"And you would doom him to the same path of suffering you now find so intolerable?"

The voice was sad beyond description. "And must I add to the intolerableness?" The question was pitifully pleading.

"Let us put it differently," Mr. Heath said patiently. "Give way to your clearer reason and better self, and you acknowledge it is better even from a worldly standpoint for your child to be a Christian. Now, acknowledging this, surrender him, feeling that, if the sacrifice is hard, it has been made through your love for him; that ever in his looking back he will remember and reverence you for it."

"He will not be allowed to remember me at all," she answered bitterly.

"Even so, let him never know you, let him never hear your name, never know you cared for him. Are you not strong enough to put yourself out of the question? Are you not mother enough to look only to the good of the child, and, subverting self, be thankful you can do something for the future of your son, for at best his future will be clouded?"

When he ceased the face opposite him had changed; there was a light and a strength in it he had never seen before, and the eyes shone. She had heard the old war cry of her youth, the cry that had urged her through her life and its sacrifices: "Are you not strong enough?"

Had her father come back? Was it not his voice she heard saying the old familiar words? She answered to the call almost by instinct.

"I will do it." The voice and the words were quiet, but there was no faltering in them. The habits and training of all her life laid their clinging hands about her, and she took her old position. Life was short at best, and a little suffering more or less did not matter; she was born to trouble; she must learn to bear her fate.

The Christian priest watched the beautiful face as the light went out of it and it seemed to settle into quiet endurance. Would she be strong enough to keep her word, he wondered, strong enough without the help of religion, without the hope of a future life?

Presently she rose. "I must go now," she said, then paused a moment before she went on slowly, "You have made me decide on what is best for my child as far as I can see. My father judged differently for me, but here I think he would have agreed with me, for the practical results of my education have been miserable. I thank you for helping me to end my suspense, although you have left me hopeless, but you must not let this thought annoy you, for it is but where I have before stood. And now, goodbye. May I come again?"

Mr. Heath took the hand she held out in both his own. "If you only will," he said gently, "by God's mercy I may sometime help you." Then after a little pause, "I shall pray for you day and night."

The words came back to her as they had been said before: "I will pray for you day and night, that God will save your soul," and the thought of that gentler sorrow that was now so overshadowed brought a mist of tears before her eyes. "I have been prayed for before," she said, "and if you think it will do me any good, I thank you. Goodbye."

Then she was gone, and the room seemed poorer and the day darker as she passed away. And the man left standing there drew a long breath, as one coming back to present things after absorbing dreams.

"And, coveting the heart a hard man broke,
One standeth patient, watching in the night,
And waiting in the daytime."

—"Brothers, and a Sermon," Jean Ingelow

CHAPTER VI

"HELEN," MRS. FELMERE SAID, one day not long after Helen's visit to Mr. Heath, "we have decided, Philip and I, that the child should be baptized."

This announcement was sudden, for nothing had as yet been openly said in the family on this subject; and now this unexpected mention made Helen feel as though her breath had left her, and something was tugging at her throat. There was quite a moment's pause before she found her voice; then she answered slowly, "Yes."

"We thought we would ask Mr. Tolman to come to the house," Mrs. Felmere went on, "and have only the family present."

"Yes," Helen again assented, still finding it hard to speak.

This noncommittal style of conversation began to have its effect on Mrs. Felmere, causing her to feel both uncertain and uncomfortable; but she persisted in her course. "I wish to name the child Philip, but my son says he thinks you wish to name him after your father."

"I did so wish," Helen answered.

"Well, have you changed your mind?"

"My mind has never yet been fixed."

"Will you then fix it, and let us discuss the matter?" Mrs. Felmere's tone was becoming stiff.

Helen thought a moment, then answered very slowly, "If the child is to inherit Felmere, I prefer his being named Hector; it has always been the name of the eldest son, except my brother."

Mrs. Felmere did not understand the apparent indecision on her daughter's part, and asked sharply, "Who else is there to inherit Felmere?"

Helen shook her head. "It is mine," she answered, "to leave as I please."

"But you surely would not leave it away from your child?"

"When I decide on what I wish the child named," Helen answered, quietly passing over Mrs. Felmere's last question, "I will tell you. After that, if Philip desires another name for him, he can suit himself." Then she left the room.

Mrs. Felmere sat thinking. Would Helen really leave the place out of the family? The very idea of having no Felmere Hall to talk about struck Mrs. Felmere as an incurable and dreadful ill. This Felmere Hall that she had so longed and yearned for, that she had planned and fought for: ah, she could not give up now; this thing must not be. Of course the child should be named Hector. Then she went to tell her son how very quietly his wife had behaved about the baptism, and how she had concluded it more wise to name the child Hector.

Helen, meanwhile, strove to calm and brace herself for this inevitable event. She had thought herself prepared, and had fixed in her own mind that Mr. Heath should baptize the child. But now she could not even think to any purpose, and after all her efforts could only decide that she would declare this desire of hers to her husband and his mother, and would the next day go again to Mr. Heath. Having come to this determination, she went down to the parlor, where Philip and his mother were in grave silence awaiting dinner.

"Aunt," she said slowly, "I have come to say that I am willing to have the child baptized, but on the condition that Mr. Tolman shall not do it."

Mrs. Felmere was too much shocked to speak, and Philip, looking at his wife in much surprise, asked, "Whom else would you have? The Bishop?"

"I do not know the Bishop," Helen answered, "and the honor is nothing to me. The person I wish to baptize the child is Mr. Heath. He is a regularly ordained clergyman of your church, so you can have no objection to him. You may ask the Bishop about him if you like."

And she gave the street and name of his church.

"And what fault, may I ask, do you find with Mr. Tolman?" Mrs. Felmere began, having partially recovered her astonishment, and at the same time found herself under the weight of a large access of indignation. "Mr. Tolman is about to be connected with the family,"

Mrs. Felmere continued, "He is, more than this, a good man and the clergyman of my church. What can you say against him?"

"I would rather not discuss Mr. Tolman," Helen answered, "it is enough that I do not like him. The point with you has heretofore been to have the child baptized. I concede that, and now make my point that the child shall be baptized by Mr. Heath, or not at all. I will stand to this, for it is no gain to me to have this thing done rather loss."

Then she left them and went back to her room. About the naming of the child Helen had been thinking much, and in the train of these thoughts came many others of deeper import. If she allowed her son to be trained a Christian, would it not be better for the child never to know her? Ought she not to carry the plan completely out and leave him altogether? And if she were going to leave him, would it not be better to let the family train and name the child to suit themselves, and let her go away back to her own home? And here she would pause in her cogitations and plans, for she could not decide. She would even go so far as to think whether or not she should leave him the old place, and give herself reasons for and against it. There was no reason why she should do it. The child would never be taught to love or reverence either herself or her father; the place would have no associations for him, no sacredness in his eyes; it would ever be represented to him by his grandmother as the home of her husband. If she should live and hold the property until after the child came of age, it would be different; for she could then send for him, and, making herself known to him, put the old house and things into his own hands; and if he had not too much Jourdan in him, he would value them for themselves, and not because they made him able to say to the world, "I have an ancestral home!"

How she despised the Jourdans! There was another thought she could never reconcile herself to: it was that Mrs. Felmere should ever set foot inside of Felmere. The place seemed to her too sacred. She could not bear to think of those cold, light eyes looking about and appraising things that to her were worth more than all the world, old things hallowed by association, and beautified by the touch of dear, dead hands. Ah, that should *never* be.

Thus her thoughts would wander off into the farthest possibilities, and finally, after long circuits of unanswerable questions, come back to the naming of the child and her first round of arguments. "If he had the place, she would wish him to be named Hector, and yet she could not know if she were going to live until her son was of age. Then, again, if he were to be brought up among the Jourdans, she would prefer his not being named Hector often ending with the wild wish to take him away and rear him as she pleased. Then she would wring her hands, or cast herself down and sob as though her heart would break. How could she how could she go away and leave him? But it was not often she let herself reach this point, for she ever strove, and wisely, to keep her mind off side issues, such as the naming of the child and the bequeathing of the place.

Mr. Heath, meanwhile, thought much about her, and often wondered who she was. Only once since her visit had he seen her, and then she was driving among the rich and fashionable people in the park, and did not see him. It was a strange case, he thought, that a woman with everything this world could give should yet seek him out in his poverty and obscurity, to tell him her sorrows, and ask his help. It certainly was very strange, and he often wondered how it would all end, and if she would really come to him again. Poor thing. He was very sorry for her.

But she did come again, and, standing in the same place, scanned him in the same way. "I am come again, Mr. Heath," she said, as they shook hands, "and this time it is to ask some questions. I will try not to keep you long."

"I am glad to give you my time," he answered, as they sat down, "and only hope I may be able rightly to answer your questions."

"They are not difficult." Then she paused. "I have consented that the child should be baptized," she went on more slowly, "and that, of course, means that he shall be reared a Christian. Now, the question is is it wiser for the child that I should stay with him or leave him? Shall I give him up body as well as soul?"

There was a moment's silence, then she went on, "My desire is that you put aside all consideration of me in this matter, and look only to the good of the child, and for you to do this justly, you should know somewhat of the child's circumstances and surroundings. He will grow up among a set of people who are nominally Christians, but Christians stamped with the 'image and superscription' of the world. This Christianity, as you will already have concluded, is neither true nor deep, and cannot have much hold on a true nature, such as I hope my child's will be; and knowing this, I cannot but think that my staying may cloud even the small fragment of faith they may succeed in inculcating. I have no desire to do this, for I am truly seeking my child's happiness, and I well know he will not find it in doubt.

"Whatever he is, let him be that honestly. Christian or Rationalist, he must not be lukewarm; for of *all* that is the bitterest suffering. On the other hand, if his nature is false, and I mingle in his life, he will prefer my unbelief, for his nature will then be untrammeled. But more than all this, will it be happy for him to learn to love a mother he will have to regard as a lost soul? Had I not better go away quietly and leave him to grow up not knowing me?"

Mr. Heath could not answer; he could not tell her she must go, he could not tell her she must stay. "I do not know what to say," he began at last. "I could not advise you to teach him yourself, for your teaching would not be true, and I hold religion far too sacred to be taught falsely; I could not ask you to be such a hypocrite."

"And I could not be," she answered. "If I stay," she added, "I shall have to stand by and see others train and teach him, and I do not know that I should be strong enough to hold myself from molding him. I do not know what to do."

If she were only a Christian, he thought, then spoke slowly, "If it is better for your child to be a Christian, I ask again, why not for you?"

And she, going back loyally, made the old answer, "Because my father did not think it best; because I took an oath to stand by him for ever."

"And you do not fear the risk?"

"I cannot really believe there is any risk; it is only a dim, shadowy possibility that haunts me sometimes. When I analyze your religion, it is as mysteriously contradictory as a fairy tale: it is to me a mass of beautiful foolishness."

Mr. Heath rose and walked to the window, and back again to the inner door, then asked, "Have you ever talked with anyone, I mean any Christians, on this subject?"

"Yes."

"And did they in no way sway you?"

"No, I only thought it all very beautiful and very comfortable, but not very reasonable. Perhaps, if my faith had been cultivated more and my reason less, I should have looked at it differently, but now I cannot."

Mr. Heath thought a moment, then answered slowly, "In that it is beyond reason, I know it is unreasonable."

"How then can you hold it?" she asked quickly. "Because it also comes down within the sphere of both reason and common sense."

She shook her head. "I cannot see this as you do," she answered, "it puzzles me; I get lost in trying to think it out. I cannot see so far as to understand why your God took the trouble to make us. Do you think he made us for his glory? Do you think he likes the wails and cries of agony that for ever go up? This God that is all-merciful and all-powerful: could he not have saved us by his word, and without all this suffering without this elaborate plan of salvation? It surely seems a great deal of useless sorrow and work."

"We do not know *why* he made us," Mr. Heath answered, "but we know we are *here*; and we cannot comprehend his plan of salvation, but we understand enough of it at least to use it to overcome our sinful natures, and so be saved from the death of sin. Look where you will, you see the whole physical universe governed by laws; would it have been wiser, do you think, to have made the moral universe without laws, without any plan, a chaotic uncertainty? Must God, because he is all-merciful, save us in spite of ourselves? Raise us from this life to a higher state, whether or not we are prepared to understand or even desire that higher state? The moral universe without laws would be in as confused a state as the physical universe without laws. We do not expect the law of gravitation to be done away with because we choose to jump out of a window, and we know that if we do so foolish a thing we shall certainly be dashed upon the earth and be killed. Why, after living a disobedient life, should we expect God to do away with the natural results consequent on broken moral laws, any more than he should do away with the suffering consequent on our dashing ourselves from a window? I cannot see, and yet on all hands I meet this expectation. The same God established all the laws, and why they should not be carried out equally seems a strange inconsistency to me. In both cases humanity is fairly warned, and why, if we believe at all, should we not believe as firmly in one set of laws as in the other?"

His tone had become as the tone of one musing, as though he had forgotten his companion, and her answer, coming slowly, startled him, "And you wish me to say I humbly receive and blindly believe these awful mysteries and laws that go to make a creed which, if true, condemns my dead father to eternal damnation?"

Her words dropped on the silence heavily, and the man before her pondered sadly. "No one can know God's mercy," he said at last, "your father may be saved."

She made a quick gesture with her hand, as though waving his words aside. "If your religion is true, there is no hope for him!" she answered. "He had all the opportunities for being a Christian, and he deliberately determined not to be one: more than this, he calmly and thoughtfully took another soul, and, shutting it off from all Christian knowledge, carefully put every known barrier between it and possible belief. Is this not a deadly sin in your eyes?"

The answer came unfalteringly, "Yes, to me it would seem an unpardonable, a damnable sin, but in another, how can I know how God in his omniscience may regard it? We do not know what may have been revealed in the depths of that poor human heart, what reasons for his blindness and weakness. His life may have been all bitterness and disappointment until his faith failed him. I do not know. I can but leave him to God. But you, you can see the light if you will; and if you *will* not . . . "

"I shall follow my father."

"And if there is an afterlife yon will forever leave your child for the baptismal cross upon his brow will be the sign of the 'great gulf' that will be set between you. His little arms can never reach you. His little voice can never come to you . . . "

Ah, the pitiful agony that crept over the face opposite him, the white speechless agony that made him wish his words unsaid. He turned away; he could not look at her. And she, not moving her eyes from his averted face, answered slowly, "And you would have me convince myself, or strive to do it, that a religion is true which would compel me to believe that my father, the only creature in all my past that was my own, is now suffering an eternity of increasing torture; or, unless I hold this, that I shall for ever lose my child?"

Mr. Heath faced her quickly, and his words fell fast and sharp, "I would have you to suffer that thought, or any other, to save your soul. Your father lived his life; he turned from the light or he hid it; he used his opportunities as he deemed best; and he is now in the hands of an infinitely merciful God. But, lying in his grave, he has no right to trammel you. He had no right to blind you and to drag you after him. Every mortal soul stands or falls to itself, and no man has a right to put another soul in bondage. I tell you again, if your father is dead as you believe in death, your keeping your promise is of no avail: if there is a hereafter," he paused a moment, and his words came more slowly, "will it make his sufferings any less that you should stand beside him to add the awful thought that he had dragged you there had betrayed your trusting innocence?"

There was an awful horror in the face of his listener, and the eyes looked almost glazed as they stared into his; then the answer came in a low-strained voice, "Now I know my father was right, for he loved me more than he did himself, and unless he had been sure, he would never have made me follow him." She paused a moment. "Could I make my child run any such risk? I do not wish him to run the risk even of present unhappiness. I am almost willing to empty my life for him by leaving him; and my father loved me just as well nay, better. In all his life he had no creature left but me, and in death I will not desert him."

It was too awful. Mr. Heath again turned his face away, and the low voice went on, "And now, as I stand here this day, suffering more almost than I am able, I can see back into my own life, and forward to my child's. If I train him as I was trained, all that I have endured he will also meet; if I rear him a Christian, then some day he will suffer the torture for me that you would have me suffer for my father. I will not put this on him. I must gather up my strength and go!"

It was almost sublime. As far as he could see, her life had been all sacrifice first to her father, now to her son. She had no God, she had no friend; and now she stood ready to leave herself utterly desolate for the love of her child.

She rose. "I must go now, but before I say goodbye I wish to ask you if you will baptize my child for me? I have come to feel that you are true; you never let the thought of my suffering stand between you and what you think you ought to say, and I value this. More than this, I think you will feel for me, and not against me. You will look on me as a suffering woman, and not as an obstinate infidel. Will you do it for me?"

"I will."

"Then, when the time comes, I will send for you, or come for you."

"And I shall be ready," he answered, then conducted her to the carriage that was waiting. Once more alone in his poor dingy room, he went again over the morning's talk. This woman and her trouble haunted him, and he could not push them aside. He wondered if she would be able to give up her child entirely, go and leave it to live and grow without any knowledge of her, and do this without any hope of reward except the child's happiness here. It was wonderful. Poor thing. How pitifully she clung to her father, "the only soul in all her past that had been wholly hers."

This father must have been a strong man to gain so powerful an influence, and create such a love. She had never mentioned her mother, and he wondered what had become of her. And while he thought of her, he remembered that even in this second visit she had not revealed herself, and was as unknown to him now as she had been at first. He did not know so much as her name, nor how she had ever heard of him; the next time he met her he would ask her this last question. Her name, of course, she must reveal or not, as she pleased. He was pitifully sorry for her, yet did not see that he could comfort her. Alas, no mortal could, but he honestly believed and prayed that God would do so.

"Canst thou not fold rebellious hands at last!"

—Unknown

CHAPTER VII

MRS. FELMERE WAS UNHAPPY, and the whole Jourdan family, except Jack and Arthur, were in a state of "I-told-you-so" and "What-else-can-you-expect?" sympathy. Long ago Mrs. Felmere had given up trying to make Philip's marriage appear a success; long ago she had given up uncomfortable ruses, and taken to talking over things in delightful conclave with Miss Esther, Mrs. Jourdan, and Amelia. This new freak of Helen's was a charming tidbit, and, being left by Philip to manage as best she could, Mrs. Felmere ordered the carriage and drove immediately to Miss Esther's. Here she found Mrs. Jourdan and Amelia; so with much alacrity she opened her budget.

Miss Esther refused to be astonished. She had expected this all along was, in fact, surprised that Helen consented at all to the baptism; and she was sure that when she heard of the proposed plan of taking the child to Europe, she would poison both Mrs. Felmere and the child, for there was no telling what unbelievers would not do once they began.

Mrs. Jourdan looked triumphantly sad. Amelia was not a beauty, nor was any great social or intellectual success expected from Jack, but she felt certain that these commonplace children of hers would afford her more comfort and satisfaction than poor Sister Amelia's child had given her. Mrs. Jourdan only *thought* this; she said that she was sure both Amy and Mr. Tolman would understand the position, and, though very sorry about it, would make no difficulty nor bear any hard feeling. It was all very sad, she thought, and the sooner Helen could be persuaded to go back to her own home, the happier for all parties. Philip and his mother could stay in Europe until the thing was forgotten, and this would not be very long.

So Mrs. Felmere went home much comforted. Miss Esther had agreed that it was best to let Helen have her own way, had appeared deeply interested in Philip, and had consented to be godmother to the child.

This last was a great point gained, but Mrs. Jourdan felt as though "Sister Amelia" had taken an undue advantage of her; for, as they had always been comrades in their intentions about Miss Esther's money, it seemed hard that the baby should be brought to play on his great-aunt's feelings when "Sister Amelia" knew that Mrs. Jourdan had no grandchild to dedicate to that unmade will. And Mrs. Felmere had an instinctive certainty of this feeling of "Sister Margaret's," but she quieted her conscience by the knowledge that all of Amy's children would be offered up after this same plan, and that where she had the advantage in time, they would doubtless have it in number. Poor Jack had lost all his chances by espousing Helen's cause, but Amy had doubled hers the day she accepted Mr. Tolman, and Philip, too, had much increased his by putting things into his mother's hands and leaving them there by turning his life and his wife over to be managed by his family.

This action was looked on as undeniable proof of good training, and a pledge to the good teachings and influence of Mr. Tolman. For all this Mrs. Felmere was truly thankful, and began to hope she might yet turn her misfortunes and disappointments concerning Helen into helps instead of, as she had once feared, hindrances. So, out of the abundance of her satisfaction and gratitude, she asked Mr. Tolman to preach a sermon on the text, "All things work together for good," etc., and Mr. Tolman said he would.

Thus Helen found her point conceded concerning Mr. Heath, but a counterpoint made about Miss Esther. "You may name the child and have him baptized by whom you please," Mrs. Felmere said, "but I wish my sister Esther to be his godmother."

Helen stood silent, thinking. She longed to defy them and refuse to have her child baptized at all, but for the child's good she restrained herself, and, though she hated Miss Esther, she gave up, not seeing the use in further contention. "I have no one to propose as his god-mother," she answered, "but I should think a younger person, who would live long enough to really help train the child, would be prefer-able, and he will have enough money without hers."

Arthur, who was sitting near, could not help smiling. Philip drummed on the windowpane; and Mrs. Felmere had to wait a few moments before she could get sufficient control of her voice to speak, and in the pause Helen went on, "I suppose, then, I may choose the godfathers. I believe a boy has two?"

"I prefer not saying anything,"Mrs. Felmere answered, "for I am insulted at every turn."

"I did not mean to insult you," Helen said, "and you cannot surely have forgotten the conversation we had on the subject of your sister's will when I first came? You did not seem then to think it was wrong to use means to get Philip favorably remembered, so I naturally con-cluded baby was to be used to make up my deficiencies in this matter. I meant no insult. But I would like to choose the child's godfathers."

"And you may," Philip answered, after a short silence. "Thank you."

Then the conversation dropped, and Arthur shortly after took his leave. Mrs. Felmere's curiosity as to the godfathers was a gnawing pain, but she would not ask, she would not stoop to such a thing. They would doubtless be chosen out of the "art ring," and one would probably be Helen's "old friend" Mr. Gordon. Philip was an idiot to have given her any such permission after she had put the possibility of refusal into his hands, but it did truly seem impossible to teach Philip tact or wisdom.

Presently she spoke, and Helen, sitting quiet, listened with in-tensity to her words, but she did not pause in her stitching nor show in any way how vitally she was interested in the conversation. "Philip, Mrs. Beaumont sails for England in May; do you not think that will be a pleasant party to go with?"

"Who else will be in the party?" Philip asked in a not very joyous tone.

"Mortimer Beaumont and his wife, and I do not know but that Amy and Mr. Tolman will be persuaded to go."

"Will Amelia be married before May?" Helen asked, wishing to help the conversation on, and if possible find out the family plans. That there was a plan she was sure; for things had been much more quiet of late, as though settled in their grooves and working toward some certain end. Of course the end could bring her no good, but she would rather know what it was to be, and prepare herself for it. She had, as far as she could, settled her own plans, but did not wish to divulge them until she had found out theirs to some extent. For, although she said she had decided to give up all and go away, yet if she found they were willing she should keep her child in any halfway fashion, she did not know that she could leave him. She would not attempt to make any resistance, for by law they could get him, and by patience she might win something, never mind how little. So she asked quietly her question, "Will Amelia be married before May?"

"God willing, she will," Mrs. Felmere answered solemnly. Then there was a pause, in which Helen wished very much to ask why the Lord might object, for she so hated this lip-piety of Mrs. Felmere and her family, but she restrained herself, saying instead, "Then I should think she would go. It will make it so much pleasanter for her to be with you."

Mrs. Felmere looked up quickly, but Helen stitched away quietly, and Mrs. Felmere wondered much how Helen had discovered the plan for her going. Then she answered slowly, watching Helen's face the while.

"Yes, and she can help me too."

Philip was watching also, but not a muscle moved, not a shade more of color came or went, and the needle did not pause in its going. They did not know by what an awful effort it was that Helen held herself in check, nor how for a long time she had been schooling herself to meet this trial, but she met it bravely, for the self control to which she had been trained came now to her aid, and she went on quietly, "Help you? Why, will you not take your maid? Will you not be very uncomfortable without her?"

Philip had stopped his drumming on the windowpane, and stood looking into the street without seeing anything, only heartily wishing himself away from before the storm he feared was brewing, ready to burst on his miserably unfortunate head. He listened anxiously as his mother answered, "Of course my maid will go, but there will be other things to do beyond her sphere."

The words fell chillingly on the daughter's heart and soul, killing all the faint fluttering hopes she had fostered with such clinging love.

She knew this work that was beyond the maid's sphere meant the caring for her child. But she did not cry out in her anguish, nor make any sign. She only felt she must be alone for a little while; so folding up her work quietly she rose. "I am sure I hope you will have a pleasant time," she said, "as pleasant as I know I shall have at old Felmere." Then she left the room, pausing on her way to glance out of the window, and to push back a vase that stood too near the edge of a bracket.

Ah, what a long breath of relief Philip drew when the door closed after her. "Mother," he said, "have you told her yet?"

Mrs. Felmere shook her head. "No, my son, but she knows."

"How do you know that?" he went on. "I mean, how does she know that the baby is to go, and how do you know that she is aware of it"

"I understand what you allude to,"Mrs. Felmere answered, "and I know from many little signs which a man would not notice that what I say is true. First, she is making for the child with her own hands an entire set of clothes, and learned to sew in order that she might do it. There is no need for this unless he is going from her. Second, she has made Annie promise to stay with him as his nurse as long as she possibly can. And the last thing, and to me the strongest evidence of all, is that two months ago she moved the child's crib and clothes into the nursery with Annie, giving the girl the entire charge of him, and only allowing herself to see him twice in a day, and never at night. Does this not show that she is breaking gradually the ties between herself and the child? What need unless they are to be separated?"

"She *is* strong!" Philip said emphatically, driving his hands deeper into his pockets.

"I call it heartless," his mother retorted.

Philip shook his head. "If she were heartless she would not need to break herself away gradually; she would give the child up easily."

"If she cared for him, she would not give him up at all, "Mrs. Felmere answered. "I know I would not until compelled."

Philip looked at her in astonishment. "Why, mother! And yet you compel Helen to do this thing. How can you?"

"I think, Philip, of the good of the child," his mother answered. "What were the suffering of ten lives compared with the loss of a soul. This is my motive, but I do not see how this can be any motive to an unbeliever, especially so obstinate a one as she is. Thus I am compelled to put down her calmness and willingness to give him up to lack of affection."

"May she not be acting for the child's good also?" Philip asked.

Mrs. Felmere smiled bitterly. "Can you imagine your wife thinking I could work good to any creature?" she said. "Does she treat you as though she considered you a success?"

Philip looked doubtful. He would like to be convinced by his mother's reasoning. It would be more comfortable to think Helen did not care for the child, and the thrust in the last clause of his mother's speech, which he knew to be true, hurt him and aided much in confirming his desire to agree with his mother; so he went on more tamely in his defense of his wife, "But, mother, if she dislikes you to this extent, the very knowledge that you want the child would make her keep him from you."

"So one would think," Mrs. Felmere answered, "unless one had found other motives."

Philip looked at her searchingly. "What do you mean?" he asked sharply.

"Only this, Philip: She asked me once on whom the disgrace fell the most heavily in case of a divorce. I told her on the woman. She is ambitious, beautiful, popular, and proud. Do you think she would enjoy being disgraced? She knows if she demurs you will get the divorce and the child too, and she thinks it better to give him up. More than this, the pathetic story she can make, that because she is an unbeliever you and I have taken her child from her, will be quite a card in her hands; for the world will not stop to reflect on the awful responsibility we feel for that child's soul. It will surely take the short-sighted view that the child could be educated a Christian anyhow, even with all her influence bearing against it, and with her example giving the lie, as it were, to all our teaching. I have thought seriously on all these points, my son, and I know them to be true. "Why, already Arthur and Jack look on her as a martyr. The next person to take this view will be Valeria Vanzandt; then all her train of artist people, and people who admire her notoriety and bow to her money. Ah, my son, your wife will have many more adherents than you will, but you will be right. More than this, she *may* have other plans. I doubt her going back to Felmere to live alone." She paused a moment, then added more slowly, "Did she not tell me Felmere was hers to leave as she pleased, and that she did not care for the child to be named Hector unless he was to inherit the place? To what does all this point?"

Philip turned very white. Mrs. Felmere went on, "Did it never occur to you that she might marry again? Divorced Christians do, and what better could you expect from an unbeliever? I tell you she *does not want* the child."

Upstairs the mother sat stitching feverishly, driving the needle through monotonously, swiftly, beating down her heart with words that kept time to her stitches, "They will take your child, but you knew it long ago. Why break your heart? Life is short. Death ends all."

Over and over again she said these words, keeping time to her stitch, and the stitches keeping time to the song the little nurse sang in the next room, "Hush, my babe."

Yes, the nurse's babe, the father's, the grandmother's, anyone's babe but hers. She was cut off she stood alone, desolate, cursed. She would sew, though sew for her little one; sew in love in every stitch a drop of heart's blood for every time her needle pierced the little garment. She would so wrap him with love that, baby as he was, he could not but remember her.

The needle snapped, and pricked her finger; a drop of blood oozed out upon the little shirt. She looked at it as though she did not know what it was, and watched it as it spread into a larger spot with a wondering sorrowful look. Slowly she folded the little garment with the spot of blood inside with the thread and broken needle still hanging. "I will put it away," she thought, "and when he is a man and I am long dead, they shall give it to him." Then she went to her writing table and wrote a note, and folding it in with the little shirt, made a bundle of it, and on the outside wrote that if she died before her son came of age, at that time this bundle should be given him. Then she laid it carefully away, and wondered if she was losing her mind.

The song of the little nurse had stopped. She wished it would begin again; she longed to hear something else than the noise of the fire and the ringing in her head. She listened; far down the street she heard a band playing; she put up a window, and on the spring-touched wind the music came to her. A waltz! She leaned her head against the window frame. How wild the music sounded in the gathering dusk, a waltz to be played in glittering ballrooms for broken-hearted humanity to dance to. Yes, the time should be gay, but the melody should be gathered from all the hearts that ever broke, the spirit from all the tears that ever fell. Poor Humanity, striving so despairingly to be happy. smiling faces over breaking hearts, dancing feet over opening graves, life and death all woven in together. Sad? How could any music ever be sad enough for them to dance to.

She put her hands over her face. Was she going mad? She would have been thankful for some tears. Alas, her brain seemed parched, her eyes dry and burning.

They were going to take her child away. She wrung her hands. Not more than six weeks then such utter, dead emptiness.

"O God!" she cried out. She stood quite still. The words came back to her time and again, echoed, and echoing from every part of the room whispered above, about, within her. *She* had called on GOD that mysterious spirit these Christians believed in. It was so silent. Was He there, in the room? She shivered. Had He heard her? Did He think she had forsaken her father?

"Never, never!" she whispered. "I tell you I have not, I do not believe. My father is all I have, all I have!"

She wrung her hands and crouched on the floor by the fire. Oh, the horror of the thought: that lonely old man, with his sad face and silver hair, and his beautiful eyes that loved and trusted her so. Never, never! They might take her child, they might torture and burn her; but *never* would she desert him.

The inner door of the room opened; a stream of light came flickering through, and in the doorway stood the nurse with the child in her arms. The mistress rose. "Bring him here," she said, then, "Annie, light the lamps."

Ah, how close she held the little one. In six weeks he would be a year old; in six weeks he would be gone. How empty her arms would be, and her heart?

"It will wring in my heart
and my ears till I die, till I die."

—Unknown

Chapter VIII

THE WORDS HAUNTED HER. The cry that had broken from her in her agony followed her day and night; she lived in a feverish dream an awful nightmare. She had called on God. If there was a God, if there was a hereafter, if her father could listen and hear, this God would think she believed her father would think she had deserted him. She would raise her hands to heaven as in defiance. "I do *not* believe I *will* not believe. There is *no* God!"

The days slipped by. Soon all would be gone, her child, her life. Maybe she would die. Ah, it was a blessed hope.

But outwardly she was calm. She stitched morn and noon; the little piles of clothes grew high and higher. The time grew shorter. Her haste increased, and still no tears came.

Philip had come almost to think with his mother, that Helen did not want the child, for she was so calm as the time drew nearer. But not so Arthur. He had had one glimpse into that poor, wild heart, and the sight had almost terrified him; what would come of it?

One day she stopped him on the stairway. "Come here one moment, Arthur," she said, "I have something to say to you, a favor to ask." And she led him into her room and closed the door. She leaned with her back against it, and he stood facing her. He watched her white hands, grown so thin and nervous, twist and untwist themselves; he watched the expression change upon her face until it seemed to him a mask had fallen off. She seemed unconscious of his presence she seemed unable to speak. At last she looked at him, saying slowly, "Arthur, I dare say you know more of what I am about to speak than I do. I do not, in fact, know anything, but I think they are going to take my child from me. I cannot help myself; for, besides knowing that the law will give him to Philip, I feel that it is for the child's good that I should leave him. But I shall not enter into these reasons; it is not necessary. I have brought you here to ask you if you will act as godfather to my child? Will you be good to him, Arthur, and watch him for me? You know the world; you know your sister and Philip; you know what that child will have to contend against. And, Arthur, if I live, will you sometimes write to me about him, and tell me how he looks and how he is? Am I asking too much, Arthur?"

Arthur shook his head. Man of the world as he was, the tears were strangely near at hand, and his voice seemed hard to find. "I promise you, Helen, to do all in my power for your child. I will watch over him and guard him to the utmost of my ability, and from me he shall know you for what you are."

She shook her head hopelessly. "It does not matter much what he thinks of me," she said, "for to him I can only be a lost soul. But you will write to me?"

"I will." Arthur felt almost dazed; her last speech had opened so much to him that he had not thought of before. She went on, "Do you go to Europe with them?"

"Yes, and I shall write you at every stage. I shall be glad to do it."

"Thank you," she answered, holding out her two hands, "thank you very much, Arthur. It would not be any use for *me* to say, 'God bless you,' but if there is a God, I hope He will bless you for all your kindness to me, and now to my child. You have been very good to me, Arthur, and I hope you will be very happy, and that some day you will be repaid."

Then she opened the door, and Arthur, scarcely knowing why or how, went downstairs and out of the front door as in a dream. Poor creature, was there no help for her?

A few days after this interview, Mrs. Felmere asked Helen if she had yet decided on the godfathers for the child, and on his name. "I have asked Arthur to be one," Helen answered, "and I hope Mr. Heath will be the other, but about the name I have not yet made up my mind."

Mrs. Felmere was frowning. "Who is this Mr. Heath?" she asked.

"He is my friend," Helen answered, "and will be baby's godfather, I hope."

There was silence for a few moments, then Mrs. Felmere spoke. "And when is the baptism to take place?" she asked.

"On what day shall you sail?" was the counter-question.

Mrs. Felmere answered deliberately, watching the face before her as she spoke, "On the first day of May."

"On the morning of that day, then, he shall be baptized." The voice and answer were disappointingly calm.

That afternoon, as Mr. Heath sat preparing his sermon, the slatternly housemaid brought him a note, saying the messenger was waiting for an answer. He took it from her, and, seeing through the window that a servant waited outside, he sent the girl away, saying he would give the answer himself. When the door had closed behind her, he tore open the envelope.

"Mr. Heath,
If you will be at home tomorrow at twelve, I shall be glad to come and see you. I wish to ask you something for my child.
Helen Felmere"

He put the note down slowly as one in a dream. "Helen Felmere!" He looked at the name as though it were a ghost, and pushed it from him. It was doubtless from his unknown visitor, but was that beautiful, rich woman really Helen Felmere? Then he remembered it was her marriage name. She might have been Helen Brown or Smith before that. He turned and walked up and down the room once or twice. There were Felmeres in the city, he knew. He had seen them more than once a mother and son; and this must be the son's wife. But the sudden sight of the name had given him quite a shock. He stopped. He would answer the note first, and think it out afterward.

"Mrs. Felmere,
I shall be at home tomorrow at the hour named, and will gladly do anything in my power to help you.
Very truly,
Percival Heath"

He handed the note to the servant, then returned to his cogitations. Helen Felmere? She must be Philip Felmere's wife. He stopped
still in his walk. She said she had married her cousin. He put his hands
over his face, and had been educated an unbeliever by her father.

For a long while he stood thus; he did not move, he seemed
scarcely to breathe. One or two knocks came at his door and went
away unanswered; still he stood there. At last there was a sound, a
little whisper, "Mother, mother, you were wrong." It was only a whisper, but the concentrated sorrow in those words was inexpressible.

Again the beautiful woman stood within the dingy room, and
the man there waiting for her looked on her with different eyes. She
sat down wearily, and her face looked worn and thin and her eyes
were unnaturally bright. "I have come," she began abruptly, "to ask a
favor at your hands, and you must not hesitate to refuse me if you
think best to do so; will you promise?"

"Yes."

"It is that you will be one of my child's godparents—more than
that—his friend. He will live here near you; I shall go away to my old
home. I am afraid it will not be a pleasant position for you, but I have
a wish that you should take it."

"And I will take it."

"Thank you." Then she paused a moment before she went on,
and her voice was lower, as though she was more carefully weighing
her words, "And will you make him an undoubting Christian? If one
is brought up to it, he can believe it all, and if one can believe it all, it is,
I think, the happiest state. Either that, or where my father stood, an
undoubting unbeliever."

"And you think it easier to be an undoubting Christian than an
undoubting unbeliever?" Mr. Heath asked.

"Yes."

"Why?"

"Because all the world believes, and it is hard to stand out against
it."

Mr. Heath shook his head sadly. "I am sorry to be compelled to
differ with you on this point," he said. "All the world does not believe.
On the contrary, unbelief is quite popular. One only needs to say, 'I am
not quite sound, I lean rather to the scientific side than to the religious,' to be considered well educated and of high mental attainments.
To me it is pitiful. If you wish your son to be well considered in the
fashionable world, let him be educated an unbeliever; for this thing is

growing, and by the time he is a man will, I am afraid, have firm hold of this country. Then it will be easier to be an unbeliever than a Christian, perhaps."

His listener looked at him wistfully as she asked, "Do you not *wish* my child to be a Christian, that you so often, in a manner, dissuade me?"

"I certainly do wish your child to be a Christian, Mrs. Felmere, but I do not wish to get him under any false pretenses. If you are going to make him a Christian solely for his present comfort, I must tell you I think unbelief more immediately comfortable, especially for a rich man of the world. The life of a Christian is by no means an easy, even flow of happiness. There are many pleasant things you have to give up, many temptations you have to withstand, many trials you have to bear patiently for Jesus Christ's sake," (there was a reverent bow with his last words), "so, that you must not make the mistake of thinking your son will have no trouble."

Helen listened intently and watched him closely, and the reverence that came so naturally as he mentioned the holy name impressed her: it was so different from Mr. Tolman's patronizing manner. It seemed so honestly done, an almost involuntary humbling of himself. Then she said, "But when all this is over, you have your reward?"

"Not if you do it from that motive, certainly not," he answered quickly. "You must ever act from a higher motive than self-interest, from the love of the true and the good, from the love of God. In fact, I do not believe that one can be a true Christian from hope of reward or fear of punishment alone; for the essence of Christianity is love; and this not love of self, as acting for a reward would imply, but love to God. I think it wrong to teach Christianity as a system of rewards and punishments."

"And yet," Helen said, "it was not so very long ago that you told me the moral universe was governed by laws, as the physical universe is; and as certain results followed certain actions in the physical world, so in the moral. Is that not law? Is that not a system of rewards and punishments?"

"I grant all that," Mr. Heath answered, "and those intuitions of right and wrong that were created with us, or were given to us in the last stages of development from brute to man, you may put it as you please, are the laws of the moral universe. If we do right, goodwill result; and if we do wrong, evil. These laws have existed ever since man stood upright facing his Maker. But Christianity comes under a higher dispensation, and the keynote of it is, 'If ye love me, ye will keep my commandments,' a higher revelation that says, 'Love your enemies, bless them that curse you, do good to them that hate you, and pray for them which despitefully use you and persecute you.' Are these intuitions? Do these laws naturally govern the moral universe? I think not. We seem to have by nature only a sense of justice more especially to ourselves and a sense of truth. Charity and mercy come in with Jesus Christ."

Again Helen saw the humble little reverence follow the holy name, and she felt, as though compelled, to wait a moment before she could speak. This man seemed to feel that some other presence was there, as though Christ himself stood beside him, and his feeling impressed her. At last she said, "But your Christ surely teaches reward and punishment? I have read the New Testament often, and all through I found this system."

"And so any one must," Mr. Heath answered, "for Christ came under the law, and fulfilled it in every particular. And so do our rewards and punishments come under that same law. But Christ's teachings are all love: there is a fullness of joy and a happiness that comes in proportion to our love and faith in Jesus Christ, that is over and above the cold just reward of keeping the law, a wonderful beauty and gentleness that was never known before."

"But are you not punished for not believing in Jesus Christ?" she went on.

"Why, Christianity *is* Christ. Our belief is this, that the Eternal Son of the Eternal Father took our humanity into his divine nature, so that two perfect natures, the human and divine, coexist in the one divine person. As all men were in Adam, so the Son of God has taken the whole of our essential humanity into Himself. Thus he was not, strictly speaking, *a* man, but *the* man. As any individual man was essentially in Adam from the beginning, and yet had to be *actually* born into the world, so each of us, being essentially in Christ, has yet to be born into Him by the sacrament of Holy Baptism. And as, after we are born into the natural world, food and other things are needed to sustain our new life, so, when we are regenerated or born spiritually into Christ, He has provided spiritual sustenance for this new life in Him chiefly in the mystical food of His Body and Blood, the Sacrament of the Altar. Now the salvation of man is the object in all this; but it is salvation from *sin*, and not merely from the penalties of sin in the future. You will see, then, how necessary it is to accept Christ and to do His will if we would have the salvation He has provided, and how meager and wrong it would be to say we are *punished* for not believing in Christ."

"Yes," she answered slowly, then asked, "Are these your own original views?"

"No, by no means. I have only given you what has always been held by the one Holy Catholic and Apostolic Church." He paused a moment, then added more slowly and gently, "As I have told you, the keynote of Christianity is love, not fear. The blessed Master is all love. There is no heart so humble, so ignorant, so sin-stricken, that He will not receive if it comes to Him; nor is there any heart that will not be able to love Him if it has any desire for purity and truth."

"But what has made you think this is the Christ? The Jews do not believe in him."

"Because He is the only one who has ever fulfilled the law, thus making His life the most perfect, pure, and holy life that has ever been lived. You may not believe the prophecies, or not believe that they point to Christ, but you must believe in the pure and glorious beauty of His life, and holding this, you must accept the miracles, or believe Him an impostor, and in accepting the miracles you must look on Him as divine."

"And do you accept the miracles, and the Incarnation, and the Resurrection, and the Trinity? Do you really believe them as you believe this is a table?"

"I do."

She looked at him curiously. "It is strange," she said, "and it strikes me more forcibly in you than in any other Christian I have ever met. Out in the world where I live, they *say* they believe all these things, but I cannot think they *really* do; for it seems to me that there are few of them who ever give a thought to these subjects, and less than few who can give a 'reason for the hope that is in them.' But I really think you earnestly believe, and it seems so strange that you *can*."

Mr. Heath smiled sadly. "And yet," he answered, "your belief seems quite as strange to me, much more so, in fact."

She looked at him quickly. "You surprise me," she said. "I thought it was my lack of belief that was strange; for what I believe is perfectly reasonable and logical; there is nothing strange in it."

"Is it not strange," Mr. Heath asked, "that from a blind, *unintelligent* Force should be evolved the marvelous intellects that guide the nations, and the high and beautiful moral laws that lift us above the brutes that perish and the worms that crawl? Is it not rather a new and strange idea to have more in the *effect* than there was in the *cause*?"

She listened thoughtfully, and answered slowly, "We get all that through association of ideas."

"The first idea must have come from something."

"Very well, and that first idea was evolved and developed slowly."

"And there must have been some germ in the original Force from which it was developed Everything begins from something. Admit the germ, or admit that there was a fresh creation of intellectual and moral powers which were added to this Force. In this case there was something greater behind Force something moral and intelligent. I will call it God. You may call it what you please. If not this special creation, then these germs of morality and intelligence were contained in this Force I grant this also, and this blind Force becoming moral and intelligent, I call it God."

"Do you believe in evolution?" she asked.

"I shall if it is scientifically proved. There are some alarming gaps in the theory now, but if proved I shall not object to it. To me it would be a beautiful manifestation of the wonderfulness of the Intelligence that governs us. But with evolution I must also believe that at some period during these transitions there was a moral sense put into man, that the brutes have not a time when there was breathed into him the 'breath of life.'"

"And do you hold spontaneous generation?" she went on.

"I shall hold it also, if it is proved, and shall be no less a Christian; for my foundation is sure."

"Tell me your foundation."

"My foundation lies bedded in myself. I know I am moral and intelligent. I see about me thousands who are also moral and intelligent. I know that the sum of all morality and all intelligence must have been contained in that from which it was developed; and that containing substance, be it what you please, is to me God. For what greater can I conceive than that which contains all intelligence and all morality?"

There was a moment's silence when he ceased. Then she said, "And yet you say you believe that unbelief will lay hold on this whole country. Unless there is truth in it, why be afraid?"

"That is the trouble," he answered. "There is so much truth in it that the majority, for the sake of this truth, will accept it *all* and look no further."

"But you," she said, "discriminate, as far as I can judge. Why should not they?"

"Because very few have the time to devote to investigation, even if they were fitted to make the examination. More than this, many would rather believe it because it is new, and Christianity is old; others are carried away by the beauty of the scientific investigations; others will follow for the fashion, and yet others for the reason and common sense they claim to find there. But the strongest weapons in your hands we have put there. Our churchmen, through ignorance of the scientific side of the question, and through devotion to the old theological grooves and ruts, are not meeting the question rightly. They attempt to ridicule it, or attack it angrily. I cannot think these the proper modes of refuting it, or of doing anything but injure ourselves. It is far above ridicule, and to rush against it furiously only convinces people that there must be a great deal in it to cause so much anger. To me it would seem wiser to meet it quietly and examine it thoroughly, carefully sifting out the truth and accepting it, and *proving* the false for what it is. I am not afraid of any truth being found anywhere that will overthrow my belief. I do not, therefore, hesitate to examine closely."

"Have you ever doubted?" she asked.

"No, but through peculiar circumstances I was led to examine, not only unbelief, but the creeds of the three great branches of the Church." Then his words came more slowly, and his voice was lower as he said, "My father also was an unbeliever."

Helen looked up quickly, drawing a sharp, short breath of astonishment. "Did he die an unbeliever?" she asked.

"Yes."

She looked at him in silence. How strange this was. "You were not educated an unbeliever?" she went on.

"No, I was brought up a Romanist."

A feeling of bewilderment was creeping over her. What was all this leading to? Whom was she talking with? Again she spoke, "How, then, are you an Anglican?"

"The Romish Church, or rather a mistaken priest, made my mother commit a great wrong," he answered slowly, "and I could no longer tolerate or trust its teachings. It was a bitter trial to forsake the religion of my mother, but truth compelled me to."

Helen covered her face with her hands. She could not collect her thoughts; she seemed groping with the light shining all about her. At last she put her hands down and looked at him. "I feel so bewildered," she said, "I have had so much of late to trouble me, that I do not think my mind is quite clear; so tell me plainly, is there anything behind all this that you wish me to know?"

"Only this," he answered, laying his hand on hers, "that in your trouble God has guided you not to a stranger, but to your brother, for help."

She looked as though she did not quite understand him. "Your name is Heath?"

"That is my name," he answered, "the maiden name of my mother, which she took again after she left her husband. I was baptized Percival Heath Felmere, and also by that name ordained, but I am always called Heath. Will you not believe me? Wait, I will bring you proof," and he left her quickly.

She did not move. She could not think connectedly. She only wondered in a dull stupid manner. She had known there was some strange tie between her and this man from the first moment she looked at him; she had seen and felt something in him that seemed hers; he looked like her father, and like the picture of her grandfather he was the image of that. It seemed to her now that she could have told him this long ago if she had not been so worried and troubled about her child. How unnecessary in him to bring proof to her. His voice was enough; sometimes it had seemed as though her father was speaking to her; this she had observed long ago. She wished he would come, she was so tired of waiting, and she needed no proof.

He was not very long gone, although it seemed so to her. He brought with him two miniatures and a package of letters.

"I know you are my brother," she said, looking up at him as he stood beside her. "I could have told it to you long ago—long ago—if I had not been so tormented. Your voice is like our father's, and you look like a picture I have of our grandfather. Oh, I am so glad, so glad." She took his hand and looked at it. "My own flesh and blood, a hand I have a right to, a hand that I can love and call *mine*. Oh, I have been so lonely, and now I have a brother."

"Yes," he answered, looking down on her sadly, "a brother who is all yours, who will devote his life to you, who will love you as sister has never been loved before. All my life I have thought of you and loved you. All my life I have longed to go to you, for I was so afraid for you. And now I have found you, and oh, my sister, you will not make me look on you as worse than lost. You will not put that awful gulf of unbelief between us?"

She raised her hand imploringly. "Hush. Do not mention that yet. Leave me my joy for a little while undimmed. Let me forget all differences, for I can never do away with them." She turned from him, and took up one of the pictures he had laid down. "Is this my mother?"

"Yes, and you somewhat recall her to me; your face has haunted me ever since I saw you on the cliff. I first thought it was your great beauty, but now I know it was this dim resemblance to our mother."

It was a sweet, sad face she looked at, with a shadowy, colorless beauty about it, that seemed to fade away on closer examination, and a mingled expression of strength and weakness that was remarkable. "Did she ever speak of me?" Helen asked, as she looked at the picture.

"Often and often. The thought of having left you seemed to haunt her day and night, and all my childhood was filled with descriptions of you and charges about you. For a long time she thought of you as dead; then she heard from a priest who lived near Felmere that you were alive and well, and the longing to see you nearly broke her heart. In her last illness I begged her to let me go for you, but she would not."

"Poor mother, to have to leave her child." Suddenly she closed the picture sharply, and put it down. "She did a great wrong," she went on bitterly, looking up at her brother, "she brought all this sorrow on us, and, if you are right, she left me to eternal damnation."

Quickly her brother's hand was laid on her lips. "It was wrong," he said, "but you must not say so. And now the matter of your salvation lies in your own hands. Your trials have come to you in such wise as to make you look into these things, and you can now choose for yourself."

She shook her head wearily. "It is too late," she said, "too late to turn back from the choice I made long ago, from the vow I took in my youth. Faith has never been cultivated in me. All my training has been against it. I cannot believe. I cannot leave my father."

She rose and walked to the other side of the room, then back again, and stood before him. "You never knew him, you never loved him, or you could not quietly stand here and say to me, 'He will suffer eternal punishment.' I will not believe it, nor any religion that teaches it. The other day in my agony I cried out, 'O God!' and ever since I have been haunted with a mortal terror. Ever since I have been afraid there was a God, and that He heard and believed me. Ever since I have been afraid there was a hereafter, and that my father thinks I have deserted him. I tell you it has ever since been an awful horror following me. I do not believe, and I will not believe. I know there is no God."

Her voice was low and tense with excitement, and at the last she raised her hands up solemnly as though taking an oath against her brother's God. He sat quite still, feeling almost at peace when he thought she had called on God, that to this extent she had acknowledged Him. God was merciful, and God would judge her according to her light.

She stood looking in his face with eyes full of defiance. "Have you nothing to say?" she asked at last. "Do you not try to persuade me that this is a morbid imagination; that I am over-excited; that I am under an unnatural strain, and my nerves are giving way? I know all this; I have said it over and over again; but that does not lessen the clinging horror that is about me, and it can not lessen the knowledge this horror has brought to me, that even in your heaven, your eternal progression from yourself to God, this feeling would drag me down with a more terrible anguish of remorse than you can imagine, a remorse for leaving my father. Ah, you never knew him; you never saw his beautiful, strong face; you never saw the trust in his dear eyes when he looked on me; you never heard him say 'My darling,' nor felt his soft tremulous hand wandering about your brow and hair, never. And you ask me to desert him?"

She turned away, and Percival still said nothing; he could not say anything, for his sympathy all went with this poor torn human heart, this strong soul, so true and loyal to the teachings and love of its youth to its oath made in ignorance. He watched her as she stood leaning on the table, and loved her with a pitying love that was absolute pain. What should he do? How could he help her?

Presently she turned. "Can you not help me?" she asked. "Can you not tell me that your God did not hear me? Or that, if He did, He believes that I honestly defy Him? Tell me something, help me in some way. You are my brother, and you said you loved me."

"And I do," he answered, as he came and stood beside her. "I do with all my heart love you; but how can I help you? I believe there is a God, and I believe He heard you. If you do honestly defy Him, He will know it; if your defiance is not honest, He is merciful."

She looked at him a moment in silence, as though striving to calm herself. "You are so good," she said, laying her hands on his shoulders, "and so true; in my deepest anguish you never mitigate the truth. It is so like our father, and I love you for it. And now I tell you I am right in giving up my child. I would do a great deal more than give him up, if that were possible, to save him from what I suffer now. And to you I leave him, to protect him and to care for him; for I do not think I can live very long. I hope I shall not. But one thing I charge you: never let him suffer for me as I suffer for my father; never let him be able to say, as I say now, 'This suffering is my mother's fault.' Promise me this."

"I promise that this shall be my endeavor," he answered. "Thank you." There was a world of earnestness in her tones. Then she went on, "And now I must go. It is late. But tomorrow you must come to me. You must come and see my child. You must come and let me learn to love you more and more, let me learn to realize this one joy left in my life, and talk with you as I cannot today, for I am excited and weary. Will you come?"

"Without fail. You are now my first thought and duty, and, next to God, you have my dearest love."

Then she stooped and kissed him fervently, hurriedly, as though she did not dare trust herself, and gathering up the letters and the pictures he had brought her, she left him. Left him standing alone in his dingy room, miserable with a misery that was hard to bear.

"Dreamed; for old things and places came
　　dancing about my brain,
Like ghosts that dance in an empty house;
　　and my thoughts went slipping again
By green back-ways forgotten to a stiller circle of time,
Where violets, faded for ever, seemed blowing as once
　　in their prime."

　　　　　　　　　—"Last Words," Robert Bulwer Lytton

CHAPTER IX

A T HOME IN HER OWN ROOM, Helen sat down and tried to think over the events of the day, and to look quietly on the discovery she had made. No one could know how glad she was; no one could appreciate what a relief it was to her. For now she could feel that a true loving care would be about her child when she was gone. Now she need not feel so desolate. There was someone in the world who loved her, and to whom she had a right; someone who would take care of her, and to whom she could leave Felmere Hall, and who would love and appreciate it almost as she did.

She looked again at her mother's picture, and a gentler feeling of sorrow for her mother came over her. She looked so weak and so pitiful, and yet had had the strength to leave her child, whom she evidently thought dying, leaving one to save the other, and finally losing both. Poor mother. The other picture was of her father in his earlier youth, handsome, but without the beauty of that perfect calm which she remembered, and without the soft love in his eyes she always met there. But both pictures would prove Percival's identity to her husband and his mother, and, more than all, establish Percival's right to love and train her child. They would not like it, she knew; but this thought did not in the least trouble her; and, though she looked on the feeling with contempt, yet a little shade of triumph would creep up and mingle with her joy, a feeling of triumph in that she could partially foil her aunt's plans.

The bundle of papers proved to be the marriage certificate of her father and mother, Percival's baptismal certificate, and two or three letters from her father to her mother, written during his last absence from home, at which time she had left him. Yes, these would be quite enough to satisfy them that she had found her brother, and she would disclose the fact at once.

So, when the summons came for dinner, she took the pictures and letters down with her, and laid them by the side of her plate. The conversation was never very easy during dinner, and today Mrs. Felmere's curiosity was so excited by the old letters and pictures Helen had brought with her, that she remained for long intervals silent. At last, when the servant had been dismissed, she turned to Helen saying, "Has Mr. Heath consented to be the baby's godfather?"

"Yes," Helen answered, "and today, in my conversation with him, I have made a discovery which renders my choice of him the happiest thing in the world, in fact, nothing short of marvelous."

"What do you mean?" Philip asked sharply, and Mrs. Felmere was all attention.

"I mean that I have found in Mr. Heath my brother Percival."

There was an utter silence for a few moments; then Helen went on, her voice and quick words showing something like triumph and much suppressed excitement. "These letters and pictures are the proofs; you may look at them if you please," handing them to Philip, who opened them slowly. "I shall leave him everything I own in trust for my child, if not absolutely. I tell you this, aunt, as you asked me to whom I would leave Felmere. It will now, with everything else I own, go to my brother. More than this, I will say that, unless my brother has a fair share in the training of my child, the property I leave shall go to some charitable institution at his death. It is all mine, you know, to dispose of at pleasure."

Mrs. Felmere listened in silence. She wished to hear Helen's full plans, and, besides this, her anger was so great she would have found it difficult to speak. But, when Helen finally paused, she said coldly, "Do you intend to die immediately?"

"To my child I do," Helen answered, "but you know this, and need no answer to your question. And far better than I can tell you do you know that ever since my child's birth you have been plotting and working to take him from me. Now you have succeeded. I could have driven you to the law, but for my child's sake I have not; I would rather he should think of me as dead. Beyond this, I think it more for his present happiness for him to be trained a Christian, and if I were with him he could not well be so trained, or, if he were, he would have the bitterness of looking on me with pity or horror." She paused a moment, then continued with the same strained self-possession, "If I believed in a future life, I do not think I could be content to leave my child in your hands, aunt, for your religion and your life do not seem to me altogether consistent. But, now that I have found my brother, I am satisfied even on this point; for I feel sure my child will be trained to something definite and consistent."

She did not let her awful doubts and trouble appear on her face, nor in any way let them see the depth of her bitter unhappiness; she would rather they should think that the fear, for the child's sake, of the disgrace of a divorce made her give him up.

While she was speaking, Philip appeared to be reading the letters she had given him, and Mrs. Felmere, leaning on the table, listened with a look of bitter anger on her face.

"And now," Helen continued, as she rose and held out her hand for the letters and pictures, "I wish to hear nothing more about this thing. I have consented to go away and leave my child entirely, as though I were dead, but consented on these terms that his uncles Arthur and Percival shall exercise all my rights in his education. If this at any time shall not be allowed, I shall come back if I am alive, and, if I am dead, you will find this point carefully covered in my will. If his education is such as I desire, all my property will be his; otherwise not. And now, having secured him as far as I am able an honest training, I wish him named Hector. He shall be baptized on the day you are to sail, and go with you. I shall go to my own home, and find what peace I can until death releases me."

So saying, she turned and left the room. No comment passed between mother and son; they did not so much as look at one another. They were triumphant inasmuch as they had gained their point, but their victory was accompanied by unavoidable and bitterly humiliating conditions, almost enough to rob the success of all its meaning. They separated as soon as possible and in silence — Philip to the club,

Mrs. Felmere to her own room, there to calm as best she might her ruffled feelings.

Helen, up stairs in the nursery, busied herself and astonished the nurse by moving the child back into her own room. "You must not talk about it among the servants," she said to Annie, "but I have agreed to give up my child and let him be trained a Christian, and next week he goes to Europe with his father and grandmother, and I go home. So, Annie, you must stay with him as long as you can, and watch him for me. And Mr. Heath, Annie, the clergyman of your church, has turned out to be my brother; so he will help to take care of my baby."

The girl stood mute, listening to the wonderful story. Then her eyes filled with tears as she watched her mistress with the child, and listened to her pitiful talk.

"He will be mine only a week longer, Annie, and every moment of that time I want him for my own. I have been trying to break away from him, but I cannot, and, if I live a hundred years away from him, at the end of that time my arms will be just as empty and my heart just as freshly broken as on the day he goes. I can never become used to being without him; therefore I had better have all of him that I can in this last week. I will myself do everything for him, and I will give you time and money to prepare for your journey. Oh, Annie, if I were only you. Will you do all you can for him, Annie, just as though I were by? Or, more than that, just as though he were your own child? You shall be paid any money, Annie, if you will."

"Indeed, ma'am," the girl answered, kneeling by her chair, "I will do all I can for the child, and not for any more money than I now get, but because I love him. All his life I have taken care of him, and I promise to do for him as if he was mine, and I promise you, Mrs. Felmere, honestly. I do."

Then the girl went down, and Helen sat there alone with her child, singing to him softly, and soothing him to sleep. Only a week more, she thought, only a week more, and he would be gone; her heart would be broken, her arms empty. She would go back to old Jane at Felmere, and try to find some rest, go back to her old life, to the old books and walks, to the old studio. She bent her head until it rested on the child, and let her thoughts float back to the old things and places.

She would go back just as though she were again the old Helen Felmere. She would absorb herself in study and in painting. She would make herself a name in the world of art, so that when her son heard of her he could be proud of her.

She wondered if anything at Felmere had changed; if Jane had moved the book her father had left open on the library table the last thing his eyes had read. She wondered if her little childish garden was still there; if Peter had kept it in order for her; and if the martins came as they used to do in the summer evenings to fly about the old house. And would the marsh hens quarrel, and the bitterns cry as sadly as in the old times?

Of course they would, and she only would be changed. Jane would seem a little older, and there would be a little more moss on the old tombstones, and a few more rocks fallen from the old wall. It would be just the same, and she would go back like a spirit from another world, like a ghost haunting old scenes. The river would be singing the same song, and the sea making the same moan, and the maple tree would still be keeping its lonely watch among the dead. And the winds would still wander all about the flats, and whisper, to her the same old stories. And the storms, and sunshine, and seasons, and years would come and go, and she would live there desolate and a mystery.

She would live there until her hair grew white and her strength forsook her, until death should come and lay a friendly hand upon her, and she could go to rest beside her father. This would be her life. Could she live it? Alas, she could not help herself. And yet Felix had said she would be happy somewhere. Poor Felix. How could he know? He had only put his hope in the shape of a prophecy. Alas, she had no hopes of any happiness; she was born to misery, and the fates were all against her. Better, if she could, to stand quiet and not even make a sign.

"Two eyes with coin-weights shut,
And all tears cease:
Two lips where grief is mute,
And wrath at peace."

—"Now and Afterwards,"
Dinah Maria Mulock Craik

CHAPTER X

THE LAST DAY, A DARK AND RAINY ONE, came in its turn, and all things were in readiness for the journey.

With her own hands, Helen had made every arrangement for the child; she forgot nothing that could possibly add to his comfort, or that could possibly lessen the trouble he would give his attendants; only asking in return that the nurse should be sometimes allowed to send her a few of the child's worn-out garments as a remembrance of him.

And now the company had assembled in the library—all the Jourdans, Mr. and Mrs. Tolman, Mrs. Vanzandt, and Percival Felmere. The luggage had all gone on in advance, the carriages stood in readiness, and the party only waited for mother and child to come in.

At last the door opened, and she came among them, calm and still as though all life had gone from her. She took the child and held him while the service went on, held him close through the prayers, through the promises and answers, until her brother paused and held out his arms to take him. She clutched the child closer and drew back. This meant for ever. Once that cross upon his brow, and they were eternally separated. She looked from one to the other like some poor hunted animal. Would no one have any mercy on her?

Mrs. Vanzandt hid her face. Others turned away. A perfect silence reigned. One deep, sobbing sigh sounded through the room, a sigh as though from the rending apart of soul and body; that was all, and she put the child in her brother's arms. She stood as rigid as stone, and watched him as he was baptized in the name of the Trinity, "signed with the sign of the cross," and pledged a "soldier of Christ."

And when he held out his little arms to come back to her, she turned away and pushed the nurse forward in her place. "Take him to the carriage, or he will cry for me," she said, and the nurse obeyed.

Then there were hurried farewells, and gathering up of shawls and hats; for they were late and might be left; they had waited so long on the service that only a few moments remained in which to reach the faraway docks.

"Take me away," Helen whispered to her brother, all the while putting on her hat as though in a frenzy. "I have heard one carriage go; take me away before the rest leave, or it will kill me!"

Once down the front steps, she paused to whisper one last charge and farewell to Arthur as he stood on the step of the last carriage, where were Mrs. Felmere and the child; then Percival hurried her off.

But they were not quick enough, only a few steps farther on they walked, when the last carriage rolled swiftly past them. One sharp cry, "My child!" One quick spring, one moment's mad clutching at the wheels, and the poor, wild creature lay among the trampling horses and crushing wheels, helpless in the hurrying crowd.

There were hushed voices, and hurrying steps, and horrified faces in the sumptuous house where Death waited so patiently at the door. Messengers came and went, but too late to stop the travelers. Physicians came and went, and Death stood there unheeding. At last there came silence, broken only by the heavy breathing and now and then the low, weak moan of the beautiful, wrecked creature.

The brother watched, watched and prayed in an agony of fear. What if she should die before he had time to make one more appeal for her soul, before he had time to plead yet again for her salvation? So he watched until night fell, and only a dim night lamp flickered in the room.

Then the moans ceased, and the breath came and went more gently. Was this death, he wondered. He bent over her, with his hand resting on the poor tired heart. Would God not grant her yet a little time?

The wind outside was rising, and rattled the windows as it went, shook them like some angry hand seeking entrance; and the rain came in great swirls and rushes that in the silence of the night the lonely watcher heard hissing through the air.

Slowly the sad, pain-stricken eyes opened under his gaze, and a whisper came to his ears, "Will it wreck the ship?"

He shook his head. "I do not think there is any danger."

How heavily her heart beat, as though every stroke was a labor, how heavily and slow. There was no time to lose, and yet he could not speak; the wistful gaze of those dying eyes seemed to paralyze his heart to silence.

Then she spoke again, "I am dying, ah, I am glad, glad!"

"And will you leave me without hope for your soul?" broke from the brother in a sudden cry that smote sharply on the silence. "Oh, my sister, will you die without saying 'I believe'?"

There was a little negative movement of the head, and a whisper, "I cannot leave my father."

"And your child?"

A wild light of pain came into the eyes, a shiver seemed to go over the poor, crushed body, there was a moment's waiting, then the dying hand closed over his and a moan broke from the white lips, rising high, and tremulous through weakness. "I cannot leave my father; it is too late, too late!" There was a pause, a catching of the breath, then a whisper, "Your God will not save me. I have not learned to love Him. I have defied Him."

"God will forgive," the brother said. "He who wore the crown of thorns has felt and known all your sorrow. Only lay your hand in His, and He will lead you into rest."

Ah, how eager and hurried his words were, and the answer came so weak and slow, the voice was so weary, as though she wished to die in silence. "I cannot say I believe. I only fear losing my child."

"Do you believe in God enough to fear Him?" the pleading voice went on. "Only say 'I believe.' Oh, for the love I bear you, do not leave me hopeless."

"I cannot leave my father."

On his knees by the bedside the brother prayed aloud, cried out to God in his agony for mercy on the blind, starved soul, that through all its days had wandered in the dark land of unbelief. Then he bowed his head on the clinging, dying hands close clasped within his own, and his words fell gently, "For your child's sake?"

A little sob broke from her. "You took him from me," she moaned, "and signed him with the cross."

"That cross need not separate you from him. Only say 'I believe,' only pray that God in His mercy will save your soul this night. Think of suffering through all the waste of eternity, a lost, hopeless soul. Think of meeting God face to face before this hour goes, meeting Him alone, and without help."

Ah, the strained gaze of the eyes looking up into his; the burning, eager intelligence that shone in them; the terrible flickering light of death that seemed to rise and fall as life ebbed. How the poor hands clung to him, and how the fading mind seemed to strive after his words. He was running a fearful race with Time and Death for this immortal soul, and his strength was almost gone. "I have prayed for you," he cried, "and I know that God has heard me. I have carried your soul to the mercy seat, and Christ I know will save it. You called on God in your agony, and I know he heard you."

There was a wild striving to push his hands away, and a cry went up that clove the silence like a sword. "Hush! Hush! You shall not drag me from my father! Even now his hands hold me, and my child is gone oh, my baby!"

Ah, the piteous breaking of the dying voice, the wail that came with this bitterest memory. Then the weary iteration, "I cannot leave my father." The poor dying heart was still loyal; the poor struggling soul still clung to its oath.

And still the brother pleaded, "Our father chose his own path; he put aside the light; he blighted your life. Oh, my sister, do not follow him. You have gone far enough through all this waste of hopeless years; do not cling to him through eternity. Say 'I believe' for your child's sake, say it. Or else for ever wander soul-stricken and desolate, with him who has murdered your soul, wandering with longing cries for help that cannot come. My sister, think!"

"So let it be," she said. "I have defied your God." The voice was very faint; each breath seemed the last.

"God is merciful!" the brother cried. "He will forgive. He can save!"

"I," then the voice failed; the beautiful, death-darkened eyes looked at him mournfully like some stricken animal that longs for words with impotent despair; but speech was gone.

Ah, how he prayed wildly despairingly. Outside the storm howled, and far away, out on the wide sea, the ship tossed and the child wailed in its sleep. And as the brother prayed, an awful terror gathered about the face and in the dying eyes, as though some horror laid hold upon her. "Have mercy, Lord!" he cried, "have mercy!"

A mute upraising of the dying hands, a little gurgling cry, a shiver. And out on the wild storm wind the soul took flight.

Once more the grating door of the Felmere vault swung open, and Helen Felmere was laid to rest beside her father. Old Jane and Peter shed some honest tears, and Percival stood there crushed and broken. It was not long, then all left her and went their ways, and, as in the days gone by, the wild winds wailed about the desolate flats and lonely church, the only voice to sing her requiem.

In the summer evening, a stranger came, a stranger with sad gray eyes and a heavy step. He paused beneath the maple tree and on the riverbank; he sat a long hour in the library, and upstairs in the studio he shed some bitter tears over a little sketch he took from off the wall, a little sketch he had tacked there long years ago. Then, lingering in the church until nightfall, he went his lonely way.

THE END

QUESTIONS FOR DISCUSSION

1. Helen adheres strictly to her father's beliefs and the promises she made him on his deathbed, while many other children rebel against their parents. How did the beliefs of your parent(s) shape your own?

2. The author devotes a long paragraph on page 114 to musing over what might have been going on in Mr. Felmere's last moments as he lies dying, alone. Do you think it possible he changed his mind about faith at the very end?

3. Helen acquiesced to "family habit" in attending Christian worship for the first time (on pages 136-137) and found it "cold unto death" with nothing in the sermon or music to attract her and the whole thing far from her grand and solem ideal of how the faithful might act in their holy place. How does this fit with your own experience of worship services?

4. Arthur tells Helen on page 143 that from his observation of results, "the religious training of the present day is rather ecclesiastical than biblical." From your observation of results, what are children learning in church today?

5. Helen answers Mr. Heath on page 258 that it is easier to be an undoubting Christian than an undoubting unbeliever "because all the world believes, and it is hard to stand out against it" while he insists that "unbelief is quite popular." How does the culture today make being either an undoubting Christian or an undoubting unbeliever easier or more difficult?

6. On page 276 and following, Helen dies tragically. Was this a fatal accident or suicide?

7. As her brother implores her to say "I believe" on her deathbed, on page 278 Helen only gets out the word "I" and then her voice fails. In this, the author left the barest chance that Helen might have within her mind been declaring that she believed even after her speech was gone. Do you think Helen came to faith in her final moments? Why or why not?

8. Helen lives her life proclaiming her unbelief and a reliance on what can be logically proven true. Yet, can you point to ways in which her actions are more Christ-like than those of the Christians with whom she interacts?

9. Helen finds the pastor of the free church and his congregation to be more genuinely Christ-like than the Christians she encoutered previously. Why might this be so?

10. Helen remains faithful to her father's teaching and will in spite of everything, even her child and the man she truly loves. Do you find this loyalty admirable or foolish? Why?

11. Have you ever remained loyal to a belief, a cause or a person despite what others may have thought of you?

12. What point or points do you think Sarah Barnwell Elliott hoped to make in writing *The Felmeres*?

www.ingramcontent.com/pod-product-compliance
Lightning Source LLC
Chambersburg PA
CBHW020407110726
47899CB00006B/1891